BONE DANCE

TERRY HAYMAN

fiero PUBLISHING

First electronic edition July 2020.

First paperback edition July 2020

Book design by Fiero Publishing

ISBN 978-1-927920-28-2 (paperback)

ISBN 978-1-927920-26-8 (ebook)

Published in 2011 by Fiero Publishing as Driven, by James Kinsak

Published by Fiero Publishing

www.fieropublishing.com

THE HANDWRITTEN LETTER Nicole Baker had opened an hour ago felt like it was chewing through the breast pocket of her suit jacket, trying to get to her heart.

"Family?" said the balding man riding the elevator up with her.

Nicole gave a tight smile and didn't answer. Couldn't. If she spoke, she'd crack.

The elevator thunked to a stop, the doors hummed open, and she hurried out onto the dim ward, leaving the balding man behind. As she passed the nurse's station, the woman there raised her eyes to watch Nicole pass.

She knew somehow. They all knew.

Nicole clicked along faster, pulling a hair band from her purse and jerking her thick mane back into a ponytail. She reached the door to her mother's private room and pushed it open. Stood there.

The room lights were off, but lights from outside the room's window threw harsh shadows over IV tubes and poles, monitor wires, an oxygen hose, and a frail body in a hard bed.

"Mother?"

There was a dragging sound from the oxygen mask as the old woman turned her head. Her face was cadaverous, the skin bluish gray from two years of a high CO_2 count.

Her mother's fingers jerked up now and scrabbled at her oxygen mask, gasping and coughing as she pulled it down. Then one hand fumbled for the pull cord to the light over her bed. She tugged it until it clicked and suddenly everything in the room was clear and horrible.

"Nicky," the old woman finally managed then coughed like it was dragging her lungs up. It took her another minute to catch her breath before she said, "What a nice surprise."

After a long hesitation, Nicole strode forward. When she reached the bed, she pulled out the letter, hating how her fingers shook, how her legs felt like spaghetti. She thrust the three sheets at her mother. "Is this another one of your jokes?"

Her mother coughed again and took the paper. "What...?"

"It was delivered to my office this morning."

"So you're back working. That's good, dear. I'm sure Paul—"

"Read it!"

Blinking hard, her mother unfolded the sheets and squinted at them. The handwriting on the paper was spidery, shaky, but not her mother's, damn it.

Dear Nicole, the letter began. *I'm writing to tell you who your real parents are...*

It took Nicole's mother a full five minutes, then she laid the papers on her chest, pushed her mask back up to suck some oxygen, and relaxed her head back. She closed her eyes.

Nicole jerked the mask down over her mother's chin again. "Well?"

The old woman took a rattling breath and opened her eyes, but she didn't look at Nicole. "True as true."

"What? I was born in someplace called Goldrock, Colorado to a girl named—"

"Betsy Müller."

There was a silence. "You're going to lie there and tell me..."

"I had a thing with my ovaries, sweetie."

"What thing?"

"Poly-cystic ovarian disease." Carefully pronounced. Rehearsed.

It made Nicole want to gag. Or grab her mother's frail shoulders and shake her. "So?"

The dying woman waved her hand and sucked in another breath. "I couldn't have kids. But your daddy Nigel wanted them so bad. So one time when we were driving down through the Rockies, you know..."

"No!" Nicole snatched the letter off her mother's chest and stuffed it back into her inside jacket pocket. "I called Sibley Memorial. They said that if I had a birth certificate issued by them, I was born there."

Her mother's smile had gone wistful, staring up at the ceiling. "We were checking out old mining towns. Some still got people, you know. Found this little girl with her own child. Starving. Asked us to adopt it."

No. No, no, *no*. "Who'd you get to write this for you?"

"The girl couldn't take care of it. No one else would. So we took it."

"'It.' You mean me?"

Nicole's mother, no, her *adoptive* mother, Suzie Jane Baker, nodded and took another long, rattling breath. "Cutest little thing you were. We got a new birth certificate."

"You can't do that."

"Your father had connections."

"What? Like criminals? Jesus. I paid for a private room for you. I've been in here every single day since you came in. My law practice is a shambles. Paul is...well..."

"A goddamned...man!" Her mother laughed then gasped and a spasm dragged her into another round of coughing that seemed to build as if her very lungs were trying to turn themselves inside out. A chunk of phlegm, greenish purple and bloody came up. She spat it sideways to the floor, coughed and spasmed again, jerking her IV tubes. The heart rate monitor beside her jumped erratically.

Nicole couldn't move. She should call the nurse, scream, something. But her legs were bolted to the floor and something inside her head shouted at her mother, *Go! Go on, you liar!*

But the coughing subsided as it always did and Suzie wiped her mouth, gasping. Nicole stepped to the bed. "Okay, Mom. Just tell me the truth for once in your life. No more games. Look into my eyes."

Nicole's mother fumbled for her oxygen again and Nicole batted the old hand away.

"Tell me."

"Sweetie. I like your hair."

"*Tell* me."

"You don't believe me? Go to Goldrock." Her eyelids fluttered and her pupils rolled up. Her breathing jerked to a halt.

Nicole frowned and reached down to squeeze the old woman's shoulders. Again. "Mom?"

Then she threw herself at the nurse call button beside the bed and stabbed it over and over.

THIRTY MILES WEST OF TULSA, in the little town of Ruston, where the main scenery was corn and dust and everyone but the locals were just passing through, the chief cook and manager of the Big Fry lumbered to the back of her kitchen to find her sole waitress, bottle-blond Georgia, clutching the edge of the dishwashing machine's feeding arm with one hand, her eyes wild and unfocused.

"Twenty-*five*, twenty-*six*, twenty-*seven*, twenty-*eight*..."

"Georgia?"

"Twenty-*nine*, thirty, thirty-*one*..."

"Georgia, honey."

"Thirty-*two*, thirty-*three*..."

"Georgia!" Bella Fry grabbed one of Georgia's skinny arms and shook her. Only then, when Georgia turned her pretty face to Bella in blank-faced fear, did Bella notice the creased sheet of paper Georgia held in her dangling hand.

Bella reached down and grabbed the paper, raised it up, and read. She frowned and read it again. It was plain, white bond paper, unsigned, and there was no return address other than "Goldrock, Colorado." It looked like a woman's writing, all fine and spidery. It read:

Your children miss you, Georgia.
It's time to come home.

· · ·

Bella shook the paper at Georgia. "What do it mean, child? This some kind of joke? You said you never been outside of Oklahoma."

Georgia blinked at her, looked at the letter, and slowly found her bearings. "I...was born in Goldrock," she said in her slow drawl. "My two kids are there."

"Your two kids? Lord..." Bella was struck dumb. This pretty girl, maybe in her thirties but perpetually a shy teenager, like she'd been struck by a truck and run inside herself to hide. This girl who'd dyed her hair and even her eyebrows blond ever since she'd first come to Bella's nine months ago. This girl was a mama? Lord.

"What you going to do, child?" Bella said finally.

"Do?" Georgia said with a puzzled frown. She reached up with shaking fingers and took the letter from Bella. "Like the letter says, o' course. I'm going home."

Josh BURST into the U of C dorm room he shared with Ari Siegel and jumped up onto his bed, then bounced up again to spin around so that his red hair flew out like a bitchin' god...of...fire!

"I is done, Ari-dad!" he cried. "We're outa here!"

Which at least got Ari to turn around from his desk. But whoah. Josh's friend, also short and long-haired, but with brown-eyes and wiry black hair, could be painfully shy and way serious. But this attitude went even past that. Right now Ari was, like, totally tweaked or something, blinking at Josh with a "Hunh?"

"Our shifted reading week, dude. I just finished my last class. Elwood's picking us up in, like, two hours. Where's your head? Where's your board? Elwood says the slopes at my folks are *waistie!*"

Josh's own duffel and snowboard were laid out on the floor at the end of his bed, but he couldn't see Ari's anywhere. "Really, dude. Where's your board?"

Ari looked like he was having trouble concentrating. "Uh...my locker?"

Josh frowned. "Say what?"

"I'm...I don't know. I don't think I can come."

"Oh, dude! Why?"

The boy stared at the floor, then slowly rubbed his nose. He finally turned back to his desk and lifted up a sheet of paper lying there. He handed it to Josh.

Josh bounced off his bed and took it, reading the spidery writing out loud. "'Dear Ari, Your Grandma Miryam has terminal heart disease...blah, blah. She won't write to you or call you...blah, but has mentioned your name to me often.

If you want to see her alive..."' Josh looked up. "This is a joke, right? Your 'Grandma Miryam?'"

"Oma."

"What?"

"My oma. My grandma. I used to be her favorite. I kind of set my course by her. But I haven't seen her in four or five years."

Josh held out the paper. "So who wrote you?"

"Don't know. There's no signature or return address."

"And don't you think that's, like, kind of weird?"

Ari snatched the letter, folded it, and stuffed it into the pocket of his jeans, embarrassed. "There was a family fight. That's why I haven't seen her. Maybe whoever wrote it knew that. Didn't want to get in the middle."

"Yeah. Just wanted to screw up our week." He held out both hands when he saw Ari's face. "Okay, look. Where's your grandma's house? Here in town? Out of state?"

Ari shook his head. "In state. Tiny little place near Telluride, but none of the big tourist stuff. Goldrock."

"Goldrock. Gold— Hey! Fuck! That's like only like five hours from my folks in Gunnison, and they got skiing, right?"

"Yeah. Good skiing and boarding, but—"

"Soooo... We drive to my parents, stay two or three days, then borrow Elroy's car..."

"I don't know, dude. That would be awesome, but...like...the road getting to my oma's place..."

"Is nothing! I've been doing snow since before time, okay. We'll bring chains."

Ari blinked slowly, running his hair back from his face with one hand. "You're sure?"

"Adventure, Ari-dad!"

"Visiting my dying grandma?"

"Living by new slopes. New snow. Right? We on?"

"O...kay."

Josh punched his roomie's arm. "Then get your gear together, dude. Holiday of a lifetime!"

"You don't talk much, do ya?"

The big man following her out of the car didn't say anything. Mary Jane laughed as she fumbled in her purse for the keys at her bungalow, then giggled nervously. The man had stepped right behind her, blocking the porch light so she couldn't see a damn thing.

"N-not good at it," he stuttered. "Muh-muh-muh—"

"S'all right, Japhet, that you're not a big talker. Tha's all right."

Oh poo, now she was slurring her speech. She didn't know how to *do* this. But—ha!—she had the keys. Right there in her fingers. With a sly smile she pulled them out and jingled them up at him. Now he was supposed to applaud, say he was sure glad she'd found them or something. 'Cause single moms, you know, they weren't quite as secure in their sex appeal, weren't so sure what the right moves were for this kind of hanky-panky.

He reached for the keys and for a second looked like a towering ape, thick and threatening. A chill shot through Mary Jane's buzz. She stumbled back from him.

He dropped his hands and stooped apologetically. "Your k-kids?"

Her tremble eased back to a smile. The stutter, the 'Aw shucks' stoop, the balding head of a man in his forties—they were what had first reassured Mary Jane when he'd asked for directions to the bus stop outside Tulepa's only bar. And even after she had him walk her back to her dark brown Ford Taurus that still smelled of cat vomit from Gilligan's little accident, he'd said he "r-really" had to get home to Goldrock, Colorado. Even showed her a letter with spidery little writing. From his mama, he said, demanding he come home. But she'd told him there no more busses until morning, so...

"Kids're at my sister's," Mary Jane said, fingering her hair back behind her ears.

And, after all, how long had it been since *that* happened? And her bringing a man home. It made her tingle in all her nethermosts. She stepped back to the door and managed to get her house key into the lock. With a grunt, she opened the door and stumbled inside. It smelled like kitty litter and old pizza. Gilligan greeted her with a purr and brush against her leg, then the man's. Mary Jane reached for the light switch.

Japhet grabbed her hand. "Don't."

"Wha—?"

"C-c-curtains. All ar-round."

She smiled sloppily at him in the dark kitchen. "Okey-dokey."

When she got back, the first thing she made out in the darkness was that he'd brought in his battered brown suitcase and toolbox from Mary Jane's Taurus. He was sitting, the suitcase a black lump on the floor beside him, the toolbox on the kitchen table and...open? Something smelled wrong. Kind of sharp. Kind of...

"Gill'gan?" she said.

"That your cat?"

"A shorthair." The booze felt very thick in her mouth but she noticed something else. Japhet not stuttering?

"Turn on the lights."

She flipped them on and saw Gilligan. He way lying beside the closed toolbox, his head flopped upwards in an unnatural position. But before Mary Ann could quite figure out why, Japhet stood and began swishing a long, black-bladed knife back and forth against his pant leg. Wet?

Mary Jane's gaze rose stupidly to his face. "Tha's a big knife," she slurred.

Then he was on her.

One quick stride and he had hoisted her off the floor by the front of her silk blouse—*Fifty-five dollars for that blouse. Shouldn't have worn it.*—and spun her sideways, slammed her back into her fridge. Her older son's artwork crackled under her shoulder blades. A tube of glitter glue clattered to the floor. Cal was so creative. Richard was just starting. Morgan was still— A second glitter glue clattered down.

Mary Jane felt a pricking down near her belly, then a tugging ripping sound and air. He'd cut open the top of her skirt.

Thwack! above her head. He'd slapped down the knife on the refrigerator. His free hand now pulled down her skirt, helped by the rough edge of his shoe at her knees. The hand went back for the panties. Yanked them down and off. Came up to the hand still holding her by the blouse and grabbed the material there to rip open the front of her blouse.

But as he loosed the hand pinning her, Mary Jane started to slide down the fridge. Cal's picture ripped behind her back and she finally remembered to scream.

He hoisted her up with a hand around her neck, under her chin, and backhanded her across the mouth. It stung and her mouth filled with blood. She gulped it down, staggered her feet under her to stand, and sputtered, "Don't. P-please. My boys–"

"Shut up!"

His hands ripped open her blouse fully now and yanked it down and off. He reached behind her, ripped the catch off the back of her brassiere, then brought his hand back to jerk the front so hard that her arms wrenched forward as he yanked the worn lace off her. He threw it away and slapped her bare breasts hard.

Mary Jane screamed again. Tried hard to focus. Last chance. "The letter. Y-you said you're going home. To your mama."

Suddenly the knife was back in his hand. His knee drove into her stomach so she gagged and the thick fingers of his free hand grabbed her tongue, pulling it out as far as it would go. "Don't you laugh at me!" he said.

Then the tip of the knife flashed under her nose. Stuck. Burned. She tried to scream. It jerked. And what was left of her tongue snapped back into her mouth in a gargle of blood.

5 / GOLDROCK

Midnight.

The woman stood in the snow just off Goldrock's main street and wrapped her cloth coat more tightly around her. She gritted her teeth and glared up at the banner that stretched across the sleeping street to announce the town's centennial.

Irrelevant, except as a goad.

For the true years that mattered were thirty-two. For it was that many years ago that the evil had seeped into the town, corrupted every person here, tainted every sheet and flowerbed, and come bursting out into the plain light of day for *every*one to see. Inescapable. Undeniable.

But what had happened? It had been *denied!* Shoveled over. Buried. The simplest part of the cancerous boil had been lanced while the rest had been left to fester in the darkness like a great pulsing infection, covered with lies and fear. In the town. In her. For thirty-two long years.

But it's time was up.

It was time to end it. The children had been summoned and she knew they would come in all their innocence and in damnation. They would meet. The ugly truths would spill out, a little at a time or all at once she didn't know. But they would spill. And it would hurt.

Yes—she ground her teeth and smiled—it would hurt good.

DAY ONE
WEDNESDAY

Montrose, Colorado. What a nothing place, Nicole Baker thought as she stomped her boots in the snow of the car rental lot while her husband began packing up the rented Jeep Grand Cherokee.

There was rumbling sound and she turned to watch an airplane take off. It seemed to squeal as it inched into the sky, folding up its landing gear and beginning its climb towards the northern mountains, abandoning Nicole and Paul here to their three hour drive.

Which was stupid.

This whole thing was stupid.

When Nicole's mother had died there in her hospital bed, the first thing Nicole should have done was burn the letter and ended things right there. What did she think she was going to find in Goldrock? The love she never had? A sense of who she really was, finally, that couldn't be shaken?

Fantasies.

Yet even as she'd arranged her mother's funeral, she'd made more phone calls. Met more dead ends. Then she'd booked a flight out here, God help her. Without telling Paul why. Too ashamed, too frightened by what she might find to tell him why.

And he'd insisted on accompanying her anyway. Probably because *he* was too ashamed and frightened by the possible repercussions of his infidelity to let her go off alone.

She turned to watch him thump their ski boots into the back of the rented gold Jeep Grand Cherokee now, snugging them in tightly between his suitcase and the wheel well and double-checking that all the buckles were folded down, nothing rubbing. He whistled as he worked, her Paul. Always buoyant and efficient. A cinnamon skinned, meticulous, even-tempered...cheater.

And the second strike on that thought decided her. There was no way she could drive with one person who'd rejected her in order to turn up evidence that another person, her biological mother, had done the same. It was insane. And while she was emotionally raw and hadn't been functioning well because of it, she was not insane. She could make more phone calls. She could hire a private investigator to figure out her lineage while *she* figured out her marriage. It had just taken flying out here, coming right to the brink of madness to get her priorities straight.

Down south of them, the highway through Montrose to the southern mountains moaned in the wind. The clouds swelled black over the peaks.

"This is a no go," Nicole said. "Checked my phone. Weather's going to be bad."

Paul pulled his head out of the rear hatch of the Jeep where he'd finished wedging in the ski poles and backpacks so they wouldn't move. "What's that?"

"I'm going to tell the rental guy we're cancelling."

"What?" Paul stepped back out of the Jeep looking flustered. "We've signed. We're packed. We're paid. What's going on?"

Nicole tugged her mitts on tighter over the red sleeves of her jacket and stuck out her jaw. "He was supposed to give us maps, and it been what? Twenty-five minutes? Look at the clouds. I'm going to say it's weather and breach of contract."

Paul looked evenly at her and Nicole shook her head hard. Then she stomped off towards the booth. Let him attribute the flip-flop to her grief process. If she paid for the Goldrock investigation from her own bank account, Paul would never even have to know. And it was entirely possible, after she'd had some time to get her head clear and work through the issues of Paul's cheating, he wouldn't even be living with her when she got the answers.

But as she approached the Hertz booth, she had a sudden intuition it might not be that easy.

The door was hanging open and there were two people inside. The young rental clerk whom she and Paul had talked to was frantically looking through the rat's nest of papers that covered the north end of his booth. Sneering at the clerk was an older man with an overstuffed face, a head of combed-over gray hair, and a weedy mustache.

Uh-oh.

The older man saw Nicole coming, looked her up and down appreciatively, then turned back to poke a finger into the back of the rental clerk's back. "You see?"

The clerk fluttered his hands up and began trembling. "I put them right...uh...right..."

"Sure you did." The man rolled his eyes dramatically for Nicole.

"Yeah...uh...."

"Want to blame it on the car accident?" He turned to smile as Nicole reached the open door and Nicole saw his name was Simms. "What can we do for you, Ma'am?"

Cancel the trip, she thought. *You don't need it. This is not a smart move for you. Not right now.* "The weather..." Nicole began.

"I got it!" Dade said and thrust a printed sheet past his boss and towards Nicole. The weather report.

"But no maps," Simms said without looking away from Nicole. "'Everything you need.' That's our motto. So if you want a discount or a refund, just ask."

Nicole frowned, caught, despite herself, by the desperate young clerk's eyes. The helplessness and frustration there—she'd seen it too often in her clients not to know what happened next. If Nicole cancelled, the clerk got fired. And then he lost his next job, and his next, and then his self-esteem, his family and friends...

He's not your client. Let it go. Just cancel the rental. Walk away.

Like she'd ever been able to do that. She reached out and touched the arm of the boss. "Car accident you said."

"What?" The boss man looked down at Nicole's fingers on his sleeve. He licked his mustache in surprise. While Dade moaned as he picked though the rat's nest of papers on his desk.

"He had a brain injury, I bet. MTBI. Mild Traumatic Brain Injury?"

"Oh, fer— Yeah, something like that his folks say. So I help him out, right? But come on..."

"Have you read anything about brain injury?"

"Hunh?"

"You hire this boy. You know he had problems. But you read absolutely nothing about how to help him cope?"

"Well..."

"Books? Pamphlets?"

"I..."

"Nothing?"

Simms folded his arms over his flabby chest. "My wife told me to give him a chance. I gave him a chance."

"Okay, then here's the primer. You bonk the brain hard enough, even if you don't leave marks, and you get mood swings, concentration difficulties, memory problems, difficulties making decisions. Okay?" *Kind of like what you get when you lose a mother, catch your husband cheating, and find you might be adopted all within the same week.*

The boss didn't look convinced.

Nicole closed her eyes and took a deep breath. "This boy—Dade?—isn't stupid and he's not crazy. But because of what's happened to him, he needs a special environment. Less stimulation. Itemized tasks. Help in setting up systems. He's great with people. He sold us on your top-of-the-line rental. There has to be a need for that."

Simms frowned at her. "You a doctor?"

"Lawyer," Nicole said. "I deal with a lot of brain injury cases. There's a good argument that it's a recognizable disability which can't be discriminated against in the workplace. *Capiche?*"

The manager's mustache bristled out. "Unless he loses us business, right? He losing us your business right now?"

Nicole stared at him, felt everything click backwards in her brain to an earlier set of decisions she'd just finished proving to herself was insanity. She quickly weighed everything she'd argued against Dade's future and decided she was a crybaby.

"No," she said. "We're taking the rental."

The manager blew out between his lips, shrugged, and shouldered his way out of the booth, stalking off towards the airport terminal buildings.

Dade swallowed and stepped out of the booth with the invoice Nicole had filled out fifteen minutes ago. "Thanks...uh..." He looked down at the invoice "...Ms. Baker. You really have a map to get to Goldrock? 'Cause GPS, most times, doesn't work out there."

Nicole nodded, noting sickly the clouds they'd be driving towards looked even darker than they had moments before.

"You know they got a party going on there this week."

"Party?"

"Goldrock's...uh...uh...centennial. I got a friend there. But he's doubting they'll get many people there with the weather coming. Already a lot of snow through Lizard Head and Red Mountain Pass. You sure you want to go?"

"We go through either of those passes?"

"No, but you might want to pick up some chains and a shovel. These small mountain towns, you know. Don't want to get stuck or...dead or anything."

The words sent a little shiver of fear through her, but it broke the back of her tension and she laughed. She leaned forward suddenly and kissed Dade on the cheek. As she pulled back, he blushed. She said, "I'm not taking this trip to get dead, okay? I'm taking it because I need to know for sure where I come from. I think a person needs to know that sort of thing before they can make the right choices going forward, you know?"

He nodded doubtfully and Nicole turned to go while she still had the courage.

CHAPTER 7

1 1 0 MILES SOUTH, on the Colorado 666 from New Mexico, a stolen brown Ford Taurus driven by Japhet Bone sent up a trail of dust that followed it north.

But twelve-year-old girl Chipeta Toop'weets did not know the car was stolen or who drove it as she sat in her lawn chair and watched it approach from a mile off. She pressed the back of her chair against the cracked plywood of her family's craft stand and slouched down. Maybe it would just pass on by. Chipeta's mother and father were both gone to Cortez; no more than an hour, they'd said.

All around the craft stand were the flat desert and low mesas, blowing with the dusty, sweet smell of sagebrush. It was warm enough for Chipeta's short-sleeved cotton dress, plus her mother's shawl which Chipeta might take off when the sun warmed things up mid-morning. Far off to the north, the purply line of San Juan mountains were like a second, looser shawl, around her.

The Taurus was slowing.

It pulled off the highway and crunched up along the dirt and stones. Chipeta pulled her mother's shawl tighter around her and shrank back into the straps of the chair. Her braided ponytail bunched up uncomfortably behind her head.

There was something about the car. Maybe the white sidewall tires. Maybe the dust that said it had come through the red rock lands of the Navajo and Ute Indian Reservations. The license plate was personalized to read, "MJ & 3," whatever that meant.

The car jerked to a stop just past her and dust puffed off it like flies from dogshit.

Chipeta could hear the windshield wipers still going, *whup...whup*, but couldn't see them from where she sat.

The wipers stopped. The driver's side door opened. A man got out and straightened to a stand, and Chipeta gasped. The man was enormous, like some great ape. He must have been four full heads taller than Chipeta's father.

But more than just tall, the man had sloping shoulders and a thick head on top of them like a great ball of suet, with short, oily black hair as if he hadn't bathed in many days. He turned his head and looked across the roof of his car and Chipeta sucked in a breath. Because he looked so...meek.

His round face was fatty, stubbled, and sunburned like he worked outside. A swatch of peeling skin lay across the cheeks and nose. Maybe a vacationing farmer or hired hand? His short-sleeved shirt was sweat-stained and revealed arms as flabby looking as the rest of him. But big, like there might be some muscle in there maybe.

Raising his left hand to shield his eyes from the sun, he gave Chipeta a careful smile. No missing teeth. "Am I on the r-r-r-right road to G-Goldrock? Past T-T-Telluride?"

"Yes," Chipeta said.

"Hunh," the man grunted, pleased. Then he looked around. "Y-y-you have a w-washroom anywhere here?"

Chipeta shook her head.

"C-cell phone?"

Chipeta shook again.

"Hunh. J-just you alone out here?"

"My papa will be right back."

The stuttering man nodded slowly, then scanned the dusty desert, the blowing, empty road. When he looked back at her, he spoke with a stronger voice than before. "Mind if I look at your stuff 'til he g-gets back?"

Chipeta shook her head and the man shut his door. As he wandered over, she saw he had something in his right hand. A camera. Small digital. No case. The man's pants were polyester too, crinkled from long driving. The right pocket bulged from a wad of change that jingled as he approached her.

He saw where she was looking and smiled. Chipeta looked up quickly and gestured to the booth beside her where her mother's bright blankets and shawls lay piled on the shelf. Above that, hanging from a thin pole that ran across the top of the booth, were fifteen of her father's best aspen carvings - horses and cacti, wolves, adobe huts. Some were flat and meant to be hung, others were meant to sit.

"You want to buy?" Chipeta asked. Her voice sounded small and silly in her ears.

"Show me the best blanket."

He wanted her to get up, Chipeta realized. His eyes commanded it. So Chipeta did, leaving the shawl behind in the chair so she would have her arms free. The man watched her closely as she walked around him to the shelf of blankets and shawls. Trying to ignore his stare, she picked through the first three blankets in each of the three piles. Which would he like? Not the bright red and gold designed to ward off evil spirits. He would like browns. Grays. Blacks.

Tugging out one like that from the bottom of the middle pile. She turned and held it up, folded. "This one."

"Unfold it."

Chipeta did, having it as high up over her head as she could so not too much would lie in the dirt. The lingering sharp smell of the dye and the scratchy wool against her face and front was like her momma's shield, her momma's warmth. So it felt doubly frightening to have the man pull out one side of the blanket to look in at her, look at her standing in her cotton dress, arms upraised. "I like it," he said, voice low. No stutter.

Chipeta dropped it down and quickly snatched up the bottom from the dirt. "It is sixty dollars."

The man rubbed at the peeling skin on his nose and laughed, so different than he'd been getting out of his car. "Would you take twenty?"

"Fifty."

He laughed again. "I'll tell you what. You spread it out across the front of your stand, stand in front of it, and let me take a picture of you and this place. Then we'll haggle."

Chipeta swallowed again, but turned back to the stand with her mother's blanket. Again conscious of the man's eyes on her, she spread it out along the shelf, folding enough over the top that no part of it would be in the dirt this time.

When she turned, the man motioned for her to stand in front of the blanket, a little to one side, and he backed up so he could get the whole crafts stand into the picture.

"Good." He clicked a picture.

Chipeta turned to fold the blanket, but he shook his head. "I want another one. Closer. Smiling this time."

Chipeta turned back towards him as he stepped in closer, and she tried to smile.

"You can do better than that."

She tried harder, smiling wide and showing her teeth like she did for her grandpa when he took family pictures.

"Better," the man said. "Now grab your boobies."

"What?"

"Like this." The man demonstrated by cupping the palm of his free hand under his own flabby chest. "You got some little boobies starting there. Grab 'em."

He raised the camera again.

CHAPTER 8

Halfway between Montrose and Ridgeway, with Paul driving, Nicole's over-stressed system had given out and she'd slept, only to dream of suing the doctors who'd let her mother die. She saw herself, raven-black hair fanned in enormous sheets around her, wrestling with the doctors. Only they weren't doctors; they were Paul. And the woman on the bed wasn't her mother...

She'd woken up sweating and chilled, drunk the bitter coffee Paul had bought her at a gas station somewhere, and noted that he'd picked up tire chains and a short snow shovel. It was warm enough in the Jeep then that she'd taken off her red ski jacket and just had on a tight lime turtleneck and leggings.

"Better safe," he'd said about the chains and given her an appreciative once-over. "They're just getting what the guy called 'diet snowstorms' so far, but they're expecting more."

And they'd driven.

Now they were off the plowed roadways and following the right lane tire tracks of the road that snaked through the mountains to Goldrock. The Jeep's tires were humming as they climbed. The stale smell of their sweat, the coffee, and the leather seats was getting recirculated around the Jeep's interior by the heater fans.

Nicole stared out at the shallow field of snow and pines between them and the sharp mountainside. To the right plunged a gully. Beyond it, more mountains, no habitations in sight, overcast sky.

Don't get dead, the Hertz boy had said.

Paul's gaze suddenly flicked, annoyed, at the rearview mirror. "Oh, jeez. Not these guys again."

"What?" Nicole twisted in her seat and saw. A rusty white Trans Am, black and red phoenix painted across its hood, was swerving around on their tail. "They were back there before?"

Paul nodded. "Twenty miles back I let them pass, but I guess they stopped for something. Doubt they've even got snow tires."

As he spoke, the tailgater gave a throaty roar and pulled into the left lane tracks, its tail sliding out dangerously. For a second Nicole saw through its front windshield. A short, young male driver. Long red hair. An equally short male passenger, young and curly dark hair, hands gripping the dashboard in terror.

"Insane," Nicole breathed.

"Yup."

Then, as Nicole watched, the red-haired driver managed to straighten the hot rod out and actually accelerated past them. "Honk at them," she said.

"You kidding? They'd probably crash."

"Fine. New clients."

"We'd be defendants."

"Only you. You're driving."

"What? You'd sue me?"

"Maybe."

"It would be a conflict of interest, Nicky."

"Like you and Shelley?"

His eyes jerked away from hers and the Trans Am roared over the rise ahead and vanished from sight. It hadn't hit them, but it had hit them. It had fractured the quiet truce in the Jeep all to hell.

Nicole put her forehead to the cold passenger side window, her face red and heart pounding hard. Hey, it wasn't her fault that Paul had screwed around. And with an insurance adjuster, for Christ's sake. Had putting up with Nicole messed him up that badly?

She rolled her forehead against the glass. Come on, Baker. You're okay. A little shaken up is all. But once you get to Goldrock, you'll crush that last niggling doubt your sainted mother left you with and you can get on with things. You can then make up your mind about whether to save this marriage or...not. But whatever you choose, life will be good.

Believe.

CHAPTER 9

As the Ute Indian girl hesitated, Japhet's fingers trembled on his Polaroid camera. He realized he was changing. Where he had been so careful in the last twelve years to select each of his victims by age and isolation, he was prepared to throw that all away for this little girl.

He wanted to fuck her.

Except it came out "fug" in his head, like he'd learned from his mother. She'd been foul-mouthed in everything but naming certain body parts, certain actions, and those quirks Japhet still followed to this day. So he wanted to "fug" this little girl. Not kill, just be with. Love. Not that it was possible, what with his size now, but... Why did he want to do it?

It was as if...as if...returning home to Goldrock was bringing back the child inside him, the innocence, the early urges.

You're a cunny-sick boy, Japhet. Bugger boy.

Japhet reared his head back. No, Mama, he thought. That's just what you and the others said. But it wasn't me. It was you. All of you. Every last one of you. What you did. He shut his eyes hard and sprung them open again.

"Well?" he said hoarsely to the Native girl.

The girl jerked her chin up towards him and he could see the tips of her ears were red. Then her gaze darted left and right down the highway to see if there were any cars. Japhet knew there were none. Only warm wind rustling the bushes and blowing dust over the roads. Desert emptiness. For miles. There was only Japhet and her.

"The blanket," she said. "You will buy it?"

Japhet lowered his camera, gave her an ugly smile. "Maybe," he said, and took a step forward. "After a picture or two. Then... Is there a problem, honey?"

She shook her head quickly. Felt her ponytail shake behind her like her bare knees wanted to shake.

"Good. What's your name?"

"Chipeta."

"Grab your boobies, Chipeta."

The girl, lips trembling, began to raise her hands. Stopped.

Japhet lowered his camera again and wiped the sudden sheen of sweat that was forming above his eyebrows. He wasn't used to this either, the drawing out of the preliminaries. It was Goldrock being so close. It was messing him up. He ran his tongue dryly over his lips. "You're not listening well, are you?"

"M-my papa," she said, and pointed back along the road that Japhet and his Taurus had arrived from, the road toward Cortez.

Japhet turned and listened, heard the rumbling now too. And suddenly the truck was there, about a mile off, wobbling along in the road's heat.

The girl raised a skinny brown arm and waved.

Damn! Messing him up was right! Fug him!

With another quick wipe of his forehead, Japhet turned and walked casually back to his stolen car. He opened the dusty passenger door and tossed in his camera. Slammed the door and walked around to the driver's side.

The girl's father's truck was closer. A half mile.

He saw the girl wavering, as if she wondered whether she could now chance running towards her father's truck. She looked over at him, staring with her eyes wide and scared and angry too.

Dumb little bitch. Dumb dumb dumb.

You can't hide, bugger boy. Let them see you.

Japhet opened the driver's door, climbed in, and reached over to heave the brown suitcase up from the passenger wheel well. He sprang open its two metal clasps—*Snap. Snap.*—and stuck a hand inside it to pry up the false bottom and slid his hand in to find his Buck Nighthawk hunting knife. Six-and-a-half-inches of black-oxidized blade. Sharp, light, real precise. It felt almost alive as he considered whether the girl was enough of a threat to warrant him killing her. One quick stab and jerk and he'd be away before the father's truck was close enough to even get the model of his car, much less his license plate.

A grinding sound on the dirty passenger window made him twitch his head up.

It was her! The dumb little bitch was wiping his window clean with her bare forearm so she could stare in at him.

In...at...him!

His whole face shook then he jerked his body backwards, knife in hand. Stopped.

He could hear the sound of the truck, roaring up across the stones. The girl's father. He was too late. Too distracted. Too slow.

With a grunt that strained the blood vessels in his face, Japhet shoved his knife back into the false bottom of the suitcase and slid the case back into the passenger wheel well. Then he jerked back to an upright sitting position in the driver's seat, roared the Taurus' engine into life, yanked the driver's side door closed, and gunned the engine. The tires spat stones wildly as they fishtailed him back to the road.

He had to get out of there. Had to get to Goldrock, to Mama, before he fell apart completely. Because if that happened, that was not going to be a pretty sight.

No, you definitely didn't want to see that.

His front tires grabbed asphalt and he shot towards the mountains.

CHAPTER 10

By the time they were whirring down the switchbacks to Goldrock, Paul seemed to have forgotten their fight. He was hunched over the steering wheel. His right hand occasionally touched under the gear shift when it looked like he might have to downshift.

Despite Nicole's feelings of alienation, she couldn't help but watch him. For a 34-year old, Paul had more self-possession and focus right now than any man had a right to. It made the fine angles of his face look like polished teak. The heritage behind his last name, Kesin, had given him Middle-Eastern doe eyes that were sharpened to lasers. And the male energy of him... She remembered so clearly what it had once been like to have that energy turned on her, seducing her, making her feel like the most important, perfect woman in the universe. And that appreciative look he'd given her earlier. She felt a thin sheen of moisture break out along the top of her forehead and her fingers seemed to vibrate on her thighs. Even now, she knew, if Paul persisted long enough to fight through her silence and really touch her, draw her to him, she'd probably...

"So?" Paul said without turning his head. "Are you going to tell me yet?"

Nicole swallowed. "What?"

"Why we're here. You've never been much of a skiier."

"My mother like to ski," she lied, surprised at how easy it was.

He glanced sideways at her. "Your mother may have been many things, but she was never a skier."

"We all have our secrets, don't we?"

"Meaning?"

"Meaning... would you have married me right out of law school if you'd known me then as well as you do now?"

"What kind of question is that?"

"One you don't have to answer."

Paul pursed his lips and shook his head angrily as Nicole turned her head away.

Then the latest switchback took them around the mountain to the final descent and Goldrock spread out below them.

It was laid out roughly north and south, surrounded on three sides by steep mountains and the fourth by the narrow valley through which Nicole and Paul had entered. A lake ran across the north side. The ski runs were to the west.

But only one of the chair lifts on those ski runs seemed to be running. There were fewer than ten dots that were skiers or snowboarders weaving down the hill, probably because the gloomy light would be making the moguls nearly invisible. In the town itself, the only sign of life was a few trails of smoke climbing somberly out of house chimneys.

Nicole clutched the leather door grip, half-expecting the sight to bring back some sort of memories. But there was nothing.

Of course, how young was she supposed to have been when she was adopted out of this place? Her earliest memories only started around five, and her baby pictures were nonexistent. Did that mean anything?

It took another five minutes before they hit the last long run along the town's southern edge, and Nicole realized she'd been holding her breath for most of it.

"Happening place," Paul said, breaking the ice again, his perpetual role.

And again Nicole let it be broken. Needed it broken now more than ever. "At least they've plowed here."

They passed an Eagle gas station that looked deserted. "Yeah. Just not the hill. You can come on down, but you can never leave."

Nicole laughed uncomfortably, shivered, then jerked up a hand to point as they turned left on the main street. "No wonder it's so cold."

She was pointing to a Victorian era court house or church ahead on the right hand side of the street. Broad, salted steps lead to its front door. The walls rose up three tall stories of sandstone brick, broken only by narrow windows with arched tops. A man-sized clock-face with Roman numerals glared down from up near the peak of its roof. And the object of her comment, a red electronic readout below the clock, noted the temperature as twenty-nine degrees and dropping.

Familiar?

As they passed it, Paul gestured at something further ahead of them. "Is this part of what you're not telling me?"

Nicole looked. Ahead, strung between the lampposts on either side of the street, a garish banner in purple and gold announced: WELCOME TO GOLDROCK! 100 YEARS YOUNG.

Right. The centennial party.

Back from the banner's left lamppost was what looked like an old miner's hotel. The Grenadine. The corners were brick and the walls were neat vertical wood slats, rising three stories like the courthouse, but with a flat roof on top and a broad wooden awning over its double front doors. Stretching along the street in front of it and down the alley to its left were a bus, a couple cars, and three SUV's, all with skis still on their roof racks.

Paul swiveled his head around. "Guess we just stop here," he said, and pulled over to the right hand curb across from the hotel. Shut off the engine.

Nicole blinked at him. "I thought you booked us into a bed and breakfast."

"The Hurzgehrmines on Lift Road. They found out we were coming somehow and sold me over the phone. Said to stop in here for directions because, like the kid warned us, no GPS signal, no bars on my cell. It's pretty much rely on the locals. You coming?"

Nicole licked her lips. Her hands were rigid on her lap and little beads of sweat had suddenly sprung up on the back of her neck.

"Well?"

She looked at him, then worked the inside of her mouth to get some saliva flowing. "You go ahead."

Paul frowned. "Still mad?"

She shook her head.

"Too stiff to move?"

"No."

"Ah. The mystery. You've been here before. You had an ex-lover who works at this hotel. You sued these people once. Your mother sued them. You happen to—"

"Enough! I'll come!" Nicole reached for her red jacket in the back seat, then opened her door and slid out.

She crossed the street ahead of Paul and entered the hotel before she gave herself time to stop.

CHAPTER 11

INSIDE THE GRENADINE'S small lobby, twenty or so people were clamoring around the front desk where a handsome older man and woman, and a pretty teenaged girl, answered their questions and tried to check them all in as fast as they could. A dog was yapping somewhere.

Nicole sidled over to the red velvet chairs along the right wall. Two women in their early thirties were talking together with high voices and waving hands. One was a stylish redhead in a lime green, fur-trimmed jacket like she'd just driven in. The other wore a functional, well-used blue parka with a stringed hood hanging back. Thankfully neither paid any attention to Nicole. Just beyond them sat a short boy with long, curly dark hair who looked about seventeen, scribbling in a notebook. He raised his face and Nicole felt a moment of vague panic. She knew this boy. Did this—?

No. She placed him. It was the passenger from the Trans-Am that had almost hit her and Paul on the way in.

The boy saw her and blushed. He raised his pen and gave her an embarrassed wave.

"You get directions?" said Paul, suddenly behind her and stomping the snow off his boots. Nicole shook her head and directed him up to the desk. When she turned back towards the two women and the boy, the redhead in pink was saying, "...snowed in here, Rory will have a *bird*. Can't watch Fox News or his sports. He's very claustrophobic."

"So I'll get Al and the boys to take him out hunting," said her country cousin. "Get some fresh deer or rabbit to take home with you."

"Without a license, I bet."

"Hush."

She glanced past Nicole's shoulder and Nicole turned to see a sad-eyed, potato-faced man come in the front door. The man wore a cowboy hat and a heavy green parka with a silver star over his left breast. Lawman.

He tipped his hat at Nicole and the ladies and walked tiredly up to the crowd at the desk. There he tapped on the shoulder of one of the taller men there who turned. The second man was in his fifties and also wore a cowboy hat, but his outfit included a heavy sheepskin coat, collar rolled down around a thick neck, and a full handlebar moustache under a nose that looked like it had been broken in more than one fight. Mr. Marlborough Man himself.

The two muttered together, then the Marlborough Man pushed the lawman aside and walked to the two gossipy women. "Grace!" He stuck a finger out at the one in the parka, so much younger than him that Nicole was sure was his second or third wife. "Where's the kids?"

The parka woman looked around, startled. "Tommy? Matt!" She colored as she saw her two young boys over to the right of the desk, down on their hands and knees and trying to look up the skirt of a short, plump maid who was setting out new brochures in the wall rack.

The maid turned, looked down, and shook her head with grin as the boys scrambled backwards, giggling. "Cheeky little buggers, you are," said the maid with a lower class English accent. "Why ain't you in school?"

"Sorry, Rose," said the parka woman as she rushed over and corralled the boys back to their father.

Rose smiled and waved it off, but Marlborough Man, presumably husband Al, cuffed each boy hard on the side of his head. "Git home." As they ran out, Al turned to the parka woman. "I was just five minutes."

"I know," said the parka woman. "But I met Moira here. She and Rory are back for—"

"The big party Saturday," Al sneered. "Just don't plan on getting out next day, Moira. Big storm coming in. The marshal just asked me to keep down tales that the old town boogeyman might show up too. Dickhead." Then he took parka woman's hand and jerked her towards the door.

Which is when the long-haired kid from the Trans Am stood up. "Mr. Rawley!"

The entire lobby fell silent, even the dog, and Al Rawley turned slowly around. His hard eyes bored into the kid, whose face was bright red. "What is it, Jew boy?"

"Don't...uh...don't forget your gun!" The kid pointed to the corner by the door where a heavy looking shotgun was resting in a rack like a deposited umbrella.

Rawley worked his jaw a bit, then stepped over for the gun and picked it up. For a second, Nicole thought he was going to aim it at the kid, but then Rawley's eyes flicked around the room at the watching faces, settling at last on the lawman he'd had words with. He strode to his wife, grabbed her arm, and dragged her out the door.

As soon as he was gone, the buzz of conversations restarted and the stylish red-haired woman in lime-green got up from her seat to move quickly to the front desk crowd, presumably to find husband Rory. At that moment, Nicole saw, Paul also discovered the short, red-headed Trans Am driver in the lineup and ducked his head to speak seriously with him. The lawman listened.

Nicole turned to the kid with the notebook. He'd collapsed back down to his seat, lips sucked together, and hands shaking. Nicole felt oddly drawn to him, to the courage it had evidently taken for him to call out to the older man like that.

She walked over. "Not your best friend in town, I gather."

"The last time I was here…" The kid looked at her and then dropped his head shakily and tried to laugh it off. When he looked up, he swallowed, wiped his right hand on his pant leg and stuck it out towards Nicole. "Ari Siegel," he said. "And Ari is not short for Aryan."

"I gathered."

"Um. I'm sorry about the car thing."

"You live here?"

He shook his head. "Visiting my grandmother."

Two GQ-style guys in ski outfits were raising their voices angrily at the counter and Nicole looked over.

Behind her, Ari sniggered. "Probably checking room prices in case things don't work out for the woman in pink or…people like Al Rawley."

"And you're a writer."

"Journalism student." He shrugged, embarrassed again.

"You know everyone in town."

"Hunh?" he said, having trouble hearing over the impatient voices all through the line now. "Oh. No. Not everyone." He glanced at the teenaged girl at the front desk. She was as short as him and very pretty in a small town, curled-back hair sort of way. Nicole smiled.

Nicole raised her voice. "Know anyone named Müller? Betsy Müller?"

Ari shook his head and stepped closer. "But if she lives here, she'll probably show up at the reunion party Saturday. Reception here. They're going to open up City Hall for tours—that building with the clock coming into town. Party in the streets if the storm lets us."

He grinned, and something in the way the corner of his mouth turned up made Nicole cock her head. When he wasn't totally self-conscious, he looked older than seventeen. Eighteen or nineteen. A college boy. But...what? "Your grandma's name is Siegel too?"

He nodded, just as Paul finished finished at the front desk and motioned for Nicole to leave the growing hubbub with him. "See you around," Ari said.

She nodded, still studying him, then raised her eyes and realized that the woman at the counter was staring through the crowd at her. The woman had a bemused twist to her lips and Nicole made a mental note to question her later.

"See you," she said to Ari, and hurried to catch up to Paul.

CHAPTER 12

On one of Goldrock's residential street, well away from the business hub, Georgia stood miserably in a snowy ditch that in spring would channel the run-off from the mountains away from the road and people's driveways. In the pocket of her light green jacket, she still had the unsigned note that said her little ones missed her, poor li'l chicks. But now, staring at the house where she'd left them, she wondered if maybe she should have stayed at Bella's Big Fry diner back in Oklahoma.

She shivered so hard her teeth shook, and she wrapped her arms tightly around herself. Though it was early afternoon, the clouds seemed to have swept down to make the box canyon one big, dark ice box. Georgia's pink jacket, blue jeans, and worn Kodiaks just weren't up to it.

Story of my life, she thought. She hadn't been up to her childhood here, or out there. Hadn't been up to marrying Eddy, moving back here again, having kids. She *especially* hadn't been up to Eddy dying and leaving her alone with a little son and daughter.

And now?

Mercy. Here she was standing in a ditch, staring at the big ol' house down the way that held her kids and she was too blamed scared to go up there and knock on the door.

She flipped her dyed blond curls out of her eyes and blinked at the tears forming there. She could almost feel Bella's big black hand smoothing her hair and her deep voice lifting her from where she'd collapsed in the restaurant: *Come on Georgia. Come on, now.*

"Okay," she whispered. "Walk. One, two, three, four—"

The sound of a vehicle jerked her head around and she saw some kind of pick-up truck barreling down the quiet, snowy street that connected to this one like it was out on the highway. No, it was a new-looking 4X4, Range Rover or something, she saw as it turned the corner and rushed right at her. It passed, leaving the sharp smell of exhaust.

She shrank back, then took two steps forward as she saw the vehicle slow and turn into the driveway of the house that held her children. The 4x4 parked beside the Hurzgehrmine's pickup truck and its occupants climbed out, a dark-skinned man and a white woman. The woman glanced back her way. Beautiful. Raven-haired in a way that made Georgia want to choke. Then the driveway-side door of the house opened and the old witch, Clara Hurzgehrmine bustled out, all businesslike.

Georgia quickly dropped down into the shallow depression of the ditch, mortified. But she couldn't not watch, either, and crawled along on her elbows until she could just see over the Carlson's driveway to the Hurgehrmine's.

Around Clara, a little girl and boy danced out, flapping their arms and singing out their hellos. April and Auggie.

Georgia almost leapt up right then. Her heart surely did. Right up into her throat. Her mittened hands shook and clutched at the snow. Her knees jerked down spastically.

But that was as far as she went.

She collapsed her belly down again and trembled her cheeks onto the snow. Her children danced around strangers and didn't know their very own momma was in town, come back to get them, but too scared even to walk up and say hello.

Because how did you say hello to your kids after you'd fallen apart and walked out on them? Left them with someone else almost a *year*? How did a person do that?

So Georgia lay like that, unable to look but listening to the snatches of April and Auggie's laughter that carried over the distance. And she thought she should just creep backwards a ways until she could run on home. Home? Here? Uh-unh. Away. She'd just keep on running.

But she couldn't get up. Couldn't just leave. Her li'l chicks were calling. Her children.

Eyes brimming to blind, she lay there and tried to figure what to do.

THE FIRST THING that threw Nicole off was the children. Before she and Paul even got out of the Jeep, they came dancing out behind the old woman like woodland elves, crying, "Hello! Hi! Welcome!" A boy and a girl, maybe five and seven, though God only knew. Little anyway.

"I thought you said we were the only guests," she whispered.

Paul shrugged with a grin and climbed out, calling, "Fraulein Hurzgehrmine!"

"Frau," corrected the gray-haired woman curtly, her accent thick and heavy. She hushed the children with a sharp gesture and walked to Nicole's side of the car. She stood there waiting, her slate eyes fixed on Nicole's in a way that sent little shivers of ice through Nicole's fingers. What? *What?*

Nicole climbed out, shut her door, and gasped at the icy bite of the air. "It's cold," she said.

"You are in the mountains," said the woman as if Nicole were a little thick. Frau Hurzgehrmine, Nicole reminded herself. Their host. Not the enemy. But she'd have given the wicked witch of the west a good run for her money. Tall, stiff, brittle. Or who was that evil housekeeper in *Rebbeca*? Miss Danvers?

Nicole looked up and around at the mountains, the clouds pushing down thicker all the time. "It's very beautiful," she said.

The woman harumphed. Nicole had obviously been examined and found wanting. Frau Hurzgehrmine turned from her and returned to Paul. In chilly, even tones, she explained that Paul and Nicole would be sleeping in the third floor room and all of their gear not left in the car should be taken up there. Herr

Hurzgehermine would unfortunately not be able to assist in carrying because of his back. The children, however, were available to assist.

Then the old woman snapped her fingers at the children, pointed to the rear of the Jeep, and she herself turned and went back inside the house.

While the children fiddled with the rear latch, Nicole walked around to Paul. "You found this place how, exactly?"

Paul grinned. "I called the Grenadine Hotel, the one hotel in town. Woman there said they might be full but offered to pass on my name to a bed and breakfast. Then *Frau* Hurzy called."

"That hotel won't fill up. Not with the roads how they are and the storm coming in."

"So you'd rather go back to the hotel?"

Nicole pursed her lips and looked towards the Hurzgehrmine house. It looked blocky and solid enough—stone and thick wood. The roof had a steep slope to roll off the heavy snowfalls. And Nicole could see the ski slopes from here, walking distance. Not that they'd be skiing if the storms came in as expected. But she could use Frau Hurzgehrmine as her jumping-off point to find out why her mother had chosen this town for her final joke. The woman was about the right age. She was also German, like Betsy Müller must have been. Maybe Nicole's mother had even stayed here on one of her many travels in the last few years and talked with this woman...

"Nicole?"

She turned back to him and smiled thinly. "Why don't you unlock the rear hatch before the munchkins snap it off?"

CHAPTER 14

Fifteen minutes later, Nicole's head was pounding as she climbed up the seemingly endless narrow stairs of the Hurzgehrmine house. Even with her jacket fully open, she was roasting hot, her bag weighed a ton, and the air seemed to too thin to breathe. *You are in the mountains*, repeated the belittling voice of Frau H. in her head. Nicole gritted her teeth and kept climbing.

"How old are you?" the girl of the pair said, skipping up the stairs beside Nicole.

Nicole ignored her.

Paul, following, laughed and said, "Older than you, sweetie."

"Are you two really lawyers?" said the boy, younger, dogging Paul's heels.

"Yup."

"Do you put bad guys in jail?"

"Just little kids," gasped Nicole and promptly banged her shin with her bag.

"It's cops and D.A.'s who do that," Paul said.

"Put kids in jail?" asked the girl.

"Yeah, but only if they're really bad."

And Nicole, hands stiff, shins aching, head pounding, and stale breath coming hard, looked back to see Paul actually grinning down at the boy beside him and up at the girl. Of course. Because he *wanted* kids. He'd come from a big, happy family and couldn't imagine not creating the same. Though he did seem to realize that it was the mother who raised them. Especially if the father was always out tomcatting around with insurance adjusters from work.

She'd finally reached the top of the second flight of stairs and toed open the door there. Attic room. Their B&B was an attic room. Sharply sloped ceiling. Bare, scuffed-wooden floor with throw rugs. Creaky pine double bed.

"Isn't this great!" screeched the girl as she went flying in. "I helped mop the floor! Smell! Amomium!"

Oh, great. Nicole staggered in, set down her suitcase, sat on top of it, and dropped her face into her hands, massaging her temples

"You okay, dear?" said Paul clumping in behind her with the boy on his heels.

"Fine."

So Paul dropped his case and went down for more. Nicole sighed harshly and stood up to take off her jacket and unpack. The clothes went to the one place for them, a six foot wardrobe with drawers on the bottom. While the girl kept nattering.

"When I get older, I'm going to climb up Gomel by myself and have my very own gold mine."

Nicole pulled her underwear and socks from her bag and found that her tin of talc had spilled all over everything. She shook them out and went to the wardrobe.

"Then I'll be rich," said the girl. "And I'll have my own house. And I'll have ten dogs, and ten cats, and a pet wolf, and hamsters."

The corner of Nicole's mouth twitched grimly but it didn't slow the girl down. While the girl talked, Nicole grabbed the lower drawers and pulled. They were stuck. She tugged them harder and they suddenly came free so that she staggered back, bumping her head on the sloped ceiling near one of the dormer windows.

When she recovered, the girl was hanging off the end of the pine bed frame, zooming her legs under the bed so the bed creaked and shook. Then she scrambled out and did it again. And again. "Can you ask me a question?" she said in between slides.

Nicole gritted her teeth and rubbed the back of her head. "What?"

"Ask me what's my favorite animal or what I want to be."

"Fine. Shh— What animal do you want to be?"

The room door banged open and the girl's younger brother barreled in, sliding tummy first, under the bed. "She wants to be a wolf!" he called out.

"Hey! Now both of you..." Nicole began, before being interrupted by Paul banging their skis into the room behind the boy, almost poking Nicole in the eye.

"Sorry," he said with a grin. "More the merrier. Late lunch in five."

Both kids were jump-sliding under the end of the bed now and the pine headboard was creaking and banging into the wall over and over. In between that and scrambling feet, the kids now began giggling and yelling, "Eat!" "Food!" "I'm hungry!"

"*Enough!*" Nicole snapped and slapped the wall hard.

Dead silence.

Both kids looked out from under the bed with big moon faces. Paul turned to her with a deep frown and spoke in his very soft, 'I mean business' voice. "Nicky, this is their home. Their mother's...away. And they're just being kids."

Nicole looked into his eyes, feeling her own chest rising and falling tightly, her lips twitching around like she wanted to say something she knew she'd regret later. "Fine," she said finally. "You stay here with them. I'm going for a walk."

Without waiting for his answer, she grabbed her jacket from the floor by the door, stomped out, and rattled down the stairs. At the second floor landing she stopped and fell silent. There was something going on at the side door where they'd come in.

Breathing heavily, she saw Frau Hurzgehrmine hunched tensely at the threshold. "What do you want?" she demanded of the person standing just outside.

That person was a pretty woman in a shapeless pink jacket. She looked vaguely familiar though Nicole was sure they'd never met. She was an obvious bottle blond who'd died her eyebrows too. The woman shivered hard. Her eyes looked red from crying.

"I've come for my children," she said.

CHAPTER 15

As Nicole watched from the stairs, Frau Hurzgehrmine folded her arms across her chest like she was made of thick white lard. "No."

The blond woman's mouth drop open. "Th-they're my own children."

"You left them with me."

"Uh-unh...I mean, yes'm...but you took them. I...said I'd be back for them when I sorted things out."

"This was ten months ago." Frau Hurzgehrmine's German accent got thicker. "*Va'at* do you think your children think happened? *Va'at* do you think they believe?"

The blond woman was shifting her feet about now, her gaze flicking up past Frau Hurzgehrmine's shoulder to the hallway and kitchen, then back to the right, up the stairs to where Nicole stood. Something in Nicole's face seemed to strengthen her resolve.

"What'd you tell them?" she said.

"That you cannot take care of them alone. Look at you."

"But I can!"

"Can you?" Frau Hurzgehrmine laughed, but there was no humor in it.

"Yes'm," said the blond woman, but her certainty seemed to be slipping away as she looked pathetically up at Nicole.

Nicole closed her eyes. The helpless and the hopeless, she thought. Why were they always drawn to her? And why did she always feel like she had to step in to help?

But before Nicole could move, there was a sudden thumping rush of feet from behind and above her. The two kids, presumably this woman's, came tumbling down the stairs under Nicole's arms. They stopped short of the bottom, though, the little boy hiding behind his big sister. She stood hesitantly on the second last step, one hand on the bannister rail as if she was ready to run. And Nicole saw the similarity between her and the blond woman. April's hair was dark chestnut but with the same curls as her mother. She also had the same upturned little nose, the little valentine lips. But where the blond woman was all curves and femininity, the daughter was built more like her brother, long-boned and gangly.

"Mom?" said the girl.

The blond woman looked up, her face so open it hurt. The hope there, the guilt, the intense need. Like her daughter, though, she was holding herself back, scared to wreck things. "April," she whispered, and craned her neck to see around her daughter's legs. "Hi, Auggie. Can you both come down to your mama?"

Before the children could move, Frau Hurzgehrmine stepped directly between the mother and kids. "No. I do not know that you can look after them. If even your house has running water."

"I...uh...I...," the blond stammered.

Suddenly Paul's clear voice sounded from behind Nicole. "If it's a matter of getting her house suitable for the kids, I can go over and check it out."

Nicole stared at him as he descended the stairs past her and went to the door, holding out his hand to the blond woman and introducing himself. The blond woman said, "G-Georgia Hurzgehrmine," in return.

Whoah. Alarm bells started going off like crazy inside Nicole. Hurzgehrmine. Surely not Frau Hurzgehrmine's daughter, because they couldn't have looked more different and Frau H. would never have named a child of hers Georgia. Which meant Hurzgehrmine was probably Georgia's married name, but the son was obviously out of the picture. So, in Georgia's battle with her mother-in-law, Paul was going to step in to help? True, like Nicole, Paul was constitutionally a defender of the weak. But in this case, the defense was too quick. Too easy. Because the person in need, while maybe lower class in manner, was beautiful.

And alone.

And a mother.

As an afterthought, Paul looked at Frau Hurzgehrmine and then Nicole. "That would be okay, wouldn't it?"

"The children will stay here while you go," said Frau Hurzgehrmine curtly.

"Of course," said Paul, still holding Nicole's eyes.

"Fine," she said finally. "I was just going out for a walk around the town anyway."

"Can we go with *you?*" said the little girl, April.

"No!" snapped Nicole. The girl shrank back from it so much it was as if Nicole had slapped her. Nicole could feel every adult eye staring up at her, all of them disapproving. Frau Hurzgehrmine's gaze, in particular, seemed to sear into her with something beyond even contempt. Loathing. Like now Nicole wasn't just lacking, but seedy and vile.

Nicole tried to ignore the woman as she reached out and touched April's shoulder. "I'm sorry. But there are places I want to go, people I want to talk with, that you'd find really boring."

"But—"

Nicole shook her head. She stepped down the stairs past the children, put on her boots and jacket, and slipped out past the blond. Her last thoughts as she left were that 1) Frau Hurzgehrmine was never going to help her, and 2) the stepdaughter, Georgia, might be all torn up inside but still managed to wear a nice floral perfume.

Paul liked nice perfume.

CHAPTER 16

HIGH UP in the Lizard Head Pass, well south of Goldrock, the lines of the road were nearly invisible. The snow around Japhet's stolen Taurus howled and pushed at the sides and rear of the car like a wild animal.

Inside, hunched forward over the steering wheel, Japhet felt the tires slip and a quick shudder of fear went through him. It was like the little Indian bitch and her folks back at the border were doing some kind of weather dance to get him.

But they weren't going to get him.

Uh-unh. Not bugger boy.

Why had Mama called him that? He'd never once. Never. So why had Mama...?

Fug.

He made himself laugh it away and turned the heater's blower up until the car had a good burnt smell. No, the snow wasn't going to get him. Because he was locked in an unstoppable endgame now. Finally going home. No more running.

His mind wandered back to his last kill, Mary-Jane Pulver, and he realized that he'd started getting sloppy even there. If they found her sooner, rather than later, they'd send out an APB on her car, and Japhet hadn't been able to ditch it yet because of this storm.

Then again, nobody would be able to follow him out here in this storm either. And even if they did, even if, he'd be in Goldrock by then, he'd have found Mama, and nothing else would matter.

He rubbed his eyes and hunched tighter over the wheel.

CHAPTER 17

As Nicole tromped off through the snow somewhere, Paul drove the Jeep one road over and down three blocks to get him and Georgia to her address. He pulled into the unplowed driveway behind a beaten-up Chevy pickup.

"That yours?" he asked.

She nodded and shivered while Paul shut off the engine and stared at her home. It looked like an oversized shanty with cheap blue siding. Its one distinction was a shaky-looking bell tower rigged up on one end of the roof like the original builders had wanted the place to become a church.

"A bell inside it?"

She shook her head. "Don't think there ever was."

Depressing. Paul kept staring at it mainly to keep himself from staring at Georgia. "Let's go in," he said finally.

A moment later, he stood behind her as she bent over, fussing with the keys to her bungalow on Chickopee Lake Road. This time he couldn't not look. The light pink jacket she wore rode up her back and exposed the whole curve of her middle and behind like she was posing for *Playboy*.

Inarguably delicious.

"This was all we could afford when Eddy and me moved back," Georgia said as she wiggled the correct key in, making her backside twitch. She opened the door and turned around, gesturing him in.

"That's your husband? Eddy?"

"Was," Georgia said, blushing and touching her bleached-blond hair. "Eduard. He died last year. Backloader fell on him."

Paul held her eyes a moment and said, "I'm sorry."

"Yeah. Well," Georgia said, looking down and straightening her jacket self-consciously.

Paul nodded and entered, toggled on the front room lights, and looked around. Unlike the exterior, the inside was cozy. The front door opened into the living room. A couch and armchair took up the right wall. A window and old-fashioned woodstove with a bin of split wood beside it took up the wall opposite the front door. To the left of the woodstove was a narrow kitchen table, and left of that, an almost galley-style kitchen squashed in behind a door.

Completing the circle was a hallway immediately left of the front door. It presumably ran to the house's bedrooms, bathroom, and laundry. The air smelled a little dank.

"It's nice," Paul said.

"You think so?" Her southern twang seemed enthusiastically more pronounced now. She smiled at him and flicked back a curl of hair from her eyes. She still looked shaky, but was finding her feet. "It's not much to look at, I guess, but it's solid."

Like herself? Paul wondered. Georgia Hurzgehrmine, even dressed in a sack, would always be something to look at and knew it, holding his gaze just a little too long. Paul tried to drag his eyes away, but it was half-hearted. After the cold-shoulder Nicole had been giving him for almost six months, he deserved a little looking. And a little flirting? A little daydreaming?

Of course, that was all he had done with Shelley Collard—they'd never so much as kissed—and look what it had gotten him. Nicole's blackest wrath. Her judgement, with no appeal, that he'd had an affair. And no one could find you guilty quite like Nicole.

He doubted Georgia would ever do that.

"Eddy added the woodstove, but it's mostly gas heating," she said suddenly and turned to show him down the hall. He followed and she pointed him into the tiny room that held the laundry, furnace, and hot water tank. She and Paul both still had their coats on because it was as cold in the house as outside. "I shut it all off before I...um...left last year. But I called hydro and gas yesterday to get switched back on. So the lights work, but..."

Paul knelt down to the little slot near the bottom of the furnace. Squinted in. "Pilot light's out." He turned the knobs for it and the hot water tank. The hiss and smell confirmed that gas was available.

He straightened back up on his knees and looked up at her. She was just as lovely from this angle. Tantalizingly close in the confined space, her bust line just above his eyes, the perfume of her filling his head. "Did you shut off and drain the water when you left too?" he said.

Nicole wouldn't have had a clue how to do that in their Maryland house, but Georgia nodded, shifting on her feet so that her body seemed to curve towards him slightly.

"Then you should be all set. I'll try the sparker. Might also need some matches."

"And you'll...um...light my fire?"

He held her gaze and there was no mistaking the awkward invitation. Paul felt his head go light and a thin trickle of sweat ran down the back of his neck. "We'll get this pilot light going," he said thickly.

CHAPTER 18

THE SECOND SHE'D stepped outside, Nicole had almost turned around and
volunteered to go with Paul and the poor Marilyn Monroe wannabe.

Then her stubbornness had kicked in. She was not going to second-guess
Paul. She was not going to show to everyone they met how insecure she was
about his love, how paranoid, how just plain jumpy about everything.

She was not.

Instead she struck out through the darkening afternoon, feeling like the
thicker clouds overhead were pushing down on her, making the thin air saw
coldly in and out of her lungs. *You are in the mountains*, sneered again in her
head. No one wanted her here. Everything was foreign and shut to her. It
wanted to hurt her.

But she plowed on, reached Main Street, and headed towards the lights of
the Grenadine Hotel. Her goals were simple. She had to find out how to get to
the town's birth records, presumably in Goldrock's town hall. (When she'd tried
over the phone from back in Maryland, she'd met such intransigence she'd
almost blown a gasket.) She also needed to question anyone who might recall
either Suzie Baker or Nicole's supposed "true" mother, Betsy Müller.

The simple goal was to turn up the source of her mother's last awful lie or
establish somehow that there was absolutely nothing to it. That her mother
might have been all mixed up about her past and present, but Nicole did not
have to be. She could affirm where she'd come from and who she was. Which
would let her, God willing, find a way to get past her wild insecurities with Paul,
deal with him honestly, face to face, heart to heart, and see if they truly had a
marriage worth saving.

Nicole reached the front door handles of the Grenadine and forced herself to stop and breathe, still the annoying hammering of her heart, her dry mouth, her flushed face.

"You forget something?"

Nicole whirled to see a short shape step out from the wall of the Grenadine. "Wha—?"

The shape was dressed in a hi-tech blue-and-yellow snowboarding jacket, his hands shoved into the jacket pockets. He stepped closer and Nicole recognized it as Ari, the college kid from the hotel and the Trans Am. His wiry curls still tangled around his shoulders. "You look like I feel," he said.

"Which is—?"

He shrugged. "Nervous. Not wanting to face something?"

"Like your grandmother? You haven't been there yet?"

"I sent Josh to the ski shop. I figured I'd talk to that girl in there first. Only I haven't found my opening line yet."

Nicole smiled wryly. "Go to your grandmother's first, Ari."

The boy hesitated, then nodded, looked down, and left. Nicole pushed her way into the Grenadine lobby.

It was empty now. No one at the front desk. Yet even the line of little brass lamps on the walls and the red velvet chairs seemed to challenge her. As if everyone and everything in town—

A high-pitched motor whined to life at her left. A second later, Rose, the buxom maid from earlier, entered pushing a vacuum cleaner. She ran it cheerily behind the desk before she saw Nicole and shut it off.

"Sorry, Miss!" she shouted, then lowered her voice, embarrassed. "Have to get me work done while it's clear like. Storm coming, you know. Could lose power."

Nicole grimaced. "Is that common when a storm hits?"

"Oh, yes." Rose brought in the cord and plugged in between the red velvet chairs. "Most folks here got gas-fired generators for the basics, though. Barmy not to."

Nicole asked for the woman who'd been at the front desk and Rose went to get her. She emerged a minute later with the woman who'd given Nicole that bemused smile earlier. She was disconcertingly older than she'd looked from across the room, Nicole saw. Perhaps in her sixties. Late sixties? It was hard to tell because her silver-tinted hair was cut in an attractive bob, her dress was expensive burgundy wool with a single string of pearls, and she walked on high heels with the poised look and grace of a movie star. When she saw Nicole, her eyes lit up.

"You know me?" Nicole asked.

"You were talking with that boy, Miryam Siegel's grandson. Is he staying with her?"

Nicole frowned. "Ari. Yes. But...you don't know *me*?"

The woman tilted her head, amused. "Should I?"

"Or Betsy Müller?" No recognition. "Suzie Baker? Nigel Baker?" Still nothing.

"You look disappointed, Miss...?"

"Nicole Baker," said Nicole, holding out her hand and still watching the older woman's face with a glimmer of hope. But the fine eyebrows merely raised in acknowledgment. The slender fingers that gripped Nicole's briefly were cool and smooth.

"And I'm Elizabeth Severin. Perhaps if you told me what it is you're looking for, Nicole..."

So Nicole told her the whole story.

The woman's face tightened in concern as she listened, one manicured hand going lightly to her collarbone and the pearls there. When Nicole was done, she shook her head. "That is...some tale, and a fascinating investigation. But you know I'm not really the person to help. I was born here but moved away very early."

"Your husband? Is he from here?"

"My first husband was. But George, my second and only true love, was born in Michigan, of all places. We only moved here to take over this hotel seven years ago."

"And you don't remember, in that time, a Suzie or Nigel Baker passing through?"

"But I thought it was thirty—Oh. I see. If your mother was lying. No, I'm so sorry. But I could give you a list of names, older people who might have met them, or who'd know if an adoption went on back then. It's a small town, after all."

She walked back behind the reception desk, found a notepad and pen, and wrote down eleven names and addresses. She ripped off the paper and handed it to Nicole along with a town map.

Nicole thanked her, noting fatefully that Clara Hurzgehrmine was on the list. "Do you know if there a way to get into the town hall?"

Elizabeth Severin gave an ironic smile. "You would think so, with the centennial celebration this Saturday. But His Honor is on vacation down south, as are most of the staff. Bob Pritchett, our town marshal, might have keys." She gave him Pritchett's address.

"One last thing? The teenage girl who was working the desk with you. Is she...?"

Elizabeth Severin smiled. "My stepdaughter, Wendy. She's just finishing high school. Off to the University of Colorado next year."

"She's pretty."

The stepmother (*another one!*) bowed her head as though it were her own doing.

"Ton of boyfriends?"

"Just one. Though you might let Ari know that any girl heading off to university..." There was another quick smile, and Nicole decided that she could come to like this woman, obviously educated and doing her best in the middle of nowhere with a stepdaughter she'd obviously taken on even though she herself looked too old to have a high schooler in the family.

"If I see him," Nicole said, "I'll do that."

"And if you have any more questions..."

Nicole nodded and walked to the door. She looked back as she left and saw Elizabeth Severin watching her, her hand again at the pearls on her throat, and the strange look in her eyes...wistful?

Small towns. Nicole shivered and left.

CHAPTER 19

Nicole followed the map to the town marshal's office first.

It was a few blocks north down Main Street, a single-story, flat-roofed hunk of concrete that obviously served as the town lock-up as well as Marshal Pritchett's office. But the potato-faced marshal wasn't in. And the town doctor, whose two-story clinic/residence was almost right across the street, didn't answer Nicole's knock either.

Disturbingly, the doctor's office seemed to spark a vague déja vu. Why would that be?

She shivered from cold this time, beat her arms around her, and turned down one of the side streets she recognized from Elizabeth Severin's list and map. She stomped through an unshoveled front walk to bang on a door. An old lady answered. Nicole got herself invited in, asked her questions, and got non-sequiturs in return. Either the old woman didn't want to answer, or she was having serious focus problems.

Frustrated, but at least warm again, Nicole said goodbye and headed back to Main Street. She walked south to Mawpester's Food Fresh where, Severin had said, Herbert Mawpester had been the town's grocer forever. A self-serve laundry on one side and pizza place on the other hit her with warm, doughy smells as she stopped out front.

Through the Mawpester windows, she saw the stereotypical stout old man with glasses and a white-fringed pate stocking the back shelves. Working beside him was a tall, thick-necked teenager with a buzz cut, a crooked scar on his chin, and a grocery store apron. Something about the teen tickled her memory again and she frowned. A large boy, the hills, a doctor...

The man and teen didn't notice as Nicole slipped in.

"...enough to ride it out," the boy was saying.

"Depending."

"On how socked in we get. Sure. But everything's out, right? You won't need help stocking."

"What are you getting at, Jeremy?"

"Well...uh...I was wondering if I could have the day off, sir. Telluride's cancelled school for the storm and a few of the kids are going to go boarding up on Warsaw, and...uh..."

"Wendy too?"

"Yes, Sir."

The man Nicole assumed was Herb Mawpester straightened up, saw Nicole and nodded at her with a twinkle in his eye. He turned back to Jeremy with a frown. "I don't know, son. I hired you because I needed someone reliable."

The kid's face dropped so low he looked about twelve, less steroidal, even with the chin scar, and Nicole suddenly wondered if this football jock's "Wendy" was Wendy Severin, the inn-keeper's daughter. Which would make him the one boyfriend.

Really small towns.

Mawpester winked at Nicole then pushed up his glasses and said to Jeremy. "Now, Jeremy, I really do need you here. But if you promise you'll do at least one jump thingy that impresses the heck out of every kid there, then...I guess you can go."

Jeremy's head popped up. "Yes, *sir*. Thanks, Mr. Mawpester."

Mawpester rolled his eyes as the kid peeled off his apron and ran for the back of the store. Nice butt, Nicole mused as she watched too. Then Mawpester turned to her. "He and his friends will just go up to one of the hill ski shacks and smoke dope, but what can you do. And what can I do you for, young lady?"

Nicole smiled, instinctively warming to the man. So, as with Elizabeth Severin, she just told him everything straight out, about her mother, her claim that Nicole had been born in Goldrock. "And," she added hesitantly, "I have this strange memory of climbing rocks as a girl with some bigger boy chasing me. That...doesn't make any sense, does it?"

The grocer's face, so warm and open a moment ago, had stiffened into a concerned frown as she'd talked. "You'd be about how old?"

"Thirty-three."

"Why you don't look half that old."

"Thank you. But Betsy Müller? Suzie Baker? Either name ring a bell?"

Mawpester looked back down to the slit boxes he'd been taking cans from to put on the shelf. They were all empty and it seemed to disappoint him. "No one like that here."

Something in the way he said it made Nicole's heart beat faster. "Was there ever?"

Mawpester began stacking the empty boxes, then paused and his shoulders seemed to collapse a little. He studied the boxes like he didn't want to turn around "Maybe."

"Meaning you remember someone? My mother and father coming through here? Talking to people? Look, you can gather that my mother has always been strange. Did she do something while there were here? Cheat you or something?"

Mawpester started gathering up the empty boxes again. "You talk to Marshal Pritchett?"

"He wasn't in."

"Hunh."

"And he didn't look old enough to remember back that far anyway."

Mawpester carried the boxes to the back of the store, kicked open a door and tossed them in. Then he turned back to Nicole with a carefully blank look on his face. "You're right, there. He's too young to remember."

Nicole stepped up to him, her head humming. "Remember what? Are you trying to hint that what my mother said is true? That I was born here and given up to two people who just happened through town? Look, Mr. Mawpester..."

"Herb."

"Herb. Is that what you're saying?"

He looked at her finally, his eyes both sad and scared. "Ms. Baker, I'm not really saying a thing. Don't know a thing. But..." He looked away from her, suddenly finding it necessary to clean the door handle of his storage room with his apron. His voice dropped down as if he feared someone might be listening. "There's a house back on Chickopee Lake Road you might want to check out. Number twelve. Blue. It's a bungalow with a couple scrubby pines out front. Little old bell tower on top."

"Who's living there now?"

"I don't know."

"But—"

"I think it's empty."

"Herb."

"You know what?" the grocer said brightly as she pushed off from the storeroom door and turned to the front of the store. "There's a big storm coming. Very big. You'll want to be getting back to wherever you're staying tonight."

"Herb, this is my whole past we're talking about. My family."

"Right! I've got my family to get home to as well. Close up now and I may just make it home for dinner."

He stared at her with a walled-off smile that reminded Nicole, for some reason, of Elizabeth Severin. "Twelve Chickopee Lake Road," she said finally. "Thank you."

She walked back to the front of the store where big flakes of snow were falling against the glass window and door. Pushing open the door, she headed out into it.

CHAPTER 20

At 12 Chickopee Lake Road, Paul crawled out from under the kitchen sink where he'd been banging about with a pipe wrench for twenty minutes. Georgia was waiting, sitting back against the narrow kitchen table, watching him.

The kitchen was small enough that when Paul stood up, he was just a step away from Georgia and could smell the light sweat under her perfume. The furnace had heated the place up nicely over the last hour and a half and both Georgia and Paul had removed their coats. Georgia was in an open-throated purple jersey that clung around her curves invitingly.

"So?" she murmured.

Paul cleared his throat. "Water's running. Nothing's frozen. Your heater should do that big tank of yours in a few hours."

"Which makes my place livable again, right?"

"Basically."

"So y'all can just leave me now, right?"

Nothing in her face or body looked like it wanted him to leave, Paul thought. In fact, under the way she squirmed against the table in invitation, he sensed a desperate fear. Loneliness? Or something else. And in himself there was an urge that seemed to rise from more than just this woman's in-your-face sex appeal. It was almost like he'd known her long before now.

He grabbed a rag from the counter and began wiping slime rust off his hands and glanced out the back door to his left that led outside. Still snowing. "Do you want to come back with me now and get your children?"

Her face blanched and she looked away. "I...could now, I guess. Couldn't I? Yeah."

"What's the problem?"

Paul saw her swallow. It drew his attention to the milky smoothness of long neck. Then she bit her upper lip and his gaze shot there. Too easy to imagine...

"You know," she whispered, jerking his focus back, "some of us ha'nt had the easiest time of things."

Paul nodded a made a sympathetic sound in his throat.

"When Eddy brought me to this town..."

"That was your husband?"

Her wide eyes shot up to his like a frightened doe. "That's right."

"When he brought you here...?"

"It took some adjusting."

"Like?"

"Like..." She shook her head, compelled to move. It drove her off the door-frame and she brushed past Paul to get a glass of water from the sink, seemingly oblivious to what the sudden contact did to him. Then she brushed by him again, her breasts pressing against his arm on her way out into the living room. There she paused before stalking to the living room curtains and swishing them open for a second as if challenging the darkness outside. A beat later she jerked them roughly closed, breathing hard.

"What?" said Paul behind her.

"You know what it's like," she said, "to have everyone staring at you all the time? Even before I got pregnant? You know what that's like?"

Paul's hands hovered over her warm shoulders, beside the milky neck. Her perfume filled him. "Tell me."

CHAPTER 21

THE SNOWFLAKES WERE FALLING down smaller and harder on Nicole than the fat ones outside Mawpester's but Nicole almost didn't feel them. For the first time, as she walked, the possibility that her mother had been telling the truth became real.

That Nicole had been born here. In Goldrock. To a mother who'd given her away like a piece of trash.

She stumbled and almost tripped. Her mouth was filled with the same sick feeling she'd had when she'd left her mother after one hospital visit four weeks ago and walked into the Baker & Kesin downtown office to find Paul kissing Shelley Collard.

Radical reality readjustment. Everything flipped upside down. Knees wobbly. Balance gone.

Nicole grit her teeth and sucked the biting snow in through them. It made her cough and stagger to a stop. *Get a grip.* There had been nothing in what Herb Mawpester had said that confirmed the unsigned letter Nicole had received. Nothing that confirmed her mother was anything but a delusional liar. Mawpester hadn't even confirmed the existence of anyone named Betsy Müller. He'd merely hinted that something—it might not even have anything to do with Nicole—had happened in Goldrock thirty-some years ago. Well, hurray for Goldrock and go and check the damn house.

She plunged on and by the time she reached Chickopee Lake Road, she was convinced all over again that her mother had simply lied one last time and this entire trip was an expensive exercise in proving it.

She was almost ready, in fact, to bee-line it back to the bed-and-breakfast where she and Paul were staying. He'd be back by now. The Hurzgehrmines could whip up some hot tea. Or dinner. She hadn't eaten dinner. Then tomorrow, if the storm weren't too bad, she'd talk to Clara Hurzgehrmine, make a few phone calls, confirm she wasn't in any of Goldrock's town records, and then either stay and ski or just grab Paul and head straight back to their home in Silver Spring, Maryland.

The mystery of 12 Chickopee Lake Road could wait for another day...or year.

But even as she thought it, the wind blurred the snow up around her so that leaving the marked road was suddenly not an option.

Which meant she had to walk down Chickopee Lake Road anyway. Fine. She ducked her head and plowed on. Six, eight... She'd just stop for a second en route to–

Her boots stuttered to a halt.

Ahead to her left, ghostlike, wavered a little bungalow with a bell-tower knob jutting up on one end. And in front of it were two vehicles – a beaten up old pickup truck and a gold Jeep Grand Cherokee.

Their rental Jeep? Had to be.

But that meant... It meant... What? That Paul had come here. Why? Because he somehow *knew* about Nicole's mission here in Goldrock? He'd finished with the widow Georgia Hurzgehrmine then done some of his own investigations? Ended up here?

But...if he knew about this place, how long had he known and who'd told him? Nicole's mother? If so, what else might she have told him? What else had Paul been hiding from her?

Feeling all the sickness of her earlier disorientation rush back, Nicole walked towards number twelve.

It felt like a death walk, like the walk of a condemned woman, her noose waiting up ahead in a snow-whipped little hut. *Be ready*, sang a voice inside her as she clumped forward. *Be ready for your life to fall apart.*

Nicole was at the front driveway. She stopped beside the Jeep and rubbed the snow off the side windshield to look in. The Montrose weather report she'd thrown in the back seat still lay there.

She turned back to the house. She had to simply go to the front door now, knock, and ask, "Is my husband here?"

But the sick fear inside wouldn't let her do that yet. So instead she clasped her gloved hands together like a silent prayer, hunched her shoulders, and walked across the front lawn to the small window to the right of the front door. The lights were on inside and the curtains had been drawn roughly so there was a gap in the middle.

Nicole walked to the gap and looked in.

Be ready.

Inside stood two people, coats off, shirts and pants wet with sweat, rocking back and forth with their arms wrapped tightly around one another.

Paul and Georgia.

CHAPTER 22

On the far southeast side of town, in a two-story house with ornate Bavarian eves and that distinctive old person smell of unwashed skin and talcum powder, Ari Siegel and Josh sat on an uncomfortable yellow brocade couch, waiting.

But while Josh grinned around at the cathedral wood ceiling and knick-knacks, Ari was clutching his fingers between his knees. He needed an excuse to get him and Josh out of here today. Because his grandmother, his oma, Miryam, did not look sick at all. This whole anonymous letter thing, he suspected now, had just been a ruse to get him here for Passover.

There was also...something else. Ari could feel a tension in the air, an uneasiness he couldn't quite put his finger on. Maybe it was nothing. What did he know? But the feeling remained that his oma was going to ask him to do something.

Ari could already smell the bubbling chicken soup from the kitchen where his oma was getting them some tea. The soup would be for dinner. There'd also be chopped apples, cinnamon, and sweet wine in there, he knew. The parsley. The matzoh. The lamb bone. Passover.

Ari jumped up to pace around the living room. Maybe it was just that his oma was planning some sort of all-out offensive to win him back to the Jewish faith. Because Ari's Jewishness had always been his oma's big thing, hadn't it? Ari's mother was non-Jewish. Ari's father didn't really care. So Oma had taken it upon herself to always inundate Ari every time he visited. They did Passover, Yom Kippur, Hanukkah, prayers, songs, stories. Sometimes his mother would participate, as a kind of cultural study on her part; sometimes she'd sit apart and fume, or just not visit.

Ari's mom had put her foot down to stop Ari from doing a bar mitzvah, though. And that had simmered to the blow up at Ari's fifteenth birthday party.

"Shicksa!" Ari's oma had spat at his mother, pointing a bony finger at her like it was a curse. *Shicksa*—a filthy, non-Jewish woman who's done something awful, like marrying a good Jewish boy.

End of family visits. End of Oma's influence.

Until this anonymous letter arrived and compelled Ari to go to Goldrock. Okay. Yeah, thought Ari, as he fumbled his wiry curls back into a ponytail. Yeah, that was it. It should have been obvious. She wanted him to do his Bar Mitzvah. Maybe there was something about squeezing it in before you turned nineteen.

Still on the couch, Josh had let his head fall back so his red hair looked like a giant Brillo pad spread on the couch back. "Even with no wifi, this is so cool. Like Heidi in Colorado."

"Hodel, maybe," Ari said.

"Hunh?"

There was a bump on the other side of the kitchen door and Ari half leapt that way. "Oma?"

But the door didn't swing open and Ari stopped.

"Should we go check?" Josh said.

"Not yet." Ari made himself sit. "My grandma's small, but she's strong as a bull. She's just—"

There was another bump on the kitchen door and a small clatter, as if a tray of dishes had almost fallen. This time Ari and Josh jumped up together and ran to the door. It was on a two-way hinge, and Ari grabbed the doorknob and pulled.

His oma sat slumped down on the floor inside like a wizened doll, one hand holding a tray of tea pot, milk, and sugar on her lap; the other hand clutched her chest.

Her face was scrunched in pain.

CHAPTER 23

ARI DOVE DOWN to his knees beside his grandmother, suddenly noting every wrinkle in her face, ever bump and age spot on her skinny bare arms. And he slapped himself inside for his doubts. She was sick. Dying maybe. While Ari could only think about himself.

Josh had ducked down to grab the tea tray. "Is she...like...?"

Ari held up his hand. "Oma?"

Miryam released her clutching hand to push him back and Ari started breathing again. "Oma?" he demanded again. "Can you hear me?"

"Not yet, *shkapeh*," she mumbled under her breath, disoriented, as if the words were to someone else. "I must be here."

"What?" Josh said.

Ari shook his head at him and nodded at Josh to put down the tray and take her legs. Together they carried her back to the couch and laid her down there. Ari was shocked and scared by how feather light she was. Standing, she was barely up to Ari's nose and had no fat on her, but even so...

When she was propped up, half sitting on the couch, her face winced again but her eyes looked clear as she smiled up at Ari and Josh, sitting on the two armchairs opposite. "You know, *bubbeh*," she said to Ari, "I cleaned the whole house before you arrived."

"I saw that."

"Top to bottom, especially the kitchen. To my neighbor, Duncan McKintyre, I have arranged to sell all the *chametz*."

"Chametz?" Josh asked.

"Non-kosher food," Ari said tensely. Sick or not, forcing Ari back into his

Jewishness was definitely on her agenda. "You saw all stuff from the kitchen? She's preparing a Passover dinner for us."

"A *Seder*," Miryam corrected. "For tomorrow night."

"Cool," said Josh.

"Once," Miryam said, "Ari would visit every year. His papa would bring him and his brothers here, sometimes with their mother, sometimes not. We would light the candles, read the *haggadah*, search and find the *afikomen*..."

"Hidden piece of matzah bread," Ari said.

"...and dip our vegetables in salt water to remember the flight of the Jews from Egypt."

"Because of, like, the big Dead Sea opening and closing thing?" asked Josh.

"Yes."

"Wailin'."

"Yeah." Ari stood up abruptly. Then, partly out of loyalty to his mother and partly because he just felt his oma was hiding something from him, he said, "I'm not doing it, Oma."

"You're not..." She looked at him, stricken, and reached over to clutch his hand. "Ari, *nein*! This year you must. This year more than any other."

Ari frowned hard to keep his resolve. His whole body was vibrating like a giant warning buzzer was going off inside him. "What's going on, Oma?"

"The first Passover. The blood on the door. You know what this was for?"

"Yeah!" Josh interjected. "So God would skip their houses when he came in to snuff the Egyptian kids."

"The first born sons. Yes."

"So?" said Ari.

His oma looked up at him. "So we must light candles tonight, bubbeh. There is so much evil in the world these days. We must make ourselves right with God."

Ari pulled out of his oma's grip. "Which means what? That I'm somehow evil?"

"You?" She frowned as if not understanding, but Ari caught something there and went after it.

"Yes, Oma. Like you called my mother evil. Unclean. You think that got passed on to me somehow? You want to get me all sorted out somehow before you die?"

His oma blanched and Ari bit his tongue. But he couldn't back off it now. There was something she wasn't telling him, and he be damned if he was just going to dance along to her tune in the dark. He wasn't a kid anymore.

He stuck out his chin. "Well?"

"Hey, dude..." said Josh slowly.

"Ari," said his Oma. "When you called to say you were visiting..."

"Because a letter told me you were dying."

His oma went even whiter and her hands trembled as they pushed her fully upright. "I did not send you this letter."

"But you know who did, don't you? And there's something you're not telling me. What?"

"I—" she began, but shut her mouth, staring up at him with a stricken expression.

Ari pulled back from her, swallowing dryly. "I need to get some air. I'm going to show Josh around the town."

Josh scrambled to his feet. "Dude, shouldn't we help your grandma clean up? What about dinner?"

"We'll eat out. And Oma has everything under control here. Don't you, Oma."

His grandmother looked at him beseechingly, then seemed to change her mind and set her lips in a straight line. "Go. This is the way of your generation, yes? Get lost in the snow."

Ari grabbed Josh's sleeve and tugged him towards the door. A minute later they had on their snowboarding jackets, lightweight, high-tech blue and yellow, and were gone.

CHAPTER 24

NICOLE STAGGERED BACK from the living room window of 12 Chicopee with her mouth wide, finding it hard to breathe.

No. No. No no no...

She swayed, then stumbled forwards again and sideways around the house, hands seeking blindly for the weathered blue siding, using it both to guide her and keep her from falling. Finally, when she'd rounded the corner and could not be seen from the front, she stopped, sucked in a deep wail of breath and let it shudder out of her body like it carried her whole life with it.

This was it. What she'd always unconsciously expected. Paul doing to her what her own father and stepfathers had done to her mother over and over and over again. And while Nicole had left home early, rarely visiting, she could still remember the arguments. See them. Smell them. There was Daddy bursting through the door late, bringing in the snow and smell of cedar wreaths, arms full of presents. And there was Momma Suzie rushing out from the kitchen, jerking up some feminine item or other which she'd found in his car last night, and waving it at him. And Daddy laughed at her, his cheeks red, mustache bristling out like a wire brush. He winked up at Nicole, watching from the top of the stairs, as he tossed down his presents and went to Momma Suzie. He brushed her blows aside and explained over and over in such reasonable tones, finally swept up Momma Suzie into his arms, kissed her neck, caressed her back.

Nicole remembered the tingles that had sent through her. The relief. And the doubt. Could Momma Suzie be wrong every time? Finally Nicole recalled the despair she'd felt as Momma Suzie had given in without pushing harder.

And the anger.

Yes, anger at the betrayal and the weakness that let itself be betrayed. Nicole tried to draw on some of that now to stiffen up her backbone. She straightened and pushed away from the wall. Momma Suzie had never pushed for the truth because she couldn't have recognized truth if it hit her across the face like a board. Her world was made of lies and half-truths, most of which she'd passed on to Nicole.

But Nicole didn't have to keep them. She had the skills and training as a lawyer. She'd find the truth, goddamn it. About Paul. About her own parents. About life. Everything.

She heard a door close somewhere and took two hard steps backwards. Suddenly she was against the trunk of a half dead pine, the dried branches snapping around her like a mummy shell sucking her in.

Nicole gasped and stepped forward again.

The wind was picking up, howling now, with the sound of an engine starting up? The darkness was coming down hard. If she wanted to get the truth about Paul, at least, she had to move now. She touched the ends of her gloved fingers against her eyes to make sure they were dry and stomped back through the snow to the front of the house.

The Jeep was gone.

CHAPTER 25

It took Nicole almost twenty minutes to walk back to the bed-and-breakfast because she missed the connecting street for Lift Road and ended up going all the way to the end of Chickopee.

When she finally pounded on the Hurzgehrmine side door, Paul jerked it open and pulled her in, brushing the blown snow off her and fluttering about like a worried nursemaid. Guilt?

"I saw you," Nicole said.

"Pardon?"

"I saw you at Georgia Hurzgehrmine's house. In her arms."

Paul stepped back and Nicole could feel his skin burning. A sour smell rose off him too, like his body had just released a panicked flight response. "That wasn't what it looked like."

"Wasn't it? Where's her husband?"

"Dead."

"Who's dead?" said a new woman's voice, cultured and precise, and Nicole looked up to see Elizabeth Severin walking down the hall from the kitchen. That explained the extra pickup truck in the driveway. Never walk when you could drive. Particularly if it would mess your hairdo and pearls.

Picking up Nicole's mood, the hotelier smiled and slid past both Paul and Nicole to retrieve her heavy, long black coat with a fur-trim collar.

"What were you here for?" Nicole asked her.

"Visiting my friend, Clara," Elizabeth Severin said. "Did you have any luck with your questions?"

The interest was genuine and Nicole felt her hostility towards the woman ease away. "No."

"That's too bad. Maybe you're right. Maybe your mother's story was just that after all. A story."

"Maybe."

The older woman, fully dressed now, put a reassuring hand on Nicole's arm and exited into the swirl of snow.

"What story of your mother's?" Paul said when she was gone.

"Better than whatever you could tell me about you and Georgia."

"She was falling apart, worried about her kids. She needed reassurance."

She needed reassurance?

Nicole angrily shrugged off her coat and boots, then felt Paul watching her. She was still wearing the lime-green turtleneck and tight leggings they'd arrived in, a sexy outfit she'd subconsciously chosen to because she knew Paul liked it. But as she tucked in her shirt and shook out her hair, she had to fight the feeling she looked crushed and throwaway. The blond widow, who was Nicole's age or older, didn't have seven years of stress-filled thirteen and fourteen hour days practicing law behind her. She didn't have the premature wrinkles around her eyes and mouth, the permanent ice in her eyes.

Paul eyes raked over her, though, excited. As if the poor boy had been sexually awakened, teased, and now here was his wife whom he was supposed to have access to. Nicole could probably use that right now to lead him upstairs and start the first lovemaking she and Paul had done in...how long? Months?

Maybe that would somehow pull him back.

But the thought of undressing before him gave her a shiver of fear. To be vulnerable before this betrayer? She shook her head. "Later." She pushed past him down the hall toward the kitchen where she could smell dinner waiting.

It was—breaded veal cutlet, sauerkraut, and salad. Nicole smiled at the Hurzgehrmines and the children, and sat down determined to be cheerful. She still had to question Clara Hurzgehrmine somehow.

But Frau Hurzgehrmine was obviously having none of that. She kept scowling between Nicole and Paul as if Elizabeth Severin's visit and Nicole and Paul's confrontation in the entry hall had both proved her guests unreliable. Nicole lasted only half the meal then excused herself.

She'd barely had time to get out her bedclothes, however, when a timid knocking sounded on the door and April's voice asked to come in.

Nicole went to the door and opened it, admitting April, with Auggie in lock-step behind her.

"Um..."

Nicole waited.

"Sorry," April said quickly, and Auggie blurted, "Sorry," behind her.

Nicole frowned. "Sorry about what?"

April looked back at Auggie and he stepped out, looking at her and sucking in his lips. "You know," April said. "For whatever we did that made you leave earlier."

"You think it was something that you did that made me leave." Not wholly untrue, Nicole thought, but they'd only been a small part of it.

Both kids nodded. "Like we made our mom leave."

Nicole's heart slammed up to her throat. "Whoah. Why do you think you made your mom leave?"

Auggie popped out his lips. "Nanna," he said, and began playing with the doorknob.

April still stared at Nicole as if she somehow trusted Nicole to tell her the truth. "She says our mom's really sick and couldn't take care of us," she said, "but we don't think so. We think it's us."

Nicole's sympathies flip-flopped yet again. She remembered seeing Georgia beg for her kids on the doorstep, so pathetic and needy. Then Georgia had seduced Paul and become an amoral bitch who'd had it too easy in life. Now the pathos had widened to include the kids and their mother's weakness. It made it impossible for Nicole's anger to have a simple focus. Except maybe this town. Goldrock. Her dead mother.

With a heavy sigh, she sat on the edge of her and Paul's double bed and patted the bedspread beside her. April hurried over and, after a second, so did Auggie, jumping onto it to bounce like a stiff-legged dog.

"Hey! Don't—" Nicole started. But Auggie had already stopped, face afraid. April looked frightened too.

Damn it. Part of her wanted to give these two children a hug, but that wasn't something she knew how to do. Instead she just laid it out for them.

"I believe," she said, "that your mom's having trouble being a mom. But I think...she still loves you, okay? I think she loves you, no matter what's happened. No matter what you did or she did or anything else. She'll come for you."

Nicole put an awkward open hand on April's tiny back, wondering suddenly at the pain it must have given Georgia to leave her children with a stepmother who despised her. And the kids – what must they have felt when she did it? It gave Nicole a squeezing feeling in both her womb and her child's heart. How could any mother lie to her kids, abuse them, abandon them? How could the kids ever trust that mother again?

Then April threw herself suddenly into Nicole, wrapping her skinny arms around Nicole's waist, and Nicole understood on a gut level. None of what had been done in the past mattered. Any abandoned child, including Nicole, just wanted their mother back.

CHAPTER 26

MOTHER.

Mother.

Mother.

It seemed to pound out through the night, rising finally from the fitful dreams at the Hurzgehrimines' to mix with the waves of snow howling through the mountains. By fifteen minutes to midnight the temperature had fallen to zero and turned the earlier flakes to driving powder.

Drifts were forming against houses and rocks, parked cars, lampposts. In Goldrock nobody stirred outside. Few houses were lit. The street lamps down Main still functioned, but only two commercial buildings showed any life. One was the Dead Man's Saloon, with a few die-hards unready to face the storm outside or at home. The other was a second floor office in which two contract software engineers worked on into the night, weather irrelevant against a shipping deadline set in Seattle.

The streets borders were vanishing.

Mother.

And then...two headlights tracked slowly down Slider Hill. Approaching Goldrock.

It was a late-model, brown Taurus sedan, so covered with snow and grime that its color was indistinguishable. Its windshield wipers swept back and forth brutally, trying to clear the snow before it even hit.

As it reached the bottom of Slider Hill, it swerved through a snowdrift there then weaved slowly forward. The car was obviously having trouble picking out the line of the road. It only found it for sure when it hit Main Street, guided by the string of signs coming into town.

The car turned left onto Main Street and crawled slowly along it pushed through a drift too deep and just stopped.

Its engine chugged to a halt and its front left door opened. A large lump of a man lurched out into the blowing snow. He held a small, battered brown suitcase in one hand. Looked up at the front of Goldrock's City Hall. Swore at its lit-up clock tower. Slammed the car door. And staggered through the storm until he reached the front doors of the Grenadine Hotel.

Further down the street, a banging sound over the wind made him jerk his head and he saw what looked like two teenagers in blue and red stumble out of a saloon.

The man turned back to the hotel, the Grenadine, yanked its front double doors open, and plunged in, the snow whirling in behind him.

CHAPTER 27

HE'D MADE IT.

Japhet Edwin Bone took a deep, shuddering breath of the air in the Grenadine Hotel's lobby, then coughed roughly on the undertone of cigarettes and air freshener. The red velvet of the place rolled into him like a scald but he staggered forward into it. Nothing could stop him.

She had tried to turn him back. With the sudden storm. The snow. The damned City Hall with its clock tower glaring down at him. And it hadn't been the little Indian girl *she* either. Japhet had been wrong about that. The *she* who'd sent the storm and tried to run him off the road was Japhet's mother. That made no rational sense, he knew and kept telling himself. But on no sleep and the strain of driving nearly blind for the last three hours, his gut insisted it was still true. It was like how his mama had been running his life remotely for years. All those little letters trying to apologize, driving him to every greater furies just when he thought he might have himself under control. His mama and her gang had set his course for him early and he had merely followed it.

Like how he'd followed it back here now, when she'd sent for him. She wanted to see how he'd grown up, Japhet guessed. Push him some more. Fiddle with her favorite toy.

But he had a surprise for her. He was going to show her how he was his own man, then kill her. Hunh-hunh-*hunh.*

No one was here in the lobby. He should call out for them. But when he opened his mouth, not even his usual stutter came out. The tension of the drive and the fierceness of the storm seemed to have made the great vortex inside his throat even stronger, sucking every last word away from him.

Mama.

That was *her* doing. Her favorite trick.

Japhet slapped his hands over his temples like he could pop the memories of his mother right out though his mouth. Pow! Like a cork. Out of him and skittering across this carpeted floor, bouncing off the wood-paneled walls on the right and rolling to a stop at the bottom of the stairs in the far right corner. What would the memories look like? All slimy purple and red. Throbbing.

"Open your eyes, Japhet. I won't have you hiding from what you are."

"Yes, M-m-m-mmama."

"And don't you go trying to cover yourself. Dogs don't cover themselves and we don't let horny little boys cover themselves either, do we, Sarah?"

Japhet's one little sister, hiding behind their mama's skirts shakes her head as she stares, wide-eyed, at her naked brother.

The linoleum grit is cold under Japhet's bare feet. The hot wind from out in the backyard is blowing in around his young, hairless butt. "L-l-l-lot of people at the f-fence, Mama."

"All my friends. Waiting for you, bugger boy. Go on now."

Japhet slapped his temples again.

Shut. Her. Off.

He snapped his jaw closed and surveyed the lobby. Stairs to the right. Heavy reception desk ahead, deserted. A hallway led back out of sight behind it. The left wall had a door to the hotel restaurant. Brass lamps with little orange lampshades stuck out from the walls everywhere, but gave no warmth. The room was chilly. And that stink of cigarettes and floral air freshener, lilies, like his mama had used. He hated that smell.

And it was too quiet.

He drew his body up with a loud snuffling breath, shook the snow off the brown pigskin bomber jacket he'd pulled on to come in here. He was proud of that jacket, weathered and scored, tough and hard like the ones the sheriff and his deputies all wore back in Juarez, California where Japhet worked now. Puffing himself up on that, he called out, "Hey!"

There was no response and he shambled up to the reception desk to bang on the little bell there. *Ding.*

"H-hey!"

There was a muffled bark, then nothing. Not a sound from above or down the little hall behind the desk on the left. Just the ache under his right leg from all the driving. The stiffness in his back. The bad smell of the air on his tongue. The dead, dull stink. Nothing else.

No, not true. There was also a quiet electric buzz, constant, coming from somewhere. Japhet swung his gaze around, finally found the simple round wall clock up on the wall behind the reception desk. Electric. The second hand swinging endlessly around. Eleven-forty-five. *Buzzzzzz.*

"P-please!" Japhet thumped his meaty hand in desperation.

There was another muted bark, and at last a shuffling sound from the hall that ran back left of the reception desk.

CHAPTER 28

THE MAN who walked out behind the Grenadine's reception desk wore slippers and was still tying his robe. His hair was silver and brushed-back. He had a perfect little nose, and sky-blue eyes like a has-been movie star.

Japhet saw him blink, run his eyes slowly over Japhet's battered suitcase and soaked, size-fifteen Adidas. The man's eyes lingered on Japhet's creased polyester pants, the bulge of change in Japhet's pocket, and the thick brown leather bomber jacket.

Japhet tried to smile. "You g-g-g-got a spare r-r-r-ruh..."

The man's gaze jerked up to Japhet's face as if he were amazed Japhet could talk. "Room? Of course. I'm...sorry about not having someone at the desk. I really didn't think anyone could come into town tonight."

"It's pretty b-bad out there," Japhet said. "Got s-s-stuck on the highway just outside. Had to go s-somewhere. This was closest."

"Ah."

There was a pause and Japhet bounced his chin around. "So you g-got a r-room?"

"Oh. Yes. Just a minute." The man fussed at the desk, looking through his book. As he did, Japhet clenched his teeth together, and rocked forward on his toes. He could kill this man so many ways. The telephone cord, the desk pen into his temple, or the letter opener on the desk, one of the lamps smashed across the man's skull, the man's own shirt gagging him, Japhet's hands crushing the guy's windpipe...

Except he didn't do men, did he? *Bugger boy.* Just pubescent girls and women. Daughters and their mothers. The watchers. And even these he wasn't doing now. Not anymore. Because he just wanted the original watcher, the evil bitch herself—Mama. Then it would all be over. Forever.

"Daddy?" The light female voice came from the same hallway the hotel keeper had shuffled out of. "Daddy?"

As Japhet rocked back, a pretty girl appeared out of the hallway, carrying a little Scotch terrier in her arms. She had shoulder-length chestnut hair, the sky-blue eyes of her father, and a chipmunk mouth with full lips. Through her tee-shirt, Japhet could see the outlines of a bra. She had still-growing tits. Small, delicious hips. Maybe seventeen or eighteen...

And he shouldn't care.

Except...maybe she could help him. Maybe she knew where his mama lived in town. Yes. That sent a shiver through Japhet's groin and made his upper lip break a cold sweat. He licked it and met her eyes. He could spend some time with this girl, get her to tell...

The girl twitched, the Scotch terrier growled at Japhet, and the inn-keeper looked up from his books. "Wendy? What are you doing up?"

"I was reading. Can I help?"

"Um..." The hotel keeper yawned. "Just let me get a credit card number from this gentleman and—"

Japhet jerked forward. "N-nnn-no. I...uh...I g-got my wallet stolen back in D-Denver. Got cash. How mm-much you need?"

The hotel keeper blinked. "You have no i.d.?"

"Just the car r-registration. Outside. You nnn-need it right now?" He made his eyes pathetic.

"No, no. Tomorrow will be fine. But I do need a cash deposit. Do you have five hundred dollars?"

Japhet breathed a showy sigh of relief and reached into the pocket of his bomber jacket. Pulled out a thick money clip and counted out four fifties and fifteen twenties, "donations" he'd collected from his last two kills.

The hotel keeper smiled and nodded. "Thank you. Your name and perma-nent address?"

With his stutter helping to hide any stumbling, Japhet gave his name as Mack Morris, from an address he made up in Winslow, Arizona. He'd liked Arizona, the women there.

"Alrighty then. Room twenty-seven. My daughter will show you up."

Japhet nodded, picked up his battered suitcase nervously, and turned to the girl. She didn't meet his eyes as she motioned him to follow. But as she climbed the stairs in front of him, she made her jean-clad bum twitch back and forth, sending the blood tingling through his groin again. He could grab her upstairs, force her naked, take some pictures...

She'd reached the top, strode down the worn green carpet and turned to wait for him at door twenty-seven, the door already open. Her little dog lifted its lips at him as he approached. Japhet would love to punch out those little fangs.

"You'll like your room," the girl said, stroking her little dog's head so it bobbed under the weight. "It's got a view of the Warsaw runs."

Japhet raised his eyebrows.

The girl laughed. "Sorry. You didn't come for the skiing, did you?"

"Just trapped by the s-s-storm."

"Well it's good you made it down here." She smiled sweetly and motioned him in, but he didn't move yet. He thought how when he took her it would be like pulling apart a rose.

"How long before the p-plows usually get down to shovel a road out?"

"You mean shovel 'the' road out? After a dump like this, it might take a few days."

"Hunh." Nothing had changed.

Japhet strolled in slowly, lingering as he passed her. He felt her heat. Smelled her musk. Felt the little tremor that ran through both her and her dog. Then the little terrier growled, turned and nipped at Japhet's arm, catching the leather of his jacket.

Japhet spun to glare down at the dog, and it brought his body around with his coat open, pinning her. As the girl frantically apologized—"I'm so sorry. Max doesn't ever do that. I'm sorry. Are you all right?"—the heat and squirming of her made his cock spring up, ragingly hard. He just...needed to...

No! He wasn't here for her. And with the town socked in like this, no one entering or leaving, he couldn't risk that by messing around, even to supposedly "question" this girl. No one died until he had things planned out.

Swallowing hard, Japhet said, "Forg-get it," and pushed by her into the room. No!

Except maybe that fugging dog...

He turned to see the girl had hurried in with her dog, set the room key on the table by the bed, and already hurried back out.

"There are three shared washrooms on the floor," she said quickly. "Lots of hot water."

"Thanks, Wendy." He didn't stutter. She was afraid of him.

The dog growled again but she shushed it and started to leave.

"Wendy?"

She stopped.

"You're very pretty. I'd like to take your picture sometime."

She gave him an uncertain smile, then turned with her furry armful and hurried off down the hall.

Japhet walked to the door, closed and locked it, took off his jacket and threw it over to the bed, and suddenly felt naked.

"You turn 'round slow for them, Japhet, or I'll throw you back in that basement and chain you like a dog. Call back your daddy on you. I swear I will."

He popped his hands over his temples again and spun towards the window. He remembered the saloon out there, and the gazebo-sized work building he'd seen on the edge of town coming in.

Yeah, they all could keep pushing him, but it wouldn't be for long now. Not long at all.

A plan was forming.

DAY TWO
THURSDAY

CHAPTER 29

It had snowed all night and though it no longer howled sideways in a blur, it showed no signs of stopping.

That's what it looked like to Nicole.

Huddled in a chair by one of the attic windows of the Hurzgehrmine house with her slippered feet pulled up and her arms wrapped around her knees, she stared out at the steady, straight fall of white. No one outside. Everyone was trapped inside their little burrows.

She could hear the sounds of Paul, the kids, and the two older Hurzgehrmines banging about far downstairs at the breakfast table. They'd all seemed to sleep well and wake with healthy appetites, but Nicole had tossed about all night. And in the shadow of Paul's guilty nerves and Frau Hurzgehrmine's glare this morning, she'd been able to eat only a pear and piece of toast. Her insides were in knots. All the disoriented terror she'd felt when she'd seen Paul and Georgia together last night had come rushing back to her this morning. Losing Paul. The possibility of losing her own identity.

This town... It was like some demonic white abyss. Something bad had happened here a long time ago that still scared the older locals. And it had happened right around when Nicole was supposedly born or taken away from here. It was as if her mother had made up a story that would fit her neatly into a horror novel. Endlessly creative, Nicole's mother had been.

Sounds of an argument downstairs made her lift her head.

Shouts, male and female. A screech. A child crying. What the hell?

Eager suddenly to be out of her own problems, Nicole hopped off the chair and went to the door. Opened it. The shouting had stopped, to be replaced by sharp bursts and pleading with an Oklahoman drawl. Georgia. She'd returned for her children.

And for Paul?

For just a second Nicole hesitated, then she opened the door and thumped down the stairs, determined to confront at least one of her demons this morning.

Georgia had pushed her way into the kitchen where the children still sat at the breakfast table. Auggie had a half-eaten piece of toast on the plate in front of him, bits of raspberry jam around his mouth. April's hand still gripped the knife she'd used to spread it for him. The little girl's eyes twitched desperately to Nicole as Nicole entered behind Georgia's back.

"You have ten seconds," Frau Hurzgehrmine was saying to her stepdaughter. *You haf ten seh-cons.* Her face was white and she gripped the back of the chair April sat in. "Then I will call Marshal Pritchett. I will charge you with child abandonment. And hitting them."

"I never..." Georgia began but stopped as Herr Hurzgehrmine, normally a quiet shadow to his wife, picked up the receiver from the wall telephone.

"Clara," Paul said from between Georgia and Frau H. "Horst. You don't want to do that. Please think it through. You'd lose and might have charges thrown back at you. Do you really want that?"

Frau H. whirled towards him. *"Vas iss? Vas?"*

Georgia clasped her hands together. "Clara, ma'am, you said when my home was ready for them, I could take them back. You said."

"But *you* are not ready," Frau H. shot back.

"How do you know that? How—?"

She stopped as Nicole put a hand on her arm. Then Nicole stepped farther into the room, stomach churning, but possessed of an icy calm that made the others stop and watch her. She pointed at April and Auggie. "Who gave birth to these two children?"

In the stupefied silence, Georgia finally whispered, "Me."

"And does she, other than leaving them in your care, Frau Hurzgehrmine, truly have a record of beating them, leaving them unattended for hours at a time, not feeding them, emotionally attacking them?"

"No," Georgia whispered.

Frau H. squeezed April's shoulders so tightly the little girl squirmed. "I have cared for them almost a year."

"And now their mother is back to take them home again." Nicole held up a hand before Frau H. could say more. "Has anyone asked the children if they want to go back with their mother?"

Silence.

Nicole turned to April and Auggie. "Do you want to stay here or go with your mother?"

Nicole could barely hear April's murmured "Mommy," but Auggie's followed with quick assurance and his pointed finger left no doubt. Frau H.'s face looked as if they'd just spat on her. Then it began to harden again. "You," she said to Nicole, glaring at her with the expression that had turned from loathing to pure, unadulterated hatred.

Nicole raised her chin. "Clara and Horst, I understand why you're concerned for these your grandkids. You've looked after them. You've loved them. So I think you should send someone with Georgia to make sure that for today, at least, they're properly cared for."

Frau H. sneered. "You could not—"

Nicole shook her head. "Not me. My husband. He's already fixed up Georgia's house. He could go with them for a few hours. Make sure everything's okay."

Both Frau H. and Paul frowned in surprise. Nicole's accusations last night hadn't exactly been private. Herr Hurzgehrmine dropped his eyes in embarrassment. Behind her, Nicole heard Georgia breathing short high breaths. Hope or dread?

"So?" Nicole said.

Frau H.'s head jerked down, then she gave April's shoulders one more quick squeeze and walked to the sink to push her husband aside and take over the dishes.

Paul looked at Nicole. "You're sure?"

"Two hours. Agreed?"

He nodded, there was a gasp of delight from Georgia and both children burst out of their chairs to run to their mother.

Nicole didn't even look at the reunion as she clenched her teeth and walked towards Clara and Horst Hurzgehrmine. Clara bared her teeth at her as she approached, but at the last second Nicole stopped and turned to the wall phone.

She had work to do in the next two hours too.

With the sounds of the children, Paul, and Georgia collecting up their things in the background, Nicole deliberately pulled out of her pocket the list of names and phone numbers that she'd gotten from George Severin at the Hotel Grenadine. The first four were crossed off and Clara, at least for this morning, would have to wait. Nicole lifted the receiver to dial number five. Jiggled the disconnect a few times.

The line was dead.

CHAPTER 30

Along the highway that formed the northern border of Goldrock, Japhet Bone hunched his way out of the gazebo-sized metal work building and grinned into the steady snowfall. In his right work glove, a lineman's heavy yellow leather, he clutched the wrench he'd used to detach the coupling that connected Goldrock's phones with the cables that went up and over the mountains. It had taken him just ten minutes. Skills he'd learned from a stint with Fresno Power and Electric seven years back.

Step one.

Now his mama probably expected him to hunt madly for her, but he wasn't going to do that. Instead he was going to try what the police had tried with him before—little mind fucks. With the phones cut out and the town closed in, Japhet was ready to begin.

He tugged the zipper of his leather jacket right to the top, turned up the collar, and trudged back through the heavy snowdrifts towards town.

CHAPTER 31

NICOLE PUT down the telephone receiver and frowned.

"What is it?" asked Horst Hurzgehrmine, standing less than a foot from her elbow, holding his dishtowel. Clara Hurzgehrmine was scowling over her shoulder at Nicole, unwilling to turn around.

"Line's dead," said Nicole. Her gaze jerked to the front door as Paul slipped out behind Georgia and her two kids, shutting the door behind him. Her distraction of phone calls suddenly gone, she thought for a second about running after them. Mawpester had hinted that Twelve Chicopee, Georgia's house, was somehow connected to whatever had happened in Goldrock thirty-some years ago. Maybe Georgia knew something about it. Good reasons to go with them.

Nicole gave her head a little shake. No. Enough people were lying to her; she couldn't start lying to herself. She was simply scared about Paul and Georgia. And it would only make things worse if she tagged along. Better to interview at least these old people on her list, then try to get into the town hall. If she could just kill off her mother's deathbed lie, she could easily handle Paul and Georgia.

Resolved, she turned her eyes back to her list of names and considered Clara Hurzgehrmine's again. She was right here, after all. If Nicole just grit her teeth...

"Frau Hurzgehrmine?"

The older woman almost snarled at her as she turned and Nicole took a step back. Fine. She'd go to the others on the list first. She turned to Horst instead. "How long would it take me to walk over to Town Marshal Pritchett's office?"

Horst glanced at his wife. "On a nice day it takes you maybe fifteen minutes. But this is not a nice day."

"No," Nicole agreed. "It's not."

She folded her list and walked to get her jacket and boots.

CHAPTER 32

Wednesday morning at Oma Siegel's house.

Ari staggered downstairs, clutching his head. His hair fell around his eyes like a tangled black carpet. Every footstep felt like a loud boom on a bass drum.

So this was what a hangover felt like. Holy crap. What had possessed him to bluff his and Josh's way into the Dead Man's Saloon last night? He'd never bluffed his way into an R-rated *movie* before. And then the way he'd started talking to total strangers after a few drinks... Because that's what journalists did, right? Drank booze and talked to people.

He heard his oma bustling around in the kitchen. Josh, hair pulled neatly back, was placing three bowls of a lumpy, dark porridge on the dining room table.

"Whassup?" Ari croaked.

"Haroset!" Josh said. "Apples, walnuts, sweet wine, cinnamon. It's a Passover dish that makes us remember the mortar the Israelites used to make bricks as slaves in Egypt."

Ari pushed back his hair to stare blearily at him. "Wha—?"

"We're going to have it with our Seder tonight, *nu?*"

"*Nu?*"

"Yeah. Like a Jewish, 'Yoh?' I'm expanding my cultural talk, dude. Sit. Have some of the apple salad."

Ari looked at the haroset again and gagged. It brought the taste of all those rum and cokes swimming back. There had to be a better way.

"Ari!" said his oma happily as she pushed through the kitchen door with a large platter. "You eat your haroset and then we have eggs and potato pancakes!"

"Oh, man," Ari said from between clenched teeth and he suddenly turned and ran to the washroom at the bottom of the stairs.

After worshiping the porcelain god for fifteen minutes, Ari felt like he'd woofed everything he'd eaten for months but his stomach still clenched and squirmed. Dry heaves. He shakily pushed himself to standing, splashed away the sourness around his mouth, and found some mouthwash to gargle with.

Through the closed door he could hear his oma, her voice raised now so Ari could hear.

"Different Jews celebrate the Passover in different ways. When Jonathan and I were in California, we would throw grass, coins, and candy for our son and his friends to pick up. These were symbols for the reeds of the Red Sea and the wealth the Israelites brought with them out of Egypt."

"Shakin'," Josh said.

"But all these things we do, they are more than just tradition. They remind us that God remembers and protects us."

Josh mumbled something.

Ari's oma laughed. "*Tokhis oyfn tish!* Put up or shut up."

Ari didn't want to know what his friend had suggested—Josh was freaking him out more and more on this trip—but dredged up his own Yiddish from somewhere back in his childhood. "*Tokhis leker,*" he mumbled into the sink for Josh. *Ass kisser.* Dragged into his oma's net.

Pushing himself up, Ari gargled again, washed his face, then pushed open the bathroom door and walked, still cringing at the harsh light, the booming sounds, the smell, even the feel of the hard wooden floor under his sock feet.

Josh and his Ari's oma were seated at the table. Josh turned and spread his arms out towards Ari. "The prodigal son returns!"

"Christian touchstone," Ari croaked. "In ours, Jacob's mother tells him to steal everything from his father. He does, splits, and stays away until all the old folk are dead."

He looked at his oma and her face went pale, lips tight. Josh looked from her to Ari and shook his head. "Hey, dude..."

Ari waved a hand in front of his own face. "Yeah, well...that about sums up things here, doesn't it?"

"I am not dead," his oma said.

"No?" Ari squinted around the room, not believing he was being so cruel. But all the dark wood. Pictures of Opa. Pictures of old, dead miners. Polished silverware and candlesticks over there. And she'd chopped liver in the kitchen, right? The bitter herbs (*maror*), the lamb shankbone (*zero'a*)... "Then what,

Oma? Just scared you're going to be? Need to get in one last wail to God? One last chance to nail your grandson into place?"

"Dude…"

Ari's oma was slowly pushing herself to her feet and Ari saw she was trembling with anger now. "Everything I do here, I do for you. I do to protect you!"

"I don't need protecting," Ari mumbled. "If I hadn't come here…"

"But you are here now. And while you are here, in this house—"

"Then I won't *be* in this house!" Ari said and clutched his head. Spinning around, he staggered sickly back towards the door and fumbled for his boots. "Stupid." Couldn't get them on. "Secrets." Had them on the wrong feet. Fixed them, yanked them on, tied them tight. "Friggin' Goldrock." Head pounding. Went for his coat and gloves.

"Ari-dad?" said Josh, suddenly close.

Ari turned, coat on, and fixed bleary eyes on him. "You want to come?"

Josh shook his head. "I'm going to stay and help your grandma prepare for this Seder thing. You sure you don't want to stay and help out, man? We could really use you."

We could really use *you*. Ari was made the outsider even here. And by a *shabbos goy*, of all people. Someone who was sycophantically nice to the Jewish people. A *shaygetz*. It was too much.

Ari squinted his eyes and tugged on his gloves. "I don't think so," he said. Then he grabbed the door handle and was gone.

CHAPTER 33

Just outside the Severin residence in the Grenadine Hotel, in the alleyway that ran along its north side, Japhet stood half-hidden by a stack of discarded vegetable crates as he watched Wendy Severin through her ground floor window.

She'd been up for two hours and was almost ready to go out. Her hair done and minimal lipstick applied, Japhet saw her sling her tiny purse over her shoulder. He watched as she checked herself in her closet mirror and tucked her top more securely into her jeans. Nice bum. Nice little boobies. He remembered the feel of them pressed against him in the doorway.

Wendy hesitated for a second as if aware she was being watched, and Japhet drew back out of sight. When he looked again, she was frowning her pouty lips slightly and checking her purse. Then she headed out her door.

Japhet slid out from behind the pile of crates and crept to the head of the alley. There he watched until he confirmed Wendy's departure from the Grenadine, walking out through the snow in her little purple hat and mitts. He crept back to her window and studied it thoroughly. Nodded.

Slapping some snow onto his face and rubbing to give himself a ruddy appearance, he returned to the front of the hotel. It was time to go in, ask enough questions to establish where he was going to be for the next few hours, then go there.

Proper planning, Mama. Planning. Testing. No mistakes.

You're an idiot, bugger boy. A shit-for-brains, mentally retarded gorilla.

You think so, Mama? You think so? Is that why you grab at me so much?

CHAPTER 34

N‌ICOLE BANGED her gloved hand on Marshal Pritchett's door then checked her watch. It had taken her just thirteen minutes to plod her way over here. Good start.

When the marshal answered, he was still tucking in his shirt and his hair was unbrushed, sticking up on the right side of his head. He waved her in awkwardly and turned away like a hound dog sniffing for something lost in his office. Nicole shut the door against the snow, stomped her boots clear, and watched him.

He rattled open the bottom door of the spare room's single desk and sighed, "Ahh." He pulled out an unopened box of unbleached coffee filters, slit the plastic on the box with his thumbnail, and struggled one out to stick into his three-cup Braun coffee machine.

"Want a cup?" he said, gravel rolling over each word.

Nicole shook her head but waited quietly while he fussed through his ritual. He wouldn't be fully with her, she suspected, until he had a warm mug in his hands. In the meantime, she pushed back her hood and walked around, noting some stairs and concluding that Pritchett obviously slept up there in the same way the doctor supposedly did – a room over the office.

He was just as obviously a bachelor. The office bathroom was filthy. The single jail cell through the door in the back looked like it hadn't been swept in a week or so. The cell had a bolted-on bench upon which lay a rag-eared copy of MAD Magazine. Pritchett's reading or his prisoners'?

"Didn't figure many people would be up early today," Pritchett called from the main office.

Nicole wandered back into the main office to see him leaning back in his wooden swivel-chair, nursing a cup. He was trying to look relaxed, but Nicole noted he'd found a brush and water somewhere and tried to comb down his rooster hair.

She smiled and shook out her hair. Pritchett was clearly in his mid-forties with a receding hairline and middle-age spread, but he was not above trying a little harder for an attractive woman. That would help. "I'm looking for some information for a friend of mine, Marshal. A Nicole Baker, maybe born Nicole Müller?"

A spark of recognition flickered in Pritchett's eyes so she went on. "She recently found out she was adopted and...thinks she might have been born here. To a woman named Betsy Müller."

The recognition was definitely there, but Pritchett shook his head to hide it. He looked at his desk and blinked his eyes back and forth like the answer to Nicole's question might be written there somewhere. "About how long ago are we talking here?"

"Thirty-one years," Nicole said casually, her heart beating hard. "Maybe thirty-two."

Pritchett got a sick look on his face and pretended it was the coffee. He set it down on his desk in disgust. "Sure. There was a *girl* named Betty Müller lived here back then. Got pregnant out of wedlock. Bit of a scandal. She went to the same school I did. Thirteen years old. Had a miscarriage, though. Why're you asking all this?"

Nicole felt the blood drain from her face. A miscarried child? What had her mother been trying to do with this? "Who was the father?"

Pritchett swung his chair a bit and peered up at her sideways, looking like he wished he'd just denied knowing anything at all. "Well now, I was just a kid at the time remember."

He said it hopefully, like that might be his way out. Nicole wanted to reach across his desk and slap him. Instead she subtly shifted onto one hip and flipped her hair back with a finger. She saw Pritchett's pupils widen. His unshaved jaw slackened unconsciously.

"But...?" Nicole said.

"What? Oh...uh...nothing." He shrugged and colored. "I mean other stuff happened around then too. I think. But like I said, I was just a kid."

"Did the 'other stuff' involve Twelve Chickopee Lake Road? Or did Betsy...Betty Müller live there?"

"No!" he said, too quickly.

"You want to tell me about the other stuff that happened?"

Now Pritchett was chewing on his lips and staring at his coffee cup, perhaps wishing he hadn't play-acted that it tasted horrible. Finally he looked up and met Nicole's eyes. "Okay, look, I can't. It was just police stuff. And the whole thing's closed."

"Closed."

"Yup. Don't even have a file on it."

But you remember it, Nicole wanted to say. *Just like Herb Mawpester remembers, and probably most of the people on the list I've got in my pocket.*

Instead, she flipped back her hair again and dropped into a voice she despised when used by other female lawyers, or insurance adjusters like Shelley Collard. "All right, Marshal," she sighed. "On a whole separate thing, would it be possible for me to get into the town hall and look at the birth records there? You could come with me, let me in, be with me the whole time."

The lumpen man almost emasculated himself by the quickness with which he scrambled up from his chair. "Yeah! Uh...yes! Certainly! Just let me get...um...keys... um...Miss...?"

"Suzie," Nicole said and smiled sweetly. "Suzie Kastonopolos. It's Greek."

CHAPTER 35

As Nicole followed Pritchett through the deepening snow of Main Street to Goldrock's town hall, Ari Siegel trudged, head down, through the even deeper snow that layered the back streets in the north end of town.

He'd been eating snow and rubbing it over his face as he went and it seemed to have helped. He still had a headache, but the pounding and nausea were receding. He even began to look up occasionally, squinting throw the falling snow to see where he was.

What he saw was that, other than the occasional curl and smell of wood smoke, Goldrock looked totally deserted. The snow in places had been up to his knees. His body was now shivering, he realized. Probably had been for the last while now. His toes were starting to hurt with the cold. And...he was lonely.

Oh, man, he was lonely.

Not that he'd ever been a real group person—that was too draining—but this last year in college, he'd come to really like having Josh around in his room. And his family had always been his mainstay.

Now he'd alienated both Josh and his grandmother. Why? Being drunk? Maybe. But fear was a big part of it. His oma was dying in pieces before his eyes, desperately wanting something from him, and Ari didn't know what it was or if he could give it.

Especially if it was against how he'd been raised. His stridently feminist global political mother, for example, wouldn't be too happy if he suddenly chose the life of an insular Talmudic scholar.

He rubbed his throbbing head then looked up to zip the Gore-Tex collar of his coat to the top. Snow got in his eyes and he blinked it out. Looked around.

The side road he'd turned down had opened up to a parking lot. Some kind of gray and green community center, two stories at the back and new since he'd visited last. There was the sound of thumping music and laughter from inside.

At 10:30 a.m.? *I guess with no school and all outdoor activities shut down, all you had left to do was party?*

Curious, Ari got close enough to smell the chlorine from a swimming pool somewhere. He could hear the country-rock beat and yelled conversations, and saw a bunch of teens jerking about in the room left of the front doors. There were only six cars in the parking lot. The other partiers had to have walked.

As he hesitated at the double front doors, a corn-fed WASP boy about Ari's age but with this whole football, vertical-scar-on-the-chin thing going, suddenly rushed out of the party room, pushed open one of the doors and said too loudly, "Hey! C'mon in!"

Ari stepped forward and was suddenly dragged inside against a wall hung with dripping boots and coats and smelling of sweat, chlorine, chips, and pizza. Not exactly Ari's—

"You Ari?" Corn-fed asked over what was clearly now good ol' high-energy, country and western, Reba McEntire/Travis Tritt-style groaning.

"Uh...yeah."

"Fuckin-A! Mindy was right! She thought she saw you out here! Heard you were in town calling out her uncle again! Fuck, you got balls!"

"Mindy Dolk? She's in there?" Ari shook his head and started turning back for the door.

"Hey!" Corn-fed laughed and grabbed him. "She's grown up now. Not jail-bait. Least come say hi."

Jailbait. Like Ari had ever chased the girl, or any girl for that matter. He'd always figured that was pretty much left to the hulking football types like Corn-bred here. Mindy Dolk had actually targeted *Ari* three summers ago when he'd been here. And the anti-Semitic crap he'd gotten from her father's family, especially her town leader uncle, Al Rawley... It had only occurred to him much later that maybe that's what Mindy had wanted all along.

Oy! as his oma would say. And now he was supposed to go in there and start the whole thing up again. It made the pounding in his head resume full force.

Corn-fed released him. "Hey, look. You wanna be chicken? Fine. Go."

Ari hesitated.

"Didn't think so." Corn-fed grinned and stuck out his hand. "Jeremy Buckster. C'mon. Ditch the coat and I'll show you around. I'll even make sure Mindy behaves."

Feeling suddenly stupid and dorky, Ari brushed the snow out of his hair, hung up his coat, and stuck out his own hand only to get it squeezed so hard the bones felt like they'd crack.

Buckster laughed and dragged him into the party room—long and narrow like a brightly-lit subway train. Shiny green linoleum. Window benches in the four bay windows. It seemed to rock back and forth to the twang of *Achy-Breaky Heart* as a double line of gaudily-dressed young teenagers were two-stepping for all their grunting little hearts were worth. Line dancing, by God. It was like time had passed this place by.

There were two adult chaperones supervising the drinks table too, which he assumed meant almost no booze. Thank goodness. The corners of Ari's mouth twitched up as he was dragged along. Maybe he could survive this after all. He'd just hang out here, eat some pizza, meet some locals closer to his own age, maybe even use his university cool to somehow fit in.

Yeah. That Ari Siegel. Phat ruler dude.

Buckster stopped him at the group of older teens who were gathered in a circle of overstuffed armchairs at the far end of the room. All khakis and mesh, short-haired guys, heavily made-up girls. And Ari suddenly felt like an alien again. His long curls felt goofy, his nose too big, his body too soft. Despite his and Josh's boarder talk, their kind really were computer geeks and SF buffs, the keeners and wieners, always last chosen for sports teams, always left out and—

The girl who had been twisted in her chair to talk with someone behind her now turned around and Ari almost swallowed his tongue.

It was her. The girl from the desk of the Grenadine Hotel.

CHAPTER 36

Buckster was introducing Ari around at this mid-morning community center party, but Ari didn't hear it because his eyes had locked with those of the girl from the Grenadine Hotel.

Up close, it was obvious she was younger than Ari. Something about the naive innocence she projected. And the hair, a clean-washed, silky brown that spilled down in front-curled ringlets to her shoulders just like a cowgirl's should. Round face. Startlingly blue eyes that seemed both fascinated and full of questions. Small nose. Small mouth with big lips that parted a little to show two big front teeth.

"And my girl, Wendy!" Buckster concluded and plunked himself down in the one remaining free chair, which happened to be just to the right of the Grenadine girl, and dropped his arm around her shoulders. Wendy shifted uncomfortably and broke eye contact with Ari.

Ari shuffled awkwardly and looked around at the other faces he'd presumably been introduced to. The girls were hiding their smiles. Two of the boys were shaking their heads like Ari had his head up his rear.

"So is our boy Ari hot, Min?" Corn-fed said to the girl Ari had been trying to avoid looking at in the circle.

Mindy Dolk left her chair and stepped awkwardly towards him. She was a big-boned girl with a flat, Slavic face, long nose, blond curls, and thick legs. And she still looked barely fourteen. "Hi, Ari," she said, and put a hand on his arm.

Ari jumped and all the boys and girls howled, especially Buckster.

Mindy herself broke into giggles and retreated back to her seat, red faced. "I'm kidding, you know. Hey?"

"Right," Ari said, his own face burning.

"You visiting your grandma again?" Mindy asked.

He nodded, feeling Wendy watching him intensely from under Buckster's arm.

"From where?"

"U of C. University of Colorado. This is kind of a late spring break."

"I'm going there next fall," said one of the boys on the far side of the circle.

"Me too," said Wendy with a light sweet voice that seemed to connect right to the base of Ari's stomach. "September."

"Me too," Corn-fed said.

"If he gets accepted," Wendy said.

"I'll get accepted."

Wendy leaned forward, away from Corn-fed's arm, and turned to look up at Ari. "What are you studying?"

"Journalism," Ari said too quickly. "Doing a piece on the Goldrock anniversary while I'm here." He grimaced towards Buckster as a peace offering but the big boy was looking from Wendy to him and back, really pissed, his chin scar all red.

As the next song started, Buckster leapt to his feet and dragged her up. "Let's dance."

"Um..."

"Come on." Buckster pulled her so that she stumbled. She gave an awkward smile to Ari, then followed her boyfriend out to the dance floor.

Ari's swivelled to watch. When he turned back, all the other kids were staring at him. "Tell us what happened at the hotel," Mindy said at last.

So Ari did. A few of the boys nodded, "Cool." Feeling bolder, Ari started telling them about his idea that people coming back here would find they'd changed and couldn't get past that. It got blank looks. "Oh, uh, you all probably haven't, uh, been away much."

There was an awkward pause. Finally Mindy licked her lips nervously and half-stood. "Wanna dance?"

"No," Ari said quickly. "I mean...um...I don't dance." The boys in the circle shook their heads at him again as Mindy said back down, a hurt young heifer. Ari kicked himself. *Stupid again. Loser. Loser. Long hair. Socially clueless. Wearing snowboots. Short. Geeky. Jewish.*

Oh, man, Ari thought. He pushed his hair back again, started to speak, then gave up and withdrew into pained silence. Later he got up and cruised the snack table, had some cold pepperoni pizza and Sprite, checked out the dance floor, looked out in the vestibule. He found the washrooms, went in, and pulled back his hair with an elastic. It didn't help. He looked out the front door...

Wendy and Buckster had vanished.

Forty minutes later, Ari finally headed for his coat.

Steering from the snack table along the wall to the door out, he was suddenly stopped by a dark-haired girl stepping in front of him. *The* girl.

"Wendy Severin," she said over the music and tossed back her curls. "Remember?"

Ari's heart jumped into his throat and his mouth went dry. "Yeah. Uh...Jeremy's girlfriend."

"According to him." She shuffled, embarrassed and tense, as the music changed to a slow dance and someone lowered the lights. Ari noticed the only two windows of the room had been covered with what looked like blankets so no daylight, however weak through the falling snow, could interfere with the mood. Ari was suddenly aware of the smell of smoke and sweat, the trembling sheen on a lot of the faces and bodies of the dancing teens as they came together. The sheen on Wendy's face.

"Ari?" Wendy said. "I'd really like to leave. Now. Can you walk me home?"

"What?" Ari blinked and if felt like his head was suddenly floating off his body. "Sure."

"Good." She dropped her shoulders in relief and smiled like he'd just saved her. "There's something I want to talk to you about."

CHAPTER 37

In the Dead Man's Saloon on Main Street, Japhet jerked up from his bar stool. He grabbed his leather coat from the empty stool beside him, knocked over his line of empty shot glasses on the counter, and staggered his six-foot four inches back into the tables area.

"Wh-wh-where's the little boy's room!" he bellowed, almost falling over like he'd actually drunk all the shooters he'd secretly poured onto the floor. "I gotta p-p-p-pee!"

A mustached man in a ten-gallon Stetson who'd been sitting a few seats down, finally swivelled off his seat, annoyed. He clumped over, and grabbed Japhet's elbow roughly. "Thuh-thuh-that way," he sneered. He pointed towards the dark corner on same wall as the door.

"Thanks, Al," muttered the bartender.

Japhet stared down into the man's hard face and the man stared back, frowning like he almost recognized Japhet. It was the big bully, Al Rawley, whose dad had owned half the resort businesses in Goldrock when Japhet lived here. Good twelve years older than Japhet. Broken nose. Mustache and sideburns all flecked white now. And everyone here still let him lead.

Japhet yanked his elbow away, "Well o...*kay!*" He weaved right, and slammed a hand down on an occupied table top for balance.

The woman at the table stopped her high chatter and drew back to look up at him with her upper lip pulled back. She was maybe ten years younger than Japhet. Her hair was a weirdly bright shade of red and she had a lime green jacket with darker green fur trim draped over the back of her chair. Seated at the table with her were two attentive younger men, which Japhet found interesting because the redhead wore a wedding band, but neither man appeared to be her husband.

Slut.

Then Al Rawley was behind Japhet again, pulling him up and shoving him towards the bathroom. The air vent up on the wall chugged out stale air as Japhet stumbled passed it and brought himself to a halt against the wall. He blinked back at Rawley and the redhead.

Then two smooth-cheeked young men in glasses entered the saloon with a load of notebook computers and papers under their arms. "Hey, f-f-fairies!" he called at them with a shit-drunk grin before he turned back to the bathroom door. They were the types who'd note the time.

He pushed on the door twice before yanking it open and staggering in.

As soon as the door shut behind him, Japhet straightened up. He turned and locked the door.

The clock was ticking.

He'd scoped out the exterior of the bar before loudly entering, so he knew the bathroom was a one-person unit with swing-out windows up at head height. Awkward to get to, but large enough for a man to squeeze through if he were determined.

He shouted, "God-d-damn!" and made a retching sound to give everyone a sense he might be a while.

Then he stepped to the window, shoved out his leather jacket, jumped up on the toilet bowl and sink, and dove and squeezed out like a bat out of fugging hell, tumbling down onto the growing snowdrift behind bar.

Step two of the game began.

CHAPTER 38

Twelve minutes later, George Severin peeked into Wendy's bedroom that was just north of the kitchen in the Grenadine Hotel.

"Max?"

He thought he'd heard the miniature terrier barking a minute ago and had finished his bookkeeping as fast as he could to check on it. Besides, Wendy had asked him to make sure Max got outside to go pee sometime this morning. Max had been acting very skittish since last night, scared to leave Wendy's room. And now...

Severin sniffed and caught a faint whiff of urine. He pursed his lips in sudden guilt for not checking in sooner. The room was a mess too. Wendy's bedspread was half-pulled off her bed though Wendy herself had been taught to be neat in everything she did. Her little bobbing-head dog that looked like Max had been knocked from her bedside table too. The closet door was open and clothes pulled out of it.

Goodness. Max had been almost frantically skittish since that Max Morris character had arrived up last night, but it wasn't like him to create this kind of mess.

"Here, boy. Come on out. Nothing to be afraid of."

And there wasn't. It was easy to be a bit scared by Mr. Morris, but the big man had left the Grenadine almost an hour before Wendy had headed off to the Community Center. Needed some air, he'd said, and shrugged out into the heavy snowfall in that thuggish leather jacket and running shoes.

"Max?"

Severin got onto his hands and knees to check under Wendy's bed, then put one hand on messy white cotton bedspread and pushed himself to standing. He groaned at the stiff pain in his knees. Sniffed the air again.

Yes, there was definitely a caustic urine smell from somewhere, but he couldn't pin it down and he couldn't see or hear Max. There was a light whushing sound from somewhere too and a chill in the bedroom air. A draft sneaking in?

Severin went over to the window to check it, and was surprised to find it not fully cranked shut. Hence the draft and wind noises. Severin grabbed the crank and turned, then frowned to find the crank seemed to be broken. Gripping the inside window edge with his fingers, Severin managed to pull the window tightly into its weatherstripping. The draft stopped.

The broken crank troubled him, though. Wendy was such a responsible kid. If the crank had broken in normal use, he would have expected her to tell him about it. Unless she was nervous about doing so? Had she maybe snuck out the window one night, breaking the crank mechanism? Or snuck back inside some night and been forced to break the crank to open the window from outside?

Severin shook it off. Ridiculous. There had to be some very simple explanation for it.

As there no doubt was for Max's skittishness this morning as well. *Phew*. With the window closed, the smell of dog urine was stronger. Maybe that's why Max was hiding.

"Max. Come here, boy."

A minute later Severin found the trail of dog urine that led out of Wendy's closet across the pulled-down clothes.

But no Max.

CHAPTER 39

SOMETHING really bad had happened in Goldrock, Nicole fumed as she finally stomped to a halt in the middle of Main Street. A murder, lynching, something. What she'd found in the town hall hinted at it, but Pritchett still wasn't talking.

The marshal stopped beside her, looking like a fawning ghost through the falling snow. "You want to...uh...come back to my office and ask me some more questions?"

"Would you answer them if I did?"

"Um...uh...about...?"

"Yeah, about that."

"I can't. Like I told you. When I took this job, there were certain agreements. Contracts."

Jesus, Nicole thought, staring at the frosty breath coming out of his mouth. It was a frigging conspiracy. And what made it sting was that her mother had tied her story of Nicole's birth right into the middle of it. Because Betsy Müller was certainly involved. It wasn't recorded in any of the musty card catalogues and filing cabinets that reached from floor to ceiling in the town hall's enormous basement, but Nicole was sure some local paper down there held it. Because Bob Pritchett remembered. Herb Mawpester remembered.

It made Nicole want to scream. She wanted to jump on dough-boy Pritchett and beat the story out of him, hiring contracts or not. She'd already tried seduction and toughness and reason when they'd been inside the town hall, but whatever had sealed Pritchett's lips was stronger right now than she was.

And it was still goddamned snowing. Like this town was determined to cover everything up any way it could.

This was beginning to really tick her off.

"Uh...Ms. Kastonopolos? Suzie?"

"What?" She turned to see Pritchett's tired, bumpy face looking at her hopefully. Like he'd love to spend more time with her, go as far as she'd let him. Just maybe even be persuaded to talk. Would Shelley Collard have put out like that to get what she wanted? Would sweet mother-of-two, Georgia Hurzgehrmine?

"Are you sure I can't...uh...?"

Nicole shook her head, looked at her watch, holding a hand over it to keep the snow off. For all her efforts, she'd only managed to speak with three of the twelve names on her list and discovered just enough to know this wasn't going to be easy after all. It might, in fact, be damn hard. She couldn't do it alone. She needed help. Paul? He'd be such an effective ally if she could honestly tell him everything. If he wasn't already lost to her.

That possibility caused a stabbing ache inside her. Damn her pride anyway. Whatever emotional stuff they had to work out between them, she *needed* Paul in her corner. As a partner. As a friend.

The decision galvanized her and made everything clear. When Paul returned from helping Georgia and her kids, Nicole had to be there. It was critical. Timing was everything.

But even as she thought it, she saw a dark shape hulk into the middle of the road further into town. It was maybe thirty feet away, its outlines blurred by the snow so that Nicole almost wondered whether it was an illusion of the snowfall. The shape looked too big to be a man. It was more like an abominable snowman, a big hulking *thing* that had emerged from near the Grenadine Hotel.

Then it was gone, ducked away somewhere through the whiteness.

Nicole blew out a frosty breath and slapped her hands together. Again the town's penchant for hiding things.

She needed Paul *now*.

She turned to the hovering town marshal and thanked him for his time. Then she squinted back along the route she and Paul had driven when they'd first come into town yesterday, stopping at the Grenadine, driving on to the Hurzgehrmine's. The falling snow was swirling up against every fixed object. If this kept up, it was going to be very dangerous, soon, to be walking around out here.

Nicole began to jog.

CHAPTER 40

"George?"

George Severin looked up from contemplating the mess in Wendy's room to see Elizabeth, his wife of six years, step into the doorway. Her immaculately made-up eyebrows and lips were taut with tension, as they had been ever since he'd told her about the guest who'd checked in here late last night. Her usual grace had turned stiff, her manners curt.

"I was looking for Max," Severin said.

"Did he pull all these clothes out?" Elizabeth's finger stabbed towards what George now realized was an illogical number of garments pulled down in the cupboards and strewn around the room.

"Maybe?" It troubled him, this not knowing. And something about the urine and the window...

He bent down to pick up a pair of Wendy's panties from the floor. Stood with them and turned to Elizabeth. Her gaze flicked to the panties and for just a second her stiff lips trembled. He read her thoughts and illogically had a pleased reaction. She obviously cared about her stepdaughter. Though neither she nor Wendy could bring themselves to be close, Elizabeth cared.

Her voice quavered now as she asked, "Where's Wendy?"

"She went to the Community Center. A bunch of the teens were going to throw a party. She asked me to look after Max."

"Can you call?"

"The phones are out."

"And that new guest, the big one, is out of the hotel."

"So?"

Elizabeth set her jaw and looked out the window. "Get your boots on, George. I want you to go and get Wendy."

CHAPTER 41

Ari and Wendy got as far as putting on their coats and boots in the vestibule before Jeremy Buckster and three of his male friends who'd also been missing from the party came staggering down a corridor to surround them. Buckster el al. were a little off balance and giggling, but they were still towering hulks. They reeked of pot, explaining the smoke Ari had smelled on Wendy earlier and where they'd all been.

And the looks in their eyes. Oh, no...

"Hey, Ari, right? Where ya going?"

Ari's quick glance to Wendy told him she was determinedly looking down, still tying up her boots. No help there. "Um...just...back. Walking Wendy home."

"Walking Wendy home." Buckster said it with wide-eyed disbelief. "Well it's a good thing we came out when we did. Right, boys?"

The other boys snickered. The one just to the right of Buckster, who had the same buzzed haircut and a bad case of acne, started weaving his head back and forth and singing softly. "Ari-the-fairy. Ari-the-fairy."

Buckster hit the singing boy on the shoulder, but grinned widely, so the other two picked it up too. The noise of it drew a few curious faces to the door of the party room, then a few more. A cold sweat ran through Ari, prickling his scalp.

"I don't think you need to walk Wendy home anymore, Fairy. I mean Ari." Buckster giggled at his wit. "We'll get her home."

Ari looked at Wendy and she was still keeping her head down, afraid. So what do I do? he gulped. What do I do?

"Um...I don't think Wendy wants to go home with you," he said.

"Aw, sure she does," said Buckster. He skipped loosely her way and reached his big hands down to her shoulders.

Wendy jerked upright and Ari saw she wasn't scared. She was furious. Her face was bright red as she shook off Buckster's hands. "Just leave, Ari," she said. "I can handle this."

Ari stepped over. "No. Um...look. Maybe—"

Buckster suddenly shoved Ari backwards. "Fuck off, Jew boy!"

"Jeremy!" said Wendy.

Buckster closed on Ari, easily a foot taller and probably twenty pounds heavier. Not to mention the two others boys backing him up. And Ari was eight years old again, facing Diego Mendez, a grade older than him and fixated on beating Ari up once a day on his way home from school. Ari's neck broke out in a sweat, remembering. Ari's father had said just walk away. His mother had risen up in a fury and said no. It was she who'd then taught Ari to duck a punch and throw his entire weight behind a counterpunch. "Aim for his belly or his groin," she'd said. "You're going to be shorter. You can't afford to miss."

Now Buckster took a swing at his head, just like Diego had.

Ari ducked his head back and the fist swished past.

It staggered Buckster forward towards Ari just as it had Diego.

And, just as he'd done exactly once before, eleven years earlier, Ari clenched his right fist and drove his body forward, twisting it to drive the punch into Buckster's gut. It connected with a thud that shook Ari to the back of his skull and wrapped his fist and arm in pain.

But when he lurched back, he saw Buckster fall to the ground (like Diego had), face twisted in agony, trying to catch his breath.

Ari jerked his sweaty face around to take in the rest of the stoned goons and saw they were all blinking back in shock. The acne-faced one said, "Fuck me..."

Then he looked up at Ari.

CHAPTER 42

"I DIDN'T—" Ari began, but Wendy grabbed his elbow and dragged him out through the front door.

"Shouldn't we...check on him?" Ari said outside. He had to shout because the wind had come back in the last hour. It whistled the still-falling snow around their faces and kept blurring everything. Even the road out of the parking lot kept vanishing.

Wendy shook her head. She'd pulled on a purple snow hat and mitts and pointed towards what looked like an open field. Ari nodded, heart still pumping hard. She took off that way and he followed, pulling up his thin hood and boarding gloves as he did. At the edge of the parking was a six foot snowbank. Wendy struggled up it and Ari scrambled after her. At the top, he looked back towards the Rec Center and saw that their tracks out were already getting covered over.

"You know where we're going?" he shouted through the wind.

She nodded, and they both jumped.

They landed near the bottom of the snowbank and went in up to their waists. They looked at each other and struggled forward, red-faced with effort by the time they were wallowing knee-deep across the field. It wasn't until they reached the backs of the nearest houses and rounded the corner of one of them Wendy finally came to a stop. They were out of sight of the Rec Center and out of the wind.

She bent forward and gasped for breath. Ari bent over beside her.

"Can't believe...you did that," Wendy wheezed.

"Crossed a snowfield?"

"You know."

Ari nodded and straightened, puckering his lips in and out in the cold. "My mom showed me how. They're going to come after us, aren't they."

Wendy pulled him away from the wall. "Let's walk."

They left the house and went for a ways down the snowed-over road without speaking. The wind whistled, died, and rose up again, mimicking Ari's heart. On the one hand he'd just escaped a beating and was out alone with a beautiful, strong girl who actually seemed to want to be with him. On the other hand, that girl seemed angry with him. Maybe because he'd just punched out her boyfriend? Proven himself a thug?

Wendy had pulled ahead of him. He hurried up beside her and put his hood next to her face. "I'm sorry!" he said over the wind.

She stopped and looked at him, eyes wet, their noses almost touching. "For what?"

"Punching your boyfriend?"

"He wasn't— He had it coming." She bit her lip and turned away to start trudging through the snow again.

Ari ran after her and grabbed her arm, amazed at his boldness. "Why are you so mad at me, then?"

When she turned to him, he saw she was crying. "The University of Colorado—am I going to feel stupid when I get there?"

"What?"

"I lived in Lincoln, Nebraska until I was nine, but I've spent the rest of my life here. We haven't traveled much. I've been to Grand Junction a few times, Santa Fe, and I even went to Boulder just after I got accepted. But..."

"You're scared?" Ari shook his head in disbelief.

"Don't laugh at me."

"I'm not. I mean it's just so ironic that someone like you should be scared."

She frowned into his eyes. "Why?"

"Why? Because... Because..." Ari shook his head again, his mouth suddenly dry, his heart pounding in his ears. Wendy's skin glistening with tears and melted bits of snow, her petal mouth just inches from his. If he put his arms around her right now...

"Why?"

He made himself look away and slapped his gloves on his pants. "You gotta know how pretty you are. You've got this wholesome *glow* thing, like you know what the world's about and your place in it. I went to university with nothing like that. The opposite, in fact. It's just...funny to hear you say you're scared."

"But I am."

"Yeah."

"You're not."

Ari blinked and blew out. "You're kidding, right? I'm scared of everything. I'm scared every time I meet someone I don't know. Sometimes even when I do know them. I'm scared of failing. I'm scared of succeeding. The only reason I punched your boyfriend back there was because I was scared if I didn't, then I'd never get a chance to see you or—"

He stopped, shut his mouth tightly, and started to turn away from her. She found his hand and squeezed it until he turned back. "You've got to meet my dad, my family," she said.

"If the guys from the party don't meet us at the front door."

"There's a back door," Wendy said and smiled. "Come on."

As they approached Main Street, Wendy led him through a snowed-in path between two houses that led into the alleyway behind Box Canyon Sports. It wasn't plowed, but the Main Street buildings seemed to have blocked at least the blowing snow, so Ari and Wendy could move faster.

The alley lay in a hush, businesses to the left, garages to the right.

As they walked through it, holding hands, Ari could smell the fried chicken aroma coming out of a blowing restaurant vent. Wood smoke from somewhere too.

At a long brick wall with small windows that had to be the back of the Grenadine, Wendy squeezed Ari's hand and stopped. She lifted her nose and sniffed. Frowned.

Ari sniffed too and understood why. There was something foul back here. Kind of coppery smell, but sharp and fecal. Like someone had taken a bloody crap out here. "What is it?"

"I don't know." She released his hand to walk to the building. She sniffed again and started making her way up the left side of it.

"Those boxes." He pointed to some vegetable boxes stacked just past one of the windows. "You put the garbage out here?"

"Not usually," she called back. "Our bedrooms are around here." She pointed. "Mine's right up—"

She stopped, frowned, sniffed, and wrinkled back her nose.

In a second, Ari was beside her. "What?"

"Look over here." She pointed at the spot directly below her window.

CHAPTER 43

ARI LOOKED and saw a bunch of half-filled-in footprints in the snow. They led from the front of the building down to this side are and up under the window Wendy had pointed out. Then there was a bunch of chewed-up snow, like some sort of scuffle or rolling around had gone on here.

If the prints and roughed-up area had been out on Main Street, they probably would have been covered over within fifteen minutes in this snow and wind. But the buildings on either side here and the Grenadine's eves had sheltered the area. There was no question someone had come in this way very recently, had stopped below Wendy's bedroom window, done something, gone back out again.

"You didn't..." Ari began.

"It wasn't me." Her voice was shaky, but she was still surveying the area carefully. "And you smell how strong the stink is here? I'm guessing..."

She pointed to a pile of snow against the building just down from where her window was. It would have looked like all the rest of the irregular drifts against the wall except that the area around it was all roughed up, like someone had scooped snow to make the drift deeper.

Without talking, both she and Ari walked to the piled-up drift and began kicking at it with their boots. They wrinkled their noses back as they worked because the stink got worse. It smelled, Ari thought, like the bloody chopped liver his own grandmother was preparing for the Passover Seder tonight.

When they reached the pinkish snow, there was a muted whine and Wendy stopped for a second and put a gloved hand on the wall to steady herself. Then she joined Ari again, furiously clearing the area with side swipes of her boot. Finally Ari's boot hit something solid that gurgled and whimpered when he pushed it. He saw why when he'd brushed off more of the snow.

Blinded and sliced open from neck to anus, a miniature terrier twitched its legs feebly back and forth in the red-black slush of its entrails.

CHAPTER 44

THE DOOR at the bottom of the stairs that led up to the Hurzgehrmines' attic guest room was bolted. The attic room itself was beginning to steam with animal moans.

On the bed, Nicole rolled onto her front, naked and glistening, hair damp around her head. She spread her legs wide for Paul, who'd arrived back at the Hurzgehrmines' exactly when promised. Nicole felt him snake one arm under her quivering belly now and she dug her fingers into the soft pillows. Then he hoisted her up and with the same hand guided himself into her. She panted as he filled her even more deeply than he could from the front.

He grabbed one of the pillows away from her hands and shoved it under her belly so he could keep her open to him without holding her. And he began to thrust.

"Oh...yes...take...me...," she gasped to the rhythm, smelling her breath, raw and hot, feeling the words inflame her husband. Inflame *her*. It was her submission to his dominance. And it had been so long it was almost like he was a stranger. In total control. Huge inside her. "Take...me..."

Then he suddenly fell forward over her back and his hand slid under her sweaty right hip. "Huh...Paul?"

His fingers found her vagina, still filled with his hardness, and slid around the opening until they located her clitoris. Lingered and played. Until waves of electric pleasure engulfed her groin, shot through breasts and nipples, down her back, through her buttocks and legs.

She clenched around him, but he didn't stop. His thrusting had become a gentle rocking and his fingers slid around her labial lips, back to her clit. Nicole felt a gush of heat down there, so wet that a part of her felt a wave of shame. Then she swallowed dryly and left it go as she was swept away by the sensations possessing her.

Possessing. All through her. Nipples, clit, belly, muscles. The shocks and waves rode up, higher and higher until she thought she could not take it a second longer.

Had to stop him.

Had to release.

Had to scream.

Had to...

"Yauugh-gh-gh!" Japhet yelled to make the thumping on the saloon's bathroom door go away. Then he slammed his own forehead against the tile wall beside the sink, clutched his sex rod, his nasty doodle, his *thing* tighter, and pumped hard.

He had to get out of here, but...he couldn't. The saloon clientele knew he was back. He'd stumbled back to his table. But the dog, the killing, had primed his blood and he'd had to come back to this washroom for release.

"Yaugh!" He changed it to another puking sound and thought of his mother. *Sonofabitch! Sonofawhore!*

"Y-yaugh!"

The yelp slipped from Nicole like a plucked-out cork as her body began to spasm. And as she shook, she felt Paul yank out his fingers and begin pumping hard into her from behind, the sudden thumping in her womb a final trigger that sent the waves of pleasure gushing even faster through her. Until she felt she was exploding deep inside her, her blood bursting through her limbs and head, and most of all her center.

It rode and shook her, on and on. And just as she was coming down, she felt Paul explode inside her too, in a burst of hardness and that gave her a final, guttural kick that made her clench the bedsheets.

"Yauuuuughh!" Japhet yelled as he released a load of his nasty sauce against the bathroom wall.

Then he looked down at it ferociously and began to smear it about. Like he wished he could have done with the dog's guts. It was too quick. Too quick.

He was still hard.

This wasn't over yet.

CHAPTER 45

WITH BOTH OF THEM SPENT, Nicole suddenly wished that she was on her back with Paul between her legs so she could wrap her arms around him and pull him close.

It was time to tell him everything.

As if sensing her thoughts, Paul whispered, "One, two, three," and suddenly pulled out of her, shoved her arms up high above her head, rolled her onto her back, and amazingly managed to reenter her, still hard. His groin clenched for a second and he shuddered in a final little aftershock. Again. Then he buried his mouth into her shoulder, breathing hard.

"Now that was a trick, counselor," Nicole said and chuckled as she brought her arms down to his. He raised himself up slightly and she traced her fingers down his burning-hot chest. *How to begin?*

"Wasn't it just." He smiled down at her and his face glimmered like a shadowed bronze satyr in the room's strange half-light, his eyes huge and dark like an animal's.

Just begin.

But she was suddenly aware of the wind noises again against their small windows. The cold snow. The way the afternoon was all grayed out and getting darker.

She felt him softening and shrinking inside her. "Sorry," he said. "All gone."

Sorry? *Sorry?* Nicole suddenly began to quiver all down her back and buttocks. If she told Paul about how truly screwed up her childhood had been, how she still didn't know for sure who her parents were, would that slip by with a little "Sorry" too? She'd be exposing her greatest weakness. She was not only imperfect; she was a broken, needy thing. And she'd lied to him. Had done so because she was terrified of losing him.

The vulnerability of it went so deep that the lovemaking they'd just done seemed casual in comparison.

"Paul...?" She licked her lips and tried to swallow.

"Just a sec'," he said. Without sliding out of her, he stretched way over to the left of her, reaching for the box of Kleenex he'd placed beside the bed. Placed there even as she'd been half-ripping his clothes off in abandon. Because he never lost control, did he? Never worried or procrastinated. Being caught in Shelley Collard's arms or in Georgia's—those weren't moral lapses in his mind. They were just...getting caught.

He warned her, counted to three, and pulled out, holding a Kleenex under him to avoid dripping on the bedsheets. Nicole took her own two Kleenex in a choking, shaking motion and held them under her as well. Because that was the deal, wasn't it? Keep things bottled up. Clean. Organized. Show no weakness.

How could she tell him?

"Now," Paul said as he cleaned himself and strutted nakedly to the corner to throw the Kleenex in the garbage, "I'd like to talk."

Nicole tensed on the bed and pulled the bed sheet up over her. "About what?"

He turned and smiled at her, then slid in one movement onto the sheets beside her and pulled down her covering. "I want to see you," he whispered. "You're beautiful."

Nicole swallowed dryly and let him examine her for five seconds more, then pulled the sheet up again. "What?"

"Kids," he said simply. "I love you. I want to have children with you. I know we talked about how tough that would be with you working, but it always will be. We'll find solutions."

"You're forgetting something."

"Mm?"

"Shelley Collard. Now poor little Georgia Hurzgehrmine. You think I'm going to let you swell me up like a balloon while you go out and..." She bit her tongue and stared at the ceiling.

There was a long silence while Paul worked his jaw back and forth. Finally he said, "It's because of them that I want children. With you. I miss you. All the things we planned—"

"You planned."

"We talked about this."

"You don't even know me, Paul."

He looked up to the ceiling and crooked his hands that direction, shaking them like he wanted to wring her neck. "Yes I *do*. You're scared. You help other people fix up their lives but you're too damn scared to just reach out and take a life for yourself. And you keep blaming it on other people. First I thought it was because of your mother, but now she's gone and you're still stuck. What exactly is it that you're waiting for?"

"I'm..." Nicole took a deep breath. "I'm..."

"What? Barren? Chronically depressed? You never want to have kids?"

There was a darkness to the question that seemed to swell up towards Nicole like the snow outside. Without taking her eyes off the ceiling, she put her toe into the darkness. "What if I don't?"

"If you don't?"

"That's right."

"If you..." The bed creaked as Paul suddenly rolled away from her to sit on the edge, facing the far wall. "Goddamn," he whispered.

Nicole shivered, then was suddenly overwhelmed by her own stink, the smell of the sweat and semen and passion that she'd thrown herself into here. And she'd been about to tell him everything? Expose her soul to him? Oh, God. She was losing her marriage. The sudden loneliness of that swept over her made her want to curl into a tight little ball and gag.

Instead she forced herself to roll up off the bed and grab the thin robe she'd packed for this trip. Silk. Sexy. Just in case she wanted to tempt Paul to take it off her. Now it was a shield, helping her keep her face set hard.

He looked up at her slowly.

"I'm going to take a shower," she said. "Then see if Clara or Horst can make us some late lunch."

Paul said nothing. He was still staring at her when she left the room.

CHAPTER 46

In the Severin's living room in the Grenadine Hotel, Town Marshal Bob Pritchett fumbled his thumbs into his belt loops to look casual as he walked slowly back and forth and questioned the Jewish boy about the dog.

"Well, now," he said. "Let's go over it again."

The boy rolled his eyes where he sat and Pritchett bounced on his toes, annoyed. Oh, sure, everyone was happy to drag the town marshal out into the snow—first Suzie Kastonopolos twitching her ta-ta's at him, then George Severin calling him frantically on the phone—but answer *his* questions? Oh, no. Elizabeth Severin and the cute maid, Rose, couldn't even be bothered showing up for the questioning. There was just George, Wendy all curled up in an armchair with a warm blanket, and this greasy-haired boy on the couch, Ari Siegel.

"What are you looking for, Bob?" said George now, fussing with a pot of tea he'd just brought in, the pot covered with a baby blue knit warmer.

Pritchett chewed his lips. That was another thing. No one in town called him Marshal, never gave him the respect he was entitled to. It had been easier in Grand Junction where he'd been part of the police force, had the weight of all that backing him up. But when he'd moved back to Goldrock to take over as marshal, there was only him to deal with all these messes. Too many people, it seemed, thought they could take advantage of that.

"You know," he said now to Severin, "we had a bunch of animal mutilations like this back thirty years ago. 'Lizabeth could tell you. Bet this boy knows, don't you, son. From your parents? You grandma or grandpa?"

The boy opened his mouth as if to retort but then just closed it again, suddenly white-faced. He knew. Anyone who spent long enough in Goldrock found out at least some version of it. Only exciting thing that ever happened here, other than the discovery of gold in Minsk Mountain back in 1898. Memory of it was obviously still echoing around too many people's heads.

"Right." Pritchett hiked up his pants and began pacing again. "So when's Elizabeth getting back, anyway?" he asked Severin.

The hotel keeper frowned and poured the steaming mint tea. "She left just before I did, but out the front. Missed the kids, obviously. Hopefully she'll check back soon."

"M-maybe it was Jeremy," Wendy said quietly from her chair.

Pritchett turned. "What?"

The girl's face was pale. Pretty little thing, but the death of her dog had really shaken her. She was trembling and white-faced. Maybe in shock. Severin brought her some tea and Pritchett waited while she took it and warmed her face over it. The girl's eyes stared far off through the carpet.

"Ari told you about the fight at the Center," she said at last. "Maybe Jeremy and the others ran back here ahead of us."

"And cut up your dog? That's pretty nasty stuff."

"They were stoned," the boy interjected.

"You said."

"And maybe...maybe trying to scare us," the boy said. "Or just Wendy?" He was leaning forward on his knees now, his brow furrowed and mouth open, like it was all becoming clear to him. Certainly wasn't to Pritchett, that was for damn sure.

"Why would they do that?"

"Copycatting?" said the boy. "Like you said, everyone knows the legend about the Goldrock freak. The way he cut up all these little animals, then—"

Severin cut him off. "That's enough, Ari." He handed the boy a cup of tea.

The boy's face had dropped in horrified guilt as he looked at Wendy; her face a scared question mark. "I mean...all I meant to say," the boy said, "was that maybe Jeremy and his friends weren't thinking straight. Maybe Jeremy figured they could, you know, recreate some of the freak's crimes. Scare Wendy. Then Jeremy would come around and comfort her."

"Or you could do that?" said Pritchett.

"What? How?" said the boy, red faced. "I was with Wendy."

"For how long, though?" said Pritchett, feeling like a real investigator now, standing over the Jew boy and leaning forward to intimidate him. He took the teacup Severin offered at the same time.

"Like an hour or two. You think Wendy's dog lived with its guts ripped up for that long? Sorry Wendy."

Pritchett wiped his nose and leaned even further forward, almost spilling his tea. "Maybe you slipped out of that dance, came back here, did it, then went back."

"Fifteen blocks, in the snow, with nobody noticing?" The boy was chewing his lips, scared, but obviously thinking Pritchett was stupid too. Pritchett didn't like that.

Before he could straighten the kid out, though, Severin suddenly clinked down the teacup he was pouring and said, "Mack Morris!"

Everyone turned to him. "What?" said Pritchett.

Wendy nodded. "That's the name of this new guest who came in last night. Almost midnight."

"And Elizabeth..." Severin finger-combed his silver hair, trying hard to remember. "When she found Wendy's room messed up and Wendy gone, the first thing she asked about was Mack Morris."

"Like he's the copycat?" said the boy.

"Or...the actual Goldrock freak himself," said Severin. "Come back to get us. He's about the right age."

"Starting with the dogs?"

"He hated Max," said Wendy. "Max snapped at him to protect me."

"Mack Morris and Max the dog."

"Now just hold on!" said Pritchett, snapping out his hands, almost losing his cup, and sloshing his tea all over his right hand. He yelled as his entire hand felt like someone had ripped all the skin off at once. "Ow!" he shouted, whipping his eyes around desperately. "Burn!"

Severin grabbed him by the arm and dragged him from the living room to the bathroom in the hall and Pritchett ducked his hand down into the sink, hissing the cold water on full blast and almost crying in relief.

When he finally made it back into the living room, his hand covered in aloe vera but still stinging hard, he nodded, embarrassed to all the three others and asked where he could find Mack Morris.

Severin told him where Morris had said he was going and Pritchett nodded. He picked up his coat, shrugged it on, and looked at the two kids with narrowed eyes. "And I'll be checking on Jeremy, and with your grandma, son. It's not some old bogeyman from the past. It's someone here and now. And we're going to find that person right quick."

No one looked convinced.

CHAPTER 47

In the Dead Man's Saloon, Japhet Edwin Bone sat at a table in the corner furthest from the feebly-pumped pop of the cd jukebox. He hung his head over a beer, apparently half-blind with drink, and watched the door through which Al Rawley had finally just left.

Japhet's brown leather bomber jacket was draped over a chair beside him. His shirt and pants dripped from him cleaning off the dog's blood, but still stank with his self-induced vomit—his alibi. Airtight.

Now he was waiting for confirmation.

The table where he sat was sticky, lacquered wood. It wobbled whenever Japhet leaned his big frame onto it. His chair creaked too. Over the drone from the jukebox, he could hear the clickety-click of the two geeks on their laptops, the horsey guy at the bar, the giggling from the red-head whore with the lime green, fur-trimmed jacket.

When will they come for me?

He dropped his face forward and caught it with both hands, elbow on the table, and stared at the frosted glass mirror behind the bar. There were six-shooter museum pieces wired up on the wall between yellow "Buffalo Bill" flyers and old mining stake papers behind glass. And over everything hung the smell of stale beer smell, cigarette smoke, and washed vomit.

And if you sniffed hard...

Semen.

Mama's mad at him for coming so quickly, so she's cleaned off her hands and pushed him out to the kitchen naked. Now she's ringing the roof bell and Japhet sees her line of girls and mothers sucking up to the chain-link fence around the little back yard.

The mountains lean in from behind for a look-see. We haven't done this in a while.

The bell stops.

Mama shows up and prods him.

So Japhet, naked and red, creaks open the screen door of the kitchen and walks down the weather-beaten boards of the back steps. Down to the packed dirt and grass of the backyard, hot under his feet. The flies buzz around him in the noon-day haze, drawn to the trickle of his sweat and semen. A few of the flies settle down on the slick fuzz that's grown earlier around Japhet's nasty doodle than any other boy's his age. Some of the girls gasp.

Jesus fugging Christ.

Japhet ducked his head almost down to the sticky saloon table so no one would see his face. He made himself listen to the redhead with the two younger guys. The redhead was just thirty-some, he'd found out. She died her hair. Her name was Moira. Drinking schnapps out of one of those pinkie glasses. She was an old-time townie who'd married a guy named Rory Buchanan to get away. Shit-for-brains Rory. He'd tried to run himself and Moira up Slider Hill in their SUV early this morning and gotten the damn thing stuck in the ditch.

The two young men chuckled in their stretchy ski pants with suspenders. Those clothes were apparently the only wardrobe they'd brought to Goldrock. They were shit-for-brains too.

Japhet raised his head slightly and looked over at the redhead to find her looking his way, licking her lips.

He dropped his head into his hands again, furious. Whore! Like his mother. Screwing everything she could, but then slapping Japhet around like...like...

The inside door of the two doors to the saloon opened and a pear-shaped guy stepped in. Lumpy face and hip length coat that hung open to reveal a town marshal's badge on the chest pocket of the man's shirt. He was nursing his right hand as he stomped the snow off his boots and looked around. Settled on Japhet.

At last.

Japhet sat up to bleary attention as the law man sauntered over.

CHAPTER 48

"MIND IF I...?"

Japhet showed the law man an open palm then grabbed his beer and took a drink. Bitter. He sloppily wiped his lips. "Whah c-c-can I do for you, Sheriff?"

"Ah...that's Marshal," said the man with a quirk of a smile. He sat down opposite Japhet. His right hand had a large red mark over it.

"Yeah, okay," Japhet slurred. "There's a county sheriff, though, right? You'n him p-p-probably cover all these t-towns."

"Well...no, actually. I just cover Goldrock."

"Whah?"

"Grew up here. Had a chance to come back, so...you know."

Japhet looked at him with drop-mouthed stupor, then looked down at the table like he was embarrassed for the man. "But y-y-you're the only law here, r-right?"

"Well..." The marshal sniffed and wiped his nose. Bit of a bulbous nose. Skin all lumpy with acne scars. Deep set eyes with dark bags under them like the man never slept from worrying about things. Tragic. "I still have to report in when something important happens."

"Yeah." Japhet shook his head in drunken understanding. Then his eyes flickered toward the door and he frowned slightly. Some kid, long curly black hair with a big nose, baggy blue, and yellow jacket—underage?—had slipped in and was staring at Japhet and this cop.

"Except...uh...the phones are out," the marshal was saying.

Japhet brought his focus back to the law man. "You still got r-r-radio contact?"

"Oh, yeah." The marshal nodded, embarrassed. "Tower up on Minsk, that steep mountain to the east. But the repeater's down. The snow, you know." He sat back suddenly and glared at Japhet. "Do you know why I'm here?"

Japhet swung his big head sloppily from side to side, uncomfortably aware of the kid watching. "The c-car, right?"

"The car?"

"Parked in a 'No p-park', didn't I? Couldn't get past that big old clock tower. Just parked where she stopped. Won't s-s-start this morning. F-foot of snow over it."

The marshal's shoulders relaxed visibly and he sank back with a chuckle. "Well, now. I don't think anyone's about to come out and tow you anytime soon."

Japhet stared at him wide-eyed, then let himself understand and smile broadly. "Guess not, hunh?"

"Guess not."

"Phew."

"Yeah." The pear-shaped marshal grinned.

Japhet stuck out his hand and spoke loudly enough for even the kid by the door to hear. "Mmm-Mack Morris. Winslow, Arizona. Got a sheriff there who's a real A-A-Adam Henry on traffic stuff. Measures his day by the number of tags he gives out."

The marshal took off his ski gloves and stuck his hand out across the table. "Bob Pritchett." Japhet shook. "You talk like a cop. Were you ever?"

"B-bud of mine did hubcaps with the Winslow sh-sh-sheriff. Small town."

Pritchett nodded and Japhet waited, took another weaving sip of his beer, glanced at the boy. Some kind of assistant? The marshal's son? Didn't look like him.

Finally the marshal built up his nerve and said, "Look, I gotta ask you. Where were you about hour ago?"

"Hunh? R-r-r-right here." He squinted his eyes down at his empty beer glass. "Hiding out from the storm."

"Right. Right. Um...how long you in town for?"

"'Til the *f-fugging* weather clears up, pardon my French." He raised his squint to Pritchett. "Why you asking me this stuff? What w-went down?"

Pritchett shook his head. "Oh, stupid stuff, really. A cut-up dog. Scary though. Tongue and eyeballs were cut out. Couldn't find them."

How hard did you look? "Sliced up d-dog?" Japhet shook his head in a drunk's imitation of Pritchett. "The way some folks get off, hunh?"

The shit-pop song on the jukebox ended and the marshal looked around as one of the silk underwear guys stood and ambled over to it. The other guy was hanging all over the redheaded whore now, sniggering with her, playing with her sticky schnapps glass. The boy still stood silently by the door. Pritchett looked at them all appraisingly, frowning as he finally noticed the boy. He gestured to the silk underwear guys and the redhead. "They're visitors too, aren't they?"

"The g-g-guys, I think."

"Should question them then. Never know, right?"

Japhet nodded. "R-R-R-Right." He fumbled up to his feet. "Excuse me, Bob. I gotta shake the s-s-s-s....."

"Gotcha." Pritchett nodded and stood.

"...S-snake."

"Good meeting you, Mack." They shook again and the marshal headed back to speak to the boy, sending him outside. Then he ambled to the silk undershirt table.

Japhet had reached the bathroom door for his third time that morning. He pushed inside, straightened up, locked the door behind him, and did a final check to make sure he'd left no blood anywhere. Satisfied, he walked to where he'd jacked off earlier, staggered suddenly against the wall, threw back his head, and opened his mouth to take deep gulps of air.

Step two, slicing the dog and leaving it where it could be easily found, had been done for two purposes. One was to shake up Japhet's mama a little more, let her know he was back. Two was to test Goldrock's responses.

Goldrock had just failed this test.

Which mean that Japhet was free to move onto step three. Another little blow to his mother's calm. Doing some shit in her own backyard, so to speak. Her own backyard...

Mama pushes Japhet out into the backyard, where he staggers in his nakedness, then tries to stand up straight like his mother says, not covering himself.

Two of the girls watching, girls from his school, start to snigger uncomfortably.

More join in. The mothers too.

And the sniggers are like little knives being thrown into him. Bleeding his skin. HURTING HIM. Until finally he buckles in the middle and he falls over onto the dirt. There he curls his arms around his legs, trying to shut out the giggling of the watchers, the sharp little stones under him. He won't cry. He won't cry.

Until his mother kicks him once. Then harder.

He begins to cry big snotty tears .

Japhet popped his hands over his temples and snapped his teeth shut. It was time for Step Three, to show his mother that he wasn't a helpless little boy any more. And for that, the redheaded whore drinking schnapps, Moira Buchanan? She'd do just fine.

CHAPTER 49

Pritchett's head was damn near exploding as he dragged the Jewish boy around the side of the pub out of the wind and poked his finger into the kid's chest. "You figure you're gonna make yourself look better somehow, coming into the bar like that and watching me?"

The boy's hands went up, scared, but even that bothered Pritchett because the boy was dressed all in these space-age Gore-Tex, baggy snowboarder getups. Blue and yellow, with little stars and stuff, all getting whuffled around by the wind even in the partial protection of the pub's front . His gloves were some kind of webby, metal-looking things.

"I just wanted to see him," the boy said.

"Morris."

The boy nodded. "Is he Bone? That was the Goldrock Freak's name, right? Something Bone? You got any old photos of him?"

"One," Pritchett snapped. He wasn't going to tell this snot nose that it was an old school photo he'd confiscated from Clara Hurzgehrmine when she'd been showing it around a few days back, stirring some of the folk up with predictions of Bone's return, putting ideas into their heads. Enough that Pritchett had had to speak with Al Rawley yesterday so the man didn't catch wind of it and rile up the whole town. Then that Greek beauty, Suzie Kasto-whatever, this morning. Then this dog thing. "The freak was just a kid," Pritchett said. "Totally normal-looking other than being big for his age. Could look like anything now."

"Okay. Okay. So I've got an idea."

"An idea."

"Those two guys in there on keyboards," the boy said. "They're programmers here on sabbatical from Qualifran in the Bay Area."

"Bay Area..."

"HP, Intel, AMD, Oracle, Cisco, Apple, you know. The big guys. Silicon Valley."

"Yeah. Duh. How'd you find out they're from there?"

The kid ignored the question. "They do most of their work in the saloon, but they've got a satellite uplink in the office they rented. It doesn't need a phone line, just a little clearance in the skies."

"So?"

The boy stared at him like it was obvious. "You could call the feds! They've probably got records on the Goldrock freak, right? Followed him. If he's active, they've probably got an open file. At least a picture. Right?"

Pritchett stared back for a second, wondering if somehow the kid had found out about the FBI visiting. Then he shifted his weight back and tried to cross his arms. It was too hard to do in his marshal's coat, so he just settled for hitching up his pants. "Watch a lot of TV, do you, son?"

"No," the boy said, annoyed. "I read. Books."

So he didn't really know anything. He was just a smartass. "Books. Yuh. Well, look up and tell me what you see."

The boy did, then back at Pritchett. "Lotta snow. No clear skies. No chance of satellite. For now."

"And all we got here's one dead dog too. Got it?"

The boy looked like he'd just tasted something bad. He turned to leave.

"Where you going?" Pritchett said.

The boy turned back. "I don't think it's police business, but I'm going back to the Grenadine to make a date." He stomped off.

"I'll be watching you," Pritchett called after him.

"I'm sure you will," the boy said without turning. Something else too, but the wind carried it away.

Pritchett ground his teeth together. Yeah, the kid was a smartass and a troublemaker. Kind of like whoever had actually cut up Wendy Severin's dog. Because that's all this was. Some hyped-up joker who thought he'd throw a scare into the town for the centennial. Pritchett might catch him if someone talked. More likely this would all just fade away now that the joker had had his fun.

Yep. Pritchett hitched up his pants again and sniffed at the whirling snow. Soon as the centennial party passed on Saturday, this would all be forgotten.

"HA!" Nicole said and poured herself more red wine from the bottle on the Hurzgehrmines' kitchen table where she and Paul sat on one side and the two Hurzgehrmines sat on the other. Paul frowned at her from under lowered brows and she laughed at him again. What she wanted was to pick up the remains of the greasy wiener schnitzel on her plate and throw it at him.

So impolite. So out of control.

And not her fault at all. It was too hot in here and the wine at the Hurzgehrmine's lunch table was too red, cheap, and sweet. Worse, Nicole was failing herself at every turn. First upstairs in bed with Paul, then, when she'd come down to lunch...

When she'd come down half an hour ago, who had been in the kitchen with Frau H., but the elegant Elizabeth Severin, the hotel keeper. Talking about Nicole again, no doubt. Nicole should have grabbed both women right there, used Elizabeth Severin's presence to get Frau H. talking, answering the questions that Nicole desperately needed answered once and for all.

But...Paul had gotten down to the kitchen ahead of her. And Frau H. had glared at her, while Elizabeth Severin had given her a raised-eyebrow smile that seemed to suggest she knew what had just gone on up in the attic room.

And before Nicole had gotten her tongue unglued, Elizabeth Severin had turned with her straight-spined elegance and swept off down the hallway for her black coat. A moment later she was gone.

As was Nicole's chance with Frau H.

So now Nicole lifted, then chugged back her sixth glass of wine, spilling some of it onto the belly of her white turtleneck. Like little drops of blood. The child she'd never have in this shitty and uncertain world. She wished she could rip the turtleneck off. She'd been chilled after her shower and had dressed in long underwear, top and bottom, plus thick socks, before pulling on ski pants and her turtleneck. She was roasting now.

She leaned across the corner of the table and jutted out her chin at the Hurzgehrmines. "Tell Clara and Horst what you told my parents when we announced our engagement, Paul."

She couldn't see Paul's frown from beside her, but felt it. Despite his delicate middle-eastern looks, his temperament fit him right in with these two stiff Germans hosts. So Old World proper. Which was to laugh, when you thought about it. Because this wonderful bed and breakfast of theirs? A sham. Frau H. was a frowning-witch evil stepmother. Nicole's and Paul's room upstairs was a claustrophobic joke. The "run of the house" meant they could join Herr and Frau Hurzgehrmine in their cramped little living room to look through five-year-old Colorado ski magazines. And the "authentic Bavarian cuisine?" Hey, here it was, served in an authentic cramped kitchen that had pots, pans, and garlic nets hanging from the walls, the hot air smelling gamey like the family goat had been butchered and popped in the stew pot.

"I don't remember," said Paul.

Nicole laughed harshly. "To my very wealthy parents—and you have to understand that my then-stepfather was a self-made Greek—Paul said that we'd be comfortable in five years and rich in ten!" Nicole sat back and slapped her ski pants with a giggle.

"Nicki..."

She grinned madly at him and held up her hand for the second punch line. "Instead, we're seven years out, childless, working our guts out to pay off the business loans, and staying *here* on vacation! Ha!"

Paul smiled weakly at the Hurzgehrmines, who were shifting uncomfortably in their straight-back chairs. "Please forgive my wife. No food, and she doesn't normally drin—"

Nicole slapped a hand down on the table beside her wine glass, knocking it over and just managing to clumsily catch it before it rolled off the table to the tiled floor. She waved it at Paul. "You're excusing me to these...these...Bavarian *wertlos?*"

She blinked and fell back into her seat. Where had that come from? German? *Worthless* or something.

Paul looked at her coldly. "I'm apologizing to our gracious hosts, yes. Now would you like to eat something, or shall I help you back upstairs?"

Frau H. muttered something under her breath and Nicole whirled on her. "What? You say something, Miss Danvers?"

But the sudden move also made her head spin and had to sit back and grip the chair. Paul reached for her arm and she snatched it away. She took in the ugly, rigid faces of the Hurzgehrmines. Beside them Paul frowned and judged her. And he didn't even know the half of how wanting she was yet, how totally rootless. Oh, God.

Feeling a wave of nausea roll through her belly, Nicole scraped her chair loudly back across the tiles and stood up. Through the little arch that set off the kitchen from the front entryway and living room, Nicole could see her red boots and jacket hung up by the door where she'd left them yesterday. "I'm going out," she said and stumbled off that way.

As she fumbled her boots on over her thick socks, she heard Herr Hurzgehrmine said, "Will she be safe out there?"

"She'll be fine." Paul's voice was tight and angry.

"*Ja*," echoed Frau H.

Exactly. Fine. Just as soon as she caught up with Elizabeth Severin and asked for her help getting to someone who'd actually talk with her. *Maybe even you, lady*, she thought back at Frau H.

Nicole awkwardly tugged on her red, down-filled jacket, found her mittens in her pockets. Then the doorknob. Turned, pulled. A gust of white swept in, staggering her back.

Fuck you, she told it. I want answers, round two.

She staggered out into the storm.

CHAPTER 51

Turning south onto Main Street near the Grenadine Hotel, Nicole Baker gasped a bit at the bite of the wind. The snow that had been gusting intermittently this morning was blowing hard now. It pushed her around, whipping the fringes of her hair out of her thin hood and into her eyes. She'd stumbled into three or four drifts beside the road so far and her ski pants were covered in snow. Her side ribs were sore from some bump she'd taken during her and Paul's lovemaking.

Not that any of this truly registered, because Paul was right about her not eating and drinking too much wine. She was truly buzzed. She kept snorting as she walked, unconsciously trying to blow out the gamey smell of the Hurzgehrmine stew that clung to the inside of her nose.

The town, this hateful town, was invading even her body!

Then, ahead, she saw the Grenadine, all lit up like a beacon of answers in the night. But as she stepped towards it, the front doors opened and spat someone out. A boy. Blue and yellow snowboarder clothes. Long curly ponytail. The boy from yesterday who had seemed somehow like her. Ari?

The boy turned his back to her and began walking. The deep loneliness in Nicole urged her to follow.

But then a second figure emerged, more stealthily than the first. A woman with a straight spine, elegant bearing, a dark, heavy coat wrapped around her down to her calves. Elizabeth Severin!

She too turned her back to Nicole without seeing her and hurried south, apparently following Ari.

Nicole followed her.

Down a long block, two, then Elizabeth Severin turned left down a winding street. Nicole had to hurry to keep up to her and to even see her through the blowing snow. She turned a last corner in the street just in time to see her pause as the woman's quarry, Ari, hesitated at the door of a heavy wooden house with enormous, jutting eves. Had to be Ari's grandmother's.

Nicole saw Ari check his watch, then enter. When Nicole looked for Elizabeth Severin again, she had vanished.

For a second Nicole wobbled in the storm. No. It wasn't fair. None of this was fair. Where had the woman gone?

Nicole stuck out her lower lip angrily and made her way to where the lady had vanished. She turned a circle there, squinting into the blowing snow, but saw nothing. Defeated again, she walked to the big-eved house that Ari had entered.

Should she knock? That made logical sense. But...what would she say? She just happened to be stumbling around in this snow storm drunk and saw Ms. Severin. Wanted to chat? Or how about that she really really wanted the company of that eighteen or nineteen-year-old boy? Yes, that was good.

Shaking her head at her pathetic state, Nicole plunged sloppily into the snow around the side of the house, lurching and sinking to her hips. She lurched forward and sank again. And again, until she finally reached a window.

There she stopped and tugged her hood tighter, stuffing her flapping hair inside it and snuffling hard. Then she rubbed with her glove at the window and, with the giggling thought that this was becoming a habit of hers, peeped in.

CHAPTER 52

"So Ari has returned."

Ari's grandmother's voice had that lilting Jewish sarcasm Ari had always hated, and he froze halfway through shrugging off his jacket. Oh, man. Should he turn around and just leave again? No. He'd promised himself he was going to make it up with his oma. Treat her right. Let her have a bit of what she wanted from him.

After he made his rendezvous with Wendy, of course. And he was going to need more clothing layers if he was going to meet do that. They'd agreed to meet down by the lake, end of Chickopee Lake Road. A little crazy in this weather, but it meant they'd be all alone. And Wendy said there were fishing huts for shelter.

He took strength from that thought to throw off his jacket and gloves and turn to face his oma. "Sorry, Oma. I was going to be back sooner, but the Goldrock marshal decided he had to interview me about a cut-up dog."

His oma froze, but then Josh came bursting out of the kitchen, wearing an apron, his long red hair still pulled back in a ponytail. "Oh, dude, did I hear right? The cops?"

"Cop, singular," Ari said. Then his eyes took in Josh, the dining room, and the kitchen through the still-swinging kitchen door. His mouth dropped open.

Flashback again. Fifteen years old this time. It had been exactly like this.

In the kitchen, exotic vegetables and ingredients were stacked on the counters, half the cupboards were tied shut with string, pots were going on the stove, the air was heavy with cooking meat and some kind of egg dish. In the living room, the dining room table had been set with a white linen tablecloth, artfully set with two tall white candles, little silver dishes of horseradish and haroset and salt water for dipping vegetables, and one plain silver goblet set out for Elijah. There was probably even a little afikomen matzoh hidden under a seat cushion somewhere.

And Ari, totally scrawny in this memory, was wrapped up helplessly in his oma's fleshy arms and bosom as she verbally attacked Ari's mother, accusing her of being unclean, of tricking Ari's father into marrying her, of stealing Ari's father away from God.

Ari's little sister wailed in fright over by the sideboard. Ari's father stood helpless. Ari's mother, his world-traveling mother, professor of political science and respected author, just took it all, white-lipped and shaking. Then she turned and walked out of this house forever.

Shiksa.

"Tell me about this dog," said his grandmother, now standing stiffly in front of him.

Ari looked at her and answered out of long training. "A dog got cut up. Wendy's dog. Someone trying to scare—"

"Who is this Wendy?"

The tightness in her voice set Ari back and he blinked. "Wendy...uh...Wendy Severin. A girl I met. She's the daughter of—"

"You will not see her again!"

The words snapped out and Ari stared at her. "I'm... You're not... Do you even know who the Severins are, Oma?"

"Elizabeth and George. I know them."

"Okay, then."

"*Nein.*"

"I'm seeing Wendy in half an hour," Ari said more firmly. "Down by the lake. In the storm. That should tell you something."

"Ari, this you must not do." Her little claw gripped his arm. Something was struggling with the anger in her face but Ari couldn't identify it. "I need you here. And she is...is..."

"Not Jewish?" Ari peeled off her hand.

"Yes!"

Josh, who'd been watching nervously, now grinned and stepped forward to put his arm affectionately around the old woman. "Oh, come on, Miryam. You're not serious."

"She's serious," Ari said, swallowing the bad taste in his mouth. "Look at her. You don't live like a proper Jew, then you're a filthy animal, right, Oma? That's why you've always cut yourself off from everyone in this town."

But his grandmother was staring at the floor now, wild-eyed, muttering, "You don't know. No, no, no, no."

"Aw, come on..." Josh's arm, still around Ari's grandmother, gave her a tentative squeeze. "You two... The Seder tonight."

"Drop it Josh," Ari said. "This isn't something reasonable. But...you look after her, okay? I've got to go get a warm sweater."

Before his friend could answer, Ari had run upstairs. When he came down again, his oma was waiting for him at the door, holding a rifle across her chest. Josh stood behind her, white-faced. As Ari stuttered to a halt, she held the gun out to him.

"What?" he said. "You want me to shoot my shiksa?"

"It is dangerous out there. Wolves."

Ari shook his head, nonplused, and began putting on his coat, boots, and mitts. "I'm just going to the lake, Oma. A little while. Then coming home. Are you going to be okay?"

"Without you here? This I do not know."

"Okay," Ari said, fully dressed. "Guilt trip, right?"

"What that letter said, Ari. That I was dying. This is true."

Ari stared at her and shook his head, fighting the urge to give in. Except that Wendy would be waiting for him down at the lake and leaving her out there by herself wasn't even a question. "You'll live until I get back, Oma."

For just a moment, the old woman's mouth strained forward and Ari thought she was going to say something else. But then she shrank back, clutching her rifle and looking very small.

"Oy vey, Oma," Ari breathed. "Josh, look after her."

He turned, pulled open the door and stepped out. As he left, he heard his oma say, "Nisht do gedachet." *It should not happen to you.*

And what, exactly, did she mean by that?

CHAPTER 53

PRESSED against the living room window, Nicole had managed to catch only muffled sounds from the argument, but all of its nonverbal ferocity. And when the boy finally turned and walked out, she saw the old woman almost collapse behind him, Ari's friend holding her up. Her nodding. Then another woman entered from the kitchen and walked over to offer a hand. Elizabeth Severin!

Nicole staggered back from the window. Elizabeth Severin had been there all along. Spying like Nicole had been spying. Why? Because she was a friend of Ari's grandmother as well as Frau H.? Friends with all the old ladies in town? How did that happen? They played bridge together? Or they grew up together? What? And why should Nicole care?

Because Elizabeth Severin was mother to Wendy Severin, wasn't she? The girl Ari had his eye on. Should Nicole tell him?

But before she could get a good fix on that, the pathos of Ari and his grandmother somehow brought back Nicole's own last days with her mother. And all the lies, anger, and guilt trips that the two of them had shared – it was all echoed here with Ari. Or maybe it was universal. Maybe everyone in the world just had a sucky time of it.

Nicole stumbled against the side of the house, feeling woozy and sick, and by the time Ari came stomping out around the corner, she was leaning back against the wood, face buried in her gloves, chest jerking as she drunkenly sobbed out her pain.

She saw Ari, jerked up her head with a snuffle, and called out.

"What the—?" he said and walked over.

He looked in the window to where his grandmother and friend now sat on the couch together, rocking together. Ari blew out angrily between his lips.

"You and me." Nicole sniffed and wiped her nose with her glove. "We love 'em, but can't stay in the same room with them, can we?"

Ari stared at her, obviously unused to the idea of opening up to people he barely knew. But he said, "That's been happening a lot this trip."

"Running away."

"Yeah."

"Tell me," she pleaded.

Ari pushed back his sleeve to look at his watch, then at the blowing storm, and finally at her. "I have to— Do you want to walk with me? It's kind of crazy, but...I have to meet someone down by the lake."

Nicole nodded sloppily, pushed off, and they walked.

Ari talked, hesitantly at first. Then Nicole took his arm, pulled herself close to him, and his words just seemed to spill out. His eyes flashed as he talked about his family. How his mother and father had both grown up here in Goldrock, what that had been like, how they'd been kept apart by the Jew/non-Jew thing and all the stuff around the Goldrock freak period...

"Goldrock freak?"

"Some guy who cut up animals and eventually killed a woman in town here. That's all I know, really. Dad says it was no big deal. They arrested the guy and sent him away. Mom won't even talk about it, though. I think 'cause the town pretty much covered it up and she can't stand that sort of thing."

"When...was all this?"

Ari blinked into the snow. "I don't know. A while before I was born. Why?"

Nicole stared back at him as her sloshed brain tried to focus and keep her upright in the snow at the same time. Yes, why? Because some girl named Betsy Müller lived back then too, got pregnant, and had a miscarriage? Or because Nicole's mother claimed Nicole was that miscarried child?

Didn't make sense. Any of it. And the connection to this Goldrock freak? What? Betsy was the killed woman? Was that why she wasn't in any of the Town Hall records? Was that what the town covered up?

"Nicole?"

She shook her head but it still buzzed. "Tell me about your parents."

So Ari did. How his mother's parents had died shortly after she'd married and she'd leapt at the chance to leave Goldrock. She'd gone back to school and excelled in everything. Started a family. Encouraged Ari to find his own path.

"And my dad's parents—well, that's Oma, and her Jewishness, and that whole thing."

"Yes...?"

He shook his head with a grin. "Your turn."

So Nicole laughed painfully into the snow, brushed some whipping loose hairs back into her hood, and told him about growing up with a mother who lied about everything— her past, what Nicole's father did for a living, what different medicines were for. Which taught Nicole to trust no one. Until she'd met Paul in second year law school and somehow leapt past that. He'd courted her so hard, revealed so much of his own tough childhood, that she'd begun to trust again, then to love.

Until, about a year ago, she'd gone through a bad time at work that had shaken her self-confidence. It was followed by her mother getting really sick. And somewhere in there she and Paul had stopped talking. Then he'd kicked her in the teeth with an affair.

"He's a jerk," Ari said.

"Truly." Nicole coughed to hide the sudden well of tears and almost stumbled.

They'd weaved their way to the northwest end of Goldrock and were on a downgrade now, passing a snowed-in school parking lot, presumably descending towards the lake. As Nicole blinked wetly through the snow, trying to see, she marveled at how good it felt to cry. Like her heart was loosening.

It was crazy. It was almost four p.m. She was in the middle of nowhere. Her ears, nose, and lips felt numb. Cold crystals beat against her face. Wind whuffled around her hood. And she felt warm with Ari, like she'd just found the long-lost kid brother she'd never had.

She grinned foolishly. Ari saw it and grinned back, which made her giggle and punch him. Had to be the alcohol. And the insanity of walking around in this storm.

The gauze of blowing snow opened for a second and Nicole could see the lake. It was frozen over and covered deep with snow—a flat, white field maybe a long stone's throw across and eight times that in length. Ringed mostly by trees on this side. Mountains rose up steeply on the other side and on either end.

For a second Nicole thought she saw something dark moving along the western slope, making a dim roar. A vehicle? Then everything got whited out again. Nicole thought she'd also seen patches of slush water that way too, though. Like the spring thaw had been well under way before this storm started.

"Chickopee!" Ari called to her over the wind.

"The name of the lake?"

"Only one in town!"

Nicole nodded, then suddenly pointed out onto the ice, concerned. "That her?"

But as Ari turned to look, she realized that there were two shapes out on the ice, too small to be teenagers. Which meant...kids? And there was something about their size, the color of their snowsuits. It was hard to see clearly from here in this storm, but Nicole found herself running down onto the frozen lake and screaming over the wind.

The kids stopped kicking at the ice and turned. The bigger one saw her, brushed back her long dark hair, and waved.

Oh, God. It was April. April and Auggie. Paul had settled them in their house with their mother just this morning. What had gone wrong?

A roaring, then an immense boom came from the west end of the lake and a shudder ran under her feet.

The ice started to crack.

CHAPTER 54

"No!" Nicole said, looking frantically back towards the west end of the lake.

"What?" said Ari, who'd jogged down beside her but obviously missed the boom.

"I have to get the children! You stay here." Nicole sighted through the snow to where she'd last seen the children and began to run.

The air cleared as she ran and the kids saw her coming. They stopped what they were doing and looked scared, about to run.

"Don't!" Nicole shouted, waving. "April! Auggie! I want to help you!"

Then she was there, sucking the air into her lungs hard.

The two children stared at her out of fake fur hoods, ready to bolt but vaguely dumbstruck, waiting for her to make the next move. Nicole spread her mitts out in front of her, palms up. What the hell was she supposed to do now? Reason with them? Grab them? Cajole them? The only approach she knew from her own mother was telling lies and she certainly wasn't going to do that.

Pursing her lips, Nicole tugged up the neck of her turtleneck, Nicole looked around. There were no more booming sounds. For the moment.

She tried to smile as she looked down to where April and Auggie had been kicking. The area was mostly clear of snow and looked like white sandpaper. "Whatcha guys doing?"

April grinned, reassured, and stepped forward. "We wanted to see if it was smooth underneath."

"So we could make a rink and go skating!" Auggie said.

"Uh-hunh," said Nicole. "Doesn't look too good!"

"It's toity!" said Auggie and began kicking a new area clear.

"Does your mom know where you are?" Nicole asked.

"Oh...yeah," said April.

"No!" said Auggie, so involved again in kicking that he didn't even look up. "Nana says you got to tell the truth!"

"Okay, no," said April quietly.

"Maybe she should go back home, then?"

"We don't want to!" said Auggie, happily lifting his foot forward in the wind and using his boot heel on the ice.

How was she going to get them to move?

CHAPTER 55

"Hɪ, Aʀɪ."

Ari had been concentrating so intensely on Nicole and the kids out on the ice, that he hadn't heard the approach behind him. Now he jerked around and his face must have shown his shock. Wendy, all bundled up like she'd been before, but wearing a soft green scarf and matching knit wool hat with a pom-pom this time, the tips of her brown hair blowing up around her face, burst into a light peal of laughter.

"I'm sorry!" she said over the rattle of the wind. "You beat me here!"

Ari nodded, swallowing. How long would he have to know her, he wondered before he stopped getting choked up and sweaty in her presence? And this in the middle of a freaking snowstorm!

She pointed out to the lake. "Who're they?"

Ari looked back out to where Nicole in her red coat was still talking with the kids. He leaned closer so he didn't have to shout. "Lawyer I met yesterday. Saw those kids out there and she went out to bring them in."

"Because of the ice."

"Yeah. But it seems okay."

She watched them for a moment, then said, "Why was she walking...?"

The wind whipped away the end of her sentence but Ari caught something in her voice. And she didn't meet his eyes. Her cheek, so close to his, seemed to twitch. "She was just...walking," he said.

"With you."

Ari blinked, understanding at last. "Wait. You think that...?" He laughed.

"What?" She looked at him with a little frown, her face pink.

"Just..." Ari grinned and waved his gloved hand around. "Well, she's *old*. And married. I mean..." He blushed himself now. "She needed someone to talk to. So did I." He jerked a thumb back in the direction of his Oma's house. "I had a fight with my grandmother back there. She just had a fight with her husband. She just—"

Wendy's laugh cut him off. "It's okay, Ari. It's okay. I'm sorry. It's just...well, you know if I'm going to dump Jeremy and piss off my parents, I just want to make sure the feeling's mutual."

"As in, like, between us?" Ari waved a hand between the two of them, his eyes wide.

"What do you think?" She was blushing again. It made the blowing tips of her brown hair seem to sparkle around her face and her blue eyes dance.

"It's mutual," Air said, swallowing.

"Good."

They grinned at each other for a moment. Then Ari cleared his throat. "Let me run tell Nicole, then...um...you and I can find those ice fishing huts."

CHAPTER 56

His heart pounding like a train piston, body going numb, Japhet's fingers and knees scraped along the west shore amidst the bobbing ice. Then they caught and he dragged himself up on the shore like a sodden dog up from chasing a stick.

As he lay on his side on the frozen bank, he couldn't believe how sloppy he'd been. Getting stuck in the dinky 4X4 when the redhead turned the tables on him and ran the thing into the lake. Trapped by his victim.

"B-bitch," he muttered, teeth chattering.

He growled at the snow and ice under his fingers and scraped his hand into a fist. Losing feeling there. Like he'd done a two week shift on the power lines and his fingers were tough inside his work gloves. Only now he had no gloves. He'd taken them off for his knife work with the redhead and lost them in the 4X4.

He was going to lose his fingers if he didn't warm them soon. And that would be bitch's fault.

Redheaded bitch, Moira. Just because Japhet killed her boyfriend, cut out her tongue, and made her drive up Warsaw naked, her mouth gushing blood. Just because he'd cut her, slapped her, then pinned her head back and cut out her eyes. He'd wanted someone to find her up there, on the side of Warsaw where everyone could see. Scare his mama. But the bitch had hit the door locks and gas, pelting them down to the lake, jolting hard as they burst through the ice. Ka-boom!

Sinking.

Panic.

Replaced by rage.

So he'd *gutted* her. Stab. Slash. Grunt.

Then he'd gotten a window down before they went under. Ungh. Fugger. Stuck the knife back in its harness.

Kicked the redhead in the head and got *out* of there.

Swam up. Floated. Almost died. Got to shore. And here he was.

But he was not only losing feeling in his fingers. No, his face and chest were becoming dull, slate things too, the shivers receding as if his body gave up on him. He sniffed and it was like sucking knives up his nose. His arms and legs ached, not obeying well. He had to get up.

He snarled back his thin lips and staggered up to his feet. His shirt and leather jacket and size fifteen running shoes dripped ice water but were also starting to crystallize and stiffen. He pushed his insensate feet forward to a thin line of pine trees and grabbed one of them, using its rough bark to hold him up.

Then he fell, from tree to tree, back towards the road coming down. There was too much blowing snow to see it, but he knew it was there because that was the road from his childhood. The road home. Japhet hadn't been stupid enough to think his mama would still be living there, not after all this time. Wouldn't do that. But still...

He could hardly see anything now as he came near the end of the tree line and the blowing snow whipped around him, suffocating him.

Was he going to die? His clothes, wet, and freezing were sucking the heat from his body. His core temperature was dropping. He remembered a guy talking about four hikers they'd pulled out of Sequoia National Park. They'd all gone hypothermic. Two went delirious before they fell asleep and never woke up. Heart attacks. One just kind of seized. The one survivor lost fingers and toes. Suffered brain damage.

Japhet shook his head. None of that. That would be like his mother had beaten him. Laughed at his little lesson for her. Laughed at his pathetic attempt to prove he'd grown up.

Huddled up, eyes shut tight, Japhet hears his mother coming banging her way outside through the kitchen's screen door. Is she going to beat him now or do something else to him?

The girls giggle louder.

"N-no."

A girl's laugh made Japhet jerk up his head and he shook it back and forth dully to clear out the weird storm mirage. Just ten feet up, walking along the bank of the lake in the storm, two figures were walking towards him. Short. Young. Teenagers. Scarves. Ski hats. Baggy blue and yellow ski outfit.

The girl laughed again and Japhet almost choked. It was the hotel-keeper's daughter. W-Wendy. He'd gotten her dog. He'd smelled her underwear. He *owned* her. Another kill before he died would drive his point home to Mama.

But even as Japhet teetered, feeling the knife he still had strapped around his chest, they were past him, going God knew where, laughing.

Japhet pushed off from the tree. A shot of rage coursed through him and restarted his body's shivers all at once. Drove him forward again. He wasn't going for the girl. He was going for heat somewhere. He was going to live.

Survival. Survive.

He staggered forward through the snow and wind, ducking his head, batting his arms out in front of him, teeth chattering hard.

H-had to find the path. The road home.

His focus had shrunk so narrow that he almost missed the three people coming up off the lake to his left. Almost blundered out right in front of them.

Almost.

But his exaggerated hunter sense had not shut down completely. His peripheral vision caught the movement and he staggered quickly right, ducked stiffly down behind a picnic table to watch, numb fingers and chattering teeth, as the threesome rose from the white-out of the lake and started climbing the hill to the road. Two children and a dark-haired woman dressed in red.

With a sudden certainty that fate was offering him a guide, Japhet pushed himself up from the picnic table and began to follow.

CHAPTER 57

SOUTH, over on Lift Road, Georgia Hurzgehrmine was in the cab of her stuck pickup truck. Sweat rolled down her face as she tried shifting the truck into reverse and roaring out that way.

Rrrrr-RRRRR-rrrrr.

She could see snow churning up around her rear wheel wells like frothy egg whites in the wind, but the truck only rocked back so far, then stopped moving. She let it roll back forward, then tried again.

Rrrrr-RRRR-rrrr.

"Come on, Blue. Come on." Georgia blinked tears from her eyes and slapped at the steering wheel.

But all she was getting was more egg whites. No more backwards movement.

She swallowed bile and took her foot off the gas. Slammed it into neutral and swore loudly. It was happening all over again and so soon. Her breakdown. Her children at risk. Stupid. Stupid! What had made her think she could do any of this?

Images flashed through her mind of all the things that could be happening back in her house right now. April, deciding to start dinner, sticks foil-wrapped hamburger in the microwave. Sparks. Fire. April and Auggie choke on smoke. Trapped.

Or Auggie plays with knives.

The ball of panic rolled up high in Georgia's chest again and she reached for the door handle. She should leave the truck and run back. Run.

Only...the snow was so bad now it would take her a good twenty minutes.

And what if the storm didn't let up and they needed the truck for an emergency? Besides, she was so close to getting it unstuck, to getting the help she needed. So close.

Georgia slammed the truck into forward again, then reverse.

Ahh...rrr-RRRR-rrrr.

Again.

Ahh... rrr-RRRRRR-rrrrr...

Not fair. Not fair. After sending off Paul, she'd tried hard to be with her children again. She'd made them soup, tried not to crowd them too much. But she'd kept touching them, hadn't she? She'd stroked their hair, ducked down to hug them, kissed their ears and cheeks and noses. Until they'd squirmed and looked at each other, never at their mother. Then they'd laughed together. At her.

Georgia had frozen, then run to her bedroom. The children followed her, tried to apologize through the door. She pushed out past them and locked herself in the bathroom. She leaned over the sink and stared at the little girl gasping and sobbing back at her in the shaving cabinet mirror. But the little girl had wrinkles around the eyes and mouth. Her hair looked like a straw blond mop with dark roots. Her skin smelled like cheap old roses. Cheap, silly...

There in the bathroom she reached her fingers up to her face, remembered all the bruises she'd had and the horrors she'd seen. She started to scratch...

But suddenly the warm round face of Eddy appeared behind her, smiling, singing to her, smoothing it all away so everything was all right.

'Cept he *wasn't* there. Not really. She was all alone. Just her. Trembling, hopeless.

She turned back to the cabinet and opened it, reached a hand inside and pulled out Eddy's old packet of razor blades so they fell into the sink with a clatter. She stared down at them a long time...

Then April called through the door. Georgia jerked away from the sink and ran out of the bathroom. She shoved past her kids and stabbed her feet into her boots. Grabbed her jacket. Shouted at the children to just *Stay here!* as she ran outside with the keys to the truck.

To here. *Rrrr-RRRRR-rrrr.* Eggwhites.

"No! I need help! I need help!"

She gulped to stop the panic. Paul Kesin would help her. He'd held her like Eddy had. He'd keep the demons away, just like Eddy. Had to. *Had* to.

She banged the steering wheel hard with her hands, then her forehead, finally resting her forehead on it and breathing deeply. "Okay. Okay. Think. Do it."

She'd already tried shoveling around the wheels. She didn't have a burlap sack to shove under them. Newspapers on the floor? Too slick. Her jacket? Same. Maybe the sweatshirt she had on, though.

Biting her lip, and breathing hard, she took off her ski gloves to remove her jacket and sweatshirt so she was just in her bra, then she pulled the jacket back on over her sweaty torso. She pulled her gloves back on, leapt out of the truck, and plunged through the snow to the rear tires. She jammed her sweatshirt under the left one, then big-stepped back to the cab.

Put it into forward. Low gear. *Rrrrr-rrrrr-rrrr.* Ease off, and, *rrrrr-rrrrr-rrrr,* again, and, *rrrrr-rrrr*–

The truck moved, kept moving... She was out!

"Thank you, God. Thank you, Lord Jesus," she whispered as she drove on, hands clenched tight around the steering wheel, trying to see the road through the snow. "I will never use your name in vain again. I'll be good to my kids. Just get me to Paul and home again. And please, Jesus, let my kids be all right when I get back."

It wasn't until she was actually turning up the Hurzgehrmine driveway, that Georgia realized two things: a) she'd left her sweatshirt back on the road so she was almost naked under her pink jacket: and b) she smelled horrible, like all her fear and panic had seeped out her pores and was rising like a skunk steam from her jacket collar.

Didn't matter, she thought as she braked and jumped from the cab. Paul wouldn't care. But his wife? *Wife?* Nicole.

She staggered for a second, then plunged ahead anyway. Banged on the door.

Paul tore open the door at her first knock as if he'd been waiting for it. His strong brown face looked down at her, confused and frowning.

"Thought I was someone else?" Georgia said, shaking snow out of her hair with her fingers, desperately preening.

He shook his head. "My wife. She's out. I—"

"Help me, Paul!" Georgia threw her arms around his neck and shuddered against him, scared she might collapse if she let go, or if he refused her now. He smelled like warm spice and male sweat. Like Eddy. Male. Strong. Able. While she... "Help me," she whimpered. "My kids."

She felt him turning back to look into the hall, maybe at Clara Hurzgehrmine, then his arms were down around her, holding her up. "Okay," he murmured. "But we'll take the Jeep."

CHAPTER 58

At Chickopee Lake, the snow was howling now. Visibility was down to ten feet. Near the broken ice at the west end of the lake, in a sturdy five-by-five fishing cabin that was barely tall enough for Ari to stand in, Ari stood and stared nervously at the hut's wood stove and metal-pipe chimney.

The former ice-fisherman here had left the bread-box stove stocked with paper, kindling, and wood, with more on the white ice beside. Without hesitation Wendy had pulled out a butane lighter and lit it as soon as she and Ari had entered. It had caught, smoked until Wendy shut its door, and now crackled nicely, throwing out heat and a thin flicker of orange around the door and chimney seal. But...

"Isn't it a little perverse," Ari said, "to light a fire when the only thing holding you up could...like...melt?"

Wendy grinned at him and tugged him down to the short bench against one wall. "Its feet keep the heat off. Trust me."

Ari sat to her right. His knees were higher than his hips.

"Long legs," Wendy said and laughed.

Ari let his boots bump forward over the iced-over fishing hole.

"Better."

Then Wendy wrapped her arms around Ari's left arm and leaned into his shoulder, making his heart suddenly speed up. There they sat and listened to the howl outside, the crackle in the gloom inside. Ari could just make out how Wendy's cheeks were still ruddy. So beautiful. The snow crystals in her hat and hair were melting like she'd been out in the rain.

"You know," she said quietly, "in about ten minutes, it's going to be warm enough to take our coats off in here."

Ari swallowed. "Uh-hunh."

She tilted her face up to him and Ari, not believing he was really here and really doing this, turned towards her. He could smell the sweetness of mint on her breath, feel the tremble in her and in himself. Her lips were wet. She closed her eyes. Ari leaned forward.

Bump.

Ari and Wendy sprang apart. It felt like the sound had come from...below them?

Ba-bump.

Definitely below them.

Ari and Wendy pushed up quickly to their feet, Ari spreading his hands nervously. "So, is this sharks or the ice starting to break up?"

"Ice breaking up doesn't sound like that," whispered Wendy.

Even as she finished, there was a long, shuddering sound, like something big scraping directly below them. Stopped, directly below them.

"We don't have sharks."

Ari nodded and dropped down to his knees. He began brushing at the nubbly ice with his hands and wished that one of them had a flashlight. Something there.

The fishing hole! It would have been kept relatively clear by the last ice fishers here and would have frozen smooth. Ari spun around on his knees and found it, brushed off the snow they'd brought in with their boots, peered down through. Something...light colored. Angular. Definitely stuck under the ice there.

"You want my lighter?" Wendy said.

"It would just reflect," Ari said. "Give me a minute."

He lay face first down on the ice, holding his nose just over the surface of the hole, and cupped his hands around his face to cut out the flickering light from the wood stove which still penetrated the ice itself, thankfully. He needed to concentrate just on what it was lighting up under there.

A minute later he breathed out heavily. "Oh, wow."

"What?"

Ari pulled his head and body up from the ice. Brushed himself off. He turned to Wendy. "We're going to have to leave and get help. There's some sort of car under there." He swallowed. "I think someone's inside."

CHAPTER 59

WELL, she'd gotten the kids off the ice, Nicole fumed, but this storm! It just did not give up. In fact it had grown steadily worse.

Walking the kids up from the lake, they'd already wandered off the road three or four times. If it hadn't been for the kids' blithe confidence they couldn't get lost, Nicole would have taken refuge behind a tree somewhere and waited it out. Paul, Ari, someone, would surely come looking for them if they just stayed close to where they'd been. Because whatever alcohol-induced stupidity had made her wander around in this earlier was long gone and she acknowledged now that she was a Harvard-trained lawyer, for Christ's sake, not a wilderness scout.

But on they went.

The wind was icy. It took your breath away and made your lungs hurt with stuck knives if you took in too much at once. Nicole stopped for a second and pulled her hood in around her mouth, turning sideways into it so she could suck in a deep breath of warm air.

Someone huge and white-faced dashed across the road between her and the children.

She stepped back and blinked. There was only blowing snow. As if whatever it was had never been. Yet as she stepped cautiously forward, she saw the tracks in the snow, already filling with blown snow. Human tracks. But so huge and far apart that she wondered vaguely if it could have been a bear. Except she'd seen the face—male, angry, and covered in frost like what? A snow spirit? She snorted at that stupidity but noticed her own mouth, with its frozen, cracked lips, was dry as a desert. Maybe even frost covered.

Which meant the face she'd seen was no spirit. There was someone out here, and he didn't want to be seen.

Nicole looked left to where he'd run but saw nothing. When she turned her face forward again, she could barely see the dark shapes that were the kids. She stomped ahead quickly to keep up.

When she reached them, they were stopped, huddled together, looking scared.

Nicole leaned in close and said, "What is it?"

"Abomible Snowman," Auggie said, his arms wrapped around one of his big sister's.

"April?"

The girl nodded, white-faced, and Nicole saw both kids' teeth were chattering. Whatever confident energy they'd had earlier had fled and now they looked ready to just collapse and freeze to death. It wasn't something Nicole had even let herself think about before, but now she saw the laughing face of Georgia Hurzgehrmine in her head, the way she'd tossed her hair at Paul, and how he was so attracted to her as this beautiful *mother*. Christ. Maybe Frau H. had been right after all. Georgia wasn't a fit mother, letting her kids out in weather that could kill.

And Nicole was little better. She'd made Frau H. hand the kids over. Then, after she'd had the chance to rescue them, she stupidly let them lead her up through this storm rather than seeking shelter. No, Nicole clearly knew nothing about being a mother. Never would, like she told Paul. Genetically incapable.

"I'm c-c-cold," said Auggie.

"Right," said Nicole, snapping out of her self-pity. "We have to keep moving, you two. Let's go." And she started to push them along...

The frost man was suddenly dead in front of them, huge in the snow, face twisted strangely, eyes fixed on Nicole from under all the ice that coated his eyebrows, eyelashes, and hair. He must have been almost seven feet tall. His body was encased in dark sheet of ice that cracked when he moved. A stiff jacket of some sort.

There was something long and black in his hand.

April and Auggie screamed. They suddenly darted in opposite directions into the snow.

"Asshole!" Nicole shouted at the frost man and dashed after April, only processing the black thing in the man's hand as a knife when she was well off the road into snow drifts. As she plunged deeper and deeper, the snow hitting her knees and hips, getting down her boots, Nicole expected to feel something plunge into her back at any second.

It was the big boy chasing her from her youth. Like a triggered flashback, Nicole felt herself running hard, but her legs weren't strong enough. The ground crumbled under them. She was going to fall and he'd be upon her.

"April!" she screamed as she stumbled.

CHAPTER 60

PAUL HAD DRIVEN the Jeep past Georgia's house and had to backtrack. As soon as he pulled into her driveway, he jumped out and began putting the chains he'd bought in Colona onto the front tires. He should have done that before coming down the hill into Goldrock. Now he was frankly worried that he'd get stuck in these back streets like Georgia had. And Nicole still out there somewhere, maybe still drunk, fallen down in the snow. He'd been stupid letting her run out, too mad to think straight. He should be searching for *her* right now.

The last chain hooked closed when Georgia came tearing back out of her house, wild-eyed.

Paul straightened up. "What is it?"

Ignoring him, Georgia jerked her eyes right and left, trying to see through the whiteness that whipped around them.

"Georgia?" Paul jogged up to her and took her arms. They jerked spastically under his fingers.

She looked at him, unfocused, with spittle formed around the corners of her mouth. "They're gone! My children! Their boots and coats! They must have... Or someone... Or... I killed them, Eddy! I killed my children!"

"Georgia!" Paul shook her hard, his own face hard. "Look at me!" She did. "Now think! Could they have gone to one of your neighbors? Could they be hiding?"

"They don't know anybody here that—" Georgia stopped, her eyes fixed past Paul. Then she shook herself loose and ran past the Jeep to the end of the driveway, stooped, and picked up something blue, the size of a small bird, from one of the tire tracks where he'd overshot her house. She stood looking at it.

Paul joined her. "What is it?"

"April's hairband. She came this way." She raised her hand and looked further south along the street. "The kids went to the lake."

Paul squinted against the blowing snow in that direction and all he could see was white. "In this weather? Why—?"

"There was a lull before I left. They wanted to go out instead of eat lunch. I said no. I couldn't bear to let them go."

And then you walked out on them, Paul thought, but didn't say it. His own behavior with Nicole hadn't exactly been sterling. "You're sure?"

Georgia nodded.

"Okay," Paul said, and pulled her again to the Jeep.

CHAPTER 61

Sʜᴇ ᴡᴀs ᴛʀɪᴄᴋʏ, Japhet thought. Like some sort of test for him.

He'd almost had her before she'd thrown herself down. He'd waded through the snow to where he thought she'd gone down, and she'd vanished.

Then he'd heard her calling for the children again. Off to his left. He'd spun around to start honing in on the sound. It was hard in this wind. It would've strained his senses if he were healthy, and Japhet no longer was. His feet and hands were lumps of ice. His face was stiff and cracked. Only his intermittent shivers told him his body was still alive. That and the dull, distant thud of his heart, driven by rage to keep him upright, driven by the need to grab the black-haired woman, no longer just follow her.

Because he *knew* her. Just...couldn't place her exactly.

Had to be the passage of time. She'd changed.

Memories.

If he could just hold her in front of him for a moment...

She called again and he tried to stomp in that direction, snow up to his thighs. When the snow drifts gradually released their hold around his legs, he figured he must be back on Chickopee Lake Road.

More memories.

He'd come down here lots as a kid. Gone to school along here. Skipped classes to cruise the shoreline and trap birds, frogs, fish, and a young deer once. He'd smeared dirt all over himself and come at the deer from downwind. Chucked a stone past it to make it turn its head, then leapt on it, locking its long slender neck in his arms and pulling its heat down with a crash. That doe had thrashed and kicked and tried to bite him but he'd hung on, squeezing tighter and tighter, too scared and excited to go for his old Buck knife, until the doe's screams became little wheezes and the legs kicked slower. Finally, as Japhet had rolled on top of the dead animal to feel its last breath under him, he'd dry-humped it until he came in his shorts. Then he'd cut the doe up good.

His very next kill, the only thing that could be satisfying after that, was a real live woman.

Killed some. Raped some.

Like the black-haired woman? Was that how he knew her?

The sounds of a roaring motor jerked him out of his reverie and he reared up. Hypothermia was making his mind wander, concentration difficult. Where was the woman? Her two brats?

There! Dead ahead of him, shapes in the shifting white. He could charge forward and have them in an instant. He was behind them and they could not smell him in this storm. He crouched lower and forced his legs to move.

Suddenly the roaring motor cut its headlights towards him. It outlined the woman and brats and Japhet himself like dead people on the edge of heaven. Japhet dropped face-down into the snow.

Voices yelled over the wind. Screams. Thumping doors.

They faded, then seemed to get closer, as if, in their joy of welcome, the angels from the vehicle had pushed the dead trio back towards him. Almost on top of him. He lay very still and did not move, hoping the snow was even now covering him up.

And his attention slipped again.

His mother is standing over him, kicking him hard in the back. "Stand up, Japhet," she says. "Little bugger boy."

"Y-y-y-yes, Mama."

Using his knee, he wipes a bunch of dirty snot from his nose, then Japhet releases his legs and uncurls them. He rolls to one knee, gets a foot under himself, and slowly rises. His mother shoves his butt before he's up and Japhet sprawls forward again, face down in the dirt. Choking on dust and grit.

His mother's foot is on his bum, pressing him down and speaking to the girls and women at the fence. "This boy ain't never going to be stronger than any of you, you got that?"

No air!

Japhet's nose and mouth were blocked with snow. Fighting both panic and resignation, he made his lumpy, dead hands move slowly to his face and claw a space there. Then he drew a long, shuddering chestful of air. He froze as he heard a man's voice seemingly right above him.

"Nicole?! Thank God!

And a shrieking voice: "Auggie! April! Auggie! You two—! Didn't Mama—? Oh! Oh!" And answering kids crying.

Then the black-haired woman's deeper, raspier voice cut through it: "There's someone following us out there. Someone big. We need to get out of here, Paul."

The voices stopped. There was only howling. Howling wind. Howling in Japhet's head, over his back, covering him, hiding him. The universe was graying. Was heaven still just ahead of him? If he stood up now...?

Bugger boy! Get up, boy! Let them see you!

No, Mama. No. I won't. I won't. And Japhet looks back through his hair and snot to the door and sees his little sister watching him, her coal-black hair spilling over her eyes just like his.

Get up!

Oh, God...

The sound of the Jeep roared into gear again, reversing, spinning its tires, moving away. Gone.

Japhet's world was spinning away darkly.

No!

Had...to...get...up.

With a numb heaving of muscle, he pushed his back out of the snow. Got his knees under him. Then a numb foot. He had to find shelter. Because he finally had slotted the black-haired woman into place. The cheekbones, the hard, haunted eyes. She was older and had taken a different name, but there was no mistaking his very own little sister.

Sarah.

He had so much to share with her, and she with him.

He staggered both feet under him and rocked in the wind like an insensate block of ice, sharp pain shooting through his upper back, his right hip, his head, like they were trying to remember how to move him forward.

He toppled sideways into the snow.

CHAPTER 62

TWENTY YARDS back along the road, just after the gold Jeep had roared by, the old woman saw Japhet's unmistakable form rise up then fall back into the snow, and she blinked away a confusing leak of tears. She restarted her truck and tried to roll slowly forward. The tires spun and she slammed the driver's shaft gear into reverse, spun the wheels the opposite direction, then rocked it back forward again. Reverse. Forward. Reverse.

She must make it move. She would not let Japhet die like this. Not when the just God who watched over these proceedings had let her return him to Goldrock and find him this afternoon. The Bone bloodline had started to come together. It could not sputter apart now.

The wind howled around the cab and she scowled out at it. In her current mindset, the wind seemed a live thing too, taking up her own desperate, coppery need.

She banged the gear shift into forward again and pressed the gas. "Gehe, verdamnt!" Move! Damn it!

And this time it did, the tires spinning the truck in a slow rock forward, then suddenly finding purchase and crunching it fully onto the road, lurching and bumping but moving slowly towards the place where Japhet had fallen.

When she saw his body, the old woman did a three point turn around him, stopped her truck, pulled on her heavy mitts and scarf, and got out into the storm. She struggled around to him and leaned over his form, checking for breath. Still living. Perhaps conscious. But he could not move, and the woman had no illusions that she could move him by herself.

For a moment, she stood in the blowing snow, then she went to the rear of her truck, stepped up on the rusted hitch, and reached into the bed to retrieve a snow-covered coil of rope. It took her ten minutes to tie one end of the rope around Japhet's ankles and the other around the hitch.

Then she climbed back into her truck and began to drive.

CHAPTER 63

In the small dining room of the Grenadine, the hotel maid, Rose Mitchell, finished a final dusting of the little captain's lamps that stuck out from the wall paneling all around the room, and wondered whether all ten hotel guests would be coming down for dinner. Like that too-dilly-icious boy in Room 22 , here skiing with his friend, also dilly.

Cor, she hoped they weren't fairies. Staying up in their rooms all afternoon.

Mind you, most of the others was too. Storm had them all quivering like. But if one of those Room 22 boys came down, she'd give them something completely different to quiver about, wouldn't she? She twitched her little duster, smiled, and plumped up her breasts in the low-cut décolletage of her forest-green maid's outfit.

"Rosemary?"

It was the Mister, George Severin, coming from the kitchen that the Missus, Elizabeth Severin, had taken over last year in a move to cut costs. The Missus had changed the menu to mostly German grub, but tasty for all that. Rose would have said so if the Missus weren't so hard.

"Yes, Mister Severin," said Rose with a curtsy as George Severin bustled out. Even dressed in a full-front cook's apron, he was a distinguished gent, was the Mister. All that silver hair. And so much younger than the Missus. It was a mystery to Rose what the Mister saw in her. It was a second marriage for them both and, judging from Wendy, the child from the Mister's first marriage, the Mister's first wife must have been a beauty.

"Have you seen either Elizabeth or Wendy?" Mister Severin said now.

"No, Mister," Rose answered, all proper. But she bent towards him as she said it, giving him a good shot of the goods, so to speak.

He ignored it. "They were both supposed to be fixing dinner by now," he said, cross and worried.

"Maybe they's together, Mister. Maybe the Missus is chaperoning the young Missus, if you catch my meaning."

"Yes, yes. Let me know the minute they sneak in, will you?"

"Yes, Sir."

Then he was gone. Rose stuck her duster in its loop holster on the side of her dress, and pulled out her soft cloth to polish the glasses and silverware. She'd come to America as a nanny eight years ago, did five years of it in New York and Colorado Springs, before meeting the Severins as they were preparing to buy the Grenadine...

A thumping from the front lobby then the sound of the door being thrown open made her stuff the soft cloth back in its pocket and scurry out to gasp.

The front doors both stood wide, wind and snow howling in, and something lay across the entrance outside. She bustled up to see a huge bloke sprawled face up in the snow with tire tracks arced up around him to the door and back to the street, like the truck had veered up to hit him.

Her flesh pimpled from the wind and she was about to call for the Master when the bloke's head twitched and he raised his arm!

"H-help me."

She barely heard it over the howl of wind, or maybe imagined it. But something in her years of nanny training and serving others, or maybe just her natural busybody nature, made her step out into the snow, grab the man by his two arms and drag him, in three staggering heaves, into the lobby. He smelled dank and coppery, like lake water. What had *happened* to him?

"Mister Severin," she panted. Then she hurried back to shut the two front doors—silence, bless her—and took a deeper breath to call out for real.

It turned to a little shriek as the man's right arm moved again and bumped her leg. His eyes were open, half-open, fluttering, trying to focus on her. "H-h-h-help me."

"I will," she assured him, stepping quickly away. "I'll get me master and—"

"No." The hand moved again. And maybe a foot twitch? The bloke was huge, well over six feet, and the white, balding head and the pouching under his jaw showed him to be at least late thirties. But he also wore running shoes (now packed in ice and snow) and what Rose had finally figured was a leather jacket, soaked, frozen, then cracked and dragged upwards in a bunch around his chest.

Something clicked as she gaped at him and she whispered, "Mr. Morris?"

"Muh-muh-muh-mmor..."

The late-arriving guest the Mister had mentioned. The big one. Stutterer. Room 27. There'd been a "Do Not Disturb" sign on it since early this morning. "You need help, Mr. Morris. Why don't I—?"

As if the heat of the lobby was somehow fanning the flicker of life in him, the block swung his hand wide and feebly tried to grab her. He managed to focus on her again. "N-n-no one else. J-just you. B-b-b-buh..."

"Bed?"

He twitched his head. No.

"Bath? To warm you up?"

The man nodded with a grateful sigh, closed his eyes and sank back to looking half dead. Rose glanced back towards the dining room door where the Mister probably still was. She just had to call.

But something in the way this man wanted just her, something in his helplessness when he was such a big man, and the leather jacket, and the mystery of his state, what had happened to him—it tickled that wild itch Rose had left nannying for and had scratched far too rarely since. Adventure. Something different, at least. And he'd asked for a bath, right? Too yum.

She hurried over to the front desk, found the double for his room key, then returned to the man and squatted down by his head. "Mr. Morris? Are you Mr. Morris? What do I do then? I can't ruddy-well lift you by m'self."

His eyes fluttered and he croaked. "I'll get up."

"You're half dead, luv."

That got him going. His long arms flexed and slid under him. Blue hands pushed on the soaked carpet. His blunt fingers sank into the little black and green flecks of the short pile. Rose gasped a bit as he drew his knees up under him, then she rushed forward ducked her shoulder under his armpit.

The dank smell and wet chill of him was almost overpowering. Rose almost gave up as they rose and staggered forward together because his weight was like a great sacks of earth slung across her shoulders. There was more of the gunmetal smell now too, like old blood, half-washed away wherever he'd soaked himself. Rose's throat felt full like she was drowning. "Turn...right."

He twitched and leaned that way, almost falling, but Rose hurried forward under him and slowed him as they reached the stairs.

"Up you go, Mr. Morris. *Oof!* One foot at a time."

He lifted a leaden right foot and Rose leaned him forward so the foot made the first step. Again.

And they climbed like this, one foot at a time, to the top of the stairs, down the hall to his room, inside. Rose herself was near collapse by the time they made it to his door and into the room, but she made him lean by the door while she slipped into the bathroom and cranked on the hot and cold water taps. She also found the room's electric kettle, filled it, and plugged it in.

Taking a deep breath, she turned to him. "Now, Mr. Morris. Me name's Rose and I need to get you out of those clothes."

CHAPTER 64

Japhet was flying in another world somewhere. One without pain or ice or snow. One of pure mind. A dream state. Floating.

Except...somehow, he knew, he was being stripped of his heavy, ice-crusted clothing, wobbling, almost falling down, being caught and steadied by the maid woman's spongy warm hands. And her voice, talking and talking, unintelligible through the wall of ice that surrounded his body, his head, his eyes and ears.

But then steam nearby. He heard the pour. Felt it roll over him.

"Lift a leg, then. There you go..." Babble babble

And he did lift his right leg—strange he still had some control over it—and a spongy hand guided it into hot wetness.

He almost fell.

Frightened babble babble. More commands. His other foot was in the bathtub as well and he was collapsing down onto his bare buttocks, his back, the hot water flowing about him, trying to strip its way in through the ice.

As it succeeded, the pain began. It jerked a guttural howl out from deep inside him, like he'd been hooked with a wire hanger and yanked hard.

CHAPTER 65

Rose was backed against the wall of the bathroom, her hands fluttering. The cry! It was like the wail of some animal being slaughtered. It grunted and squealed while the huge naked man began to jerk about in the bathtub, sloshing the water over the sides.

And the blood, all the blood. When she'd jerked off the stiff clothes, she'd seen he was red and black all over, wearing a knife holster she couldn't take off or pry open. And when he'd dropped into the water, the bath had filled with red. But none of it was his. Morris had no gashes or cuts on him. It was all something else's blood. Or some*one* else's. The knife.

"*Cor.*" Rose ran out of the bathroom as the cry continued, but jerked to a halt by the door. If she ran out now and someone saw her, and they checked this room, found this sight...

She locked the door and inched back inside, feeling suddenly light headed and lost. Trapped. The cries had subsided to moans but Rose's own breath was high and fast in her chest. Waiting for something to happen.

Looking around, she saw the room was untouched other than the unmade bed. Over on the chair by the curtained window sat a battered suitcase, with some socks and underwear, two or three shirts, and something lumpy underneath.

Swallowing, dizzy, Rose stepped over and pushed back the clothes to see what was hiding there. Some sort of cheap false bottom. She fumbled her fingers about, eyes flicking occasionally back towards the bathroom, and found a concealed zipper tucked down in the lining. She unzipped it and reached in to pull out...a Polaroid. It was a pretty woman, in her twenties, smiling nervously, pushing back her hair. Rose reached in for more and brought out a bunch at once. More women, some clothed, some nude and...tied up. Bleeding. Oh, *fook*.

Rose's hands shook and she dropped the stack, realized it contained two letters too. Unable to make herself just turn and run, she knelt down and picked up the letters. They were addressed to someone named "J. Bone," care of a California government office. Neither had a return address but they were both the same handwriting. The postmarks were different years and different states.

A sudden howl from the bathroom made her drop the letters and turn. Then the cry cut off all at once, followed by a pathetic, "Wh-where am I?" Sloshing water. "R-Rose?"

Heart spinning wildly, her survival reflex finally kicked in and Rose dashed for the room's door. She grabbed the handle, twisted, and yanked hard, almost falling down. It was stuck! No, locked! Yes, she'd locked it.

Frantically releasing the handle, she fumbled with the deadbolt. Opened it. Grabbed the handle.

Morris' dripping hand slammed into the door above her head.

She yelped into tears, ducking her head down against the door, turning the handle uselessly back and forth, back and forth, like this was all a dream.

Finally, sobbing and shaking, she turned.

He stood towering over her, wet and naked, and even in her terrified state, or because of it, she dropped her eyes to his middle. He was so huge and stiff it looked like he held a club out from between his legs.

"Ow, no. Ow, fooking no."

"Shut your eyes," he ordered and she did quickly.

"Rosemary. Me mum calls me Rosemary. Always prays for me. Every night. Every—"

"Shut up."

She did, her mouth still open and lips sucking in and out.

"You undressed me, Rosemary. And stared at me. Didn't you? Stared and sniggered."

"No, I—"

"Bitch!" His hands had grabbed the front of her dress and bra and torn it down in a movement that wrenched her shoulders and back. Rose closed her mouth as tight as her eyes, gritted her teeth. But for a second there was nothing, like a great white pause in the unknown.

Then she heard the click of the deadbolt locking behind her and, in front, something sharp scraping its way out of a leather holder. "I've got some questions I need to ask you," Morris said.

CHAPTER 66

J‌APHET FUGGED HER IN A RUSH, took her picture, then tied her to the single wooden chair in his room. There he slowed down enough to ask her questions about the old women in town. He cut her after each answer, asked more, cut her more. But he was barely able to control his knife because his hand twitched so badly. He was still shivering, naked, and in his mind all he could see was the burning eyes of his dark-haired little sister, Sarah, out in that snowstorm. Grown up. Returned to Goldrock.

Or...did she live here? Wouldn't that be a joke. Japhet's diaphragm shook jerkily as he circled around the room.

"What d'you want?" whimpered the cow-bitch on the chair again. "I told you everything. I—"

"Shut up!" He strode to her, grabbed her hair, straddled her bloody legs, and slapped the flat edge of the knife against her face just below her eyes. "You've told me nothing! You know nothing about her, do you."

"*Who?* I told—"

He silenced her by pressing the knife harder against her cheek so that a new line of blood sprang up along the edge. What was Sarah doing here? That voice out in the snow had called her Nicole, so she was obviously in hiding like their mother. No Wilma Bone. No Sarah Bone.

But maybe Mama had told Sarah that Japhet was coming. Maybe Sarah had even been spying on Japhet. Somehow she'd followed him down to that lake.

And saved him? Pulled him back to this hotel? Had that been her? And— Japhet had a blinding insight and shook his head at the shock—had this little cow-bitch maid in the chair, Rosemary, seen who had dropped him off?

He stared down at her. It couldn't be that easy, could it? The maid sees her, recognizes her, tells Japhet now where she's staying...

"Please, Sir." The cow-bitch was looking up at him with her eyes full, her teeth were chattering and her big, droopy tits were quivering up and down with her breaths. The knife, Japhet saw, had cut clean into her cheek now and was covered in red.

He drew it back slowly, tasting the smell of her blood and fear, and locked his eyes on hers. "You want to live, Rosemary?"

She nodded, sobbing once quickly.

"All right. You got one chance. I was dumped at your front door this afternoon by someone. Tell me who and where she lives."

"I..." She licked her lips, took a little gasp, and her eyes flicked to the knife. "Missus...um...Missus...Dolk?"

Japhet scowled. Useless. Making it up. Useless.

He grabbed her jaw and forced out her tongue.

CHAPTER 67

WHEN JAPHET finally finished with the maid it was almost eight-thirty and the room's walls were sprayed with blood. He'd moved the mangled body to the bed and covered her up to her neck with the bedsheet. Turning out the lights in the room, Japhet went to his hotel room window and pulled back the curtains. He was facing out onto Main Street and could actually see up and down its gloom. The storm had quit raging and settled into a silent snowfall. A tow truck was creeping south down Main Street then swinging west, probably to rescue some stupid tourist stuck in the snow.

Japhet swung his bum onto the window ledge and pulled his gore-slick knees up in front of him. There he held them and rocked back and forth. He was warm at last and momentarily content. He'd cranked the room's thermostat up. The air seemed full of a thick mist of blood, like a Turkish steam bath. It filled his nose and lungs with coppery warmth, taking away the lake smell, the mossy dankness, the ice.

He could almost imagine the sun on his back, warm dirt under bare feet...

His mother pulls him from the dirt by his ears, grunting, because even at the age of twelve, Japhet is a giant of a boy. "Now, Japhet," she whispers hotly in his ear. "You are never ever ever going to fug your sister or anyone else. You turn around and show them your pathetic little pee-pee. You show them so we can all have a really good laugh."

No. You fug everyone, Mama. You do.

He blinked back his head with flare nostrils and popped his hands over his ears but the memories kept coming.

He is standing and staggering in a circle, trying to cover himself until his mother whips his bare bum with a long, straight stick she's brought from inside. "Show them!" And he exposes his penis again, crusted now with dust, still dripping its last bit of semen.

The crowd at the fence, women and girls, start to giggle and whisper among themselves. Japhet's mother encourages them, using her stick like a pointer. "Nasty doodle!" she says like a schoolteacher, stabbing the stick's point at his crotch. "Teeny little wee-wee!"

Japhet sees Sarah in the doorway of the house, covering her eyes. The others are laughing and shaking the fence now, like they wish they could barge in and gleefully rip him to pieces.

Japhet stumbles and looks into the loathing in his mother's face.

"You want to know why I call him 'bugger boy?'" she roars, and strokes her blunt-ended stick.

Japhet wants to vomit.

Japhet popped off the windowsill to find he was breathing hard, his heart thumping again, the smell of blood harsh and choking in his mouth. His mind was whirling too, something he was not accustomed to. In the room's dark, he stared at the eyeless corpse on the bed. He gulped like a fish as he recalled the cutting, the pain in her face, the slash that had jetted out her life, and he began to feel good again. Better than good. Excited. Because this killing hadn't been planned. All his other killings had been carefully worked out in advance, even Mary Jane Pulver in Arizona.

But then...this. Right here in his own hotel room. Right where someone should have heard the cow-bitch's shrieks and summoned the law, but didn't. Because the hotel was half-empty. Because the law in Goldrock was one stupid little bug of a marshal. Because the storm had everyone scared and hunkered down. He could prowl among them like a lion, killing, taking what he wanted.

Until he found his mama.

He whirled back to the window, the revelation of his power flooding through his limbs like hard liquor, burning and making him hard all over again. The lake and storm hadn't really been trying to kill him at all, had they. They were just trying to shake him out of his caution. Get him moving.

As if to confirm this, the lights all along Main Street flickered suddenly. Japhet walked to the window and looked out. The snow must be bringing down the power lines.

They flickered again and went out everywhere. A few with backup generators buzzed back on at once. Others would follow soon.

"Not soon enough," Japhet whispered. Because for now the town was weak, scared, and huddling in the dark. And Japhet had a name to find, the one he'd heard down by the lake before being delivered. Nicole. *Little Sarah is Nicole.* Once he got all cleaned up, someone out there was going to lead him to her. And she would lead him to Mama.

The old woman was going to be so surprised.

DAY THREE
FRIDAY

Slowly waking on the lumpy pull-out bed in Georgia Hurzgehrmine' living room, Nicole groaned and rolled toward Paul's warm back. It was still dark. And freezing cold. She reached out for him, then stopped as she blinked fully awake.

Her fingertips hovered inches from his skin.

Paul had been so cold towards her after the rescue last night. Sticking her in the Jeep's front passenger seat while Georgia fawned and wailed over the kids in the back. He'd hunched over the Jeep's steering wheel and lurched them back to Georgia's house with his jaw locked tighter than a hunter's leg- hold trap.

Nicole pulled her hand back.

It had been Paul's locked jaw, not all of Georgia's teary begging, that had gotten Nicole to agree they would drive to the Hurzgehrmines' only to say she and Paul were going to stay overnight at Georgia's. Nicole realized she needed to see how Paul behaved around Georgia if she was ever going to get an accurate read on the situation. And after Nicole, Paul, Georgia, and the kids had all had a greasy meal of frittatas and smoked sausage in the kitchen, she'd had her answer.

Her marriage was in deep shit.

Yup. From the moment Georgia had started to take off her jacket only to blush and explain she'd left her top under the wheel of her stuck truck. And Paul's eyes had gone wide, following her every move as she'd gone into her bedroom to change and reemerge, giggling coquettishly. Georgia had kept flirting all through meal prep, while Paul had been all tense and flaring nostrils. Then the electricity had gone out and Paul had lit a fire in the woodstove for heat—it had clearly burned out sometime in the night—and Georgia had gotten the kids ready for bed. Finally, Paul had roughly gestured Nicole off the couch, tossed aside the couch pillows, and yanked open the bedframe that had been folded up beneath them. He'd coldly suggested Nicole borrow one of Georgia's nightshirts because her own clothes stank.

Now, in the cold chill of morning, Nicole pulled the sheets and blankets up around her neck and shivered miserably. She stared at the dim ceiling. Her eyes followed the meandering crack of a dark water stain up there. And the double-whump of where she was finally sank home.

This wasn't just Georgia Hurzgehrmine's house; it was connected somehow to whatever horrible thing had happened in Goldrock thirty years ago. Something involving a teenager named Betsy Müller. Something that Nicole's mother had picked up on or...been a part of?

What was it? Had there truly been a baby-giveaway back then, with Nicole being the baby given? Had this very house—she felt a curling in her gut as she considered it—been Nicole's childhood home?

Paul snuffled a little in his sleep and the curling in Nicole's stomach turned painful. It was as if the truth of long ago was trying to slice apart everything she was now, everything she'd built up. Her work, her marriage. It was spreading like that water stain on the ceiling...

Paul shifted again and it snapped her back to the present. These little movements of Paul's were his pre-waking routine. She knew them all too well from her past bouts of insomnia. It had to be close to five-thirty.

So what came next?

There was a high-voiced giggling from under the pull-out bed. Then a furious "Shh. Shh." Nicole's bum felt the bump of an elbow or head. "Auggie, don't. *Don't.*"

Oh, God, no. Georgia's children? Before the sun was up? Looking out the window, it was hard to tell, but it looked like it had finally stopped snowing.

With barely-suppressed aggression, Nicole grabbed the side of the bed and swung her head down. "Boo!"

Take that, she grinned, as the two kids under the bed saw her dark, upside-down, makeup-less face framed by matted black shadow, and screeched. They tried to jerk backwards in their pajamas and bumped their heads hard up on the mattress under Paul. He grunted and twitched awake, saying, "What...?" as a thump and crash from the hallway told Nicole that Georgia Hurzgehrmine was now awake too.

She came running into the living room from the hall wearing nothing but a long cotton nightgown. Her nipple bumps showed through it even in the dark like she'd just had an erotic dream.

When she saw her two kids were all right, and in fact now looked at each other and at Nicole and giggled again, Georgia pursed her lips at the two and stabbed an index finger in the direction of the kids' rooms down the hall. "Y'all get back to your rooms. Now!"

Nicole winked at them as they went, more to piss off their mother than anything else. They giggled again and ran down the hall.

Georgia fluttered her hands. "Sorry."

"What time is it?" said Paul.

"I don't know. Five? Five-thirty?"

He grunted and squinted at his watch. "It's almost seven. We need to get up. Get going. The Hurzgehrmines." Paul sat up, fully awake and bare-chested.

"I'll...uh...get dressed, then get some breakfast if you could stoke up the fire," Georgia said.

"No. We should—"

But she'd already retreated. Without turning to Nicole, Paul hopped out of bed, pulled on his pants and shirt, then strode to the woodstove, opened up the front door, and stuck some more kindling and split logs into the firebox. He knelt before it and started blowing on the dead-looking coals until they began to glow.

"Paul?"

"What?"

"About yesterday. At the Hurzgehrmine place."

Paul stopped blowing for a moment to look at her hard, and Nicole saw herself from his eyes—hair messed, no makeup, wrinkles, the extra weight on her thighs. But she refused to grab a sheet to cover herself, refused to be that weak and insecure. She closed her lips and returned his look with an automatic defiance.

He shook his head. "We'll talk about it later." Back to blowing on the coals.

"When?"

"*Later.*"

The fire lit. He adjusted it a bit with the poker, then carefully closed the woodstove's front door, stood, and strode into the kitchen. There was the sound of a match being lit, the smell of candles. Georgia joined him and Nicole followed the clattering sounds, the dull murmur of conversation, and the mouth-watering smell of oranges being cut up. The electricity was obviously still off, but the oh-so-devoted mother had not only pulled out an additional supply of candles, she also had a stock of fresh fruit to keep her kids healthy.

Nicole scooped up her clothes and went for the washroom. She found the candle there and lit it. She pulled on her bra and panties and socks, then leaned on the counter top and stared at herself in the mirror. How could she try so hard to do the right thing and keep messing up so badly?

It had started with deciding to come to Goldrock, of course. Her mother had offered her one last masochistic game to play and Nicole should have just refused. But she'd wanted the truth.

And when she momentarily came to her senses at the Jeep rental place, she could backed out there, however foolish it would have looked. But she'd wanted to save the job or a brain injury victim.

Then, even after they'd arrived here, she could have at least told Paul why they'd come and made him help her. Instead she'd tried to stay strong and sent him off to help poor little Georgia.

Even with Herb Mawpester and Marshal Bob Pritchett—she'd let them off the hook with their secrets when she should have just whaled on them until they talked.

You're always helping and blaming other people, Paul had accused her. *When are you going to reach out and make a life for yourself?*

Really, Paul? That was all she had to do?

And maybe stop drinking and snapping and moping about like a crazy woman, is what he should have added.

Her mouth twitched. None of the lines around it could ever be as soft and pouty as the ones Georgia Hurzgehrmine had, but Nicole had grit and intelligence. She *was* going to get some answers, and whatever they were she'd deal with them. But if she wanted Paul to still be there at the other end of that, she'd better get her act together. She was a lawyer. She knew how to fight. Viciously if she had to.

She grinned so her teeth showed and tugged on her smelly white turtleneck and ski pants. Under the sink she saw a pair of slippers that had to be Georgia's. As good a place to start as any.

She stepped into the slippers then strode out of the bathroom to go reclaim her man.

CHAPTER 69

Only in a place like Goldrock, Ari Siegel thought groggily as he rolled off
Marshal Pritchett's couch where he'd slept, ominously one floor above the jail,
and tugged on his jeans. They didn't arrest you in Goldrock; they just didn't let
you go, even to tell your oma and friend where you were.

Ari's phone said 7:05 a.m. Dim light outside.

He made his way to the lawman's washroom, emptied his bladder, and
found and unwrapped a new toothbrush Pritchett kept for guests or just hadn't
opened yet for himself. He brushed his teeth. Then he glanced at the dark
shadows under his eyes in the bathroom mirror. Images of last night kept
flashing up.

*Trudging blindly up from the lake with Wendy, Nicole and the kids already
gone.*

Banging on Pritchett's door.

*He and Pritchett walking Wendy home, then going back to Pritchett's place to
wait for a break in the storm.*

*Getting two guys and a tow truck, middle of the night, wind calmer, to break
up the lake near the fishing hut.*

Pulling the Toyota sport ute, a 4Runner, out of the lake.

*Two dead, frozen bodies inside. The woman is naked and all carved up. Eyes
and tongue cut out. Nipples gone. Shallow cuts all over like she's been tortured.
Deep stab wounds just below the rig cage.*

*Tow truck guy points out it had to have happened that day because there were
still bubbles of air trapped in the vehicle.*

Pull them out. Take them to the town doc.

Ari gagged at the sink as his stomach suddenly tried to leap up his throat. He steadied himself on the sink and splashed cold water over his face. Brushed back his hair. Oh, man. It had to be the same freak who'd butchered Wendy's dog. And whether it was the original Goldrock freak or a copycat, this town had a seriously sick puppy in its midst. As soon as people found out, there was going to be a massive panic. Everyone would want to leave and there was no way out because of the storm.

Ari grimaced as he recognized a part of him was enjoying this. A real killer. A snowed-in town. This was like journalism gold. And Pritchett needed him too. Ari seriously doubted whether Goldrock's marshal was up to the task of finding the killer by himself.

Pritchett apparently chose that moment to fall out of bed. Ari heard a thump and a curse. A second later there was a thumping on the locked bathroom door. "Move it, kid," the marshal's gruff voice said. "I gotta pee."

Ari spat, rinsed his mouth, and thought he really should convince Pritchett to at least go tell his oma and Josh that he was okay. Right after this one thing he needed to do.

"Now!"

Ari rinsed out the toothbrush, stuck it in his rear jeans pocket, and hurried out of the bathroom. The marshal brushed past him quickly in his boxer shorts and slammed the door. Ari grinned as he heard a crash, the splosh of Pritchett peeing, and a loud groan of relief. That came from all the beers the marshal and tow truck guys had downed once they'd smashed through the ice and pulled out the 4Runner. It had definitely taken down Ari's fear of Pritchett.

Especially after Pritchett played father and only let Ari vomit into the snow. No booze. Which was just as well. Ari had decided after yesterday morning that his one fling with alcohol was enough for a lifetime or two.

"Marshal?" Ari called.

"Whah?"

"Snow's stopped."

"Whoop-dee."

"That means the computer guys could probably get through to their satellite uplink. With this new killing, do you think maybe there's enough to—?"

He stopped as the bathroom door opened and Pritchett swung his great fleshy body out, hanging on roughly to the doorframe. He fixed Ari with his bleary red eyes for a moment, then said, "You really think they could tell us anything that'd help?"

"If they got pictures on file, yeah. If they've worked up some sort of a profile, we might even be able to predict where the guy's hiding, what he might do next, or where—"

Pritchett waved a hand at him then ran the hand over his stubble and finally nodded.

Ari ran to the couch to get the rest of his clothes.

Minutes later, he and Pritchett were nine businesses south on Main Street. Ari banged on the door. He was ninety-five percent sure this was the address the two computer guys had given him that fuzzy night in the Dead Man's Saloon. There was no answer from inside. Not surprising this time of the morning.

Ari banged harder.

Pritchett, meanwhile was adjusting his black fur snow hat and squinting around the dimly-lit street like something wasn't right.

Ari looked too, but couldn't see anything. The socked-in skies had slowed the dawn so everything was a surreal, dim silver color, and the snow had stopped. But everything else looked normal. The street stretched out long and quiet in either direction. Deep snowdrifts lay against every building, completely covering some parked vehicles, particularly where the snowplow had gone by yesterday.

Ari banged even harder and finally heard some stirring from inside.

At that moment, though, Pritchett swore under his breath. "Goddamn it."

"What?"

"Break-in at Box Canyon."

Pritchett pointed and Ari saw the scuff marks near the entrance of the sports store. Broken glass? At the same time, he heard footsteps clumping slowly down the stairs behind the door they stood at.

"Couldn't it wait?" Ari said. "Just go in here and—"

Pritchett tugged down his dark blue parka so his badge flashed on his chest. "You go in, boy. Ask your questions. You find something, you tell me. I'm thinking that the nut who did that other stuff might be right near us now."

"What? He cuts up a dog, two people, then goes and steals some skis?"

Pritchett fixed him with a superior stare. "Books don't cover it all, smartass."

"But—"

Too late. Prtichett had stomped off. The door opened and one of the computer guys (Was it Kevin? Calvin?) stood there in his bathrobe, squinting through his glasses at Ari. "What?"

Ari took a deep breath. "Hi. I know this is going to sound crazy, but I need to use your satellite link to speak to the FBI."

CHAPTER 70

On the Grenadine's second floor, Wendy Severin hummed and grinned as she picked up another set of clean towels from the linen room. Rose hadn't turned up this morning, so Wendy's stepmother made Wendy take over. This meant cleaning all the rooms vacated the day before, then, once the current guests were down for breakfast, cleaning those rooms too.

And that was all okay. Because the world was okay. Even finding what had looked like a dead body in a car under the ice was okay. Having her stepmother monitor her every move this morning was even okay.

Why? Because she was in love.

She was in love with the most unlikely of guys. Short, Jewish, long-haired, a little awkward and shy. But smart as anything. Funny. Sensitive...

Oh, my goodness. (Wendy would have put her hand over her mouth if she hadn't been holding a stack of towels.) She suddenly understood all those movies where the shy geek got the girl.

Of course, Ari was a geek who'd managed to punch out Jeremy Buckster in front of all those other football thugs. Which made him a geek with a bit of action hero inside him.

The thought made her grin even more as she stepped out of the linen room, closed the door with her foot and bounced back to the second floor landing to go up to the third floor and work her way down.

She stopped at the landing. Just a minute. There, on the dark carpets of the stair and hallway, were vaguely darker spots and streaks. She hadn't noticed them on the way up because of the dim light earlier; the generator wasn't powering the main hall lights to conserve fuel. But now, leaning down and squinting, she saw they were partial, large muddy footprints. Who would find mud to step in through all this snow? Curious, she followed them down the hall until they stopped, then suddenly jerked her nose up at the smell.

It was Room 27. Mr. Morris' room. A "Do Not Disturb" sign hung on the outside doorknob.

She leaned in and sniffed. Popped her head back again. The stink was definitely coming from here. She was surprised none of the other guests had complained. Though now that she thought of it, she realized no other guests were in the rooms directly beside this one. Her father had been spreading them out to give them all extra privacy since they had the space.

And the stink suddenly fell into place in her head. She'd smelled versions of it before—the butcher shop, Max's eviscerated body.

Lower lip trembling, Wendy started to set down her towels to knock on the door. Then she thought better of it. Uh-uhn. Mack Morris had already scared her once. Let her father deal with him.

Determinedly humming herself back into her happy love-state, she waltzed back to the stairs. She'd tell her dad about this, finish her own chores, then she was going to walk over and surprise Ari.

It was going to be a wonderful day!

CHAPTER 71

PRITCHETT'S NERVES were jangling as he approached Box Canyon Sports. Other than himself and the kid back there talking his way into the computer guys' place, there was no one else out this early. Main Street looked like a ghost town. The only sound Pritchett heard was the crunch of his boots and his wheezy breath.

He stopped at the smashed-in front window at Box Canyon Sports. One type of tracks led in. Another led out. Pritchett stepped in to investigate.

Nothing out of place up front. But in the back, behind a rack of these webby-style ski pants like the gloves the Jew-boy wore, Pritchett found a balled-up, blood-encrusted package of clothes and running shoes. The shoes were size fifteen. Pritchett's heart dropped into his stomach. He looked behind another rack and found the balled up leather jacket.

"Aw, Jesus."

Had to be Mack Morris. And the blood on all these clothes was probably the lake corpses' blood. Morris had hidden out, then come here for new clothes.

The boot tracks leading out of the store were probably the biggest ones the store stocked. And they led not onto the road where they'd have vanished, but around the side of the store, clear as arrows saying, *Follow me. Catch me if you can.*

"Aw, damn," Pritchett said and followed.

CHAPTER 72

THE GUY who'd met Ari at the door downstairs was named Calvin Beeb, and was more helpful than Ari could have hoped. After hearing Ari's story, he'd kicked his partner, Deng Shioah, out of bed and the two of them had managed to get a satellite connection despite the cloud cover.

Five minutes later, they'd arranged a direct tunneling protocol to a special agent Deng knew in Quantico's training division. From there, they got patched through to an Agent Jillian Clarke in CASKU, the Child Abduction and Serial Killers Unit. After grilling Ari over the audio hookup for fifteen minutes about his background, his relationship with the town marshal, his general knowledge-base about Goldrock history, and, it seemed, Ari's emotional fortitude and judgement, Clarke began to spill information the other way.

CASKU, Clarke said over the speakers, had been vigorously tracking a California resident named Japhet Edwin Bone for the last month. (Ari wished Pritchett were here so Ari could hit him and say, "See?") They'd identified Bone as the prime suspect on three unsolved homicides with the same signature.

"Signature," said Ari into the microphone now slung around his head. "You mean like how he kills his victims? The *modus operandi*."

"Uh-unh." Clark's voice got lost in a bit of cackles as some bytes didn't make it.

"Repeat?"

"...can use different means of killing, but the thing by which the killer expresses his anger, his fantasy enactment, stays the same."

"Like?"

"Bone likes to dominate and torture his victims. That's a pretty common signature for sexual serial killers. But Bone also likes to cut out their eyes and tongue, cut up their hands. Happened there with both the dog and woman you found, right? That's Bone. In his last few victims he's been slicing off the nipples of his women too. Very directed rage. You should find all these pieces stuffed up the victim's vagina."

Which is why they hadn't found them in the 4Runner last night. Ari felt his stomach roll over and swiveled around on his chair to see that Calvin and Deng also looked sickened. Deng mumbled something about coffee and walked off.

"But...why would Bone go back to doing animals?" Ari asked. "Could it be a copycat? Someone who just knows all about the Bone killings and...I don't know...is trying to resurrect them or something?"

There was a silence on the speakers for a bit and Ari wished Agent Clarke were hooked up to some sort of web cam so Ari could see what she was doing. Then Clark's voice crackled out again, her contralto voice quiet and serious. "You're in Goldrock. You know Bone was born there."

Ari nodded, then grimaced. "Yeah. Cut up a lot of animals here. Set fires, too. Finally killed one woman."

"That was part of it."

"Hunh?"

"He raped at least twelve girls and women there over four years before he finally killed one."

Ari frowned. "That doesn't make sense. How'd he get away with that in a town this size?"

"According to him, it's because they were all scared of him. But we contacted some former residents of Goldrock and they tell a different story. Seems a certain attitude towards rape existed in the town back then."

"What? It's the girl's fault? She asked for it?"

"Something like that. Also that if you're raped, you're permanently unclean. It's possible that some of the girls or women would have simply kept quiet about it."

"But..." Ari thought of his mother and the other women he knew who'd lived there then. If any of them... Would he even know?

"Another factor," continued Clarke, "was apparently the fact that Bone's mother was some kind of incredible seductress with a sex addiction. Slept with half the men in town and made them do things you wouldn't think good Teutonic immigrants would even consider. Could be the town leaders used their influence to hush things up."

Al Rawley. "They let it all continue!"

"Not necessarily. Some of the people we interviewed think that Wilma Bone kept her son locked up in the cellar most nights. Probably beat him. Hints of something involving a group of her women friends. She might have led them down their own dark paths. Sexual abuse probably. You can get a kind of cult-like psychopathy developing in small, isolated towns. Wilma could be considered a cult leader."

More faces flashed through Ari's mind. His oma's small circle of women friends. The anguish in her when she'd tried to stop him going out. Had that been guilt? Ari couldn't believe it. But fear maybe. "So you think it was Bone who killed the dog and this woman. You think he's here."

"We've got a string of victims in California, Monterey area, that look like his. Then one shows up in Arizona. A little girl down south of you in Colorado says a big man with a stutter threatened to sexually assault her but was scared off. The man was driving your way."

"Big man with a stutter. Can you send a jpeg?" Ari looked up at Calvin, who was curled tensely over the chair and desk to Ari's right. "Can he do that?"

Agent Clarke answered before Calvin could even jump at being addressed. "I've got a recent one scanned from when he applied to be a parole officer. Sending it now."

Ari waited tensely. A minute later, the picture file name popped up in a box center screen. Calvin grabbed the computer mouse to click it open for him.

"Mack Morris," Ari said.

The appearance of Morris' face wasn't a surprise, but it did make the reality of everything the FBI agent had said hit home. Twelve rapes and at least one murder from decades ago. Multiple ones since then. Wendy's dog and that woman in the 4Runner.

And Ari, Wendy, Nicole, those kids had all been out wandering the streets thinking the storm was the only thing they had to worry about.

Ari swallowed dryly, about to speak into his head mike, when Clarke's voice cut through on the speakers again. "I haven't told you the worst of it," she said. "The reason I'm telling you any of this at all."

Oh, great. "What?"

"Ever hear of the serial killer named Ed Kemper? Lot like Bone. Big man. Killed a bunch of co-eds around Santa Cruz back in the nineteen-seventies. His killings only stopped when he finally realized it was his mother he really wanted to kill and rape, in that order. A friend of the Arizona woman Bone killed said her friend met a guy outside the town bar, told her she was taking him home, and that he had to be all right because he was on the way to see his 'mama.'"

"Then...he just has to find her."

"There's no Wilma Bone living in Goldrock now. Unless she changed her name."

"Which is possible, right? Bone did."

"And if she's not there, or if Bone can't find her, what do you think happens?"

"What?" Ari leaned forward like he was in pain. A part of him really didn't want to know.

"Call it decompensating, shortening the intervals, changing from a serial to a spree killer. Just before Kemper decided on his mother, he'd figured on shooting everyone on the block where he lived. If his mother had been unavailable, I think that's what he would have done. Especially if there was no way for anyone to leave."

There was a long silence. Finally Clarke said quietly, "Look, Mr. Siegel, Ari, I'm sure you know this is not how we normally do things. Probably shouldn't have talked to you at all. But given the danger I believe you are all in out there, and the time crunch, I'm going with my gut. I'm going to transmit to you most of the file we have on Japhet Bone. You read it through, then show it to your town marshal. Make him get some extra help. See if you can track Bone down."

There was a long hissing sound and Ari thought for a second the satellite connection had been broken or Clarke had signed off. But then the file download bar showed up, tracking the progress of the transmission.

When it was finished, there was another hiss, then Agent Clarke's last words:

"Good luck. And if you find another corpse or two today, watch your back."

CHAPTER 73

At the Dolk house, Pritchett's eyes followed the tracks to the garage attached to the house, the scuff marks up on the roof, the heavier marks where the killer jumped back down. Carrying something?

Pritchett followed these last marks to the unheated storage shed the Dolks kept out back. The shed's lock was broken. Bloody prints led out again. "Uh-oh." Pritchett swallowed and yanked open the door against the piled snow

He reeled back again as the smell hit his nose, hard and rotten like chicken guts and machine oil. Holding his nose, he forced himself in to check out to find...

Young Mindy Dolk. She was, *had been,* a big-boned, broad-faced little flirt. Sixteen years old.

After forcing himself to confirm Mindy's naked body was mutilated like the lake corpse had been, Pritchett staggered out, retched in the snow outside, and went to bang on the Dolk's back door. Carl Dolk, a big blond Swede who was married to Al Rawley's sister, was still dressed in his bathrobe when he answered it. Pritchett looked up at him, stammered a bit, then said, "I...uh...just found something in your shed back there, Carl. Don't...uh...don't go back there. It's an official crime scene now. And just as soon as I can...uh...I'll be back to check it out."

Carl frowned. "Where you going now?"

"The...uh...perpetrator left tracks. I'm following." He pointed.

Then Pritchett retreated, leaving Dolk annoyed and confused. Pritchett should have said nothing. Nothing. Or found something to lock up the shed again. Or at least dressed the girl. The smartass Jewish kid would have probably had lots of ideas, right?

Pritchett shook his head. Nothing to do now but find the killer. Do that at least. And he trudged on, following Mack Morris' clear prints.

He found body two in the Christianson house.

Alberta Christianson was a divorcee. Looked like she'd been taken in bed while she read by candlelight. The cuts on her body were almost symmetrical, like the killer had painted a picture with his knife after taking out her tongue and eyes. And, Pritchett couldn't help his eyes noticing, her pubis looked red and bruised from hard thumping. With this one at least, Morris had done more than just cut.

Pritchett swallowed. What had Alberta sounded like when she'd tried to scream with no tongue?

He staggered outside to retch a second time, getting some on his coat this time and not bothering to wipe it off.

He followed the prints to bodies three and four, five and six, seven, eight and nine. One girl, five women, and three husbands who were no doubt killed just because they happened to be in the way. The men simply had their throats cut or large stab wounds in their backs. The stripping and carving was just for the women.

And because Pritchett knew most of the women and girls by name, it felt like his world was being disassembled before his eyes. He'd stopped retching after body three. His mind had gone numb, functioning just enough to pull out his gun and keep it at ready as he pushed out of the latest house, scanning for the killer's tracks in the snow.

The words "organized" and "disorganized" kept flashing in his brain. Some seminar he'd had once on serial killers. Some of them planned out their crimes carefully, followed careful rituals, took trophies. Others just did crimes of opportunity, unplanned, using whatever was on hand.

So what the hell were all these bodies? They were each carved carefully, but...so many. They couldn't be planned. Morris, or whoever he was, was just going wild. Which made him unpredictable. Terrifying.

I need help, Pritchett thought. But there's no time. Every extra minute I take is one more Goldrock citizen dead. And it's my fault.

Ten twenty-one a.m.

Blinking hard when he found the tracks again, he held his gun high and plunged out through the snow.

CHAPTER 74

Ari rushed, in awkward snow-straddling leaps, for his grandmother's house. He hadn't been able to see Marshal Pritchett when he'd come out of the Calvin and Deng's place, and he'd been just too scared to go chasing after him through the back alleyways. Not with Japhet Bone, the Goldrock Freak, on the loose.

No, he needed help. Needed Josh and to tell his oma what was happening, especially if Wendy came there looking for him.

Wendy!

The sudden thought of her made him almost drop his file on Bone as he spun back towards the Grenadine, staggering comically backwards to keep his balance. Then he spun again and plunged on towards his oma's. He needed Josh first. Needed to get some backup before he went anywhere. And his friend and grandmother were probably worried sick about him too since he hadn't come back last night. He owed it to them.

He reached his oma's house and tried to burst in, surprised to find it locked. Gasping hard for breath, he banged hard on the door.

Josh answered with a wild look in his eyes. "Ari-dad," he said. "You see her, dude?"

"Who?" Ari panted, suddenly afraid.

"Your oma. Miryam. She threw on this funky black fur coat and barged out of here twenty minutes ago, swearing all sorts of stuff. German? Yiddish, maybe? Told me to lock the doors and don't let anyone in except you. Took her pickup and roared off."

"Oh no."

"She didn't look too good, either. Kept clutching her chest and making her tight face, you know."

Ari staggered into through the front hall and looked around his oma's living room/dining room. He could still smell the vinegar spicing and cooked lamb from the Seder the night before. The one Ari had missed. *Oh, Yaweh, pass over us. Spare thy children.* Did she know Bone was back in town? "Did she say anything else? Anything about where she was going?"

"It was in another language, dude! But...she mentioned a name a few times. Clara-something."

Ari spun on him, pressing. "Clara-what?"

"Clara. Just Clara."

Ari squinted his eyes closed. Clara. Clara. It sounded so familiar. Why? Where had he heard it? Then it came to him. The evil witch landlady Nicole had told him about yesterday during their walk in the storm. Clara Hurz-something. German. Maybe even a German Jew like Miryam. Maybe they knew each other because of that. But still, why go there? Looking for backup like Ari had with Josh?

Ari felt a hot rush of guilt and a bad taste in his mouth. He knew nothing about his grandmother. Nothing really about her past, who her friends were in town, how she'd coped since Ari's grandfather had died. Opa. Ari's mother and father never talked of her. Ari had never asked. Now...

"I need to find her."

"What?"

Ari threw the Japhet Bone file at him and Josh caught it before the papers fluttered out. "That's a file on a guy named Japhet Bone whom the FBI thinks is here now in Goldrock. They think he sliced up the dog I told you about. And another woman that Wendy and I found last night out by the lake. That's why I wasn't home last night."

"Dude, this is, like, a joke?"

"Dead steady, Josh. Crazy, yeah, but a hundred percent steady. And I saw this Bone guy yesterday. Scary guy. Read the file after I go and you'll see he's probably looking for a mother here that he hasn't seen since he was thirteen. I'd say that puts every older woman in Goldrock at risk, including my grandmother."

Josh was shaking his head so hard his hair looked like fire. "Whoah! Dude! What do you mean, 'After I go?'"

Ari pushed past him back to the front door. "Wendy, this girl I was with last night, might come looking for me, okay? You have to go to the Grenadine—she's the hotel keeper's daughter—and tell her to stay there. Stay with her. Watch out for this guest there called Mack Morris. Show her the file."

"Why don't you—?"
Ari shook his head. "She'd want to come with me."
"Dude, where you going? What if your grandma's already..."
"I'll see you at the Grenadine."
And he was out of there.

CHAPTER 75

Ten-thirty-five a.m..

Marshal Bob Pritchett stumbled numbly out of the Amencourt's house on Pearson Crescent and leaned hard against the front corner of their house. The .38 Special in his right hand hung down like a lead weight.

That was bodies eight and nine. Doug Amencourt in the kitchen, killed by what looked like a large knife slicing over his throat that had almost taken the head clean off. And of course his pretty wife, Anne, in the living room, naked like the other women, eyeballs and tongue out, nipples hacked off, sliced all over. Blood all over. Their old shag carpet slick with it.

How many more were there? How long had the killer been *on* this spree?

Blowing his nose hard like he could somehow clear out the scent that had lodged permanently there, Pritchett raised his bloodshot eyes to survey the snow around the house. There. Tracks leading off across the back lawns, towards the back lawns of Chickopee Lake Road, toward a sparse line of spruce trees between them.

Then it struck him that the Amencourt's blood had looked pretty fresh. Morris couldn't be too far ahead. If he hurried, maybe Pritchett could even stop this killer before more people ended up dead.

The thought of an actual confrontation made him think about organizing a posse again. But again the logistics defeated him. There was no one like him in this town, balls-to-the-metal fact. No one would follow him.

He had to do this alone.

Sucking in the icy air, he plunged after the tracks.

The snow in the back yard quickly wrapped around Pritchett's thighs, even his waist in places, and he kept pushing at the bottom of his hip-length marshal coat with one hand, raising his gun up high with the other.

Ten-thirty-seven a.m.

He reached the line of slender spruce trees that separated the Pearsons Crescent back yards from those of Chickopee Lake Road and saw the tracks leading through and over to the Chickopee homes.

He paused for a second, breathing hard, his feet feeling like blocks of ice, and wondered if there was a way to get ahead of the killer.

Figure it out.

Goldrock was built like a lopsided butterfly, with Main Street as a north-south body, Chickopee Lake as the head, and mostly-residential roads fanning out on either side. But the eastern wing of roads butted up against the steep, mined-out walls of Gomel Mountain on the north and Minsk to the east, keeping it narrow. Most of the roads were on the west side, leading over to the ski lifts of Warsaw. There also lay the town's elementary school, the Community Center, many of the bed and breakfasts, and...the lake!

Maybe the killer was heading back to the lake to check on his first kill.

Roused by this insight, Pritchett strode forward. His right arm knocked a tree which dumped a load of snow on his marshal's snow cap. As he looked up, he suddenly sank into a dip between two of the trees and had to swing down his gun hand to keep him from falling. "Damn it!" He jerked the gun up, scared of getting it wet, of having it not working when and if he finally caught up to the killer.

"Hey!" he yelled at the back of the closest house.

And because there wasn't any wind or snowfall anymore, whoever was inside actually seemed to have heard him. Pritchett saw a face in one of the windows. Clear enough that it must have seen him too.

It disappeared again and no doors opened.

Well, hell. Thank you very much.

He struggled out of the deep drift with a grunting rush and stopped. The cold rasped deeply in his lungs. The sourness of his earlier vomit clung inside his nose. The gunmetal gray sky seemed lower than before.

A clank from his right made him look and he saw the tracks again, leading to the side door of the house there. And damn if he didn't know that house. His heart pounded faster.

This was Petra's house. Petra Hungerford. From high school. She'd been Petra Duglosz then. Square-jawed and big busted. A little mean, but she'd actually gone out with Pritchett twice. If Morris was in there now and he could save her...

Fingers suddenly icy and trembling inside his gloves, Pritchett raised his .38 to shoulder height and scuffled quickly forward.

He reached out and slowly twisted the doorknob with his free hand.

CHAPTER 76

At 12 Chickopee Lake Road, seated at one end of the kitchen table while Paul, Georgia, and the kids were seated down either side, Nicole smiled over the breakfast plate she'd just finished. The fruit salad breakfast was as good as any she'd had in ages, Nicole thought. The cantaloupe and early California grapes, apple, canned pears—very nice. Light, sweet, healthy.

Not that she'd tell this to Georgia or Paul. No, right now she was maintaining an atmosphere of hawk-like judgement in the room. There was no more muttering of apologies from her, no nervous gestures or weakness. Nor were there allowances for Georgia's weakness. Nicole had given a brusque thank-you for the food and decisively taken the head-of-table position when she sat down.

And Paul, every time he'd tried to draw Georgia into a conversation, had been smartly cut off, his annoyed looked burned down by Nicole's simple, unflinching gaze.

No more bullshit, was the simple message. Yes, she'd let her attention to Paul and her marriage slide recently, but that was no longer to be the way of things.

When Georgia finally clattered down her spoon and stood up to start the dishes and Paul began to rise to help, Nicole reached out and lightly touched his arm. He froze and twitched his head around. "What?"

"We'll be heading back to the Hurzgehrmines soon, won't we? I wouldn't want them to worry. Do you need to do anything with the Jeep?"

"I—"

"Warm it up, at least?"

She smiled calmly up at him as she saw the confusion and anger in his eyes, all layered over with pervasive guilt. Her sudden strength had thrown him off-balance. It wouldn't heal the rifts in this marriage of theirs, but before anything else, Nicole had to get Georgia out of the equation. And for that, Nicole needed Paul out of the house.

"Paul?" she said again, more of an order than a question.

Without a word, he stalked from the kitchen and Nicole heard him pulling on his boots and coat.

Nicole nodded to herself, determined to see this through. She saw Georgia watching her fearfully from the sink. The woman knew what was coming. But the children?

April and Auggie were still at the table with Nicole. April was on her right, Auggie on her left. Both were still in their pajamas and didn't want to go get dressed. Ironically, it seemed as if they couldn't bear to leave Nicole. Like they were somehow desperate for her approval.

April caught Nicole's eye and scooped up one of her last red grapes. "This is an eyeball!" she said.

"Yeah, a eyeball!" Auggie said, copying her. "Ah-*um!*" He popped it into his mouth.

April turned her grape back and forth in her spoon. "My eyeball sees you, Auggie."

"Kids," said Georgia nervously. "Y'all don't play with your food."

Auggie scooped up his last two grapes on his spoon and held them across the table towards April. He whispered loudly. "I got *two* eyeballs."

"Auggie!" said Georgia.

"Okay-y-y," Auggie said with a huff and dropped his spoon.

"Hey," whispered April to Nicole. "How do you bust balls?"

Nicole raised her eyebrows at her, but Georgia suddenly fluttered from the sink with her face bright red and her hands all soapy. She lifted April right out of her chair. "Time to go wash hands," she said.

"But—"

"No but's. You too, Auggie. Let our guest finish her breakfast in peace."

"I'm done," Nicole said, smiling as she finally turned 'bust balls' around in her head to become 'ball-buster.' She wondered when, last night or this morning, April had heard her mother say that. About Nicole, probably.

Auggie wasn't obeying. He'd slid out of his chair and grabbed onto Nicole's sleeve, hanging on tight. "I'm not going."

Nicole leaned down close to him, smelling fruit and milk on his breath. Why was he clinging to her, of all people? "You'd better go now, Auggie. Your mother and I need to talk." She straightened up and caught Georgia's eyes. "Right?"

Georgia mouth twitched like a rabbit caught in the headlights. "Um. Right."

The kids scampered off to the bathroom and Nicole stood to face her host.

CHAPTER 77

Ten-fifty-two a.m.

Also on Chickopee Lake Road, the front door of the Hungerford house opened with a slow creak. A warm flow of lemon-scented air rushed out around Marshal Bob Pritchett as he stuck his head in.

He wanted to call out, "Petra?" but bit his tongue. Listened.

There was a distant shuddering *thunk* sound, like a water pump straining to work, again and again.

The loud tick of a wall clock somewhere, probably battery operated.

Nothing else.

The living room directly in front of him was empty. Barely ten by twelve and crammed with furniture. No TV. The door to the kitchen was ahead on the right. That was where the tick of the clock was coming from, Pritchett realized. It looked otherwise empty.

Pritchett had, in fact, seen footsteps heading out from the front door to the far side of the house. But they hadn't been Morris' oversized prints; Morris' came up to the front door then vanished. The other prints were likely those of Petra's husband, Bradley. Had he left before or after Morris had arrived?

And where was Morris?

Pritchett's breath was coming high and quick in his chest and he opened his dry mouth and throat to breathe quieter. He cocked his revolver and held it out straight in front of him, both hands, like they'd practiced at the shooting range.

One step in, quietly. Two. The door stayed open behind him.

Still no sound.

Pritchett swung the gun right. Then left. Stepped ahead. Stopped.

He cleared his throat. "Petra?"

His voice sounded strange in the quiet house, like he was speaking into an empty cave, like he could see himself suddenly from behind, see the hair prickling on the back of his neck.

Tick...tick...tick...tick...

Nothing.

Trying unsuccessfully to swallow, Pritchett sidestepped quickly to the kitchen door and swung his gun up at the ticking clock—square, white, plastic—down around the cupboards, back towards the pantry door and fridge, as if the killer could spring out of there any second.

"Damn," Pritchett whispered quietly, hands shaking. "Damn." Then he turned sideways and quickstepped out of the kitchen, gun raised ahead of him, face sweating so hard now it was starting to drip from his eyebrows and nose. He reached up quickly and wiped it, then grabbed off his black fur hat and dropped it quietly to the floor.

Both hands back on the gun.

He started walking forward in a half crouch, feeling a quivering, crazy feeling zing through his lower gut and butt, like he had to jump up straight and run or he'd collapse into a twitching idiot. He shouldn't have taken this job, damn it. Should have stayed in Grand Junction and—

He froze. A sound.

Something shuffled down the right branch of the hall.

He sniffed and smelled something now too. For a moment he thought it was just the film of blood he'd carried around in his nostrils for the last two hours now, but then he twitched his head back and forth. He could pinpoint which direction it came from. Ahead of him, not behind. One of the bedrooms.

Damn damn damn. He fought the urge to drop his gun and just run ahead into the bedrooms. Because the smell meant he was too late again. That was why it was so quiet. The killer had come, killed Petra, and gone. The sudden picture in his head of what she'd be like, her square, proud body cut up and bloody, made Pritchett's knees wobble, and for a second time he almost dropped the gun.

Sheer fear kept the gun high. Pritchett walked slowly forward, swung his gun, straight-armed, to the left. Two doors there. Looked like a bedroom and a washroom. But the smell was behind him now. The master bedroom.

Pritchett swung back that way, took two short steps forward, and kicked the door open with his foot.

The horror of the bloody bed, the blood-sprayed walls, Bradley's stabbed corpse in the corner, Petra's body tied and spread-eagled on the bed with pieces of flesh cut and hanging from it—it thumped into Pritchett like a pile driver. *Whump!* He stumbled back into the tee of the hall, unable to breathe.

And felt a change in the air behind him.

CHAPTER 78

PRITCHETT WHIRLED AS A THICK, wet arm whipped around his neck and jerked him sideways off his feet. A searing pain slashed across his right hand so the hand spasmed and dropped the revolver. The next pain would be in his gut, he thought, or his back, or across his neck like the other men he'd seen.

But instead the bloody arm around his neck just tightened more until Pritchett couldn't breathe. His legs flailed and his fingers scrabbled at the hands. Then the world started getting red. Redder. Blurry. Gray. He could no longer feel his limbs.

Suddenly the arm dropped away and his lungs sucked in a loud breath of air. Another. Another. Until the world swam back into focus. He'd been pulled back into the tee of the hallway, still upright, held by his arms now. Both were pinned behind him and held by a grip that felt like a bar shoved up across the middle of his back.

Something sharp dug up under his chin. Knife.

"D-don't m-m-m-mmmove," the creature behind him said.

"Morris?"

"D-d-don't."

Pritchett swallowed and the motion made the blade at his throat cut in more. He could feel the blood trickling down inside his collar. Why wasn't he dead?

"Comm-m-muni-c-c-cations," the Morris creature said hotly in his ear. "How m-much reestablished?"

Communications? Pritchett thought frantically. Like what? Radio. Phone. Of course. Morris needed to know if Pritchett had called the outside world and told them what was happening. And for the first time he remembered the smart-ass Jewish boy. Wondered if he'd gotten through. "Um...," Pritchett said. "I...uh..."

The knife came away from his throat and Pritchett suddenly felt like someone had grabbed his left ear and *ripped it off!* Pritchett screamed and looked left. Screamed louder as he saw the u-shaped piece of flesh flop off his shoulder and down to the carpet.

A bloody fist the size of a grapefruit slammed back against his mouth, stopping the scream. Then the fist drew back, revealing the gore-slick black knife it held. The knife twitched back and forth in front of Pritchett's eyes.

"T-tell," said the voice by his ear.

Mesmerized, Pritchett didn't see the other black shape that had entered the house until it was all the way into the living room with its double-barrel shotgun raised and pointed straight at Pritchett's face. Carl Dolk, father of slain Mindy Dolk, held the gun. He must've seen Mindy and followed the trail like Pritchett had done.

Dolk's face was hard as hard. "You drop the knife," he said evenly.

The big creature holding Pritchett from behind twitched in one big spasm and Pritchett closed his eyes. Then, deciding he wanted to have his head neither blown apart nor sliced off, Pritchett suddenly ducked and twisted to the side.

Morris flung himself sideways too as the shotgun boomed.

When Pritchett twisted up from the floor, he clutched the bloody pulp on the left side of his head and his back burned with the smell of gunpowder. Morris was gone from the hallway. A thumping and crash of glass shattering located him. He was back in one of the bedrooms. Escaping.

Pritchett looked up at Dolk. The big Swede was standing shocked, swaying. "I hit him," he said. "The shoulder."

"Well don't just stand there!" Pritchett shouted up at him. "*Get* the bastard!"

Dolk nodded and pump-loaded his gun.

CHAPTER 79

MOMENTS BEFORE THE SHOT SOUNDED, Paul had been thrashing the last of the snow off the rented Jeep Grand Cherokee and feeling guilty as hell.

What *if*, his thoughts had run, he just divorced Nicole? Now, before they had kids.

Before this trip, he'd always been able to slough off her temper tantrums and mood swings as just part of the package you got when you married a "difficult" woman. She was highly intelligent and sensitive and had a wicked sense of humor. Not to mention the fact she was beautiful in a dark, intense sort of way, and could be sexy as hell when aroused.

Paul's mouth twitched up as he remembered yesterday's lovemaking. That was the sort of sex you only got when you married a woman with grit.

Then his smile fell as the rest came rushing back. It wasn't just the Hurzgehrmines. It was all this last year. First the MacMartin case shook her confidence. Then her mother got diagnosed with emphysema. The two together had seemed to intensify every down, self-flagellating, nasty impulse Nicole carried in her. She'd been short-tempered and forgetful with clients, insulting to opposing counsel, impossible to live with as a wife.

And the death of Nicole's mom didn't seem to have helped. One wild morning of sex didn't change the way she'd withdrawn into herself, as if everyone and everything around her was a threat.

Christ. This was the woman Paul wanted to be the mother of his children?

He fished the Jeep keys out of his pocket and stuck them into the driver's side door keyhole. He paused and leaned his head into the door of the Jeep and let the remaining snow there cool the fire in his head. Closing his eyes for a second, he imagined what it would be like to come home to Georgia. To her soft voice, soft sweet body. She was a delicate thing who'd obviously had her own share of traumas, but her reaction was to reach out for support. Paul could handle that. And her kids obviously loved her to bits. Paul could handle that too. If only...

A distant scream registered subconsciously and his eyes opened. Blinked.

The boom shot his head up from the car. Shouts. Shattering glass.

He knew those sounds. Unlike Nicole and her childhood bouncing between small town New York and posh Philadelphia, Paul had spent most of his life in and around D.C. as the member of a visible minority. You couldn't *not* recognize the sound of gunfire and mayhem.

He spun to his left and looked up the snowed-in street in the direction of the sound. He heard someone, maybe the same man who'd screamed earlier, shout something.

The houses along Chickopee Lake Road, at least this end of it, were less well-to-do than the ones on Lift. Most of the Chickopee Lake homes were bungalows, some were converted mobile homes, each on its own little chunk of property wi th the occasional aspen or pine tree, and the lawns along the fronts seemed to roll in little humps between the driveways, especially now that every-thing was a uniform, icing-sugar white.

It made it easy to spot the source of disturbance.

There! Just three houses down, a man was tearing out the front of the house, clutching the side of his head with one hand, waving a revolver with the other.

Another boom.

"Run after him!" the man screamed to someone at the back of the house. "Run!" And the screaming man himself ran, plowing desperately through the snow to the road to follow the tire tracks Paul had made last night with the Jeep. The man—Paul could now see he wore a policeman's coat and a badge. Was he a sheriff?—was running in Paul's direction, swinging his gun towards the houses to Paul's left, Paul's side of the street, trying to get a bead on someone.

Another boom from behind the houses.

And it finally clicked in Paul's brain that this awkward, stumbling violence —the bloody sheriff, his shotgun-firing partner, and whomever they were chasing—was coming toward him. Him and Nicole and Georgia and the kids.

Paul, grown soft from years of living in the quiet Maryland suburbs, finally kicked into gear and ran for the front door of Georgia's house.

It was barely a fifteen foot sprint, just enough to consider the possibilities:

1) The violence would pass them by. Hit the other backyards.

2) The runner would launch itself at Georgia's house but be cut down before he got in...

The sound of splintering wood and the crash and clatter of glass said someone was trying to get in through Georgia's back door.

Paul reached the front door and jerked it open. Could see through the living room to the right rear corner of the kitchen, the back door. The door's glass had been smashed in. Glass shards lay all over the floor and the top of the stove. The kids stood huddled against the stove there, staring into the rest of the kitchen, terrified.

Paul ran across the living room to the kitchen opening and...

Oh, holy shit.

CHAPTER 80

Paul froze.

Violence incarnate stood just left of the stove, between the kitchen sink and the breakfast table. He was a giant of a man who looked like he'd tried for camouflage. He wore hiking boots, soaked brown ski pants, and a bloody poplin shirt covered by an equally bloody green down vest. His head was balding and spattered all over with blood. He stank of it. It dripped from his open mouth like he'd been chewing on fresh kill.

And though his right shoulder looked chewed apart and bloody—Paul smelled acrid gunshot—his left arm was still wrapped around Georgia's throat, almost as if he was supporting himself there. His right hand held a long black blade under Georgia's ribcage. Both the man and Georgia were taking short, wide-eyed little gasps. *Huh...huh...huh...*

But Georgia's eyes found Paul's and shot a pleading look to her left, to where April and Auggie stood shaking against he stove.

"D-d-don't m-mmove," the madman said. His eyes were darting around the kitchen wildly, like he remembered this place and it scared him.

Back against the fridge that was at right angles to the kitchen counter and drawers, Nicole cowered in her white turtleneck, her face half-hidden by her hair. The one dark eye Paul could see, though, was burning as her hands blindly clawed around on the counter to her right. Searching for a knife.

Paul shook his head at her and her eye shot hatred back.

Why, Paul thought, couldn't the madman have grabbed *her* instead of Georgia? Then he blushed so hard at the thought that he felt chilled to the core.

"All right," he said calmly, licking dry lips. "All right. We're not moving. What d—

"Drop it!" shouted a new voice.

Paul's head twitched right to see another man at the smashed-in kitchen door. He was shorter, blocky in a thick overcoat. He held a pump-action shotgun raised to his shoulder, sighting along the barrel over the children's heads to target Georgia and the madman.

"This time you do it," the man in the overcoat said, his words squeezed with an accent Paul couldn't place, "You drop the knife or I shoot you dead."

For a second it looked like the big man was going to laugh, but then he said, "O...kay," slowly.

Keeping his arm around Georgia's neck, the bloody man slowly eased the knife away from her chest and dropped it on the floor by his feet. Auggie and April both startled as it clattered in front of them.

The shotgun man nodded. "Now let the woman go."

"Yeah. Sh-sh-sure." The big man leaned forward and eased his left arm down. Then, before anyone could react, the left arm yanked Georgia back as the madman's right hand grabbed April's hair, lifting the girl like a rag doll and hovering her screaming face inches above the glass shards on the stove top.

"Mommy!" April wriggled and kicked her legs but the big man's hand in her hair had her clamped securely.

"N-n-n-now! *Y-you* put down your g-g-gun or I'll g-grind her face!"

"Mommy!"

"Please don't," Georgia sobbed then gagged as the arm around her neck tightened.

The shotgun man wavered. There was a movement from Paul's left. And suddenly Nicole had leaped onto the big man's back, her hands wrapped around his eyes, pulling back hard.

The big man stumbled back but his face was too slick with blood. Paul watched with horror as Nicole's hands slipped and she fell backwards. The man released Georgia to regain his balance, and, with a roar, threw the little girl and himself at the shotgun man. The shotgun swung up just before April hit. Almost simultaneously, the bloody hands of the Violence Incarnate wrenched the gun from the shotgun man's grip and shoved the man and girl out the door into the snow.

The shotgun came up.

The man who'd just been thrown saw it and rolled to cover April as the gun fired. At a range of under four feet, the gunshot tore through the man's back like an explosive lawnmower, ripping through the cloth coat and flesh and spreading gore in a chunky spray over the snow beyond.

"April!"

It was Georgia, scrabbling up madly to her feet, hands to her face, ready to dive past the shell-shocked Auggie and out into the snow. But the mad giant with the shotgun turned on her now, pump-loading the shotgun with the jerk of one hand.

Paul leapt forward, grabbed her and Auggie, and dragged them both to the floor. In a mad scramble, he tried to cover them with his body like the man in the snow had covered April, expecting any second to feel the explosion in his back, tensing for it, whipping through a million frames of his life in a second, sick with fear, clench and shudder, come one, come on…

There was silence.

Paul jerked up his head just in time to see the killer looking down at where Nicole had fallen by the counters. The bloody man seemed to choke back a sob. "Suh-Sarah?"

"What?" said Nicole

"Sarah. It's m-m-me. Your brother. Japhet."

CHAPTER 81

Nicole was half-hidden from Paul by the overturned kitchen chairs, but he could have sworn he saw some kind of horrified recognition in her eyes at the killer's words.

Then the lawman Paul had seen outside suddenly hurtled into the kitchen with his gun out before him in both hands.

"Freeze!" he shouted, and wobbled back against the wall. His face was white, eyes glassy, and Paul automatically saw why. The left side of his head that he'd been holding was an open pulp of flesh, still streaming.

How much blood had the man lost?

Too much, apparently. The lawman's head suddenly lolled and he slid to the floor.

When Paul turned back towards the killer, he saw the man had pushed Nicole up against the cupboards at the end of the kitchen. His bloody left hand held her there by her black hair. His right hand held the shotgun up to her belly. But his blood-smeared face had dropped into almost childish wonder as his nose hovered inches in front of Nicole's own.

Like he's trying to look into her soul.

And rather than whimpering, Nicole had adopted an absolute calm, returning the killer's look and talking to him as if her were a frightened animal.

"...your sister, then you want to put down the gun, don't you? You want to let me go so we can talk about it, figure out if it's really true. So just slowly let me go. Put down the gun. We'll talk. Okay? You can tell me where you've been, what you remember, who..."

As she talked, Paul slowly rolled off Georgia and Auggie, who wisely lay perfectly still. Paul slid away from the killer and around the legs of the kitchen table to the revolver the unconscious sheriff still held in both hands. Slowly peeling the man's fingers off the handgun, Paul tugged it free, then crept back around the table legs, moving slowly on all fours.

He froze as the monster holding Nicole spoke. "Y-you sent letters to me. In C-C-California. Y-you did."

"No. That wasn't me." Nicole still calmly held the eyes of the blank-faced monster. Japhet, he'd called himself. "But I'd like to see the letters. Maybe you could put me down and show them to me."

There was a growing tightness in her voice now, like she was giving up hope that Japhet would respond. Like she needed someone else to do something. Needed Paul to act.

"Then they w-w-*were* from Mama. And you sent me the l-l-last one. D-different writing."

Paul felt a chill as the words seeped through and his gaze whipped back to the rear of Georgia's dyed blond head. A letter from Mama. Georgia had told him that she'd come back to Goldrock because someone had sent her a letter. Was it possible…?

"Paul?"

He almost didn't hear it, delivered as it was with exactly the same forced calm the rest of Nicole's words had been. Nicole said it a second time.

"Paul."

He looked up at her wide-eyed, to find her still holding the madman's eyes, trying to stop the odd jerking his head was doing by force of her own calm. Speaking calmly to the man's face though her words weren't for him.

"Paul, I think if you don't do something soon, I'm going to be dead. Please do something now."

The lawman's revolver was hot and sticky with blood and sweat in Paul's hand. It seemed to weigh a thousand pounds. He could just raise it now. It was probably dual-action. You cocked it by pulling the trigger halfway. He'd aim at the madman and…maybe hit Nicole?

Or should he offer up Georgia instead?

Fingers shaking with the effort, he slowly pushed himself up on his knees, raised the revolver, and called out to his wife.

CHAPTER 82

Ari ran with great, leaping steps through the snow.

Crossing Main Street, he'd heard shouts from the Grenadine and almost gone there. But then he'd seen Wendy outside the front door, held tightly in her father's arms, the shouts coming from others, some running up with guns in their hands. Rifles, shotguns, handguns. Some of the armed men had grim faces; some, excited; some, full of visceral hate.

Ari had known instantly what it meant. Bone's aftermath. He'd struck again, as FBI Agent Clarke had said he would. And the people of the town were responding. But too late. Too slow. And they didn't know where Bone was going, like Ari did.

So he'd kept going for there, rather than the Grenadine.

And he'd heard the rifle shot down Chickopee Lake Road a ways over to his right. Yells. Shattering glass. More shouts and gunshots. Yells. Splintering wood and glass. A moment later someone yelling, "Drop it!" Another pause. Then more crashing and a gunshot.

Bone was there.

Not sure whether he was drawn by the need to help Nicole Baker, or to merely see the Goldrock Freak killed, Ari changed course and headed through the back yards towards the sound.

There! He saw a large body on the snow thirty yards over, clearly dead. And what looked like Pritchett heading into the house through its back door.

"Freeze!" came Pritchett's voice, but was followed by silence, not a shot. What was happening!

As Ari waded through a sudden dip in the yards, he heard a child crying and saw a girl trying to crawl out from under the dead man in the snow.

God.

Ari plowed out of the drift and wavered for just a moment, snow up to his knees, torn between his instinct to run and help, and sheer terror that he might end up as dead as the body the girl struggled out from under.

Then he heard a man shout, "Nicole, duck!" and Ari made up his mind.

He plunged as fast as he could for the bungalow's back door.

CHAPTER 83

THE .38 in Paul's hand bucked back as he shot, making Paul blink. But he thought he'd hit his target—he was only four feet away—winging him across the back of his head.

It didn't help.

The monster roared, but only, it seemed, in annoyance. Jerking Nicole upright by her hair, Japhet swung her around in front of him and clutched her also with the arm that held the shotgun.

Paul heard Nicole grunt in pain. Then she caught Paul's eyes as he stood, gun still held up, shaking, in front of him.

"Shoot again, Paul." Nicole's voice was cracking at the edges.

"I can't. I'll hit you."

"Don't let him take me."

"Nicki..."

The monster swung out the arm holding the shotgun and Paul, in one of those moments where time slows, remembered a childhood buddy enthusing once about shotguns. How the Ithaca 12-gauge was the most popular pump action gun. Blow a man's head right off at four feet. Police versions held eight shells. Public versions were only supposed to hold five, unless you jimmied them. And Paul mentally counted the shots he'd heard outside. One before he saw the men running, then three more en route to the house, then the one the killer had used on the man outside in the snow. Which meant the gun should be empty. Unless it was jimmied, or a police version, or...

Click.

"Please don't let him take me."

Paul hardly heard her. His body was covered with a chill sweat, his head floating. The revolver weaved in the air in front of him. Heavy. Slick "I..."

"Paul." Nicole's voice cracked. "I love you."

Then she was jerked backwards as the monster threw the empty shotgun at Paul and pulled his captive out of the kitchen and into the living room.

Paul snapped back to earth as he deflected the shotgun and jumped up in time to hear the front door slam. Where would they go? Where in this snow would...?

Oh, goddamn. The Jeep. He'd left the keys hanging in the door of the rented Jeep Grand Cherokee like an open invitation.

Sprinting around the kitchen table, he ran from the kitchen to the front door and pulled it open just in time to see the Jeep start up with a roar, and back up, snow spitting forward from under chains on the wheels.

"Nooooo!" Paul ran out after it, thumping his left hand on the hood as it reached the rear of the driveway. Then the bloody monster at the steering wheel shifted gears and Paul leapt to one side avoid being run over.

The gun, Paul thought even as he jumped. He still held it clutched in his right hand. He rolled up to his knees and aimed. The right rear tire of the Jeep was spinning forward only a foot from him. Paul pulled the trigger.

Click.

Again. Click. Again. Click.

"God-dammit!" he yelled and threw the empty weapon at the accelerating vehicle. Now what? Run? Chase it? And do what if he caught it?

Then he remembered the cop in the house. Maybe he had more ammo. And the shotgun. Maybe the dead man outside had more shells. It wasn't like the monster with Nicole could get out of Goldrock, snow chains or no.

Gasping, Paul ran down the road to retrieve the revolver he'd thrown, then turned and sprinted back to the house, into the kitchen.

A teenage boy was there, hands and front smeared with blood. He was lifting Georgia up from the floor. A large red stain was spreading across her lower abdomen from a short, diagonal gash that seemed to get redder and deeper as Paul watched. Georgia's face was white and lifeless.

"Wha...?"

The boy's eyes looked up into his, scared. "I think she fell on that knife." He pointed to the black weapon Japhet had used coming in. "Bounced it? I don't know. It was under her. She's still alive though."

Alive. Yes. Paul knelt down beside her and could see the twitching rise and fall of her chest now. "Her kids?" He didn't see Auggie. Couldn't bear to look for him.

"They're hers? Jeez. I helped the little girl out from under the man outside.

Her brother's with her. Neither one will speak. Shock, I think. The marshal's still breathing too."

Marshal. Law. Bullets. Paul was going to get the law man's bullets. But if Georgia was bleeding, he had to help her.

"Someone called out 'Nicole,'" said the boy. "Where is she?"

"I... Outside." Paul waved his hand that way.

"You're her husband?"

Paul nodded. "Man took her, took the Jeep. Heading north. I was going to...follow, but..."

The boy was nodding his head. "He's freaking out and going for the old Warsaw trail."

"What?"

"An old mining road up between Warsaw and Gomel on the north side of town. Impassable, I'm sure. But Bone—the bad guy's name is Japhet Bone—grew up here. He'd know about it."

"Goddamn." Paul tugged his gloves out of his pockets and began tugging them on.

"What? You're going to *run* after them?" The kid had turned from him in what looked like disgust, tugging a dishtowel from the rack near the sink to ball up and press over the wound on Georgia's belly.

"I can see the lifts from here. Not far. And even with chains, the Jeep's going to get bogged down. Half a mile tops."

The kid looked up at him. He had a Jewish nose, wiry dark hair pulled back behind him in a ponytail that made him look silly. But his eyes looked at Paul like they were judging him. Figuring if he had what it took. "Okay. If you reach the ski hill," the kid said carefully, "check the big shed to the left of the chair lift. They used to keep a Snowcat in there for rescue and grooming the hills. Keys are to the right of the door."

"You'll..."

"Look after the woman and kids. Sure. Go." The kid tried a confident laugh. It came out sounding hollow.

Paul nodded and leaned forward over Georgia's pale face. He smoothed back her blond curls and kissed her once, softly, on the lips.

The Jewish kid flinched. "You *are* Nicole's husband, right?"

Paul nodded again and pulled back from Georgia's softness.

"So don't you think you should go rescue your wife?"

Paul quirked his head at him, too full inside to respond other than to nod a third time. He got up and went to see if the dead man outside had some shotgun shells in his coat.

CHAPTER 84

Ari watched Nicole's husband stroll casually out the back door and heard him thumping about outside in the snow. Then he was back inside and rooting through the marshal's pistol holster for bullets.

Ari wanted to grab him, say, "You stay here and *I'll* go after Nicole." This man was a total loss.

Then the blond woman in Ari's arm jerked a little and Ari came back to the situation at hand. He had to get her up and out of here. The kids, too. They were in their pajamas and slippers and standing out there in the snow beside a dead man. What was Ari thinking?

Nicole's husband left out the front door with the pistol tucked into his coat pocket and the shotgun clutched in his right hand.

Ari looked around for something to hold the balled-up dishcloth against the blond woman's stomach. He couldn't see anything so finally just lay her on her back and dashed out to the back where he'd helped pull the little girl out from under the dead man. The girl and her brother were standing together in the snow, shivering hard.

"Hey, guys."

No response. They didn't even look at him. And their faces were white, probably going into or already in shock. But they were still shivering. That was good, wasn't it?

"Okay, you two, we have to get inside. Get some coats on. Your mom needs help."

He had to physically grab each kid by an arm and march them inside, into the kitchen that stank of blood and gunpowder and death. But once there, Ari saw the girl's face twitch toward her bloody and unconscious mother, so Ari kept marching them forward, into the living room. There he stopped, swaying a bit, overwhelmed. He had to get the kids dressed and out of here before they passed out or something. But if he left their mother in the kitchen, she could easily bleed to death. And the marshal against the wall—Ari had seen that he was still breathing, but whatever had been done to the side of his head might mean he was dying to.

Which was most urgent?

He bit his lips then squatted down in front of the kids. "Okay, look, you two. I've got to go back to the kitchen to help some people. You guys stay right here, okay? Right here."

Again no response. Their eyes looked dull and glazed, but the little boy's teeth started to chatter.

Ari looked around, saw a couple of kids' coats hung on a row of little pegs beside the front door, and jumped over to grab them. He forced the bigger one onto the little girl, the smaller one onto the boy. It was like dressing floppy mannequins. Then he zipped them up. He saw and grabbed two snow hats and stuck those on them. At least they wouldn't die of hypothermia while he helped their mother.

Leaving them like little bundled statues in the living room, Ari sprinted back for the kitchen. The small cloth he'd stuck over the blond woman's wound was so soaked with blood that for a moment Ari thought her it was her entrails, somehow pumped out of the gash in her belly.

He swallowed sickly as his vision corrected, and he knelt down beside her. One knee hit the knife, the big black honking knife that she'd had fallen on, and he grabbed it to chuck it out of the way.

At that moment there was a crash at the kitchen's smashed door and Ari looked up to see two men in heavy cloth overcoats. One was sucking in his lips hard as he looked at Ari. The other, his handlebar mustache quivering with fury under his Stetson, was Al Rawley.

Ari dropped the bloody knife beside the woman's bloody body.

"Oh, shit," he said.

CHAPTER 85

INSIDE THE JEEP clanking and lurching slowly across a cup between two mountains, the frozen Chickopee Lake below on her right, Nicole gripped the dash and door handhold and stared straight ahead.

Paul had failed her.

But she was going to get out. This wasn't even a question. She could feel the lump growing on her forehead where her driver had smashed her when she'd tried to escape earlier. He'd seatbelted her in, too, more to slow her movements, probably, than for her protection. Didn't matter. Next escape attempt, she was going to punch the torn-up mush of his right shoulder first. Then she'd go for his eyes, hit the unlock for all the doors, open the driver's side door, and shove him out.

He just had to let down his guard.

The snow in her slippers and up her legs had melted—the Jeep's heater had been blowing the stink of blood and buckshot around the cab for awhile now—but Nicole shivered. All she had on up top was her white turtleneck, smeared with blood.

The Jeep lurched off the old mining road—it was barely visible as an indentation in the snow—and powder sprayed up over the hood. Nicole's captor yanked the steering wheel and floored the pedal. The engine roared. The wheels spun.

And even as Nicole watched the muscles bunch in Japhet's big arms and gut, she felt the seat dropping backwards under her and the ground tilting—*uhrrr-rrrrr!*—she had that flash of memory again—a boy chasing her up the hillside. This boy, now a man? And she'd fallen...

The wheels bit and pulled them back on track, the shoulder belt cutting a little into her neck as the Jeep lurched.

She couldn't do this. Couldn't lose her cool. She had to find something else to focus on. Something hard. Involving.

Like what had gone wrong with Paul.

Yes! Figure it out.

Second year law school.

That was the year she'd met Paul. He'd come into Harvard as a laid-back transfer student and stuck out in a class that was ninety-nine percent uptight and white. Most of Nicole's friends assumed he was East Indian. Nicole, brooding and dark by nature, had laughed with them, sharing their put-downs of him, their ridicule of the fact he hadn't been admitted to Harvard Law's first year but had only come in on some sort of affirmative action balancing.

"Fug," growled the monster beside her, which spurred another flash of...something. Nicole gritted her teeth harder.

Law school.

Her law school friends had been wrong. Paul was of Arabian descent, mixed-blood, fourth generation American, determinedly non-religious, and had grown up in one of the rougher areas of D.C. He'd gotten out with a laser-focused positive attitude that made him the first member of his family to attend university. He'd also been admitted to first year at Harvard but hadn't had the funds to attend. So he'd taken a year off to work two full-time jobs, wangle two scholarships, *and* convince the law school to let him in on an accelerated basis.

All of which he divulged to Nicole after getting teamed with her for a mooting competition. It nonplused her. What? Was he trying to impress her?

The Jeep slewed around almost perpendicular to the hill and Nicole took a terrified gasp. As soon as the Jeep was in control again...

Paul. Paul Kesin. He ran deep. The longer Nicole knew him in law school, the more intimidating he became. But somehow she opened up to him anyway. After nine months of increasingly intense discussions, they had sex. A month later, they were engaged. But even as they said their vows, Nicole shook inside, wondering what would happen when he finally discovered how petty and cold she truly was?

Now she knew.

The Jeep jolted hard as its chained wheels found the track but slurred sideways again as the hardpack broke—cold snow, spring snow, then the powder of the last two days on top. Horribly unstable. Nicole's eyes flew open and looked involuntarily to the right and back. Downslope. Her stomach flipped again.

Jesus, her captor might have chosen this escape route because he was afraid of roadblocks or pursuit up the real road out of town, but the mountains them-selves... *Don't get dead*, that young Hertz guy had said.

She cleared her throat.

"Shut up," her captor said.

They'd reached the far side and another of the faded red posts that marked a switchback . Circling slowly around it upslope, her captor squinted forward over the wheel to pick out the next higher indented line in the snow.

How long had they been climbing? Twenty minutes? Forty? They were so high that Chickopee Lake down to her left looked like a dull silver dollar. Goldrock was like those teeny towns in the glass balls filled with water and soap flakes.

"Wh-what do you remm-member from your childhood here?" Japhet asked suddenly.

Nicole blinked at him and decided it was finally time to face these unex-pected flashes of memories. Maybe they'd throw him off balance.

"I remember," she said slowly, "not having a father."

Japhet's eyes whipped towards her in triumph. "Yes! The p-prick left us when you were born."

"I also don't recall having a brother."

The creature wagged his head and snickered, sending blood drops winging out of his hair to the dashboard, the seat, and Nicole's pants. "Y-you don't remember because th-they sent me away. S-scared of me."

And then gave up her daughter for adoption too? Why? To protect her? Or to forget her? Expunge her? Nicole could feel her captor waiting for her to ask, eager for her to ask. But strangely, Nicole didn't sense it was out of wanting to control her. It was a real need, desperate almost. As if somewhere inside this brute, a damaged being was crying out for help.

To a woman who, even *in extremis* felt pathologically compelled to listen. "I could help you," she said and swallowed thickly. "Let me help you turn yourself in."

"Y-yeah?" The monster turned and grinned at her with his lips pulled back. Then he spat blood into her face and hooted, slamming a thick hand on the steering wheel.

Nicole grit her teeth. "Fuck you, then."

"Th-th-th-that's what Mama was always afraid I'd do to you." He reached for her, grabbing the front of her turtleneck.

The Jeep lurched. Nicole looked through the front windshield to see the semi-buried top of another marker pole they'd been plowing towards. They were almost on top of it.

"Turn!" she yelled. "The marker!"

Japhet's hand flew back to the wheel too late.

With a jolt, the Jeep passed the marker and lurched down to the left. Japhet yelled and spun the wheel right, gunning the engine. The chained wheels spun, whirring and clanking, trying to find purchase.

Then the Jeep tilted back to Nicole's left and went over.

CHAPTER 86

As THE JEEP crashed back and kept going, Nicole was thrown first against her shoulder seatbelt, then the side. She grabbed frantically for the dash and door grip, her blood rushing into her head as her world flipped end over end in sickening crunches. The windshield cracked. On the next hit, it burst inward in a thousand rounded beads. The right side windows followed. A huge ice chunk from somewhere rammed through the open windshield as they went, slamming Nicole's left shoulder back to her seat and pinning it.

Her head snapped sideways into the ice chunk. The left windows shattered in beads. Her head bounced back. Suddenly the ice chunk was gone, torn free of the open windshield, and the Jeep seemed airborne. The snow, the mountainside, was...under them? It must have been a dip in the hill, the Jeep aloft. Which meant it had to come...

Down.

It hit on the left rear corner of the roof, seemed to ski for a moment in that ridiculous balance, then whumped onto its left side and slid to a rest, facing upslope, snow chunks and ice tumbling to a pile-up all around the hood and windshield.

Stopped.

Still.

Nicole hung suspended on the high side of the interior.

A bashed-out grille from one of the heating vents clattered down to the driver's side door.

Still again.

Nicole blinked, dazed but breathing, her face and body flushed, her heart pounding so hard she thought it would explode out her ears. As she squirmed her body, she fell half out of her seatbelt so that her nose slid down to press against Japhet's unmoving chest. He hadn't been belted in but his huge body must have been pinned behind the wheel.

Nicole grabbed the bent steering wheel with her right hand and felt her left hand slide into something hot, wet, and chunky. She pushed up and looked. Her hand was in Japhet Bone's unmoving shoulder – chewed flesh, shotgun pellets, and bone.

Too dazed to be sick, she simply slid it back to his arm and kept pushing. She realized she had to slide her feet out from under the dash first and almost panicked. She couldn't move her feet! Then she figured out it was just her ankles, pinned by the pushed-in side panel.

With a grunt and a scrape of her socks sliding out of the soaked slippers she'd "borrowed" from Georgia Hurzgehrmine this morning, Nicole managed to work her feet loose. She pulled them up to her chest with a cry and spun them sideways and down, so she was virtually standing in her wet blue socks on Bone's body and the snow that had pushed up and in through the shattered driver's side window.

Hastily wiping the man's gore off her left hand, she undid the seatbelt's lap portion that now cinched up diagonally across the abdomen like a crazy parachute harness.

Trickles of snow fell in across her legs and she looked up through the smashed-out windshield. She could see little past the snow-pile just outside, but could almost feel it shifting down towards her, like it wanted *in*.

She fumbled with her seatbelt button. When it released, she dropped awkwardly down onto Japhet, her knees weak, her whole body trembling. The Jeep frame creaked and shifted, making her freeze in panic. But it stopped moving and she breathed again in little gasps.

Should check...if he's...alive.

But she couldn't. She just wanted to get out.

Pushing up with a cry of pain—something hard must have hit her in the side; her neck was stiff; her feet were raw—she brushed at the beads of windshield glass that covered her and felt sharp pricks in her hands. Her skin was too vulnerable. The snow outside. She'd never make it.

Forcing herself to bend down again, she tried reaching Japhet's feet for his boots. But the legs were hopelessly jammed under the steering column with a black-bladed shovel that had somehow tumbled down there during the crash. And not cut their heads off? Jesus.

With a quick sob at the blood smell—hers or Japhet's?—she rooted around further up the footwell and finally found the slippers she'd pulled out of only moments earlier. They were wet woolen lumps. They wouldn't stay on her feet. She pulled them onto her hands as mittens.

Now...Japhet's jacket?

Balls of snow bounced hard across the Jeep's hood out of sight out there, then some of the blocking snow pile shifted and tumbled in across the dashboard.

Nicole's head shot up. Oh, God. No time.

She looked at the stuck shovel and nearly screamed as Japhet suddenly grunted and rolled his head. She whirled and scrambled up through the windshield opening, pushing and clawing at the snow piled there until she was past it and out. Then she turned and furiously kicked at the chunks until a mini-landslide of them rushed into the front of the Jeep, burying Japhet inside.

She sobbed once, choked it back, and slid down off the hood to fall sideways into the snow. Picking herself up, she began wading, hip-deep, downslope and right among rolling pieces of snow. Too slow. Too slow. Her feet were going numb. Her breath came out in ragged gasps.

She stopped twenty yards down, snow up to her hips, teeth chattering, and looked back at the blown-out Jeep. It wasn't tipping after all, but with its crumpled hood, smashed in door and roof, it look even worse off than her. "Glad we opted for comprehensive," she managed and almost threw up.

Turning back downslope, she was suddenly overwhelmed by how far up she was, and how little time her body would give her.

More snow rolled past.

Then, from somewhere far off, she heard the full-throated roar of a tractor-style machine. Someone on the slopes? Rescue!

But even as she opened her mouth to call out, still more snow rolled past. Big chunks, thumping down like the Jeep had thunked down, tumbling end over end. And a clank and grunt from the Jeep sounded behind her.

"Oh, no," she breathed, and turned to look.

One bloody hand was reaching slowly out around the roof of the Jeep. How? *How?*

Then she saw the hand retreat and the black tip of the shovel come out. Digging. Unwilling to die.

Nicole stood fixed in shock as the shovel widened its hole. Another minute and he'd be free. He'd be after her.

The mountain decided enough was enough.

Layers of light and heavy snow. Gully between two mountains. Spring.

The hundred little trickles of snow and rolling ice chunks began to multiply furiously. Then a huge crack sounded from high up the slope and reverberated off the surrounding peaks. Up near the gully top that Bone had been trying to reach, Nicole saw a three hundred foot, jagged line appear, widen, then suddenly release like a skeleton dropping its lower jaw.

It turned to powdering white that billowed high into the air, and the rumble of its fall did not fade but instead became a cascading roar that grew louder by the second until her entire being shook with it.

Nicole turned downslope and began to run, flinging her body in great, leaping steps down the slope diagonally to the right. How far to the edge of the gully? Thirty feet? Forty? Maybe she should have run left. But the town was this way. The tractor sound she'd heard was this way.

Leap, feet. Throw them forward. Bounce. Don't fall. Hands and feet ice. Cold wind whuffling against the back of her head like Death trying to blow her over. Harder. Don't look back. *Run*.

Then the ground itself seemed to turn liquid and the air a roaring white around her as she was lifted...

A part of Nicole flashed to her intubated mother on the white hospital bedsheets those last weeks. *I'm already an angel, Nicki*, her mother had croaked more than once. *See? I can fly*. And she'd flapped her sheets and closed her eyes in bliss.

Nicole closed her eyes and spread out her arms.

...until she was horizontal in the whiteness. The coldness of heaven. So loud it was no sound at all.

See? I can fly.

Then a core of her that was much stronger than her mother bit into the bliss and told her to *try*, goddamn it. To swim the tide of death. Try to stay up. Stay near the surface. Stay *up*.

That core screamed silently as Nicole felt her body being turned upside down, ice crystals pounding hard against her exposed face.

She went end over end.

CHAPTER 87

A FEW MINUTES before the loud cracking sound, Josh Noony was sitting in one of the red velvet chairs of the crowded Grenadine lobby, clutching the folder Ari-dad had given him and trying hard to fade into the wallpaper.

What was in this folder was insane. But from the panic dancing all around in here—rednecks swinging around rifles and shotguns, hotshot younger dudes cocking and uncocking pistols, a posse of twelve or fourteen men bursting out twenty minutes ago—Josh was shitting himself thinking it was probably all true.

Wendy Severin had found something in Mack Morris' room, the buzz went. Enough to hide Wendy back in her room with the town doctor.

No one in to see her. No passing of messages.

Josh swiped at the sweat on his forehead, licked dry lips, and tugged back his ponytail. If this Wendy-babe didn't come out soon, Josh was going to have to slide on out of here. Guns made him nervous. 'Specially when they were being swung around by a bunch of hyped-up country dudes who were probably pissed off at every rich outsider who came in to throw down bills and ride their hills.

As if on cue, a beefy-looking buzz-cutter who looked college age but too stupid for college, snarfed over his way and stood just in front of Josh. *Aw, shit.*

"What's in the folder?" buzz-cut said, trying to sound casual. Except he held a hunting rifle in his left hand and had a vertical scar on his chin like he was used to fighting.

"Private stuff," Josh said. The dude's football buddies now crowded round the chair too.

"Private like downloaded homo pictures? Or private like a pretty high school resume?"

"Private."

"Show me." The scar-dude reached down for it.

"Fuck off, butt wad."

There was the *kuhchick-chick* of multiple guns cocking and Josh eyes flicked around at the faces aiming guns at him. Hands clammy and mouth sour, he handed over the file on Bone. Buzz cut took it, opened it, and began reading, then flipping through the pages. He finally stopped and looked at Josh, his face scared and ugly.

"How'd you get this?"

Josh couldn't help himself. "Colorado Tourist Bureau."

Buzz cut's scar went red and he shoved his rifle barrel hard into Josh's chest. "You think this is funny? You think it's funny, people getting cut up dead? I'll tell you funny. You're the killer or the person helping him."

Josh shoved the rifle barrel aside. "Right. I'm Japhet Bone? I'm just real short when I sit down?"

"You could be copycatting." Buzz cut waved the file. "That's why you got this."

Josh looked around, incredulous. "Oh, give me a—"

He was cut off by one of the front lobby doors slamming open. The big posse leader from earlier stood there, his gun half-raised in triumph. Brushing off the bottom of his sheepskin coat, he swung his Stetsoned head around to encompass the whole room and announced, "We got him."

The room exploded into cheers and whistles, but buzz cut still kept his bulk almost straddling Josh. "What's he look like, Al?" he called.

The posse leader smiled behind his handlebar mustache in a way that made Josh think he didn't smile often. "The Jew boy," he said. "Ari Siegel."

"*What?*" Josh yelled, jumping up and shoving buzz cut backwards to stomp to the posse leader. "That's insane! That's totally stupid!"

"He had a folder on Japhet Bone!" buzz-cut suddenly cried from behind Josh. The entire crowd of men in the lobby started muttering and crowding forward. "He's involved!"

"Don't do this," Josh said to all of them. "Come on, dudes. You know this is—"

"You know Ari Siegel?" the mustached posse leader cut him off.

"Of course. I came here with him. I... Aw, no way."

Two of buzz cut's friends grabbed him by either arm and there was a sudden, booming crack from what sounded like all around. Like God was real angry.

The posse leader, like the rest of the crowd, looked up and around and frowned. Then he snapped his head back down. "Pritchett's out of it," he said. "Got his ear hacked off. So take this boy to the Town Hall courtroom. This time we handle it right."

CHAPTER 88

Alone in her room, sitting on her bed, Wendy kept pressing her hands together and shaking her head.

She heard the crack of the avalanche but it hardly registered because her mind was filled with that...*thing*...in room 27. Wendy should have just told her dad, then run out to find Ari. But something had made her come back to see what the Morris had done to his room. And now she'd have to live with the memory of what she'd seen for the rest of her life.

It had looked like, smelled like...the inside of a meat blender. Yes, like Rose had somehow wandered into a room with a spinning metal blade and... Only, she'd been naked, tied. And the cuts in her, the parts cut *off* her...

There was the sound of scuffling through the right wall of her room. Her parents' room. The angry voice of an older woman that Wendy had heard before but couldn't place. "Where have they gone, then?"

An indistinct reply. Wendy's stepmother.

The other woman: "And you did nothing?"

Another reply Wendy couldn't make out but she thought she heard Ari's name.

There was a knock on her door and Wendy started. It swung open to reveal Doctor Williams, Goldrock's only medical practitioner. Wendy's father had summoned him over here when they'd keyed open Room 27 and found...Rose. But the doctor had been more worried about Wendy, it seemed, than Rose.

"Wendy? Can I come in?"

Wendy didn't respond, half caught in the conversation through the wall and still choking on the overwhelming meat rot that filled her head and eyes and body.

"Wendy, child." Doctor Williams had somehow come across the floor from her door and sat beside her on the bed. She could smell his cologne and pipe tobacco and instinctively leaned into him. But as he put a comforting hand around her shoulders, it only reminded her of Ari's hand. Where was Ari? And she had a sudden flash of Rose's slashed-up hand, her fingers clawed into the bloody sheets of Room 27. Wendy shivered.

"Are you having trouble focusing? That's normal, dear." Doctor William's hand squeezed her shoulder and he stood again. "A little bit of shock. It will pass."

"Where's Daddy?"

"That's what I've come to tell you, Wendy. Your father, all the town men, were called to a meeting in the town hall. And I have to go to my clinic where they brought in some...things. Elizabeth is managing the hotel."

Wendy felt an inexplicable chill shoot through her. "What's going on?"

"It seems," Doctor Williams said, "that they've caught two young men whom they think did a number of killings last night, probably including this one you found. Awful business."

"Two young men?" Wendy asked dully. Mack Morris had worked in concert with someone else?

"Yes. Two older teenagers. They apparently caught one of them red-handed. Your father said—"

"Who?"

The old doctor pursed his lips at being cut off. "Well now, I don't remember their exact names, but they were both staying with Miryam Siegel. You know, the elderly woman—"

He was cut off again as Wendy sprang from the bed and ran for the door.

Out on Warsaw Mountain, the Snowcat sputtered and bucked as Paul desperately worked the two sticks that controlled the right and left tracks. He'd seen the avalanche come down in the gully north of the ski hills. Like a white fist of God it had washed over the high-up speck that was the Jeep and just kept coming down, spreading, louder, faster.

And now, as Paul finally got the Snowcat up to the edge of the ski hills and roared it over an embankment to plunge into the gully, the avalanche ran out and all sound ceased. Completely.

Still as death.

"No!"

Fighting a blind instinct to panic, Paul shoved down hard on the brakes and clanked to a stop. He wiped his face with his ski gloves and was shocked by the gloves' roughness and the wetness of his eyes. Fumbling his fingers across the sparse dashboard, he tried to find the windshield wipers to clear the ice and snow from the windshield. When he couldn't, he fumbled the side door open and swung himself out, stepping on the wide metal-and-rubber tread, swinging back to the vibrating hum of flatbed behind the cab.

There he stopped and dropped his chin in awe.

The entire slope before him, the cup between the mountains looked like it had been razed by a giant child's hand. The trees Paul had picked out as he'd tracked the Jeep's progress high up the slope were plowed over, splintered and broken. Large boulders and jutting ledges of rock had been ripped loose and tumbled downhill along with huge slabs of ice torn from under the top layers of snow. But eeriest of all, this total devastation lay unmoving and silent, like it had been this way forever.

And Nicole? The woman he'd been so ready to write off only an hour earlier? Oh, God, where was she?

As his eyes raked systematically down the avalanche slide from where he'd last estimated the Jeep to be, Paul tried to swallow with a sticky tongue. He saw no signs of her.

His very first day at Harvard Law School. His very first clas—Advanced Evidence. He'd stepped in late and there, down in the second row of the seats that sloped upwards from the lectern, was slash of ebony hair that swung like clean perfection. Swish.

And then her voice, as she answered a question of Professor Langdale. It was low, quick, and concise to the point of sharpness.

Only later did he learn how the sharpness covered fear. How she cared so intensely about things that others drew back. How she constantly cared for others but couldn't believe they could care for her. A scared idealist.

And beautiful. Funny when she let herself go. Sexual as a wildcat.

Nothing. No sign.

What happened between us, Nicki? Where did your humor go? Where did my need to make you trust? Into your mother's sickness? If I had just held on a little longer and tried a little harder, would we have gotten through?

A moan slipped out as he remembered something his father had kept telling him growing up. Something about appreciating what you have or even that will be taken from you.

"Nicole!"

He'd raked his gaze over the whole slope above and across from him. He couldn't see her. Couldn't see the Jeep. And his cry seemed to be sucked away by the tumbled snow and surrounding mountains. He cupped his gloved hands around his mouth and tried again. "Nico-o-o-o-ole!"

Then...was that a twitch in his peripheral vision? He twisted his head, scanning further down the cup. Saw it again. Something dark against the snow, twitching back and forth like a blowing flower. It was hundreds of feet farther down the slide than he'd figured the Jeep could have been tumbled. Almost near the bottom of the cup, but it could be, had to be...

Paul jumped from the Cat's back to its left track and up into its driver's seat. Hitting the accelerator, he pulled the right stick a little further back and clanked up the ski hill lip for a third time.

Headed down.

CHAPTER 90

ARI YELLED in pain as Rawley's lip-sucking partner jerked back his arms, shoved him down into the chair in the witness box, and handcuffed his wrists through the back of the chair.

This was crazy. *Mishigas.* Getting into Goldrock's courtroom in its hitherto locked-up Town Hall should have saved him. Instead Ari felt like he was fighting for his life.

Because this was definitely no regular session of the court. The only people in here were male, teen to adult, mostly bundled up in parkas and heavy overcoats, all dusted with snow, every one of them toting some kind of firearm.

The air smelled like ammonia, like whoever maintained the place had been through in the last week, mopped the floors, then sealed it up tighter than a drum. Ari coughed on it, noted his breathing was getting high and tight. He tried to calm it. He had to stay cool and confident, something he'd never had a huge talent for. But if he just told the truth about what had—

There was a shuffling sound in front of him and he looked up. The crowd of surly men had spat forward a kid just a bit younger than Ari. Ari blinked cautiously as the red-eyed boy had advanced on him. He looked so familiar, but... Of course. The party at the Community Center. One of Jeremy Buckster's friends. Rich. Rick? A schoolmate of Wendy's. Wispy little mustache. Mesh shirt that—

The boy stopped a foot in front of him and suddenly bared his teeth. "You fucking killed my mom and dad!"

Ari swallowed, putting it together. "No. Look," he said quickly. "I'm sorr—"

"Shut the fuck up you twisted fuck!" And the boy was on him, punching hard at Ari's face, his eyes. Ari ducked his head and whipped it back and forth to avoid the blows but they still caught his neck and ears, his chest. *Thud. Whump. Crack. Sparks. Pain.*

"It wasn't me!" Ari screamed, aware the rest of the crowd was just watching. "I didn't do anything!"

"Shut up! Shut up!" The boy kicked him now, sending shooting pain up through his legs. An elbow to Ari's forehead snapped his head back. "I'm going to kill you!"

Then someone screamed, *"Stop it!"*

A woman. Girl. Familiar? Ari nodded his bruised face forward and squinted out to see the redneck crowd peel open around the doorway to reveal...Wendy! She stood bundled in her mismatched ski jacket and green scarf, her face red and flushed, breathing hard. Her eyes shot back and forth at the assembled men like she wanted to fry them all where they stood.

"Now, Wendy..." began one of the older gentlemen standing near the middle the crowd that had split.

"No, Mr. Mawpester. Don't 'Now, Wendy' me. I'm embarrassed for every man here. Look what you're doing. *Look* at you all."

There was a rustle of murmurs at that, but Wendy glared them down and Ari silently cheered her on. Yes. If they just kept looking at her, Ari could...*ungh!*...tried to wrench his wrists... Oh, shit! Pain. And his hands would not come out.

"Where's my father?" Wendy was demanding of Mawpester.

"Um...uh... Some people helped take Georgia Hurzgehrmine and her kids to Doc Williams' place. Think your dad was with them."

Wendy nodded shakily. She wished her father was there to back her up, Ari guessed, but was proud he wasn't one of the mob. "Marshal Pritchett?"

The sucked-in-lips guy stepped out beside Mawpester. "Marshal's with Doc Williams. Sicko here cut his ear off."

Wendy stuck her chin out. "You saw that happen?"

"Kid was standing right there with the knife in his hand."

"Meaning you didn't."

"Didn't have to. Al Rawley was there with me too. Anyone with half a brain..." He looked sneeringly around at the other men, challenging any of them to think differently.

"Anyone with half a brain," Wendy said loudly, "would have wondered how one teenager who's not exactly built like a wrestler, could do half the things you're accusing him of."

"You listen up, little lady..."

"No *you.*" Wendy spun to address the other men in the room and Ari swallowed hard. This was the girl who'd talked about being so scared? "Think about it. Marshal Pritchett's got a gun. You found a kid holding a knife. And...the other killings you think he did? The ones where he tied women up. I saw one of those women—Rose. She worked at our hotel. She was strong as a horse. No guy under six feet and two hundred pounds could have done that to her."

A few of the men around her sucked air, wavering, and Wendy seemed ready to pound home another point.

She was interrupted by someone stepping in the door behind her. Rawley. He carried his bolt-action rifle loosely in his right hand. "She's right," he drawled. "Jew boy up there couldn't have done all those things...working alone. But he had a partner."

The crowd in the room held its breath as the man motioned out through the door and Corn-fed—Jeremy Buckster—came marching into the room, leading someone bound by a heavily knotted rope.

The prisoner, Josh Noony, looked up the length of the courtroom to Ari and grimaced. "Hell of a vacation, dude."

CHAPTER 91

IN THE DARKNESS of being buried alive, Nicole kicked her frozen foot again, puzzled by the fact she could move her leg.

She'd somehow managed to protect her head as she'd tumbled—clasped her hands over her ears and hung on tight. She'd thrashed about and spun until she had no sense of up or down. Finally she'd come to rest, hands still clasped over her ears, elbows miraculously forming a tiny pocket of air in front of her in the snow, the rest of her body splayed in an arch behind her, unable to move, other than her left leg from the knee down.

And the total darkness...

She swallowed dizzily and wondered if she'd gone blind. Her head had been battered as she'd tumbled.

Except...the snow all around her. She could feel its crystalline ice, the cold against her hands, pressing up the pants of her right leg and up her back, under her turtleneck. If she was buried....

At least there was air in front of her face, hot, thin, a little pocket deep inside the snow. But which way was she facing? She thought for a minute, then chewed on her tongue to work up a mouthful of saliva. She let it dribble out and felt it run up her cheek beside her nose.

She was upside down.

Sideways?

No, upside...

She sloppily kicked her right leg again. It could be up above the snow or in a pocket twenty feet under the top of the avalanche. Did avalanches form pockets? And if not... If not...

Hard to keep her thoughts on track. Air running out.

If...if...she was so close to the surface that her lower leg was out, why couldn't she move any other part of her? Why did it feel like she was trapped in iron? Buried in concrete?

Kick.

And her bruised mouth tried to smile. Dying topsy-turvy, blind, struggling for answers and air. Like...life.

She licked her swollen lips, tasted what could be blood, blinked blindly, and thought that now, right at the gates of death, might be a good time to fix her thoughts on what she really cared about.

Not who her true mother was, whether that psycho in the Jeep had been her brother. Not what she'd accomplished or hadn't in her life so far.

Just...Paul. Paul Kesin, her husband, her love, her support, her *understander* ever since they'd met. He'd hurt her and she'd hurt him. None of that mattered. Nicole knew at last that he was part of her and would always be. And whatever he wanted, whatever he needed...

Her head was spinning. Lungs heaving.

Dying blind.

Suffocating.

Dreaming of Paul.

CHAPTER 92

PAUL WAS out of the Snowcat and on his knees, digging furiously.

It was a foot. Nicole's pant leg and sock foot. No longer moving. Had it ever moved or had he imagined it?

She was buried upside down, somehow out of the Jeep she'd been abducted in. Had the monster killed her and tossed her? Is that why she was so far downs-lope? If she was dead... If she was...

He dug harder. Plunging his gloved hands down together like a spade, curling his fingers, and wrenching the snow back and up with a guttural cry. Again. Hitting ice. Digging around it. *Again.*

Until at last her entire right thigh was clear, and her waist, and Paul could see she wasn't curled but extended, which meant her head was buried *feet* more down in the snow.

"Oh, God," Paul breathed raggedly.

He plunged his hands in again.

When he had dug a space down to her chest, Paul widened the hole until he could crouch down inside it himself. There he almost collapsed and had to stop for a second. The whiteness, the empty air here, seemed to laugh at him. She has no breath, it said, because we have stilled everything. Completely.

"No." Paul said evenly, grit his teeth, and folded himself down into the hole to dig out Nicole's arms. She'd wrapped them up—down, actually, given her inverted position—around her head and they'd been pinned there. He carefully kept his boots back and cleared the space around her head until he could her see Nicole's face, pale and still. He shook his head and kept going.

When he'd finally freed her, he wrapped his arms around her torso and pulled.

Grunting and wheezing, he got her body up over his back, then pushed with his legs and arms until his quads and delts shook like jelly. Moved her. Finally flopped her up on top of the rough snow, just feet from the still-humming treads of the Snowcat.

He dragged himself out after her and tugged her arms away from her head. Her face was bruised with one ugly looking abrasion across her left temple and forehead. There was crusted blood spattered across her face.

Heartbeat?

He pressed his ear down onto her chest. Useless. He fumbled off his right glove and stuffed it into his pocket, then pressed his index and middle fingers up to her neck to find her carotid artery. Pressed around…

There! Thready. Irregular. But that was definitely movement. A heartbeat. Nicole was alive.

Yes. Yes. Yes, thank you, God.

He propped up her head, clasped his gloveless right hand around her jaw to open her mouth, and tried to remember his childhood classes in artificial respiration.

CHAPTER 93

Blow in...two...three.
Chest falls...two...three.
Blow in...two...three.
Watch it fall...two...three.
Come on, Nicki.
Blow in...

———

Torn back from...airiness?...everything was suddenly so heavy in Nicole. Her body was swimming in mud. Blackness swirled like thick ink. Her body rocked with nausea and swung crazily around in space.

Pain thrust in and out of her chest.

———

Paul's head was swimming.

Blow in...two...three.

Nicole's mouth tasted bitter and dry under his, like death was trying to suck her away from him. He wouldn't *let* it.

Watch it fall...two...three.

Blow in...two...

Nicole coughed into his mouth and he jerked back. Rolled her onto her side towards him so she didn't choke.

She hacked again, curling into a ball, gasped and hacked a third time, then threw back her head to take long breath that sounded like she was sucking air through a half-closed pipe.

Her eyes blinked open wide as she took two more gasping breaths, then her head came back forward as her breathing evened out and her eyes slowly came to focus on Paul's.

He blinked hard to keep his eyes clear through the moisture that was getting in the way and slowly reached out to touch the side of her bruised face.

"Paul?"

He nodded. "You're all right, honey. The nightmare's... It's over."

"So c-cold."

As she said it, her breathing almost seemed to stop again, and Paul realized that under all her bruises she looked almost white. She was dressed only in a Lycra turtleneck and ski pants, her feet covered only in socks. Which was how she'd been the last...what? Forty minutes? She might already be suffering from hypothermia or shock or something. That monster might have attacked her in the Jeep. She might have lost blood. She might have internal injuries.

He had to get her down the hill and to a doctor *now*.

He slid one arm under her torso and one under her legs. With a grunt, he lifted her battered body up off the snow and staggered back to the waiting Snowcat.

CHAPTER 94

"Majorly schooled," Josh gasped to Ari as Rawley's posse clamped him down into a chair right beside Ari and roped him into place. Josh's face was white.

Ari winced as the ropes and brutal movements banged against his own raw wrists. The air in the courtroom had become so tense he expected it to explode any second.

"This doesn't change anything," he heard Wendy say.

"Like hell it doesn't, girl," said Rawley, shifting his one-handed grip on his rifle. "These two came into town just before all these killing started. Bobby Brixell from Eagle said this first one was the guy who called out Pritchett and him to a body in the Chickopee. Just 'happened' to see it down there through all the ice and snow."

"I...I was there too."

"Well, now. Maybe that's why he had to report it."

Ari looked up just in time to see Jeremy Buckster stepping toward Wendy with his face fallen. "You were out by the lake with him? The little psychopath got you out there alone with him?"

"No. It wasn't..."

Ari looked around to see the courtroom of men leaning forward licking their lips with rage. And the smell—it was like all the men were pumping acid sweat, eager for a payoff for all the fear and excitement. They knew they couldn't run away from the terror in their midst, so they were determined to fight.

He caught Wendy's eye and she nodded at him with determination. But Ari didn't buy it. Not with Bone, the Goldrock freak, ripping his way through town, dragging everyone back into those long-buried nightmares. No, Ari and Josh had been caught in the backwash of that and it was way bigger than common sense or justice could handle.

He was suddenly swept by the conviction he should have spent Passover dinner with his oma after all. *Thy judgment pass over us.*

Wendy had rallied and was confronting Al Rawley. Attacking the leader. "You've still got nothing. Lots of people came into town last week. Right in our hotel we had—"

"We found this little turd holding a ten inch knife over a cut-up woman and the marshal. Now you want to argue that?"

The sucked-in lips guy surged forward. "And the tracks leading there went through every other place we found killings. Two sets of tracks!" He stabbed his finger at Josh and the kid who'd been beating on Ari now turned on Josh like he finally figured out Josh was supposed to have been in on all the insanity.

"Which pretty much means you're it, boys," said Rawley, taking in Ari and Josh with one look. "And I think it's time to go."

"Oh, shit," Josh breathed.

"Shut up, Zit-Head!" said the boy, Rick, who'd pounded on Ari earlier. He stepped up and cracked a hard right across Josh's jaw, stunning him.

Ari drew himself up as tall as he could and shouted, "Let's lynch 'em boys! Just like the KKK! Good old American tradition! Good old—"

He barely heard the "Fuck you!" as his head was battered sideways so hard his vision blurred and his chair fell over, carrying him with it. Then someone said roughly, "Pick him up. Get the keys. Both of them."

Then...black fur? By his face. Smothering him. And a smell he remembered from his childhood. That perfume. Too sweet but comforting. Hot. And the voice. "You stand back. All of you."

"Now Mrs. Siegel..."

"*Ikh hob dir in dread!*"

CHAPTER 95

OMA? Ari forced his vision to clear and drew back his head just enough to look up and see that it was his grandmother, standing there imperiously beside him, five foot two inches bundled in black fur. But—Ari wiggled his chair back a bit on the ground so he could see better—she wasn't just staring people down. She was holding a gun. The rifle she'd tried to give Ari earlier. But her face was pale, her lips shaking like she was having another attack of angina.

Oy.

"Mrs. Siegel," Rawley said, "I think you better just lay that thing down here afore you hurt yourself with it." His own bolt action was still hanging down loosely in his right hand. He took a slow step towards her and reached out his ropy left hand.

The explosion of the gunshot jerked Ari's whole body and he blinked hard to see what Oma had shot. Scanning around, Ari picked out a chink in the ceiling. She'd fired high. But her old hands were aiming down at Rawley again, and unlike her lips, they weren't shaking at all.

"I was here thirty years ago, Mr. Rawley. I remember how you made us be quiet then. You think you can do this again?"

Ari swallowed dryly. Thirty years ago. The Goldrock Freak. And Al Rawley somehow involved in what happened?

"*Und jetz,*" his oma said, "little Miss…"

"Wendy," Wendy said. Ari saw her eyes were shining with excitement.

"Miss Wendy." Ari's oma nodded jerkily. "You will get the keys and undo my Ari. And you,"—she waved the gun briefly towards Jeremy Buckster, who jumped back from where he hovered over Josh's head—"you will untie Ari's friend, Joshua. Quickly!"

Buckster jerked forward to obey, struggling with knots he'd used to tie Josh to the chair. Wendy too stepped forward, reaching for the keys the sucked-in mouth guy had been pulling out of his pocket when Ari's oma had appeared.

"These boys need to be tried for murder, Ms. Siegel," Rawley said.

"I see your 'trial,'" Ari's oma said, and spat on the floor.

"Lot of people died last night. Daughters, mothers…"

"Then you should be out looking for the one who— What?"

Ari looked where his oma had turned her head. It was Wendy. Josh was almost untied, but Wendy and the guy with the sucked-in mouth were struggling over the keys. Or, more precisely, Wendy was pulling on them, grunting. The sucked-in mouth guy wasn't giving them up.

Ari's oma swung her rifle towards the struggle and Ari was too late to warn her about Rawley. The big man stepped through the four feet separating them, raised his own rifle and smashed the stock down hard on Miryam's gun, sending it clattering to the floor, Oma almost following.

Josh, whose upper body was untied, leapt for it, pulling the chair over behind him as he dove. Buckster got there first and turned and danced out of Josh's sprawled reach. The guy with the sucked-in lips simultaneously gave Wendy a rough shove that sent her stumbling back against the judge's desk.

When Ari looked back towards Rawley again, the man had his rifle trained on him. As did the guy with the sucked-in mouth and half the men in the courtroom. Ari could almost *feel* the itchiness in every trigger finger now. He could see the strain in the sweating faces, hear the high, shallow breaths.

"I figure," Rawley said now, wiping his brow with the back of his left hand, "that we'll take these two *suspects* back along the route they took last night. Maybe make a side trip down to the lake."

"What do you mean the route *we* took?" shouted Josh from the floor, his normal cool totally dissolved now. He was crying..

"Last time, fucker," said the boy, Rick, who saw his chance to get involved again. He kicked Josh so hard in the stomach that Josh gagged and Ari thought he was going to vomit.

"Undo them," snapped Rawley. "Then tie them together and take them out the front."

"What about Wendy and…uh…?" Jeremy Buckster said, pointing to Wendy and Ari's oma.

"Bring them along too. But keep them away from the boys."

Ari tried to catch his grandmother's eyes, or Wendy's, but a tide of angry men had swept between them and Ari. A second later he was jerked up to his feet, every part of him aching, his mouth dry and acid. Then he was shoved shoulder-to-shoulder with Josh, Ari's right arm being handcuffed to Josh's left.

For a second he managed to catch Josh's eyes, wide and scared. And Ari's mouth twitched up, trying to say without words, *Hell of a vacation*.

Then the mob drove them out through the doors.

CHAPTER 96

I'M way too young to die.

Ari stumbled again as someone gun-butted him between his shoulder blades.

Oy. Pain.

Josh, wide-eyed and speechless, pulled on the handcuffs that held his and Ari's wrists together and Ari regained his footing. He shook out his shoulders and they kept walking.

They were headed north down the plowed center of Main Street, the men from the town hall walking in a mob around them so that Ari couldn't see beyond their shifting backs or their bodies on either side.

Rawley was right beside him, though, and despite Ari being punched enough to permanently loosen a few of his teeth, Ari was determined to make the man listen to him. "What is it? You think I had sex with your niece three years ago? I never touched her. I saw her at the party yesterday. It's the Goldrock freak who's doing this. The real one. Japhet Bone. He came into town under the name Mack Morris."

"Shut up." It was barely a growl, drowned out by other men in the mob as the whole groups slowed.

"Started here at the ski shop," someone said up front.

"Gonna cut off the street here?"

"Follow the tracks."

"Rub their noses in it."

"Proof."

"Watch the fuckers' faces."

"So do it, Rawley. Jesus."

"You all shut it too."

The crowd shifted like one hot, giant slug, turning a corner, oozing between the buildings into the darkness of the back alleyway, pushing Ari and Josh up ahead of them. The clouds had moved in heavily over the last hour. The temperature was dropping again too.

"Listen to me!" Ari pleaded as he stumbled. "Marshal Pritchett saw Bone as well. Go to the doc's office and talk to him. He probably saw what Bone did over at the house where you found me."

The guy with the sucked-in lips hit Ari on the back of the head so he stumbled. When he regained his footing, Josh whispered, "Waste of breath, Ari. They got a hard-on to kill someone and—"

"Rawley!" Ari called and lunged left to butt into his arm. "Bone's still out there! He could be after your wife or your niece! You want him doing—?"

"You. Little. *Fuck!*" Rawley bellowed and knocked Ari backwards with such a whomp to the head that Ari dragged Josh down with him to the dark snow and the whole line stopped. A girl screamed further back in the mob, probably Wendy, and he heard his oma shouting. But there was blood in Ari's mouth, bright lights, and a roaring in his skull, like some big tractor bearing down on him, like his brain was going to explode.

Then he realized it *was* a tractor or something, because the roaring suddenly kicked to a sputtering and there was a clanking, thumping, like a person dismounting, stumbling.

"Kee-rist," said suck-lips to Rawley. "What's that?"

"Pritchett."

"Fuck."

"*Marshal* Pritchett, driving one of *my* vehicles."

As Ari raised his head, the giant slug of a crowd seemed to bunch forward in the alley, sealing it side-to-side, keeping Wendy and Ari's oma back. And Ari blinked blindly into the glare of two massive headlamps lighting them all. He squinted and saw that below the lights were...tractor treads? The Snowcat! Nicole's husband! Paul-something.

And he was there, but only as backup. He and Wendy's father, the hotel keeper, were standing tight behind the town marshal Ari had last seen slumped on the floor of the nightmare kitchen. All three men were backlit. The right side of Pritchett's head was all bandaged now so he looked like a half-wrapped mummy, his pale face in almost total shadow, his arms hanging darkly by his sides.

"Pritchett!" Rawley's voice called from Ari's left. Josh started to help Ari up, but Rawley stepped sideways and put a boot onto Ari's back shoving him back to the snow, Josh staggering to his knees. "What in tarnation are you doing out here? Thought you were injured!"

Pritchett's voice came back sounding weak and strangled. "Turn...over...your prisoners."

"You don't look so good, Bob," Rawley said. "These boys behind you holding you up?"

"I'm...the marshal. Turn them over."

"Now, Bob..."

"Don't 'Bob' me."

"Listen, Pritchett. You're hurt. You been cut up. You go back to the doc's office. Lie down. This ain't none of your business."

"Like hell, it's not."

Then there was a silence and a rippling through the crowd, a stiffening of the shoulders all across the line. Ari realized some of the men up front had raised their rifles.

CHAPTER 97

It stayed like that, frozen under the building press of darkness, for what seemed like a full minute. Then, Ari heard a wheezing sound and a cough, and Marshal Bob Pritchett's voice again, harsh and steady. "You better hope your boys hate me enough to shoot an officer of the law, Rawley, because if you don't turn over the prisoners by the time I count to three, I'll damn well going to shoot you."

Ari heard the click of a revolver being cocked. Pritchett's hanging right hand.

"One...two..."

Oh, shit.

Rawley's voice: "Lift them up."

Ari suddenly had two sets of hands under his armpits and he and Josh were hauled upright. Not released, though, even though Marshal Pritchett was steadily aiming his revolver at Al Rawley. Probably because that revolver was wavering and marshal, very obviously held upright by the two men behind him, looked ready to pass out. "Those...aren't...him," Pritchett said, wobbling. "I *saw* the killer. Chased him. Got my damn ear sliced off by him."

Nicole's husband said, "The killer's nearly seven feet tall. He took my wife up the mountain, got caught in a landslide. I got her out. Didn't see him get out."

"Listen to them, boys," said Severin.

The mob wavered now, some of the fever leaving it, some of them dropping back, the front line loosening. But Rawley was sucking on his handlebar mustache furiously, his hand gripping and re-gripping his rifle.

"Hey, you heard him," Josh sobbed. "It wasn't us!"

Jeremy Buckster, stepped up close behind Josh and held the butt of his gun right near Josh's mouth. "Shut up."

"Or what?" came Wendy's voice, as she was able to struggle through the weaker crowd at last. "You going to beat up two innocents some more?" She pushed past Buckster and stood directly in front of Ari, her cold hands reaching up to gently smooth his hair back from the goose egg growing beside his left eye.

"Little girl...," growled Rawley.

She whirled to him and snapped, "You could already be sued for assault and battery, false imprisonment, threats, and attempted murder. You want to press it?"

The cowboy held her eyes for a minute, then glanced back at Marshal Pritchett, his gun still at ready...barely. Then he looked up between the rooftops at the darkening skies, then at his watch. "Figure we got maybe a couple hours before the snow hits again. I'd still like to find that killer's body if we can get this gentleman here to show us where he thinks it is." He looked innocently at Paul.

Paul nodded. "Close as I can. I can cram maybe four of you in the Snowcat I drove. Just let me check on my wife once more at the clinic."

Rawley nodded and pointed to Buckster, suck-lips, and the boy who'd lost his parents to stay with him. They followed Paul into the Snowcat, whose engine was still sputtering, but Rawley took the driver's seat. There was a roar as it thunked into gear, then it back off down the alley at high speed.

In the ensuing silence, Pritchett waved his gun and coughed. "The rest of you go on home now. Anyone without electricity or water, double up with someone who does. Otherwise, get."

And simple as that, the mob split and dissolved, slithering off in all directions.

"Hey!" Josh called out and held up his and Ari's handcuffed hands.

Suck-lips walked over with the key and unlocked them without comment, flipping closed the cuffs and bringing them back to the marshal.

"Too close, dude," Josh said, wiping his nose and eyes, embarrassed. "Too—"

But Ari had already running past him. His grandmother was lying on the ground, face in a pale rictus, her hands clutching her chest. "Oma!"

His grandmother couldn't speak when he reached her, but Josh was suddenly behind Ari, saying, "Her nitroglycerine. She's got a spray at home, in the kitchen."

"Too far," said Wendy, there also. "Take her to the clinic. Doc Williams must have some."

"And if he doesn't?" Josh said.

Ari looked back at him. "You run to her house, Josh. Wendy and I will get her to the clinic. It's just about eight buildings down that way when you get back here. On the right."

Josh nodded and was gone. Wendy scooted around opposite Ari and helped him lift up his grandmother, still in pain. "Gotta walk, Oma," he whispered. "Just a bit more. It's not your time yet."

"*Ge...Gehennom*," she said tightly. Her breath was acrid.

Ari nodded, then saw the question in Wendy's beautiful eyes. "Jewish hell," he said. "This." He nodded his chin down at his oma as they began half-walking, half-dragging her down the street between them. "And everything else here except for you."

"I'm...unh..." Wendy stumbled a bit as Ari's grandmother's legs buckled and she and Ari had the full weight of her body and its heavy black fur coat. "I'm your Beatrice,"

"My what?"

"Dante."

"What?"

"Later," she breathed, her smile strained under the weight.

"Yeah."

Behind them, Wendy's father struggled along with the marshal sheriff's arm slung over his shoulder. When they were almost to the doctor's office, the Snowcat from earlier suddenly roared away from its front door and headed for the ski slopes. Paul had obviously checked and Nicole was going to be okay.

And so was his oma, Ari thought furiously. So was she.

It was like the aftermath of a bloody war. The enemy was vanquished, the craziness was passed. All that was left was to aid the wounded and count the dead.

As few dead as possible.

He looked sideways as his oma and Wendy and they hurried faster.

CHAPTER 98

OVER THE NEXT hour Doc Williams's three room clinic become recovery central for Goldrock.

The doctor tended to Miryam Siegel, Nicole Baker, Bob Pritchett, Georgia Hurzgehrmine, and Georgia's children. Ari and Josh were pressed into service directing flow of dead bodies being brought in by friends and relatives. The bodies went outside behind the clinic, where the snow and cold would preserve them. The bringers of the bodies were brought back through the clinic waiting area where Wendy and her father talked quietly with them and offered rooms in the Grenadine to those who were not emotionally able to return home. Wendy's stepmother had reappeared in the Grenadine and directed the arrivals on that end.

Up in the gully between Warsaw and Gomel...

Paul kicked at a clump of ice and snow that was bigger than he was and looked over the surreal landscape of the avalanche slope.

The Snowcat crouched like a hulking shadow about ten yards down, pointing its headlights over the area they searched. The Cat's five riders, including Paul, were spread out over that area and beyond, ranging the length of a football field, searching among an unreal landscape of jumbled ice and shadows that Paul had remembered as being so smooth.

Actually, it was, further down where he'd found Nicole. Up here, where he'd figured the tumbled Jeep and the killer had to be buried, it was rougher.

Paul looked up, remembering the close chill that had been in the air the afternoon he and Nicole had arrived in Goldrock. This was worse. The clouds stewed together overhead like thick pitch. It might have been only six p.m., but it felt like ten or eleven.

"Al!" Paul called. Somewhere on the way up here the mustached Al Rawley had decided Paul was okay and had given him his first name. Buddy-buddy. Fine. If it sped his and Nicole's way out of this hellhole and home safe to Maryland, Paul would use it.

One of the distant searchers held up his hand. Rawley, presumably.

Paul shouted, "Not going to find a thing without more light! We need to get down and come back tomorrow!"

There was a pause, then the distant figure waved his hand and called back, "Let's go!"

Five minutes later all five males were crammed back into the Snowcat, the engine snorting, the heater going. Rawley's elbow dug into Paul's side as the cowboy shoved the Cat's accelerator and lurched them forward. The breathing was heavy in the cab, the sweat strong. Then, directly behind Paul's neck, the boy who'd lost his parents to the killer, spoke.

"I found something out there."

Al Rawley's head whipped around, the movement making the Snowcat spin left too.

"This," said the boy, and pushed his hand forward past Paul's head. He opened his mitt and showed three pieces of what looked like balls of ice. "They're glass," the kid said. "Shattered glass. And you see what's on them?"

Paul studied them and now saw the dark stains. Reddish black. Blood.

At the steering levers, Al Rawley nodded and, for the first time since Paul had met him, smiled. "Not like we didn't trust you or nothing, Paul, but that nails it."

"What?" said Paul.

"What you said. Really was a Jeep up here. Tumbled and broke. And when we find it, damn but I think we're going to find our killer too. Ground up good, I hope."

"Real good," said the kid quietly behind Paul. He closed his hand and pulled back his souvenir.

Rawley nodded. "It's over, anyhow."

Thank God.

Paul blinked hard out through the darkness and steered the Cat downslope towards the few twinkling lights of Goldrock.

None of them saw the black-bladed shovel that the treads ran over and pushed out of sight under the snow.

DAY FOUR
SATURDAY

CHAPTER 99

IT WAS AFTER MIDNIGHT. The inside of the clinic was dark, muggy, and crowded.

Nicole could smell the sourness of her own breath as she pushed up from the edge of her cot in the overnight-stay room and tip-toed painfully across the tiles to the shut door that connected to the waiting room. She had to step around the IV pole that was dripping an antibiotic solution into Georgia's arm. As she did, April muttered something in her sleep and rolled off her rubber air mattress at the foot of Georgia's bed to bump Auggie. He was already lying upside down on a second air mattress, head back and mouth wide. He didn't stir.

Nicole took a step towards them, filled with an urge to straighten them out. Tuck them in. But then she pursed her lips and stepped back. They weren't hers. Nothing was hers any more.

Her bones felt bruised all over. She had a swath of bandages across her forehead and down her left temple. Every time she moved, her clothes seemed to scrape some other uncovered wound. And they weren't even *her* clothes... Someone had taken all her own wet clothes while she'd been out, even her bra, and dressed her in a pair of the doctor's old wool socks, cotton intern pants tied at the waist, and a tee-shirt.

She'd become sexless. Identity-less. Abandoned.

Paul, meanwhile, was sacked out in the waiting room along with the heavily-sedated Marshal Pritchett. Nicole knew Paul had saved her, but he hadn't stayed with her. She'd woken up here alone. Then Ari had come to bring her up to date on all that had happened, including the stuff on Japhet Bone's history in Goldrock. The probable sexual abuse of Bone as a child fit with the craziness she'd seen in the Jeep and the craziness among the townspeople. Impossibly, it made Nicole flash to wishing again that she could save the monster somehow. Lock him up. Get him help.

Then Paul had finally come to see her. He'd seemed unsure what to say, whether even to go first to her or to Georgia. Just like they'd been back at Georgia's house this morning.

And what the monster had said to Nicole there hadn't helped, had it.

It's me, Sarah. Your brother. Japhet.

Japhet Edwin Bone, Ari told her. Which would make her Sarah Bone.

She shivered. Whether it was true or not, whether the monster deserved saving or not, Paul knew somehow that this was why Nicole had brought them to Goldrock. He knew because she hadn't been able to deny it. And it meant that, like her own mother, like she'd accused Paul himself of doing, Nicole had lied about who she was and what she was doing with her life. It made her an unfit mother, an unfit wife.

And if it was actually true...

She pressed herself miserably to the door and, to make things still worse, could hear Ari all the way from the examination room off the waiting area. He was whispering again to his new girlfriend. Even after being beaten and nearly killed. Even with his grandmother on the slab there, alive but touch-and-go, and his friend, Josh, asleep on the floor four feet away.

The girlfriend laughed quietly. Ari laughed. Nicole grimaced into the door. When you were young and in love, you'd find anyplace at all to connect.

Outside, the wind started picking up. It whooshed and rattled some loose wire against the back of the building.

Nicole realized her throat was dry but the only water was in one of the other two rooms and she didn't want to disturb the young lovers or wake up Paul. She turned around and leaned back against the door.

There were issues to sort out.

First, her love for Paul that she'd discovered near death. She'd been surprised by the certainty of it. Whatever he might have done, and wherever he might be at emotionally right now, Nicole had finally figured out that, if the crunch came, she loved him absolutely and would do anything for him that was within her power to do.

Which raised issue number two—children. She knew Paul wanted them. No, he needed them. Deserved them. Would be so good as a father. While Nicole... Well, it had always been obvious to her she feared motherhood because she didn't want to become like Mama Suzie—a pathological, pathetic liar who manipulated her children more than loved them. Now Nicole realized that it could be even worse than that. If her brother was that monster she left on the hillside, Nicole had some serious mental illness in her family. And given Nicole's own unsteady grasp of her identity and worth, this didn't seem unlikely.

It did rule out children, though. For their sakes.

Which led, with inescapable logic, to a cruel possibility she had to face.

She trembled as she considered it, pushing her long hair back over top of her bandages. She looked through the darkness to the bed where Georgia lay in her slit-back hospital gown, connected by a long tube to the black pole and bag of liquid. Drip...drip...

"Georgia," Nicole said softly.

CHAPTER 100

Georgia didn't respond.

Nicole pushed herself quietly away from the door and padded in her socks to Georgia's bed. She pulled over a chair from the wall and sat in it. Leaned over to touch the blond woman's forehead.

Georgia was burning up, covered in sweat, and still gorgeous. She even smelled cleaner than the rest of the crew here. Which was ironic, given that the doctor said the knife had perforated her bowel, essentially releasing an army of E. coli bacteria into the other areas of her abdomen. Peritonitis. That's what the antibiotic drip was fighting. She'd been awake a few times since Nicole herself had come to and been told what was happening, but it didn't look like she was doing well.

"Georgia," Nicole said again and squeezed the woman's shoulder.

Georgia moaned and Nicole squeezed harder. "Georgia, wake up."

Finally Georgia's eyelids fluttered and she looked up into Nicole's eyes. Let out a little gasp of breath. Foul. It made Nicole smile weakly. "How you doing?"

"Ohhh... Sick." *See-ick.* She moved her head back and forth, eyes searching.

Nicole looked, saw a small, metal chamber pot on the ground near the foot of the bed. Empty, thankfully. Nicole reached and got it, brought it up beside Georgia's pillow, and helped the blond woman roll towards it to dry heave twice, hopefully not ripping her stitches.

When Georgia lay back, Nicole put the pot back on the floor and used the corner of the sheet to wipe Georgia's mouth. "We never got to finish our discussion," Nicole said quietly. She noted Ari and Wendy's whispering had stopped in the other room. Listening. Fine. Let them.

Georgia's eyes found hers in the dark and focused fearfully. But she nodded.

"You love Paul. Or, at least, need him." Nicole didn't state it as a question. "I love him too. I've also been married to him for eight years, but I want to put that aside for the moment."

Georgia was listening hard.

"The fact is, I think he loves both of us." Nicole stopped a little, breathed hard over that admission, then pushed on. "What we need to figure out is what is best for *him*."

"I don't—"

"Shut up, please, Georgia. This is damn hard for me and you have to let me finish."

The younger woman looked up at her and nodded, her eyes wet.

"When I confronted you in your home yesterday, I was ready to fight. I was shocked and hurt and angry. I'm still...hurt. But I've also had time to think. I...think when you realize you really love a person, you want more than anything what's best for him. And in this little scenario, that may mean you."

"No."

Nicole grabbed Georgia's shoulder and squeezed hard. "Let me finish! Paul needs to have children in his life. And you...have children." Nicole shot a wistful look off the end of the bed where April and Auggie slept. "Beautiful children. Something...I...don't think I can give him. An uncomplicated life. A straightforward family. All the—"

"Stop this!"

Georgia hissed it out so suddenly that Nicole was knocked off track. And the sweaty, flushed face in the hospital bed was shaking. Angry. All Nicole could say was, "What?"

"I left my little ones for almost a year! Did you forget that? You know why I did that? You want to know why?"

"Tell me."

Georgia caught her breath and stared into Nicole's eyes. Then she wiped a hand roughly over her eyes and began.

CHAPTER 101

"My mama and daddy," Georgia said, licking her lips and breathing high in her chest, "came from Oklahoma. They moved up to Goldrock afore I was born. Just for a while. To ride out a tough time, my mama said. My daddy was a preacher. That's why he built that bell tower up top our house. Never had money for the bell. Used to have a root cellar. Someone filled it in."

"Where you live now?"

Georgia nodded but then her eyes closed like she was going to pass out. Nicole jumped up and skipped carefully out to the waiting area, avoiding the receptionist desk that had been pushed back against the wall. Paul, she noted, had pulled his cot across the door and slept there with a shotgun held across his chest. *Where'd he get that?* Nicole shook her head and crept to the water cooler near the heavy couch were Pritchett was stretched out. She pulled out two paper cup. Gritting her teeth against the noise, because the wind had died down again and the only sound in the clinic was people breathing, Nicole filled first one, then the other.

The glug of bubbles awoke neither Pritchett nor Paul, though. Nicole tiptoed back to the overnight room and closed its door behind her.

"Thought...you'd gone," whispered Georgia.

Nicole shook her head. "Water." They both drank. Then Nicole said, "You were in the old house."

Georgia nodded, closed her eyes for a second, and continued. "I never knew my daddy because my mama slept around a lot and he finally couldn't take it and left her."

Nicole shivered. It was her own parents (if Mama Suzie and Nigel Baker really were her parents) in reverse.

"But after he left we still managed, because the house was all paid for, Mama was a sometime teacher, and Goldrock was real little. Folks stuck together."

"I'll bet."

Georgia shot a look at her. "They did. All through everything. Even though we was Oklahoma trash, they said. They still brought us meals, I remember, and candy for my brother and me."

"You had a brother?" Nicole tried to say it calmly but Georgia heard the sharp edge in her voice and seemed to draw back inside herself, afraid. Nicole had to put her hand on Georgia's shoulder and bring her face in close. "Tell me."

"H-he was older than me," Georgia finally said. "F-four years older."

"What was his name?"

Georgia shook her head and swallowed hard.

On a sudden instinct, Nicole asked, "Did he ever...do anything to you?"

Georgia's eyes went wide and blinked up furiously at Nicole. If it had been brighter in the room, Nicole was sure she would have seen Georgia's face go red. Nicole's surely was. Nicole's head and heart were swimming with the salvation Georgia's story offered Nicole, even as it damned Georgia.

"How old were you?" Nicole asked.

"F-five."

Nicole leaned back, her throat tight. But she kept her hand on Georgia's shoulder and finally leaned forward again. "Go on."

"Ah...ah...ah...Nobody liked us much 'cause, like I said, we was Oklahoma trash. So I didn't have any friends. And one day, when my mama was out teaching..." She blinked hard and her mouth worked, but nothing was coming out.

Nicole reached out and took the empty paper cup from Georgia's feverish hand. She set it down with her own to the ground by the bed. Then Nicole reached up and took both of Georgia's hands in her own. Squeezed them gently. "Take your time," she said.

"I remember I was playing in my room," Georgia said so quietly that Nicole had to lean forward to hear. "I had a doll. A little Suzie doll, like a cheap Barbie, and I was combing its hair. And when I looked up, my brother was standing in the doorway."

Nicole's head grew light. "He was nine years old?"

Georgia nodded and her breath was high and tight now, her lips shaking and her head starting to go side to side. Nicole reached for her forehead and stilled it by covering it with her own, cooler palm. "It's okay. Georgia. I'm here. It's okay." Her eyes darted nervously to the children but they still slept.

After a minute, Georgia's breathing calmed and she stared up at the ceiling. "My brother came into my room and took my Suzie doll from me. We were really poor. That was my only toy."

She paused again, her eyes twitching back and forth, remembering..

"He took my doll from me, and...he pulled out this jackknife he had. Then he told me to take off my clothes. And...I was scared he was going to hurt my doll, so...I did."

"Georgia..."

She shook her head, still not looking at Nicole. "And I remember him taking off his clothes. He was so huge I was struck dumb. Then he came over to me. He pushed me down flat on the floor. No carpet. He told me if I made any noise at all, he'd chop up my doll and tell Mama I'd been bad. Then he... It was like this giant...hot...blanket covering me up. So dark I could hardly breathe. Crushing me. Then he... Ungh. He..." Her eyes flooded. "I can't. I was five years old. I was just so...little..."

Then a choke came from somewhere deep in her belly, and she rolled away from Nicole, curling up so tightly it threatened to tear the IV tube from her arm.

Nicole reached for her, trembled, withdrew her hand, reached again. Finally she forced herself up from her chair and climbed onto the bed behind Georgia. She wrapped her arms gently around the younger woman's body and head. And she cried with her.

CHAPTER 102

Five minutes later, Nicole's body breathing in rhythm with hers, Georgia finally found the strength to continue.

"He must have raped me about ten times over the next year or so," she whispered in the darkness. "Told me he'd done it to other girls and women in the town too, more'n once, which I think was true, because Mama was getting crazier and crazier with him. He was so big for his age."

"And nobody stopped him," Nicole whispered. It had been one thing hearing the FBI conclusions Ari had recounted. It was another to actually talk to one of the victims of this monster (for it surely had to be Japhet Bone) and imagine the town letting it continue. Bone had been only nine and ten. Surely...

"Most everyone knew. But my mama was very good at manipulating people. She'd use blackmail, sex. Whatever worked."

"How long did it go on?" Nicole asked. "How many girls and women?"

"I don't know," Georgia breathed. "Lots, I think."

Twelve women, Ari had said. But Nicole guessed that didn't count Sarah, and probably counted each female only once, however many times she'd been assaulted. Jesus. The attitudes, the code of silence... Nicole felt her whole body shivering even though the clinic air was sweltering hot.

Many of the folk living here now—Herb Mawpester, the Hurzgehrmines, even this Rawley character Ari kept running into—must have known that Japhet Bone was raping Goldrock's women, raping the *girls*, for God's sake, and they'd done nothing to stop it.

Girls. Betsy Müller? Nicole felt a chill at that horrifying possibility and shoved it quickly from her mind. "When did it stop?"

"When a woman turned up dead, all cut up."

Nicole breathed out shakily. "How old were you at the time?"

"Just turned nine." Very quiet.

"And?"

"They couldn't prove it was...my brother. But the marshal took him and locked him in the clock tower."

Nicole frowned. "Not the jail?"

Georgia shook her head and just that motion made her wince. "The marshal was afraid the other men in town, if they knew where he was, would bust him out. So they gagged him and tied him up all secret 'til they could ship him off to a country courthouse and get him ruled insane. I only found out afterwards when the marshal's son, Bob Pritchett, told me. Said everything was gonna be alright."

"It wasn't?"

"It just made everyone madder—those that wanted to save him and those that wanted him dead. They run my mama and me out of town."

"But you came back."

"Not 'fore my mama left me in a store in Oklahoma and took off. Store-keeper raised me. By the time I was twenty, I'd slept with just about every boy in the town we lived in. And some of their daddies too. I felt so unclean and dirty." Her body convulsed for a second. "Then Eduard came through town one day, remembered me from school in Goldrock, of all things, and made me feel like none of my past mattered. He helped me change my name, first and last. He loved me that much. He married me and brought me back to Goldrock. We had two kids. I even started going to church and Sunday dinners with my in-laws."

"Then he died."

"Backloader crushed him. Right through his head so there weren't nothing left. And...and...I was suddenly all alone again. In this town. Right here."

"With two children."

"That I loved with all my heart, but...I just couldn't...cope. Then Eddy's mama stepped in and said she'd look after them, and...I ran away. Almost like I can't remember where." Nicole could feel Georgia taking big gasps of air as her body shuddered.

"What brought you back?"

Georgia fought for control, regained it, and said, "A letter. Someone wrote me a letter with this fine, spidery writing, saying my kids missed me."

Nicole froze. "Did they sign it?"

"What?"

"The letter. Did they sign it?"

"I don't— No, I don't think so."

Nicole said nothing, but her insides were churning again. Three letters: one to Georgia Hurzgehrmine née Sarah Bone; one to Nicole Baker whom Japhet Bone *thought* was Sarah; and a bunch to Japhet Bone himself. What the hell was going on?

"Then Paul helped me get the house set up," Georgia said into the silence. "He had the same kind of quiet strength Eddy had. He listened to me. He seemed to care. And I started to feel safe again, for the first time since Eddy died. I can be anything if I just feel safe."

Nicole stiffened and Georgia must have felt it. She said quickly, "Except...there's you. Letting Paul help me. Rescuing my children from the storm. And I find out you're a lawyer. Married to Paul eight years. Y'all escape a madman together. You let Paul save you from an avalanche." She laughed harshly. "How'm I supposed to compete with that? How'm I even supposed to *live* compared to that?"

"And yet..." Nicole cut it off and pressed her face into Georgia's back, breathing hard into the sweaty cotton of the young woman's hospital gown.

CHAPTER 103

AND YET YOU'RE A BEAUTIFUL, *loving mother*, Paul finished the thought from where he listened in the other room.

He exhaled into the thick air cot and shifted his sweaty fingers on the shotgun lying across his chest. He'd faked sleep to deal privately with the issue that should have died out on the avalanche slope—which woman did he want to spend his future with? Then he'd heard Nicole get up in the other room and start talking with Georgia. He'd heard her virtual offer to release him to Georgia and much of Georgia's horrific response.

And his confusion only deepened.

Eight years with Nicole. Ups and downs. Promises. Commitments. Paul's moral center. They should have decided the issue. But here in this remote little town, cut off from the rest of the world and coming face to face with true mortality, Paul had to ask where the rest of his life was going to go.

For a second he saw the accusing eyes of the kid, Ari Seigel. *"You* are *Nicole's husband, right? Then don't you think you should go rescue your wife?"*

But Paul felt like he'd been doing that forever.

He'd rescued Nicole. And he'd rescued Nicole. And he'd rescued Nicole. And damn it, he loved Nicole, but he didn't want to spend his life hoping she'd pull it together when another woman who also needed and wanted him with simpler demands was standing right here. Yes, Georgia would obviously take some major rescuing too. But at least Paul would get a complete family out of it.

Georgia or Nicole. Family or childless struggle.

Paul closed his eyes and found his mouth was so dry he couldn't swallow.

CHAPTER 104

"Dɪᴅ ʏᴏᴜ ᴄᴀᴛᴄʜ ᴀʟʟ ᴛʜᴀᴛ?" Wendy whispered.

"Most of it," Ari said, almost wishing he hadn't. He just wanted to extend the moments he was spending with Wendy. Right here, right now.

They were huddled on the floor against the wall with Ari's ski jacket covering them, more for intimacy than warmth, since Doctor Williams kept his clinic almost balmy, maybe because his quarters upstairs weren't separately heated. Ari's bandaged head was touching Wendy's clean one so he could hear and feel every warm breath she took, smell the lingering sweetness of her shampoo. It made up for the throbbing pain in his ribs and back and everywhere.

Ahead and above them was the examination table, propped with pillows to hold Ari's sleeping grandmother. Her attack had lasted too long to be just angina, Doc Williams had said. It had probably been a minor cardiac infarction, a heart attack. But with no EKG equipment to test, he'd had to stick with spraying nitroglycerine until the attack had stopped. Then he'd given her aspirin and kept her here for observation. Wendy's father had miraculously agreed to Wendy staying the night with Ari and Josh, watching to see if Ari's grandmother pulled through. The amount of trust it took for a father to do that...

About an hour ago, Josh had given Ari and Wendy some privacy by sitting out of sight on the other side of the examination table. Ari had turned to Wendy, she to him, and they'd kissed for the very first time. So tentative, both Ari's lips cut and swollen from beatings. And it was suddenly like they'd been starving their whole lives and finally found food in each other. Ari's wounds seemed to vanish and so did his timidity as his body ran with thrills he'd never felt before, from his toes to fingertips so that even the tips of his ears seemed alive and on fire.

His hands had sought her body then, hesitantly feeling for her breasts through the stretchy, button-up top she wore under her coat, marveling at her soft fullness. And she, breathing hard, had quietly unbuttoned her blouse and unhooked her brassiere so he could feel her completely, skin to skin, her nipples taut little bumps. Then she'd reached for him, clutched his hardness through his pants, and they'd pressed together like that, holding each other, straining and crazy, until Ari had finally drawn back, gasping. "We can't."

"I know." Her voice just as strained.

"Not yet. Not here at least." The trust of Wendy's father. Ari's own oma lying perilously close to death on the examination table ahead and above them. Josh just on the other side of that, for Pete's sake.

So they'd settled back to gentle kissing, Wendy's top still undone, Ari groaning at his different injuries. They'd whispered, and giggled and shared their childhoods, their fears, their hopes for the future, which now, cautiously began to include each other.

Until Nicole had begun talking to Georgia in the other room.

"I never realized how normal my life was," Wendy whispered.

"Better than normal, sounds like."

"Other than my folks splitting. Yeah, I guess it was. Though I always wished I had a sister."

"Bleh. Sisters aren't so great. Take it from me."

Wendy gave Ari's arm a punch that drew his eyes involuntarily down to the jiggle of her half-exposed breast. Then she turned serious again. "What are you going to do if your grandmother fully recovers and asks you to do the Passover again?"

Ari's eyes flicked up the shadowy side of the examination table where he could just see the top edge of his grandmother's body. "This morning I would have said just that I'd do it as long as Oma let me bring you along. I would have done it just to satisfy her and get her off my back."

"Now...?"

Ari looked down again. "Now it scares me. Something about that lynch mob and my oma standing up to them. Like it was a familiar experience for her. I don't know, it...brought home somehow what she's been saying about the tradition of the Jewish people. Oppressed, accused, kicked around. I'm starting to understand why they defend their Jewishness so hard."

He heard Wendy swallow before she said, "Are you going to rule me out, then? Because I'm not Jewish?"

He met her eyes in seriously in the darkness. "You know *if* I somehow rediscovered my Jewish roots or culture or whatever, it wouldn't make me stop loving you. My dad and mom... Well, I guess it would really depend more on you, whether you'd be able to handle me observing a bunch of crazy rituals, trying to understand a new view of the world. I mean, it might change me."

Wendy swallowed again. "I'd like to try." She nodded her head towards the other room. "Look at them—Paul and Nicole, right? They've been married eight years and still don't have things worked out. At least your parents and mine are still together."

"Very."

There was a silence while Wendy burrowed her head down against Ari's chest and, careful not to grab a place with bruises, held him tightly. Then she said, "Ari?"

"What?"

"What if your grandmother doesn't make it? What if she dies tonight or tomorrow?"

Ari put his hand stiffly on her hair. "That's not going to happen. Nobody else dies anywhere for at least a month."

"But—"

"Nobody."

CHAPTER 105

ALL OF THEM, Japhet thought, blinking underwater.

Every single person in this town was going to die by his hand, one by one.

He was lying back, head submerged, in the claw-footed tub of his childhood home. His slug-like legs curled up over the far end, on either side of the tap that dripped steaming water onto his exposed nasty doodle. *Tsssss!....Tsssss!*

Cleansing him. Arousing him. Like his mother sucking him. Jerking him. Putting things up his bum bum. *Bugger boy.*

He'd almost forgotten that. *Sublimated* it, as the psychs he'd been forced to talk to as a child would have said. Not that it mattered.

His eyes could see only dark murk above him, the swirl of his own blood, but still he kept himself under, curious as to how long he could hold his breath. And knowing that once he came up, once he arose this time, there would be no stopping until the very end.

He'd dug himself out of the town's second attempt to suffocate him—once in the lake, once in the mountain—and stumbled down the hill to his childhood home. He'd thrown himself, fully clothed, into a lukewarm bath like the one he'd had in the Grenadine. After, he'd arisen, stripped, made a small fire in the woodstove and spread his clothes across it to dry. He'd found and lit candles, eaten, his brain swirling as he relived his finding then losing Sarah. Then he'd finally come back to this bathroom to reflect, to clean his wounds, pick out the buckshot, prepare bandages, and run a new bath for himself, this one so hot the steam danced in the candlelight like a spirit from hell.

Here he would die and then rise again, a demon incarnate.

His chest was finally starting to hurt now, the oxygen eaten greedily by his blood, his throat starting to tug upwards. A trickle of foul water snuck in through the natural valve close-off in his nose and down the back of his throat, but he suppressed his cough. It was just more of hell seeping into him. And hell, Japhet decided as his nasty doodle bobbed stiffly out of the water, was his proper domain.

Certainly not earth, where they fucked and taunted and beat and laughed at him. Where they even ripped from him the one child he'd made. Where they pretended to be shocked at the blood he spilled and locked him up, called him crazy, and trucked him out of town in a cage. Where even his own sweet little sister didn't welcome him back, but tried to bury him in the mountain. Like a dog. A wild dog.

A whine began to gulp in his throat in his throat as his body demanded he surface and breathe.

Arise!

Bind your wounds!

Sweep through the town and deliver your justice!

Yes. The pressure sucking his throat down was incredible now. His buttocks and legs shook with eagerness. *As long as I can start with Sarah.* His body began to spasm. *Yes.*

His fingers shot around sides of the tub and he hauled himself up, gasping with a breath to suck in all the wind outside then huff it out two-fold. Again. And again. A building cycle.

It had begun.

CHAPTER 106

Hours later—he had no idea how many because he'd somehow fallen asleep —Paul startled at the sound of thumping close to his head.

His first thought was the storm. It had been growing since soon after midnight. First the wind, then the flakes had come down, hard and fast. It was going to be another whiteout, maybe worse than the first.

Thump! Thump! Thump!

He blinked his eyelids hard and rolled off the cot with his hands clutching the shotgun the doctor had given him. The doorknob rattled again. The beam of a flashlight shone against the other side of the window blinds. Someone was trying to get in, but had found the door locked. Paul had also shoved his cot up against it in case the lock wasn't strong enough, but things apparently hadn't gone that far yet.

Holding the gun with his left hand, Paul lifted the blinds on the narrow window beside the door, but could only see vague shapes in the storm outside. He considered, then finally dropped the blinds and shoved the cot out of the way with his foot. Stepping quietly over to the sleeping marshal, he shook him awake and pointed to the door. The marshal blinked in the dim light much as Paul had. He grabbed his revolver out of its holster under his pillow on the couch and sat up. Swaying a little, he swiped groggily at the bandages plastered around the left side of his head. He waved for Paul to open the door.

Paul crept up to it, just as whoever was outside thumped a third time. He turned back the double deadbolt—addicts, the doctor had explained, made the security necessary—and unlocked the knob. Pulled it open.

It almost blew him in with a whoosh, the storm had grown so fierce. And in the dark howl of snow on the doorstep stood Al Rawley and a crowd of about twelve men toting flashlights and guns.

"Need to tell you!" Rawley called in to Paul, waving at Paul and the marshal's pointed guns.

"What?"

"More killings!"

"What?" Paul felt his hands get even slicker on the shotgun barrel.

"Tons more! Killer's back!"

Paul stepped back and let the men in.

CHAPTER 107

In the overnight room, Nicole shook her head at the banging without waking up. *Japhet Bone! He was trying to get in! Get at her!*

Then the sounds of men's voices filtered through, Paul's voice, and she swam up to consciousness, suddenly jerking her eyes open and her body off her cot as she remembered where she was. She banged against Georgia's bed and almost tripped over the children's air mattresses as she stumbled to the door of the waiting room and carefully opened it.

The waiting room lights were on and the room was full of men. Ari, Wendy, and Josh had come out of the examination room. Doc Williams had come downstairs in his robe. Paul and Marshal Pritchett were standing. And the rest of the room was filled with snow-covered men in coats and rifles, some carrying heavy flashlights.

Another lynch mob?

At their front, facing Paul, was the man in the sheepskin coat and cowboy hat whom Ari had accosted just three days ago in the lobby of the Grenadine Hotel. Al Rawley. He was part of Georgia's story too, and the story Ari had told her about the near-lynching. Rawley was a grade-A asshole who might have played a big role in delaying Bone's apprehension all those years ago.

Except that in full glare of the reception room lights, the man looked like someone who'd just had his liver ripped out. His face was blanched white and his eyes were unnaturally wide and staring. He leaned forward, almost nose-to-nose with Paul, when he spoke and Nicole realized he was drunk.

"Was sleeping downstairs," Rawley slurred. "Didn't want to wake Grace and the kids when I came in 'cause...you know. Then, later, I hear something.

Wake up. Go up t' check it. An' I can *smell* it. Like hunting. You get close you can smell it." His hand shot out and gripped Paul's arm. "Y'ever?"

Paul shook his head.

"Kinda hot...metal. I run to Matt and Tommy's room and...great holy freaking ghost..." His eyes went totally glassy for a second, seeing it, as his free left hand jumped up to slash a finger spastically across his own throat, then his chest, then around his groin and down. "I go to Grace's bedroom and..." He shook his head and spastically slashed his finger over his throat again and again.

"Al...," started the pudgy man beside him and Nicole wondered where the seconds were whom Ari had described as being with Rawley—Jeremy Buckster and a guy with a sucked-in mouth. Wait, there was Buckster, hanging at the side of the crowed, staring daggers at Ari. And behind Buckster, watching uncomfortably, was Horst Hurzgehrmine.

Rawley snapped back to himself, wobbling. "So I grab my gun and go for the door. Bastard's gone, but I see Joe there, pounding on his neighbor's door. Other men and wives out in the snow. Daughters. Sons." He choked the last out.

"I heard screaming, kind of," said a man behind Rawley.

"Me too," said another.

"But he was never there when you got there."

"Ghost."

"*Army* of ghosts."

"Shut it!" Rawley said, raising his gun. Then he bored his pasty face and mustache towards Paul and grabbed Paul's shirt front. "You get what's happened? Your crazy man—he didn't die up on Warsaw. He's back. That sonofa-goddamn-bitching bastard killed my wife and son."

"Hey, Al." The pudgy man pulled Rawley back and Rawley stumbled. Then he shrugged it off, pushed through to the outside wall of the room where he reached out to steady himself and faced away from everyone.

The pudgy man said, "We found tracks, see. The snow is wiping everything clean, but we've got at least twenty-five dead. All by knife."

"Holy Christ," whispered Marshal Pritchett back to Paul's right.

"We also found one woman cut up but alive."

Nicole couldn't help herself. "*What?*"

The whole room swiveled towards her and she knew how she had to look. Borrowed cotton pants and tee-shirt hanging loose, her hair wild. "Why was she alive?" Nicole demanded.

"To tell us," the pudgy man said, "where Bone was going."

Nicole looked from man to man, avoiding only Paul. "Why?"

The pudgy man looked embarrassed. "He said he was tired, see. Satan was calling him. But if we didn't come get him soon in one of the old mine shacks up on Minsk, he was going to come back and take the rest of the town to hell with him."

There was a silence in the room and Nicole thought furiously. It sounded...wrong. In some way that she couldn't pin down. "It's a lie," she said.

"Says who?" Rawley said from the wall. He pushed off it and lurched, red-faced, into the middle of the men. "You going to listen to some woman in a doorway over what you saw? The tracks were heading that way. Straight east out of town. How long are you little puppy dogs going to wait here? Until he comes back for *your* wife, Burke? Or your kids, Andrew?"

There was a murmured agreement through the men who'd come in. A heightened energy in the air. Nicole saw even Marshal Pritchett looking at the floor seriously as he touched his head bandages.

"And you gotta come, Paul," Rawley said suddenly, fixing his eyes on Nicole's husband. "You'n Bob here are the only ones who've seen him."

"I don't—"

"You owe us, Paul. You screwed us big with the avalanche story."

"That was no story."

Rawley bit his mustache. "Okay, put it this way." He looked over at Nicole, who glared back at him. "That's the wife you pulled out of the avalanche, right? You want to let this killer keep running around until he gets to her again?"

Nicole shook her head fiercely. "Don't," she said low.

But she could see Paul buying it. He looked to her, and beyond her, to the room that held Georgia and the children, and he made up his mind. "I'll come," he said, and pushed through the crowd to get his coat from under the overturned cot.

Rawley slapped him on the back.

Pritchett shuffled to peg on the wall to grab his own parka. "I'm coming too," he said."

Someone opened the door again to the blowing snow and men began heading out. Paul was at the very end of the line.

"Don't leave me, Paul," Nicole whispered at his back, but her words were lost in the sound of him slamming the door shut behind him.

CHAPTER 108

NICOLE SLID down the doorframe between the reception area and the overnight room.

"What?" Ari said to his friend, Josh. "You didn't want to grab a gun and go with them?"

"And have them plug me 'by accident' out in the storm? No way, Ari-dad."

"Hush."

That would be Wendy, Nicole thought. She was probably pointing her finger towards Nicole, the abandoned old woman in the doorway. Because, God knew, Nicole surely felt old and abandoned right now.

There was a light patter of bare feet, then twenty bare little toes were standing right beside Nicole's raised knees. Above the bare toes and feet were little pajama bottoms – blue spaceships on one and pink kittens on the other. Oh, please.

"Nicole?"

Nicole tiredly raised her head. "What, April?"

"Is everything going to hell in a handbasket?"

Nicole's mouth quirked up and she looked back to the bed where Georgia lay, awake, too sick to do anything but watch with a worried expression. "I hope not."

Auggie said, "Is your hu'band going to die?"

Nicole frowned at him. "Why are you asking that?"

"Um... 'Cause... 'Cause..."

"Because you look like Mommy did when Daddy died," April said. Her little face was so pasty and serious in the harsh light from the reception area.

"I hope nobody more is going to die around here," Nicole answered with equal seriousness. "Except maybe the man my husband and those other men are going out to find."

"The scary man," Auggie said and blinked rapidly.

"Yes," said Nicole. *Your uncle.* "That one."

"I hope they shoots him," Auggie said.

Nicole nodded, though she knew a good parent should be horrified by the thought, horrified by all these kids had been through and what that must be doing to their sense of the world. But Nicole was beyond horror, and she was *not* the parent of these children. "I hope they shoots him too," she said.

The examination room clicked closed and Nicole saw that Doc Williams had obviously been in there and come out again. "I heard all that, Ms. Baker." He strode brusquely over to where Nicole sat blocking the doorway. "And while I don't approve the sentiment, I am glad to see my two youngest patients are talking again. Hm?"

He looked down at Auggie and April. They looked up at him with tightly closed lips, then Auggie turned and ran back to Georgia, trying to crawl up onto her bed until Georgia groaned and shook her head. Auggie ran back to Nicole and huddled in close.

"Well perhaps they won't talk to *me*," said the doctor. He reached down and squeezed Nicole's shoulder like he was sending a secret message. Then he readjusted his glasses and carefully stepped over her, smiled at the children, and walked over to Georgia's bed. "Let's see about our other big patient in here, shall we?"

As he did, Auggie crawled onto Nicole's lap and April snuggled under her arm. Nicole caught Georgia's glazed eyes and the sick woman nodded. Then Nicole saw Ari, grinning ruefully at her, his own arm sneaking up around Wendy's shoulders to give her a hug.

Josh looked at everyone, then brushed back his long reddish hair with the spread fingers of one hand. To no one in particular, he said, "Hell of night, dude."

The wind beat harder against the door in response.

CHAPTER 109

LATER, the lights in the reception area were off again but Doc Williams had turned on the outside light for the men when they returned. He'd also plugged in some phosphorescent green night lights in the reception and overnight rooms for the kids.

But despite the excitement, the moan of the wind outside, and the dull chug of the generator out back, the children were back on their cots, sound asleep. Georgia had likewise conked out. Doc Williams had retreated up to his apartment over the clinic. Josh had crashed in the cot Paul had abandoned. Ari and Wendy had gone back into the examination room where Ari's oma had slept soundly throughout.

Nicole did not sleep.

Cursed with insomnia from early childhood, the foreboding she felt now wouldn't let her sit for more than a few minutes at a time. She paced around the reception room, her arms were wrapped around her, clutching and re-clutching as she tried to understand what was going through Bone's brain.

Looking for his mother, Ari's file had said. And he wanted Nicole as his sister. Family hang-ups, then. Sexual fantasies. Sadism. Merciless killing. None of it related to the sort of wounds Nicole knew personally or met in her clients.

And yet something picked at her mind, made her jumpy like an internal clock was running down. She was missing...something.

She went to the blinds and turned them just enough to look out at the snow whistling by the clinic's front door light. She squinted at the dial of her watch, which had miraculously survived the bouncing around she'd taken in the Jeep. It showed 1:22. a.m. That made it almost forty minutes since the men had left.

Long enough for them to be solidly climbing the mountain. Long enough for the people they'd left in the clinic to have all fallen asleep again.

A large shadow seemed to pass through her peripheral vision outside the window and her head jerked up. There was nothing. She was seeing ghosts now. Nerves.

What had she been thinking, though? That it was long enough for what?

"Hey."

She started and turned her head. It was Ari. He grinned, looked back into the examination room to make sure his grandmother and Wendy still slept, then tiptoed over to her. Nicole gave him a tight smile.

"Can't sleep?" Ari whispered.

She shook her head, dimly aware of how well they matched, both their heads bandaged up, and how he was struggling to not check out her body. "I've never been a good sleeper. One more reason for people to—"

She stopped as the niggling thought burst through. It was what her brain-injured clients, herself, and Bone shared. Extreme shifts of mood. Sudden, intensities that made other people question your stability and label you unpredictable or even crazy. And when people saw you that way, they'd believe anything of you. Even something like being called by Satan and waiting up a mountain in the middle of a snowstorm for people to come get you.

It was a trick!

With all his raging through town, Bone had certainly been able to pin down Nicole's location at least. Then all he'd needed to do was remove any protections they had for...long enough. *The shadow outside.*

"What?" Ari asked.

Nicole bit her lips hard, then set her jaw and looked at him. "We need to check all the locks of this clinic again, front and back," she said.

"What is it?"

Nicole checked the window latch through the blinds, then shut the blinds. "Japhet Bone is coming here," she said.

Ari opened his mouth like he was about to dispute it, but shut it again and simply nodded. "Okay." He hurried through the door to the overnight room and she heard him unlocking and re-locking the deadbolts on the door.

Nicole meanwhile walked over to the couch where Josh slept and shook him awake. She explained what she needed his help doing. "Wha—? Y'okay," was his response. He rolled off the heavy couch and went to her end of it to help her slide-push it to the window.

Ari returned from the overnight room and ducked quietly into the examination room, coming back out with a rifle. "My oma's," he said, embarrassed.

He set it on the floor near the door and the three of them hoisted the couch up on one arm and pushed it over. The couch crashed against the wall. Wendy woke up in the other room with a cry. Ari, Josh, and Nicole waggled the upended couch along the wall until it covered the blinds. Then Nicole made them haul over the receptionist's desk to scrape up against it and hold it in place.

"Won't keep him out," Ari puffed when they were done.

"No," Nicole said. "But it might slow him down."

Wendy had finally appeared in the examination room door. "What are you—?"

"Shh!" Nicole said. "You hear that?"

They listened to a scraping sound from the back of the clinic. The wind howled, drowning it out. Settled. They heard the scraping again.

"It's the fallen telephone wire," Ari whispered. "Doc said it came down in the storm, first night."

They fell silent and all listened again. Just storm sounds. The front and back doors were locked. The only windows were here and one each in the examination and overnight rooms, both too small to climb through.

"There's nothing," Josh said and looked at Nicole doubtfully.

Nicole became aware her lips were trembling hard. The inner clock was ticking down. She could feel it. She knew.

"You sure this isn't, like, a bit paranoid?"

There was a tinkling sound out front. A clunk.

"Look," Nicole said. She pointed to the window behind the upended couch. No light spilled through it now. The outside light was gone.

"Oh, sh—"

The entire window and blinds behind the couch burst inward.

CHAPTER 110

WHATEVER HAD SHATTERED the window drew back and struck again, shattering the remaining glass and ripping through the blinds to shudder into the rear of the couch. It jerked out and there was the blur of two thick arms covered in snow and blood jamming through the ripped blinds with a savage roar, battering at the couch, pushing it, tipping it...

Ke-rack!

A chunk flew out of the blinds and Nicole whirled to see Ari holding up his grandmother's gun to his pasty white face, sighting for a second shot.

But the arms were gone, sucked back out to the storm.

"Keep your gun up, Ari," Nicole said, steelier than she felt. "Wendy and Josh, turn on the lights and look for something to attack him with. Paperweight, chair, whatever you—"

Whump! Something hit the front door so hard it shook.

Again. A crack appeared in the middle of the door. The lights went on.

"Dude's got an axe," said Josh, frozen.

Again. *Thump!* The front tip of metal was through, splintering the heavy wood. The power behind it. If he just...

Ari had swung the rifle barrel towards the front door, sweating and blinking hard. "Do I fire through the door? Nicole?"

She shook her head, her brain burning. "He's not trying to get in or he'd have gone for the lock," she said and ran to the reception desk.

The axe hit again. *Crack!* Nicole felt like her own knees were about to give way.

"He's afraid of the gun. Just keep covering the door. The rest of you get your weapons." Nicole grabbed a box of thumbtacks from the top right drawer, shoved it into her shirt pocket, and grabbed a letter opener.

Again. Splinters flew inwards.

"Josh!"

"But—"

"Josh, catch!" Wendy shouted at him too, throwing him a heavy bedpan she'd found in the examination room.

"What do I do with this? Vomit?" Josh screeched and fumbled it so it bounced to the floor and away from him. He chased it down and scooped it up.

The thumping on the front door stopped. Everyone froze. Listened.

There was only the storm again, louder now since it could whistle in through the shattered window. Then, through the pounding of her heart in her ears, Nicole heard the crying from the overnight room. The children!

"Keep the door and window covered, Ari," Nicole said and skipped back to the overnight room, slipping her letter opener into the rear waistband of the Doc's intern pants that she wore.

In the back room the lights were still out and Nicole had to blink a second to adjust. Then she saw both kids huddled, scared and crying, over by their mother. Georgia, in obvious pain, was doing her best to wrap her arms around both of them, but she looked ready to pass out.

"It's okay," Nicole lied, coming up behind them gently and touching their shoulders. So skinny. "Really. But I think I'm just going to move your mommy's bed a little bit further away from that d—"

Whump! went something into the back door and both children screamed.

"Ari!" Nicole called. He came running in with his rifle raised, aiming at the door as Wendy followed, flicking on the lights.

Whump! The door seemed to crack louder than the front door, the wood less strong.

But Bone was still going for the center of the door, not the locks. Trying to scare us, Nicole insisted furiously to herself as she clutched the railing on the side of Georgia's hospital bed. Not truly intent on getting in yet. If they could just hold out, then. Get ready for him somehow.

"N-Nicole?" Georgia said from her bed. "Where's Paul?"

"Out looking for *him*," Nicole said and fiercely jabbed a thumb towards the back door. The next expected axe blow hadn't come.

"Is...is he coming back?"

Paul or Bone? "Yes," Nicole breathed. Both, she was sure. But it was Bone she had to worry about now.

Swallowing dryly, she tiptoed to the back door and felt it where the axe had sounded. It seemed solid enough. And the deadbolts, she noted now, had metal plating all around them. Very solid. If Bone did try to come through the doors, it wasn't going to be as easy as he'd made it seem. But the blocked window in the other room? Vulnerable. And these narrow windows. Could they be breached and widened somehow?

Nicole gulped and reached, open-mouthed, for the blinds over the tiny window near the door. Lifted the blinds out just a little...

A frozen corpse glared in at her, its throat cut, its empty sockets crusted black.

Nicole screamed and dropped the blind back even as she saw Bone's hands around the neck of the corpse, holding it up, then drawing it back and ramming it like a rock into the window so the glass shattered and the window blind fluttered back.

Ari fired his gun at the space, missing the hole by a good foot as a chunk flew out of the inside wall. The children screamed and began to wail in panic. Wendy ran to them.

Then there was nothing.

The storm gusted through the hole Bone had made in the window and blew the blinds around inside with a clacking sound.

"Oh, dude, this sucks," came Josh's shaky voice through the children's yells. Nicole saw him holding up his silver bedpan like a shield. "This really really sucks."

Ari, hands so slick he had to keep adjusting their hold on the rifle, was looking to Nicole. "What now?"

Nicole swallowed and looked around the room. Everyone, even the wailing children, were looking at her with hope and trust in their eyes. "Josh, check the last window downstairs," she said. "It's in the examination room. See if you can find some tape and boards or something to seal this window too."

"I'll go with him," Ari said.

"No," Nicole said. "You keep your gun. Cover all the rooms. Especially the window in the reception area. Wendy, help Josh."

"But—"

"I'll look after the children. Go."

Wendy did.

Nicole took her place, squeezing Georgia's hand, kneeling beside the children and talking with them quietly until they quieted to hear what she was saying. And for a moment she willed even herself to hear only her voice, the children's snuffling, the wind whistling snow in through the shattered window and blinds.

Nothing more. Nothing.

CHAPTER 111

In his bedroom above the clinic, Doctor Chester J. Williams finally struggled awake through the claustrophobia of tangled sheets and bad dreams. In them, there were dead bodies everywhere—in his kitchen fridge, on his doorstep, in his bathtub. He kept tripping over them and they thumped and rolled about. Things crashed. They shattered windows...

Then he was fully awake and aware of the thumping downstairs. Like someone rummaging through all his medical supplies. Thieves!

Chester J. swung his hairy old legs in their flannel pj's out of bed and remembered the previous day and night. All his patients and guests downstairs. All the corpses in the snow out back. It was a real nightmare, a true one. The Goldrock Freak had returned. And while all those men—Rawley and Pritchett, this visitor Paul, the others—were trying to track him down, Chester had no confidence they would.

Because he remembered Japhet Bone far too well. Spooky thug of a boy. Abusing his sister. Abusing half the little girls in the town, then the women. And Doc Williams, Chester J., with the evidence of these crimes coming through his office nearly weekly for a time, had said nothing.

Why? Because young buck Al Rawley, whoring around with Wilma Bone, had threatened to close down the ski hills if anyone said anything?

No, because Doc Williams had been doing the mean thing with Wilma himself, and Wilma had begged with him, pleaded him for some kind of help for Japhet. *He's sick,* she'd said. *Help him.*

Sick was right.

Chester huffed out of his slack, white-haired old chest. He turned his head sadly to the picture of Ermeline that still sat on his bedside table. Lovely young woman. Kind and thoughtful. She'd been the Goldrock freak's first official murder victim. "I'm sorry," Chester said to her for the thousandth time. Then he creaked up from the edge of his bed to get to the bathroom, reaching down to grab his crotch to help hold it in. Damn prostate. Made it hellsabitch to pee enough before bed. Had to look into ordering some of those new drugs for it.

He stopped just outside the bathroom door and frowned. Some sort of thumping in there. Scraping sounds. Wind.

Then he remembered the telephone wire that ran from just under the roof to the pole down the alley a little. It had snapped off in the first night of storm and had been hanging down his back wall ever since. And Chester must have left the window open.

"Slab-face idjut storm," he grumbled as he grabbed the doorknob and pushed it open.

"Hi, doc."

Chester blinked. What stood there made awful sense in his half-awake state of memory. It was the thug-boy, Japhet Bone, only blown up all out of proportion, filling the entire doorway plus. And his face, his vest and shirt, were covered in snow and blood. He reeked of it. His hand held a large knife.

"You're...back," Williams said.

The man shrugged forward and drove the knife deep into William's gut and upwards, puncturing Chester's scream before he could release it. Sucked it back down and out.

Something grabbed Williams' head, jerked it back so he could see the grimace that seemed to wrap around the monster's entire being.

Then something hot sawed across Williams' throat, crunching in through this windpipe until he could no longer breathe or draw air. Then wetness. Bubbles. Choking. Drowning. He spastically gripped at his mouth and his mangled, flapping neck as Bone headed for the stairs down to the clinic.

So this was what...it...felt...like...

CHAPTER 112

ARI FOUGHT to keep his gun down as he danced anxiously into the examination room. There Josh and Wendy were just finished taping the doc's surgical instruments tray across the narrow window. Ari snorted nervously as Josh patted down his last piece of surgical tape then picked up the stapler he'd found somewhere and began stapling the tape into place.

Ari danced over to the narrow, arched staircase on the far side of the room that led up to Doc Williams' residence. He looked up it worriedly, then paced away again.

Wendy came to him. "The kids are okay?"

He nodded, studying his oma's prostrate body on the table now. "Doc must be out as cold as Oma," he muttered. "Maybe I should check on him."

"Are you okay?"

Ari swallowed a hard lump and shook his head.

"What?"

"Sounds real cliché, but...it's too quiet."

Wendy, and Josh who'd heard him, stopped moving and listened with him. Besides the dull rumble of the storm and their own breathing, there was nothing. Not even the sounds of the kids snuffling from the other room.

And a certainty suddenly came to Ari that Japhet Bone was sliding silently into the reception area around the upended couch. He was right there! Ari needed to get out there to stop him.

Ari turned to rush out but Wendy grabbed his shoulder.

"Wha—?"

Both her hands went to his cheeks and pulled his face around to hers, then she kissed him hard and long, her hands and lips warm on his clammy skin. When she pulled back, she held him just a second longer. "We'll be okay," she whispered.

Which is when two thumps sounded from the arched staircase—just enough time for Ari to look that way and let his jaw drop—and Japhet Bone, like a mythical grizzly bear, came leaping over the examination table at Ari.

He hit him before Ari could half-raise the rifle, and drove Ari backwards. There was barely time to register Josh and Wendy's screams before Ari's head hit the floor and he saw sparks. A part of him tensed for the knife he'd seen in Bone's right hand. Tried to roll. Couldn't.

Then he realized the knife hadn't come and Bone was no longer on top of him. Ari grunted his way up to his feet and saw that Bone was spinning in a circle with Josh attached to his back like a red-haired wolverine, beating at the monster's head.

Wendy was frantically searching Doc Williams' desk for a weapon and settled on some kind of saw device, rotary-ended and sharp looking. She cried out and ran past Ari to stab at Bone, making the big man howl as she slashed up his leg.

A second later Bone had kicked her backwards and slung Josh down, slicing Ari's friend across the chest as he crashed down.

Ari dove for Wendy's weapon and raised it in front of Bone, but Bone had grabbed Josh by his hair and dragged him up in front of him, knife across his gut. "I'll k-k-k-k-kill him!" he said, and sidled around the exam table to the door out.

Ari swallowed sick chunks in his mouth, remembering the gun and wondering where the heck it had fallen. "Okay," he said. "Okay."

Then Bone was in the doorway and Ari leapt at him, making him leap back rather than stab Josh.

And Ari suddenly blinked hard because the lights in both the reception area and the overnight room went out.

Nicole!

"He's coming!" Ari shouted.

CHAPTER 113

Nicole was already ducking behind the med clinic's upended couch and reception desk, pulling her letter opener out of her waistband and fumbling open her box of thumbtacks.

Paranoid instinct had gotten her out to check on Ari a second before Bone had leapt, and like a replay of the nightmare scenario she'd already practiced over and over in her mind, she'd run back to hit the lights in the overnight room, then fumbled about, cursing to herself, before she found the lights for the reception and rooms. Almost lost Josh to the delay. Then she ran across the reception area in blackness to make her last stand.

Now she swore again, "F-fuck," as a few of the tacks spilled, but heard Bone going for the overnight room door and so jerked up to her feet.

"Asshole!" she shouted.

Bone whirled at the voice and, presumably still adjusting to the dark, rushed towards her.

She flung her box of thumbtacks and saw them spread in the dark, hitting Bone in a weak patter that nonetheless made him stutter to a halt.

"S-s-s-stupid, Sarah."

"Name's Nicole."

The monster leapt at her over the edge of the desk, reaching to grab, but Nicole jumped back, stabbing at the monster's injured right shoulder as she did. She connected with a satisfying scrape of bone before she yanked her weapon out again and backpedaled to the wall.

"Ahhh!" Bone fell to the floor but rolled up again, half-clutching his wounded arm with his left hand. And rather than leap again, he pulled back his lips like a feral animal to advance slowly.

Nicole wavered, mouth dry. Every instinct in her screamed to dash forward around him to the overnight room on the right wall. But the children were in there, along with Georgia, who was too weak to even get out of bed, too weak to do anything but scream and die if Nicole brought the monster in.

So Nicole held her bloodied letter opener up in front of her with both hands and met Bone's eyes. "Stay back," she said evenly.

His response was to rush her. In one quick motion, he swept the letter opener aside with his right hand, spun her around into his right arm, and grabbed her hair with his left hand, shoving her up against the wall. He bent his face down beside hers. His breath was hot and foul, his lips still pulled back so she could see his teeth in her peripheral vision. Also his unshaved, blood-caked face, his wild eyes.

He tightened his grip on her hair so it felt like he was ripping her scalp. He shook her head, hard. "You're S-sarah Bone."

"I..." Nicole tried to focus but could hardly breathe with her face pressed so hard into the wall. "I'm not..."

"Y-y-y-you're Sarah and I can p-prove it with lights."

He began dragging her back towards the light switch...*beside the open door to the overnight room.* If he saw Georgia. If he saw the children...

It rekindled her fight and Nicole kicked and struggled, but she was too weak. He was almost there.

There was a crashing sound from the overnight room and Georgia was suddenly in the doorway in her hospital gown, clutching the doorframe and blocking Bone's way.

"Let her go, Jafe," she sighed. "It's me you want."

CHAPTER 114

Against the bottom wall of Minsk Mountain, the wind was howling fiercer now, and the snow was stinging so hard into Paul's eyes that he'd pulled the strings of his hood down to almost cover them. His fingers inside his gloves could hardly feel the weight of Doc Williams' gun in them.

And his anxiety was growing. Something wasn't right.

Shielding his face with his hands, he could see Al Rawley bounce his flashlight beam around the bottom of a broken-down sluice run. It was a crudely-shaped wooden trough that originated somewhere far up the mountainside, the third such one they'd checked out. Unlike the others, though, this slope up looked totally inaccessible, all cliff and ice.

"It has to be another one!" Paul shouted through the wind. "There's no way up!"

Rawley whirled back to him fully, swore, then took in the other twelve who'd made it this far with him. "All the others were knocked down last year! He's *here*, goddamn it!"

Paul shook his head and looked away, squinting through the stinging snow to the black hole of Goldrock, trying to figure out why he had a growing certainty Bone wasn't here. He tried to put himself into Bone's mind. Crazy mad, slashing his way through the town. Slash! Slash! Oops. Stop and tell a woman that you're going to keep going on up the side of Minsk and wait there. Slash! Slash!

Tell them I'll be there. Get them to leave where they are...

"Oh, God," Paul whispered quietly. What had he done? He'd even taken Doc Williams' gun from the clinic.

Stepping quickly over to Herr Hurzgehrmine, Paul cleared his throat and said over the wind, "Come back with me to the clinic, Horst."

"*Vas?*"

Paul held the eyes of his bed-and-breakfast landlord. "The killer isn't up here, and I need help finding my way back. Come with me."

Rawley yelled over to them. "What're you doing?"

"Horst, please. My wife's in danger. And your grandchildren."

The last decided it and Hurzgehrmine nodded, holding up his gun. It was a single action, manual loader but it would have to do. Paul thanked him and squeezed his shoulder but Rawley was suddenly there, shoving them apart.

"What's going on?"

"Killer's going for the medical clinic," Paul said.

"Said he was going to be up here."

"He said that to get us away from protecting the others."

Rawley grabbed Paul's jacket. "Cow-pucky."

Then Horst stepped up beside Rawley and reached in to grip the front of the cowboy's sheepskin coat with surprising strength. "You will let him go now."

"But—"

"My wife, she thinks it is right to let the devil play here tonight, that this is somehow justice. But I do not. My grandchildren are *innocent*."

Then Bob Pritchett was beside them, holding his hat in the wind and leaning in. "I think Rawley's right," he said. "We all stay here and look."

With disgust, Horst Hurzgehrmine pushed Rawley backwards so the bigger man staggered in the snow. Horst had his rifle trained on Rawley before he could regain his footing. Pritchett frowned and stepped back quickly. Then Horst grabbed Paul's arm and pointed down the hill.

With Horst shuffling backwards and keeping his gun trained on the rest of the search party, he and Paul began their descent.

CHAPTER 115

THE THICK ARM across Nicole's arms and middle twitched and she felt Bone's foul breath hot by her cheek again as he said, "N-no. This is Sarah." He shook Nicole's head by her hair so it felt like her scalp was ripping and she cried out.

Georgia slumped a little more against the doorframe. Her face was pale as she shook her head. "Jafe. Y'all know it's me."

"H-hair!"

"I dyed my hair."

"Eyes!"

"Look into them. You remember me? You remember...*fugging* me? When I was only four...unh...years..." She slumped down more in the doorway. "Want me to tell this woman what you said every time?"

Bone's arm was like iron around her middle but Nicole had the feeling he'd forgotten she was even there. His breath was coming fast and hot against her and she could feel... Jesus, she could feel the hard lump of his crotch twitching into her backside.

"You said, 'I'm a big boy. I'm a big boy.' Over and over. You remember."

"Y-y-y-you... Sarah."

"Yeah, Jafe. Me Sarah," she said weakly, and tried to push off the doorframe to walk to him.

Bone stopped her by jerking hard on Nicole's hair. "Show m-m-m-me."

For a second Georgia closed her eyes and Nicole thought she'd passed out. Then she reached one hand over her back and untied the top string of the hospital gown. She dropped her arm and shrugged the gown forward off her shoulder so it fell down over her bra. Then she pulled the right cup of her brassiere down to expose a long white scar that curved down and left around the nipple like a signature.

When she pulled the bra cup up again, Nicole could feel Japhet pumping rhythmically against her buttocks and Nicole's gorge rose in her mouth. Then his hand swept her head back and forth by her hair like he was about to snap her neck.

"Don't," she breathed quietly.

Suddenly there was a hard crack behind her—gunshot—and Nicole drove all her force into a kick on Japhet's shins. His hold loosened with a grunt and she ripped herself loose, rolling across the floor, seeing Ari with his grandmother's rifle—his aim was as bad as Paul's, for Chrissake—aiming again...

...as Bone dove for the door to the overnight room.

And Georgia, sweet, soft, abused little Georgia, threw herself between her monstrous brother and her children, which was akin to throwing herself in the way of an oncoming train.

Bone plowed through her as Ari swung his gun high, scared of shooting her. It made Bone, preternaturally aware and quick, spin with a laugh and jerk Georgia off the floor, then smash her sideways into the doorframe with a sickening crack. He plunged on as Georgia's body toppled slowly to the floor.

Her eyes seemed to be staring into Nicole's. Begging. Then blood trickled from her mouth. The stare became glassy.

No, Nicole mouthed wordlessly as time slowed down. *Not after all that. No.*

Time snapped back to speed and Nicole sprinted over to Ari, wrenched the rifle from his grip, and ran to the overnight room with Ari pounding after her.

She was too late.

Bone was crouched down behind the hospital bed Georgia had been in until her final sacrifice. On the bed in front of him, each with one tiny wrist gripped in one of Bone's fists, were April and Auggie.

"N-N-Nicole. Right?" he said, baring his teeth at her from behind the childrens' shoulders. "Still want to s-s-save me?"

Nicole shook her head and raised the rifle to her shoulder, sighting it to a spot in the middle of Bone's forehead. But even if it weren't so dark, she thought as her forehead and hands broke out in sweat, *could I guarantee I'd hit Bone and not the children?*

Her own breath was like a storm in her ears. In...out....

"Stand up," she ordered.

"Okay," Bone said, and scooped his arms suddenly around the children, holding them up near his face like a shield as he stepped slowly out from around the bed.

Nicole wavered her gunsight from his face down to his exposed lower abdomen and legs. She could—

"B-back off, bitch. Or I'll s-s-smash them like their mother."

"She was your sister," Nicole said, backing out the door and waving Ari back with her hands. Bone was advancing.

"Ari!" Wendy called him urgently and Nicole heard him retreat to the examination room completely. Oh, thanks very much, brave helper.

Bone paused for a second in the doorway, glancing down at Georgia's crushed body. "F-families mean dick," he said. Then, as if he knew these words would stun her, he suddenly twisted his body so that Auggie rolled down his arm with a shriek. Bone's large hand caught him by his pajama top, though, and heaved him at Nicole.

As Nicole lowered the gun to catch Auggie, Bone was already running at her, plowing her down much as he'd done Georgia, but grabbing the rifle as he went, not Nicole.

Then Nicole was on the ground with Auggie and Bone was grunting a violent laugh as he threw back the bolts of the clinic's front door. "Y-you want the kid, b-b-bring me my mama. Twenty minutes. Just you and her. Top of the t-town hall."

And he was out, the storm whipping the door back to crash against the outside wall, the snow howling into the clinic like a triumph of cold over warmth, blackness over light.

CHAPTER 116

"Arɪ!" Nicole called, fighting hysteria. She gulped down deep breaths and held Auggie to her as she struggled her feet under her.

Ari stepped from the examination room with his face blanched white. He saw Auggie wrapped around Nicole's neck and his eyes twitched around the rest of the room. "The girl?"

"He has her! He's taking her to town hall. I'm supposed to bring his mother there."

"Why the town hall?" Ari asked dully.

"You have to help me find his mother!" Nicole lurched up and towards him. Auggie was clutching both his arms and legs around Nicole now, quivering and making strange yelping sounds, head buried into her shoulder. But Ari made no move to help. What the hell—?

"My oma," he said to her. "Miryam Ava Siegel. She's dead."

"Oh," Nicole said, and felt her heart, which she'd already thought dropped as far as it could go, hit the bottom of her gut. Not only for the death—another death, another love killed, another loss—but also for the vanished faint hope of using Ari's grandmother somehow to trick Bone.

Now she was gone. Hope was gone.

Wendy stepped out behind Ari. None of them were looking at where Georgia lay slumped and absolutely still. Not even Auggie. There was no need. "You have to go with Nicole," Wendy said shakily, then bit down hard on her lower lip to keep control.

"What?" Ari said dully.

"I'll look after the boy," Wendy said, "and Josh. You need to go with her because...well, because she's going after the little girl." She looked, scared, at Nicole. "Aren't you?"

And even as she said it, Nicole knew it was true. Because there was no one else here. And Georgia had looked at her in her last seconds. And if Nicole didn't go, little April Hurzgehrmine was going to be killed by the same man who'd just killed her mother, saying, *Family means dick.*

"I'm going," she said.

She took a breath and murmured in Auggie's ear that she'd be back soon. Then she peeled Auggie's scrambling feet from around her waist, his desperate hands from around her neck as he cried, "No! No! Stay! *Stay!*" She held him at arms' length while Wendy hurried forward to get him and hold him to her.

"Take my jacket," Wendy said, nodding to the examination room, and Nicole went in to get it. She reemerged a moment later wearing a pair of boots she'd found and the parka, tight around her shoulders and riding high on her taller frame.

"Check the pockets," Wendy said.

Nicole did and found mitts, a snow hat, and something small wrapped in a bunch of paper toweling. She pulled it out, unwrapped it, and saw a wicked looking scalpel Wendy had obviously snagged from the Doc's operating supplies.

Wendy shrugged and Nicole nodded. She rewrapped it and stuck it back in the right pocket. She pulled on the hat and mitts.

She saw that Ari had finally snapped out of his shock and pulled Georgia's body out of sight into the overnight room. He had his own blue and yellow coat and gloves on, and carried the silver bedpan Josh had fumbled in one hand, and a blood-encrusted butcher's knife in the other. He looked at the knife and shrugged, "I've been caught with a knife of his once. I may as well use it this time."

Nicole nodded, shuddered, and together they stepped out the door and into the storm.

The wind and snow howled around them. The only was from the clinic and the occasional building further up Main Street, including, ironically, the lit face of the Town Hall clock.

Ari turned towards her and shouted over the wind. "So what do we do when he asks where his mother is?"

"What?" Nicole yelled back.

A dark, graceful shape suddenly stepped out from the south corner of the clinic and walked towards Nicole and Ari, resolving into a woman Nicole recognized as she stepped in close enough to be heard and spoke with cultured precision.

"He asked," she said, "what little Jafey Bone was going to do if you show up without his mother." Elizabeth Severin gave Nicole a smile that drove the storm chill straight through her.

CHAPTER 117

Up. And up. Tick tock.

Japhet stumbled a little, almost lost his grip on the girl. Weakened right arm. He leaned his head against the lower stairway wall of the Town Hall and used the wooden bannister to ease the weight of the little girl snugged under his arm. He sucked in the red glow of the emergency exit lights, one at the top and bottom of each stairwell. Pushed himself off the bannister. Kept climbing. The auto-loading rifle he'd taken swung in his left hand.

How many bullets left?

The elevator was out. The whole place had been shut down and abandoned for this storm. The stairs, stinky with ammonia, went up forever.

"Are you going to kill me?"

It was the girl speaking. Little voice. Pale red face under his arm. Almost like he remembered Sarah's face, peeking out from behind Mama's skirts.

Mama.

Mama stank. Didn't wash. Hurt him.

Bugger boy.

She'd be coming soon. Nicole would bring her.

"I won't kill you, I don't think."

"You look sick."

"Uh-hunh." And Japhet stumbled again. He'd mentally blocked out the burning in his right shoulder, the back of his head, the scraped right shin, and all the screaming bruises and cuts he'd received in the avalanche. But he couldn't will back strength that wasn't there. Or think really straight. He was bleeding heavily. Might slip into shock again and bleed to death if he didn't tend the wound soon. But Mama. That woman was going to bring him his mama.

Then he was on the third floor. The clock was at the front of the building. That was...this way. No. This way.

Stumbling to the end of the dark hall, Japhet dragged the kid to a halt and looked around. There had to be. There was.

He tried the knob to the narrow attic door, found it locked, and took a step back to raise his stolen rifle and fire directly into the lock. Then he reared back and slammed his boot into it.

The mechanism splintered.

Japhet pulled the door open and took the girl up.

CHAPTER 118

"You're her!" Nicole said to snow swept ghost that was Elizabeth Severin.

The older woman reached up to elegantly tuck some whipping hairs back into her black hat. "The woman who sent letters to you both? Yes. And to Japhet and Georgia. I was going to send one to your mother too, Ari. Did you know that? But she'd never come. She'd know it was me and stay away. You're here as her proxy, you might say."

Nicole shot Ari a look and saw the same confusion she felt. "What? Why?"

"Let's just say I've been following Japhet's progress for years. All over California. All the way here. All across town tonight."

"And you didn't stop him!"

Severin laughed harshly into the wind. "Why would I do that?"

Ari stomped forward. "Because Wendy could have been killed, for one thing!"

"So?" Severin said. "She's not mine. She's just a bit of unfortunate baggage that came along with George. Not that my own slut of a daughter was much better."

Georgia, Nicole thought, itching to drag this woman inside and lock her in the overnight room with her daughter's corpse. And maybe all the ones that were frozen out behind the clinic. She settled for locking eyes with her now and baring her teeth to say, "You're coming with us. Now."

"To see, Japhet. Oh, I don't think so, however fun that might be." She suddenly had a pistol in her hand that she'd pulled from her coat. It was aimed at Ari who had stalked around beside her, clearly intent on dragging her along if necessary.

"You're his mother," Nicole said.

"He has no mother! He's just a cancer that pollutes everything it touches. It spreads outwards through the generations. Infects everything. It made me…sick. Corrupted my daughter. Corrupted this town. Drove me out. Do you know how many towns I lived in? How many men…?"

She paused for a second as her gun hand shook, and she stared at it, blinking hard.

"Until I realized that the only way to deal with an evil cancer isn't to ask its forgiveness like Miryam did with her yearly guilt letters. No, you have to go back to the diseased heart of it. So I returned here. I reunited with my guilty friends. I plotted with them how to bring Japhet back, and bring back his whole cancerous bloodline."

"Us?" Nicole asked with a frown.

"You," Severin said, her head jerking up. "And Georgia. And Ari. But the whole town too. Every trace of Japhet Bone's deviance has to be wiped away so it can't hurt anyone anymore. It must be utterly expunged. It's Japhet's mission: to kill and be killed, in that order."

She was pointing the gun straight at Nicole now, and Nicole mentally urged Ari to jump her. Because however confusing this woman's madness was, April needed saving. Now.

But as Ari tensed to move, Severin suddenly stepped backwards and aimed at him again. "You don't need me," she said coolly. "Because I have one final gift to give you, Nicole 'Baker.' You asked me once if I knew you and I said I didn't. That was a lie. How could I not know my own granddaughter, the butcher's one putrid child?"

CHAPTER 119

"No," Nicole said, fighting a feeling of panic.

She wanted to rush at Elizabeth Severin right there in front of the clinic on Main Street and demand she unsay it, deny that Japhet Bone had ever fathered a child. And certainly not with someone named Betsy Müller.

"He's not old enough," she said. But even as the words came out, Georgia's story came back. Japhet Bone had raped Georgia/Sarah when he was nine. By the time he was sent away at the age of thirteen, he'd raped at least twelve women and girls. One of them was presumably Betsy Müller.

The ages worked.

Elizabeth Severin, aka Wilma Bone, had no doubt seen Nicole work it out in her head and now smiled cruelly at her. And just like that Nicole knew in her gut it was true. Like the cupboard door she'd been picking at in the dark since Mama Suzie died, had just sprung open to reveal a whole host of monsters—Japhet Bone, Sarah Bone, Wilma Bone, and...

Nicole Bone.

She reached for Elizabeth Severin through the snow, but the woman was backing away, smiling cruelly, her gun still up, her glance flicking to the dim circle of the tick-tock place in the distance.

"Get her," Nicole croaked to Ari. "Bring her to the clock."

"But—"

"Say hi to your daddy for me!" Elizabeth Severin called over the wind, then slipped around the corner of the clinic. Ari took off after her.

Nicole, shaking her head and swinging a mittened hand in front of her eyes as if it could clear her vision, finally huffed out loudly and began to run.

CHAPTER 120

In the back lane behind the clinic, Ari panted to a stop in the snow, his head jerking right and left like his thoughts.

Why had Elizabeth Severin gone after his mother? Desperately enough to attack her through Ari? It had to be more than just being "polluted" by Bone thirty years ago. Elizabeth Severin had said "bloodline." Did that—

There! He saw the black strip of Severin's long coat disappearing between the buildings towards Main Street. Like she knew where Japhet Bone had gone and was weaving her way towards the Town Hall to be there for the big finish after all.

Great. That would make it easier.

He set off after her.

CHAPTER 121

SLOGGING through a whirlwind back alley towards the clinic, Paul and Horst were both breathing raggedly and covered with sweat. Paul furiously swung his rifle butt back and forth like a kayak paddle as he threw his feet forward through the snow.

They rounded the corner almost directly in front of a running black shadow and jerked up their rifles in unison.

"Don't shoot!" said the runner and jerked to a halt, raising his arms up.

"Ari?"

"Paul? Thank God! Come on!" The boy's arms were waving frantically. "We have to catch her!"

"Who?"

"Bone's mother! And Nicole!"

"Nicole's out here? What about Georgia?"

Ari dropped his arms by his sides like Paul had just beaned him, but his voice came out with a colder fury than the storm's. "This is *it*, Paul. Georgia's in danger at the clinic back there. Nicole's in danger further down Main Street. Which one do you choose?"

"But..." Paul jerked his head back and forth between Horst and Ari, finally identified the knife and bedpan Ari carried in his hands. "Tell me why. Has Bone shown up?"

"It doesn't matter!" Ari shouted. "You have to choose, now and for good! Who is it?"

Paul swallowed the swirling snow, the brutal cold and night, and realized that when he was up on the mountain with Rawley and the others, his desperate need had been to come down and save Nicole, not Georgia. Maybe because of the eight years they'd spent together. Maybe because underneath their troubles they were matched intellectually, morally, spiritually. Maybe because he simply loved her. And the reason he'd rescued her over and over again was that he wanted her with him, above all else. Above, even, a family.

"I choose my wife, of course," he said.

Ari visibly sighed and then picked himself up. "Then come on, both of you! I'll fill you in en route." He whirled and plunged off again.

They got as far as the Grenadine on Main Street before Rawley and his posse cut them off.

CHAPTER 122

At the south end of town, the decision-making nexus of Goldrock's power lay shadowy under the glow of its giant clock face above, lit by emergency reserve batteries to shine out through the darkness of the snowstorm.

That's where Bone would be, Nicole knew. Up where they'd taken him before they shipped him out of town the *first* time they thought they'd ended it.

Nicole struggled over the snowplowed barrier in front of its door and reached for the Town Hall's double doorknobs, half-hoping she'd find them locked.

The right one turned.

She entered.

The front hall was quiet and empty and smelled of ammonia. As she closed the heavy door behind her, though, she imagined she could hear a creaking from somewhere overhead. Because of course that's where the big clock was. Where she had to go.

But where was Ari? What could she possibly do on her own against Bone?

Hands clammy, she stripped off her borrowed purple mittens and hat, left them on the floor by the door as a sign for anyone who followed, and went for the stairs.

CHAPTER 123

"Well look what we got here," Rawley bellowed as his posse spread out across the road and brought their rifles to bear on Ari, Paul, and Horst. "Two turncoats and filthy Jew boy!"

"Now, Al," drawled Pritchett when it was clear whom they'd stopped. "Let's not go off—"

"Shut up, Bob!" Rawley snapped. "You asked me earlier if my boys hated you enough to shoot a law man. Well I'd say enough crazy stuff's gone on tonight that I could shoot you dead between the eyes and explain it away. Right, boys?"

There was some uncomfortable shuffling, possibly because Paul and Horst still had their own guns raised and pointed at Rawley. Then Jeremy Buckster, who looked to have been whispering with someone, suddenly stepped forward through the line and pointed to Ari with his shotgun. "Look what he's carrying!"

All eyes, even Paul's and Horst's, went to the blood-crusted butcher's knife and Ari went white. Oh, dude, as Josh would say, he thought. Here we go again.

CHAPTER 124

THE SECOND FLOOR of the Town Hall seemed to breathe as Nicole stood still, listening. The floors and walls in the dim wash of the exit lights, the functional green leather couches—the all seemed to be watching her, daring her to keep going.

A close scratch of sound made her start until she realized it was just the arm of the parka Wendy had given her to wear rubbing against the body of it. She was so tense her tongue was pushed up tightly to the roof of her mouth. Her feet felt hot and wet inside the felt lining of the boots she'd borrowed from the clinic.

Listen.

There was nothing except the dull moan of the wind outside. Where was she supposed to go now? How did she get up to…?

Her sight fell on a black spatter on the floor. More beyond, streaked. She knelt down and felt its stickiness. Smelled it. Blood. Fresh. Presumably Bone's. Had they been on the stairs going up too, or was he getting worse?

Forcing herself to creep forward, Nicole followed the dark spatters down the hall then saw a smudge on the wall at what would have been Bone's head height. Nicole's heart jumped. He *had* come this way. And he was weak enough he'd had to stop and lean on the wall.

Two minutes later she found the shot doorknob, the door hanging open, and she stood at the bottom of the stairs, looking up. There was no door at the top, but no lights either. Just blackness. An attic. Probably big enough to stand in since it had to house the clock mechanism and have stairs up to it. But dark. A last refuge for Bone in a place that had once been his prison. A wounded animal's retreat. With a gun and little girl hostage.

For just a second Nicole flashed back to her old self, the one who agonized over who she was, what life owed her, and how she could never be a good mother because of her own mother's lies.

The corner of her mouth pulled up in a pained rictus. Just what the hell did worries like that matter in a situation like this?

She began to climb.

CHAPTER 125

Come. Come. *Come.*

Japhet could hear the footsteps on the stairs as he sat collapsed in an ancient, moldy couch that had probably been stowed up here as far back as when they'd brought him up here and hog-tied gagged him. Left him lying on the filthy wooden floor for the rats and bugs to run over.

Japhet's left hand covered the mouth of the little girl.

He wondered vaguely why he heard only one set of steps, but he couldn't puzzle it out because his head was stuck in the little whirring click, click, click of the clock mechanism that ran on some minimal allotment of the backup power. The mechanism was a dusty, huge-man-high tumble of dark gears, boxes, and poles that humped up against the glowing yellow circle taking up the end wall—the inside of the town hall's clock face. The gears looked like they might have been steam driven once upon a time. Now a simple cord ran into the rear of a central black box and the arm-thick pole that held the clock's two arms ran out the other and through the wall to the outside.

All of which was lit up by a set of corded spotlights on the floor that shone up at the inside clock face, a good twelve feet in diameter. It was like being inside a glowing moon, Japhet thought. Once you came around the tumble of stuff at the top of the stairs, you could see the lights, the huge round face with the Roman numerals all backwards. Time all backwards. And watch out for the shadows.

Click...click...click... Japhet struggled up to his feet.

C'mon, Mama. I'm waiting for you.

CHAPTER 126

Outside and a block down the street in the swirling snow, the standoff was getting more and more insane for Ari.

"Look!" he screamed out to the line-up and stabbed his gloved finger in the direction of the Town Hall. "He's up there now. Japhet Bone! And this guy's wife!" Ari jabbed a thumb at Paul, who was still leveling his gun on Rawley.

"And how exactly do you know that, boy?" Rawley called back.

"How do I know? How do I fucking *know?*"

"Watch your language, boy!"

"And you watch your gun, asshole!" Through being polite *or* afraid.

"You just better—"

"Hey!" Ari suddenly leapt forward, but not at Rawley, for the person he'd seen lurking behind him.

Rawley and Buckster caught him and threw him back, but Ari jumped up again. "It's *her!*" he yelled, pointing at the black-coated Elizabeth Severin who now casually squeezed up beside Rawley. "She's Bone's mother! We have to take her up there! She can end this!"

Rawley looked from Severin, who was raising her eyebrows innocently, back to Ari. "You serious?"

"She...said it," Ari said, but the looks he was getting from the older men in the posse and even Horst Hurzgehrmine made him suddenly unsure.

"Bone's mama was named Wilma, boy! Curvy as bottle of beer and about that much class! You think that describes Lizzie here?"

"So she got a nose job or something! That..."

He never got to finish the sentence because a crash of breaking glass that sounded even over the storm, drew every eye back to the Town Hall clock. A bright hole had appeared near the bottom right, just above the number seven. As they all watched, stunned, something came out through the hole and dangled out in the storm, screaming.

A little girl's scream.

"*Mein Gott,*" said Horst beside Paul. "April."

Then he and Paul and Ari were pushing through the gathered men and running for the Town Hall, praying desperately that Bone would not let go.

CHAPTER 127

"Y-y-y-you LIED TO ME!" yelled Bone at Nicole, and his face was mask of blood-caked fury. "Y-you said you'd bring M-m-m-m-mama!"

He shook April again in the storm, and she screamed, trying to grab with her free hand the awful fist that held other wrist, her hair whipping about in the blowing snow.

Nicole, only feet back from Bone, could see it all through the hole in the lit-up clock face, just as she could see the figures running down the street toward the Town Hall and knew that they would be too late to do anything.

As soon as she'd reached the top of the stairs, Bone had leapt from the shadows and dragged her into the attic, then shoved her so she stumbled backwards and fell against one of the cobweb-covered walls. As she did, Bone checked that there was no one behind her, then roared and shoved an old couch that sat right by the attic door through that door so it went thumping down the narrow stairs, blocking it up. Then boxes of books, sacks of things that crashed like glass. Dust flew. The dank smell that had hit Nicole coming in was now joined by the sharpness of urine, probably from mice or rats, and dust filling the air, making her cough. This attic space had obviously been used for storage as well as the clock mechanism that took up, with motor, rods, gears, and moving hands, maybe twenty percent of the space.

But it obviously wasn't well maintained. More taken for granted. A secret place. A place to temporarily lock up out-of-control maniacs. Or shelter them.

Bone worked feverishly, grunting and sweating and swearing with pain at the exertion each time he threw something more down, careful to stay between

Nicole and little April, who cowered back near the clock workings with her face young white and shaking.

Bone had finally limped back to grab April, then the rifle he'd stashed near the clock face. He'd used the rifle butt to smash an isolated pane of glass out of the clock face, and suddenly shoved April outside.

Now Nicole dropped back down to her knees and held out her hands to him, her heart beating at one-eighty a minute. "Please...Japhet. Bring her back in. Listen to me."

"N-n-no!" he yelled again, but in the horror of his face Nicole thought he saw a brief flash of question, a wavering.

"Why haven't you killed me?" Nicole said quickly, jumping on it. "Or raped me?"

A definite twitch.

"Yes. Take me instead of the girl. Bring her in. Let her go and...I'll let you." *Like fucking hell, I will.* But Nicole remembered all her adoptive mother's tricks now—how to soften her voice and lean her head forward with sincerity—even as it sickened her to feel how natural the tricks were, how she'd probably even used some of them in her law practice. "You'd like that, wouldn't you? Doesn't that intrigue you? To have a woman who actually *wants* it from you?"

The bloody face twitched hard now, looking out at April hanging from his left hand, his good arm. Looking back at Nicole.

"Bring her inside, Japhet," Nicole cooed, deliberately staying on her knees. "Come on." She unzipped her borrowed parka halfway down, felt the cold rush in, and ignored it, pretending she was eager, hot for him. She tried to lick her lips but her mouth was too dry.

"I c-c-could fug you," Bone said, as if the thought had just then occurred to him.

"But only"—Nicole's hand zipped her parka back up a notch—"if the little girl is safe."

Bone lips curled back, exposing teeth as crusted with gore as the rest of him. The smell that rolled towards her on the wind was of sweat and stink, blood gone rotten, and the sharp smell of blood still fresh. Nicole almost gagged.

She smiled instead. Beckoned him.

And at last he came, pulling April inside and dropping her, forgotten, by the clockworks. He dragged his rifle with his bad arm as he approached her, crawling, hopping with his left arm until he was directly in front of her. The he drew himself up on his knees to tower over her like some terrifying primordial beast. His eyes raked over her.

All softness was gone from his face. All intelligence. All the pain. There was just lust, though whether that was for Nicole's body or her pain, she didn't know.

She let her eyes dart sideways and saw April huddled mere yards away, staring wide-eyed and silent, curled in an upright little ball as if she could make herself so small she might not be seen.

Nicole shot her eyes angrily to the left and mouthed *Hide!*

The little girl ran.

Then Japhet's hands were on her. They roughly unzipped Nicole's jacket and grabbed at her breasts through the tee-shirt she wore, grunting and squeezing them painfully. He pushed her backwards over her knees so she hit hard on her butt and tailbone and almost smacked her head as she went down.

He was over her knees then, reaching down to jerk down her intern's pants, no panties beneath. He laid down the rifle to tug down the front of his own brown ski pants and flopped out an erect penis so large that Nicole momentarily thought he'd packed an iron bar in his crotch.

She craned her neck to see it, gasped involuntarily, then darted her eyes up to meet his. "There's one thing you have to know about me first," she said shakily.

"Yeah," he said, his stutter gone.

"I'm your daughter, you *sonofoabitch!*"

She jerked her right knee up so hard into his balls that she literally hiked him momentarily off the floor.

He screamed and rolled over sideways, spitting bloody saliva from his mouth and clutching his groin. But even as Nicole had tugged up her pants and jumped to her booted feet, he was back on his knees, glaring at her with an intensity that made him look like the devil himself.

Then he got one of his own boots under him, used his left hand to balance as he rose, and lunged at her.

Nicole ducked back around the old clock machinery, her jacket almost catching on a sharp corner, as Bone leaped across the space between them. She grabbed a big, immobile valve on the side of the power box and used it to swing over a bunch of pipes and cogs so that she ended up in front of the machinery. She was among the spotlights, the lit clock face behind her, the storm whistling through the hole in the glass by her right thigh.

"Bitch!" Bone screamed after her, his voice awkwardly high, like some vessels had popped in his throat. "You're not mine! I never had a daughter! Never!"

"You did!" Nicole shot back. "From a girl named Betsy Müller! Young little girl! Only—"

Bone had found his way back and lunged around the corner for her, but Nicole was faster, dancing back over the lights and swinging around the machinery to where Bone had thrown her to the floor. The gun. Where was it?

He limped out around the corner, lit from below by the spotlights. Monstrous. "I threw it aw-way," he said. "We don't need it. Do we...daughter?"

Nicole finally made sense of the sounds she'd heard earlier. The thuds and scraping were the men downstairs, Paul, she hoped, and Ari, and a hundred others. She doubted, though, they'd even be able to get the first item Bone had thrown down for them, the couch, out through the narrow doorway.

"Fuck you," she said to Bone.

He grimaced. "M-mama always said 'Fug,' you know. More polite." And he lunged again.

Nicole danced sideways again, spitting at him as if this were all a game to her too. He was wounded and slow. She was younger and quick. She could do this for as long as it took.

Except that it didn't work that way, she knew. Her heart was pounding so hard she felt she could have a coronary any second. Her hands were slick. Her muscles zinging with crazy adrenaline. She could slip any time. She could trip on one of these pipes, a bolt on the floor.

Or Bone himself could lose patience and find the rifle again. Or April.

She had to *do* something.

As she was trying to figure it out, she realized she'd made another one-eighty around the clockworks and stood in front of the lit inside of the clock face again. She heard a grunt, then her face jerked up as something huge went whistling past her head—a metal gear? An old wagon wheel?

It hit the central strut in the face behind her and went through, shattering the high panels of glass on either side and bringing a whistling gust of storm in and sideways as if it wanted to suck her out in to the night.

Bone rushed at her again.

Nicole turned and ran around the outside of the clockworks to the middle of the attic and stopped there, facing him as he hulked slowly towards her. "Just stop!" she shouted, her whole body shaking with it. "I'm your daughter! Jesus! You're my father! Doesn't that mean anything to you? Do you want to just die without anything at all of you to carry on? Because they're going to kill you. You know that, don't you? And if you kill me, there'll be nothing left of you. Nothing!"

He was closer now, almost within leaping distance. And Nicole just...could...not...run anymore. "I'm your daughter," she whimpered and jammed her hands into the pocket of the parka Wendy had loaned her.

Bone stopped, swaying there before her, almost two feet taller than her, with his bad arm hanging and a look of fiercely insane amusement on his face. "Yeah. Nicole, right? Okay then, Nicole. Here's what we do. You've got two minutes. You find the rifle. Y-you bring it back here and put it to my head and kill me. That way you save yourself. And you save the little girl."

He licked his lips and leaned closer, his breath hot and sour.

"But I don't think you can. You know why? 'Cause even if you find the rifle, you won't be able to use it. Because I'm your father." He was swaying harder now. "You can't kill me, no matter how much it needs doing. No matter how much I deserve or *want* to die."

He was right in her face now and Nicole almost expected his eyes to be wet. Because that's what he was trying to do with that speech, right? Convince her he experienced some moral feeling or regret? Bit his eyes weren't wet. They were just big-pupiled with excitement.

"Or maybe," he said, "you just don't think you deserve to live in this world."

In the right pocket of the parka Wendy had loaned her, Nicole's hand had finally worked the paper toweling off the scalpel that was there, and closed her fingers on the handle.

"You know what, Daddy?" she said with trembling lips. "I think I do."

And she whipped the scalpel up and left under his chin, slicing Bone's carotid artery so cleanly that all his blood seemed to come out of him in one long, seamless ribbon of surprise.

"Goodbye," Nicole said as he pitched forward over her.

CHAPTER 129

IT TOOK ALMOST an hour for the men from downstairs to clear the way up to the attic, but they'd taken Nicole and April down the outside with a ladder long before then.

This time the gathering place became the Grenadine, its warmth more inviting than the medical clinic, with all its broken windows and dead bodies.

Nicole huddled against a wall in the dining room with April and Auggie and two blankets and pillows. She stroked their hair and watched the other people of Goldrock who'd been cut off during the night gradually filter in. The newcomers hung around the lobby or trickled into the dining room. They whispered and cried on each other's shoulders. Then those who had been put up in the upstairs rooms somehow found out what was happening and came down, until the ground floor was bursting with people too frightened or traumatized to be alone facing this dawn.

George Severin, Wendy, Ari, Paul, and eight other able-bodied helpers were passing around blankets, coffee, tea, hot chocolate, and cookies.

At five a.m., a ripple of shock went through the survivors huddled in the dining room when Herb Mawpester, who'd been with the attic clearing crew, brought word that Elizabeth Severin was dead. She'd shown up in the final stages of the attic job, climbed up past the wreckage to see Japhet Bone's dead body, and shot herself right there beside him.

Nicole left April and Auggie momentarily to stand with Ari and Wendy. The pretty girl shook and held her father's hand as the hotel keeper broke down.

Paul came up behind Nicole. He touched her shoulders. She hadn't spoken to him since she'd come down, hadn't been able to speak to anyone but the children. And she still couldn't. Not yet.

She gripped his hand tightly, kissed his fingers, and sent him back to his coffee duties.

She herself went back to April and Auggie and snuggled into the blankets with them. Fifteen minutes later, she'd finally managed to rock both children into a restless sleep.

Sometime around seven a.m., Marshal Pritchett drew up a chair and humbly asked for her story. And Nicole finally told it because she was too tired not to and because she knew she would be telling it for days when the road finally opened and other law officers got through.

She stumbled at the part about Elizabeth Severin, though, because Ari had told her the old woman was not Bone's mother after all. Pritchett hemmed and hawed at that, rubbing his mouth, when suddenly the cold German voice of Clara Hurzgehrmine cut in from behind him.

"Elizabet, I, and Miryam were friends," Clara said, striding closer and darting her gaze over the sleeping children on Nicole's lap. Nicole wondered what had taken her so long.

"They all thought you would be dead," said Horst Hurzgehrmine who had stepped up behind his wife and, Nicole sensed, had forced her forward in the first place. "Now that you are not dead, Clara *will* tell you what is your right to know."

"*Nein.*"

Pritchett said quietly from behind Horst, "Oh, I think you better tell it, Ms. Clara. Either here and now or in jail later."

"My son, Eduard, married the sister of the *Teufel*," Clara Hurgehrmine said and spat sideways onto the floor. "This sister, Georgia, she is dead now, yes?"

Nicole nodded coldly. "She died saving these children of hers, saving your grandchildren."

Clara's face twitched as that registered.

Horst prodded her and she finally spoke again, cold. "Elizabet would have done that also, for her child, Betsy. But she could not. And so Betsy Müeller bore the devil a daughter. You." Clara made to spit again but her husband grabbed her arm.

Nicole fought to stay steady as she said, "Elizabeth Severin was Elizabeth Müeller, and she was my grandmother?"

"And Betsy lived with you in Elizabet's house," Clara said. "Do you know what that meant? Every day Elizabet saw you, she saw the evil that had been done to her family and would not go away! More than once, *die Teufel* tried to claim you."

"I remember being chased up a hillside by a big boy..."

"Elizabet rescued you again and again. Until she had enough. Through a friend, she sent out word you could be adopted. Two people came a week later."

"Susan and Nigel Baker."

Clara Hurzgehrmine nodded stiffly and turned to Horst, discussing something in German with Horst as she vigorously stabbed her finger towards the two sleeping children. He shook his head and said something that made Clara close her eyes. She frowned sourly and began to leave.

"Wait!" Nicole raised her hands to her and Pritchett stepped in front of Clara, making her stop.

Clara turned back to her, waiting.

Nicole's mouth was so dry she could hardly speak. "What about Bone's mother? And Betsy? Is my mother still alive? Where is she? Please!"

For just a second Nicole caught a flicker of compassion in Clara's hard features, then she said, "Wilma is dead, I heard. I hope. But Betsy... This is where Miryam has suffered. Her son, Moshe Siegel, he would visit Elizabet's house with his mother. He fell in love with Betsy and one day they eloped. Started a new family far away from Goldrock."

Nicole's head spun. It was too much too fast.

Nicol's eyes flickered around the room for a second before stopping where Wendy comforted her father. Behind both of them, talking with what looked like an apologetic and utterly broken Al Rawley, stood Miryam's grandson, Ari.

THREE MONTHS LATER

NICOLE GRIPPED both sides of the passenger seat as Paul brought their new minivan to a slow-rolling halt. They'd driven halfway across the country, over three thousand miles, and were now on a dirt and gravel road under a spreading apple tree. She could smell the apples through their open windows, for God's sake. She could feel the sun and clean air fill her lungs. Great Falls, Montana was twenty miles south of them. The Rockies, reminiscent of the San Juans in Colorado but more distant and gentle, rose up in a purple and blue dawn to their left. A white board house was just ahead of them to their right.

Paul swiveled around in his captain's seat to check on April and Auggie. They were still sleeping peacefully. Auggie clutched the teddy bear he hadn't been able to let go of since the horrors of Goldrock. Give it time, his counselor had said.

April contented herself now with just her blanket and pillow, but had been unwilling for almost three solid weeks to let Nicole out of her sight for more than a few minutes at a time. The nightmares still woke her up frequently. She still had bouts of crying and silence.

But these would also pass with time, the counselor said.

The main thing was that the children needed to be out of Goldrock. And April, at least, clearly needed Nicole. Even Clara Hurzgehrmine had finally conceded that.

What most surprised Nicole was her own growing need for the children. As if it had taken surviving this horror with them, fighting for their lives and her own, to finally allow herself to love like a parent.

But there was one final step.

"Well?" Paul turned and looked at her expectantly.

She tried to smile. Paul was hers and she was his now in a closer way than she'd thought possible, but he was still maddening in his cheerful confidence. Nothing fazed him. The bad stuff was just...done with. The future was just there. Take it.

"I'm afraid," she said quietly.

He reached over and covered her hand. "We'll be right here. Just give the signal when you want us."

She nodded and finally released her fingers from the seat. With one more glance back at the kids and a tight smile for Paul, she climbed out of the van and began walking, thinking hard.

Betsy Müller had survived because Moshe had taken her so far away from where her horrors had happened. And after six years of fruitless searching with Moshe, Betsy had even managed to give up the memory of the daughter who'd been taken from her. She'd taken a new name. She'd successfully begun her life again. She'd gone back to school, gotten a degree in political science, then a masters, then a doctorate, as if she'd been driven to prove she was worth more than Bone and her own mother had believed.

And now?

She was no longer Betsy, Nicole reminded herself, almost tripping as she missed a step. Nicole had to remember to call her Judith, Judy, Dr. Judy Siegel.

Nicole's lips, her legs, her whole body was trembling as she reached the front porch, touched back her hair, and stepped up.

Ari came bursting out of the screen door and threw his arms around her before she could say a word. After a squeeze that almost took her breath away, he bounced back off her, still holding her arms, and looked her up and down with a wild grin.

"You look great!" he said.

"And you cut your hair."

He stepped back and hand over the short-shaven look and grinned again. "New year, new look. Wendy says it's sexy."

Nicole ran a hand over it. "Very."

His gaze flicked back towards the van and he shook his head. "Never thought I'd see it. They okay?"

She nodded.

"And you?"

"Getting there." The fear suddenly rushed back into her. "She does want to see me, doesn't she? I sent her letters and she answered, but..."

"She wants," Ari said softly. And before she could change her mind, he spun, jerked open the screen door and shouted up, "Hey, Mom! Dad! I got someone down here claiming to be my long-lost sister! She'd like to say hello!"

Thank you for reading one of my books!

When I finished an earlier version of this back in 2011, I was so overwhelmed by the complexity of it that I pretty much rewrote it from page one. And when I finally published it through Fiero Publishing that first time, I did so under a pen name I reserved for my darker stuff.

Fast forward nine years, thirteen books, and a dozen screenplays, and I can now see character arcs and themes my unconscious stuck into this story. It may be darker than the stuff I usually write under my own name, but the themes of facing loss and despair head on, and finding dignity and meaning in what you do and how you love—those are all very much me. Hence the minor revisions and re-release under a new title and my own name.

I hope some of it resonated with you, and you became a little more alive in sharing this world, this story, with me. If so, I'd really appreciate you leaving a review of the book on the site where you bought it. Reviews from readers like you can be so influential in helping others decide to give the story a try.

Thanks, and may the good things in your world always overcome the bad.

-Terry

ABOUT THE AUTHOR

Terry Hayman lives with his family in the Pacific Northwest, where he writes screenplays, novels, and short fiction. You can find more about him and his work and subscribe to his newsletter if you so desire at www.terryhayman.com.